MW00883471

LYCANTHROPY
and the
Single Girl

A Novel by
DEE SARAH FISH
Book One

Edited by Laurie Foster
Special Thanks to Heidi Whistle,
Sabrina Pandora, Erica Freeman, & Sue Aguilera
Copyright © 2023, Dee Sarah Fish

Whistlefish Creations
Oil City, PA 16301

www.lycanthropyandthesinglegirl.com   deebrisbyfish@gmail.com

Chapter One

·)）◉（(·

The room was a discordant mixture of color and sound. The beat of some overproduced, poppy dance track was assaulting her ears, but she didn't care. It was all an invasion; the sights flooded her eyes, and the sounds pummeled her from all sides.

It was the smells, however, that were the most vivid. Every single one was telling a story of uncompromising detail that she was tired of knowing. Taking another swig of the rum and coke in her hand, she worked hard to try and drown that all out.

The night wasn't about knowing; it was about forgetting, and as she put the empty glass on the counter, she held up two fingers for more. She surveyed the room as the voices all fell into an indecipherable hum of background noise. The effects of the alcohol were finally deadening her ability to pick anything apart.

At that moment, it was all she wanted; to dull her mind and take away the near-perpetual anxiety she had felt for so long. The bartender returned with a fresh drink, and she grabbed it, placing a five-dollar bill on the counter. She had lost track of how much she must have spent to get as drunk as she was.

For the time being, however, she wasn't thinking about her somewhat unique problems. The feeling of relief made the rest worth it.

Moving with her drink out to the dance floor, she let the music and her desires carry her. She wasn't much of a dancer, but at the moment, she didn't really care. She just wanted the experience of freedom to continue.

That was when she noticed him. The man at the other end of the floor was looking at her. His eyes were locked on her as she moved, and she found herself liking the sensation. She wanted the attention that she had spent so long trying to avoid. Across the room, she could feel his desire, and it reignited something in her that she desperately wanted to succumb to.

For just a moment, that pit of anxiety that all but lived in her stomach tightened and tried to warn her off. Not wanting to care anymore, she downed the entire glass of rum and coke and smiled at the man. He wanted her, and she knew it. Taking a heavy breath, she locked her eyes on him and began to walk over with one thought in her mind. She had a longing that hadn't been satisfied in what felt like forever, and she was tired of denying herself.

She was hungry.

"Oh shit, oh shit, oh shit. I can't believe I frickin' did that!" The disheveled woman thought, hours later, as the light poured into the window and across her face. Some mornings, she was happy for her ability to wake up with the sun, but this morning, all she wanted to do was stay in bed and sleep. She moaned and looked at the ceiling.

Expecting a headache, she was surprised to feel… essentially fine.

"Really?" Claire mumbled. It felt very much as though the sun had a personal grudge against her as it streaked through the glass. "This is *it?* No hangover?"

There was the slightest bit of fuzziness in her head and a familiar cottony taste in her mouth—sensations she remembered well enough from late nights drinking during her art school days—but those were the only symptoms. Blinking, she reached over to her nightstand to check what time it was. Her phone glowed to life as she blinked some of the sleep out of her eyes. It was a good bit shy of seven in the morning, which was par for the course. Claire sighed.

"I mean… you worked *hard* for that endrunkening. So much for getting shitfaced and forgetting the…" Claire muttered as her eyes went wide. Jerking up in the bed, she finished her thought with a decidedly more concerned tone. "...NIGHT! SHIT!"

The bed next to her looked untouched, so she felt the sheets with her hands. They were cool to the touch; she was fairly sure that nobody else had been there. It was a minor relief as the memories of the previous night began to pour in.

What were you thinking, Claire? Bringing some random asshole home?! Are you nuts? Claire furrowed her eyebrows as she thought about the evening and just how inebriated she had been. Looking around her room, she squinted and tried to piece it all together.

Sniffing, she noted that the godawful Axe body spray he had all but bathed in still wafted through the apartment. Her senses always seemed to have their volume cranked up to 11 the morning after…

Wow, that is just vile. He was marinating in that stuff on top of everything else. It's gonna be in your frickin' nose for days. You have achieved a new level of funk; congrats. Mariska is going to have a field day with this.

Ugh… she thought, rolling her eyes. *Smells like hormones and sadness.*

Any other night, she'd have avoided this guy like the plague. Last night, however, was different. It was almost as if she had responded to his interest in order to spite herself…and now she had to deal with the aftermath.

Pursing her lips, she looked to the hallway and shook her head. In spite of how strongly his odor lingered in the room, she remembered what was waiting for her in the living room. It was impossible to overlook, lingering in the other room like a hammer about to fall. She concentrated on ignoring it.

Being in her own bed was a plus. As she lay there, the only thought in her head was that she wanted to stay right where she was. It had less to do with the non-hangover and more to do with her feelings of embarrassment. Sitting up slowly, that familiar knot of anxiety in the pit of her stomach started to tighten. It felt something like a massive ball of rubber bands coiled together, threatening to snap.

It had been a good long time since she had gotten that drunk, and how normal she felt was irritating. It was a sobering reminder of exactly why she felt okay and why she had tried to feel anything but the night before. She gave a resigned shrug.

The cute skinny jeans she had been wearing were neatly folded on the seat of the plush old chair in the corner that had quickly ended up becoming a catch-all for laundry, both dirty and clean. The brand-new top she had found at that little thrift shop with Mariska was folded over the edge of the easel she hadn't painted on in ages.

She scowled at the otherwise empty easel. It had been a little over a year since she had really worked on her art, and she often feared she might have lost that part of herself entirely. The idea only served to further irritate her.

She looked over and saw that there were tears along the seams of her top and pants, and visibly popped stitches in the waistline of the jeans. "Oh, frickin' hell? Really? I liked those jeans."

What did you think was gonna happen, Claire?

Sighing again, she dragged herself out of bed, noticing that she was wearing a fairly long nightshirt she didn't remember changing into. Considering the neatly folded clothes and her current attire, Claire pulled the neck of the shirt up to her nose and took a whiff.

Mariska.

Pulling off the shirt and tossing it on the bed, she walked across to the door to her little bathroom, pausing for a moment to peer down the hall to the living room at the far end. To where she knew what had happened, and where she was still trying to ignore it.

She snapped the light on. It was an old, ornately decorated overhead fixture that had a bad habit of flickering due to the building's ancient wiring. It was a price she willingly paid for the charm of the vintage architecture.

Yikes. This is gonna take a little work, she thought, as she surveyed the damage in the old thrift store mirror she had hung up over the sink. As the bulb warmed up and the flickering died down, it seemed to accentuate every pore, wrinkle, and blemish. With a groan, she decided she looked like more of a mess than usual.

Running a hand over her slightly round face, her big, hazel eyes looked more amber around the edges for her stress and were ringed by dark circles. Her skin was soft, and she was a bit more thickly built than she generally preferred.

At a smidge over six feet tall, she hunched down out of habit to look herself over in the bathroom mirror as she worked to piece together more of the past evening. She gave herself the evaluation that always followed a night like this. Her somewhat unique 'time of the month' seemed to come earlier this time thanks to the circumstances of the past evening.

She blamed the rum and cokes.

"Shit, I JUST got my frickin' hair done." She muttered out loud, her voice slightly more hoarse than usual; another indication that last night had been wilder than planned. Considering what day it was yesterday, it wasn't a massive surprise.

You shouldn't have ditched Mariska. You shouldn't have tried to deal with it yourself. Or… not deal with it… as the case may be.

As she rubbed her face, she looked at the grown-out ends and ragged bangs that dangled into her vision, and grunted. She had known that getting a haircut was a meaningless luxury. She had set her heart on treating herself and now was regretting the decision. That annoying voice in her head told her it was a waste, but she simply wanted to do something familiar and relaxing.

Her hair currently looked like a proverbial rat's nest. A rat's nest that hadn't seen a pair of scissors, much less a pick, in its existence. Her frizzy, knotted locks were clinging to her face haphazardly.

Anger started to spiral within her and she felt her eyes get hot, but she knew rage would just make her morning worse.

Okay. Focus. You can fix this. Just… a little do-it-yourself trim to cut it back. You've done it plenty of times. Yeah, you look a little ragged, but that's not a huge deal. You drank too much. People DO that. Shit, you've done it plenty before this and it's nothing you can't deal with. Take a nice, hot shower. Breathe. RELAX. You've got this. You've got the hair kit in the cabinet and you can tweak this so it looks better right after you get out of the shower.

Stepping in, she turned on the water and the shower was exactly as good as she had hoped. A few months ago, Mariska had talked her into making a somewhat significant investment in a miracle shower head that made it feel like a million tiny hands were massaging every inch of her. She was always a little raw after a night like the one she had just experienced, and a good shower was an almost cosmic-level reset switch that made her feel human again. The familiar process was soothing as she washed the stink of the prior evening out of her hair before applying a liberal amount of conditioner. Letting it soak in and do its job, she thought back on the epically embarrassing events of the evening.

The night was spent in Ybor City, club hopping with Mariska to blow off steam after a particularly crappy day at work and *the* anniversary she was trying desperately to forget. Claire could remember breaking away from her friend in the club that they frequented during a particularly dense outbreak on the crowded dance floor. Mariska had been trying to distract her with a fun night and turn her stress into a reason to celebrate. For her part, Claire just wanted to escape herself and cut completely loose. As much as her friend had meant well, Mariska reminded her of too much of what she was.

As the warm water washed over her, rinsing the residue of rum-twinged sweat and stray hairs, she recalled ditching Mariska at the club to cut over to another. She remembered ordering drink after drink after drink, actively trying to beat her own metabolism. She remembered a guy she saw dancing who she thought was cute. She remembered an upbeat, autotuned song that Mariska would probably hate.

The song began to play on a loop in her head, just one chunk of the chorus she couldn't identify, repeating. She had no clue as to the rest of it. Trying to place the tune, she knew it was going to be stuck in there until she got into the car and could replace it with something else from the radio.

Walking out of the shower, she toweled herself off and quickly got to work trying to fix the issue with her hair. It was something that she had unfortunately gotten used to. Pulling out the little blue case from the cabinet behind the door, Claire grabbed the rat-tail comb and long, silver scissors. Brushing out her locks, she carefully tried to remember what length they should be and sized out the rest with her first two fingers. "Okay… you are actually kinda good at this. It's second nature, Claire. Just… don't go all crooked…"

"Again," Claire whispered as she nervously trimmed the curling edges of her bangs off. Breathing a sigh of relief that it looked to be a good cut, she moved on to the rest of her hair, trimming back the ends to where she figured it would look best.

Not having the patience for a blowdryer, she frowned in the mirror as she towel-dried her hair. It would leave her frizzed out for sure, but that was what ponytails were for. Her stomach growled and she decided to pick up the pace. She never let herself get too hungry.

Hair wrapped up in the towel, she rummaged through her closet looking for something to wear that would fit and obscure the fact that she still looked a bit rough. It was a routine she had gotten fairly good at over the last year as she laid out a few different options on her bed.

Okay! This will do. She picked a pair of comfy jeans and a dark blue blouse that hung off of her like a cute smock. For now, with time constraints and a meeting at lunchtime, it would do just fine.

As she looked the outfit over, her stomach growled again in protest. *C'mon, give me a minute and I'll feed you, all right?* She thought to herself while looking at her middle with a sarcastic pout.

The rest of the affair was a cotton-headed blur as she struggled to manipulate herself into a clean-ISH bra that was draped over the top of the dresser. Next to it was a series of fairly well-maintained house plants that littered the space. Pulling her still-damp hair back into a loose ponytail, she threw on the most basic face she could manage in the mirror over her dresser. She resigned herself to her fate. *Okay, this isn't bad. I mean, it's not TOO terrible. You've looked worse overall. You've got this.*

The little apartment overlooked the bay, but not the particularly pretty part. Through the window in her bedroom, she had an unparalleled view of a bank of massive fuel storage tanks used by cruise ships. They created an unpleasant smell at least once a month when they picked up and dropped off tourists at the nearby pier. Grabbing her barely-charged phone, Claire shut off the lights in her bedroom and made her way to the kitchen.

The narrow hallway was somewhat of a mess too, a few more garments clearly having been discarded along the way. Tossed along the floorboards were her socks and the cute leather boots she had been wearing the night before. Not wanting to fuss around in the closet again, she swept down and grabbed the boots as she passed.

Moving into the kitchen, she once again ignored the living room and tried to stay focused, but the tension was building. She could smell the pile of dishes from Wednesday's dinner still collected in the sink and a couple of empty wine glasses on the countertop of the bar that led into the living room. Something else she would have to deal with when she got home. On the face of the refrigerator, Claire figured was older than her own twenty-nine years, was something that caught her eye. Between the menus for the local pizzeria and the Chinese food place a few blocks away, was a yellow Post-It note that she knew she hadn't left there.

With a raised brow, the slightly frazzled-looking young woman pulled it off and gave it a quick read...

'Glad you're safe. Took care of it. See u tonight. :)'

The message was written in Sharpie, with black lipstick kissed on the paper that smelled distinctively of Mariska's signature perfume. The same scent she had noticed on the shirt she'd slept in, which confirmed what she had already figured out.

8

Did… did I call her when everything went tits-up? The last events of the night were still a bit too fuzzy for comfort. Checking her phone, which had only a 14 percent charge, she looked to see if there were any drunk, late-night texts or calls. Claire sighed and rolled her eyes as she found the last text sent at 2:43 in the morning:

til

"i fucked ut!!!@! I brought some guy home and it happened. Pleese come. Help!!"

She put the phone back into her rear pocket and the Post-It back on the fridge for now. It wasn't the first such note her faithful wing-woman had left for her after a difficult night, nor was it the first panicked message she had sent. It was, however, always appreciated and always a relief.

Predictably, the fridge was a mess, with a half-finished box of wine blocking most of the actual food. In the back, a set of silver cans rattled as she rummaged around them for something to eat quickly. She grabbed the little carton of leftover egg rolls from earlier in the week that she could scarf down in the car, figuring she could grab a coffee at the office. It was cheap and the creamer was that powdery shit she didn't care for, but it would do the job. Perhaps she could run through a Starbucks if she hurried.

Fresh, hot coffee sounded lovely and was a goal worth shooting for.

She grabbed her purse from the counter and headed to the door, but stopped in her tracks in the small, modestly appointed living room. Looking at the floor in front of her, she finally had to deal with what she knew was in there. What she could smell from her bedroom.

The mess.

The throw rug in the center of the room was stained with a few drops of now-dried, brown blood that she hoped she could get out. She had an industrial-sized tub of Oxi-Clean in the laundry closet for just such a situation. Surrounding it were small piles of tufted, brown fur that had been strewn all over the room. Enough fur to fill a pillowcase or two covered most of the blanket-covered, hand-me-down furniture. She rubbed the bridge of her nose with her thumb and forefinger.

Goddammit, she thought, eyeing the mess in the room that confirmed what her admittedly alcohol-stained memory had already told her. As much as she wished she was capable of blacking out drunk, she always eventually remembered everything. She groaned loudly and tried to compose herself.

Okay. Okay, Claire. Calm down and breathe. It's just a frickin' throw rug, not the actual carpet. The furniture is covered for a reason. Yes, you brought a total stranger home, and yes he SAW. But Mariska came and her note says she took care of it. Everything's okay. Do NOT freak out, you've got this. It's okay.

She grabbed her keys and ran out the door.

I swear, though. Sometimes being a frickin' werewolf is such a pain in the ass.

Chapter Two
⦾⟩⟩⦿⟨⟨⦾

Pulling into the parking lot of her small office, Claire took a breath to relax. She was having a hard time focusing thanks to the events of the last evening, and her mind drifted back to a year prior; to the day after the night she had been trying to forget. Her memory flashed to the secluded hotel where the ginger woman had sat on the end of her bed, cold green eyes glaring as she spoke to her like an angry parent. Her Scottish lilt sounded irritated, like the voice of a woman who would rather have been anywhere but there. "This… like it 'r not… is what ye are now, and ye cannae turn off what ye are."

"Everything will be louder for ye, now. Sights, sounds, smells. You'll feel... overwhelmed all the time if you let yourself be, so ye need to find things that help ye control tha' input a bit." Sighing, the put-upon redhead shook her head as she continued in a flat, matter-of-fact voice. "Simple things. *Real* things. Flowers by yuir bed so ye c'n focus on tha' scent an' push everything else out f'r a time."

"It'll get t' be too much, ya ken? Ye dinnae have t' transform to feel the wolf, girl. Yuir never NOT the wolf, but th' wolf is never not you, either. So listen t' what ye hear. Take it all in and learn to understand it all. Ye may not be hairy but once a month unless ye choose t' be, but those gifts… an' they ARE gifts even if ye don' always think they are… are a part of ye, now. All the time."

"You're late," Marcia said, as Claire came in through the main door of *Pixel Monkey Marketing,* two coffees steaming and fresh in a brown, sculpted paper tray. Only about 6 minutes late, the slightly frazzled young graphic designer was prepared.

"This is true, but I've already provided my penance, Marcia. Behold, French Vanilla with Snickerdoodle cream," she said, holding out the flavor she knew her employer preferred.

Marcia Bryce was a lean, athletically built, middle-aged woman with a short shock of silver hair she wore with confidence. She had a stern professional facade but, as far as bosses went, was otherwise fairly personable and generally even-handed. Her few employees were given extremely wide berths to do things like occasionally be late or goof around, so long as deliverables were furnished and they put together good work. Looking Claire up and down for a moment, she quipped,

"Bribery will get you everywhere in this company, Miss Gribbald. Thank you."

Popping her own cup out of the holder, Claire turned toward the main body of the office. It was a small, reclaimed space in an older, Spanish-style building that used to be a home before it was converted. The brunette's own little cubicle was tucked in the back, her chair up against the rear window, which overlooked a small patio and picnic area behind the building. The top shelf over her cubicle and the narrow shelf along the side was adorned with a rather dense collection of houseplants she had brought in to make it easier to relax at work. The position of her desk had been chosen to ensure that the veritable jungle would get good sunlight throughout the day.

Scattered between the plants was a clutter of tchotchkes, mostly liberated from thrift stores; little shot glasses, snow globes, and assorted miniature buildings from vacation destinations she had never been to. On the cubicle wall were photos of her with friends, her sister Ellie, and one of her with her nephew, Grant, at the Smithsonian a few years ago. Below them, there was an *Edvard Munch* calendar reprinting some of her favorite pieces from the artist.

Tucked halfway behind her computer was a plastic faux-medieval mug she had acquired at a Ren Faire a few years ago, now filled with pens, only half of which had any ink left. A few assorted thumb drives were strewn about around the stacks of used printer paper she wrote notes and doodled on.

Shondra commented regularly that she was crazy to have so

much light on her screen as it washed out the true representation of colors on the graphics, but preternaturally keen eyesight was a perk that Claire couldn't help but enjoy regarding her somewhat unique condition. As such, her work never suffered, and she adored the feeling of warmth from the light that seemed to have a restorative effect on her. While her morning had been stressful, being a werewolf did occasionally have its advantages.

Sliding into her desk and turning on her workstation, Claire took a sip of her coffee and closed her eyes for a moment. As she did, the scents of the Silver Drop eucalyptus and jasmine that framed the edges of her desk filled her senses and helped settle her nerves a little.

"Wake up, Claire." Shondra McKay's somewhat bubbly voice floated from the cubicle across from her own, the cubicle wall blocking some of the light from the window. "Hey, sorry. Could you, uh, get me the layered files you were working on for the Microbrewery brochure? Got an email that they totally need to change all the prices AGAIN and Marcia wants me to take care of it. Thanks!"

Sometimes, it seemed meaningless, going in and working like her life hadn't been completely changed forever. Sometimes she wanted to run away from everything and start over. But, like her plants, it was a way to keep herself centered and grounded; to remind herself not to get lost in the often tumultuous details of her new reality. Besides, she genuinely liked her regular life and sought to maintain it as best as possible. "Huh… Yeah. Hold on, I'll send that over, Shondra."

"Thanks, Claire," Shondra replied, with a beaming smile on her plump cheeks as the two women went to work. The marketing firm tended to keep Claire busy more often than not, and while she had studied fine art in school and wanted to be a painter, graphic design proved to be a useful way to make a decent living off of what she had studied. As such, the job didn't feel like it was a complete waste, allowing her to at least be partially artistic. And unlike her painting, she didn't seem to have as much of a creative block with it.

"Soooo, I see you're wearing your *'hangover ponytail'*. I'm guessing you, uh, had a fun night last night?" Shondra said with a bit of a conspiratorial tone as she leaned across the narrow aisle that separated their desks. "C'mon, Claire. Don't make me go digging. What happened?"

Blushing a deep shade of pink, Claire stammered a bit. "W... what, no. No. I don't have... Shit. I'm fine and last night wasn't all that."

"Oh, c'mon," Shondra said frankly with an almost childlike grin. "I've known you since art school... practically forever... and I *know* when you're... y'know... specifically not talking about stuff. All I did last night was, y'know, run a few task forces online. What happened?"

The two women had met at a small, independent art and design trade school when they were both fresh from high school, and had become fast friends as well as roommates for a time. The shorter, stout woman with the mane of bouncy, auburn curls had been one of Claire's closest friends, and they had shared literally everything for years. It was a closeness that Claire couldn't help but feel a bit of melancholy for, as there was now a massive part of her life that she struggled to keep secret for fairly obvious reasons.

Where once they had gone to those Renaissance fairs together, they now barely saw each other outside of work. The days of dressing in extravagant costumes or spending late nights together talking and watching the over-the-top fantasy, sci-fi, or horror movies that Shondra adored seemed to be gone.

"Ugh... really?" Claire mock-groaned as she clicked through her files, saving them to the cloud as she rolled her eyes a bit. "Well... I *may*... emphasis on *MAY*... have had a bit too much to drink last night, but... there was this guy. He was dancing and he was kinda... cute."

While the evening had been a massive blur when Claire had woken up and she was still in mild panic mode, the embarrassing events had reconstructed themselves as the events replayed for her like a dramatic reenactment on a crime show. "We hit a few bars last night and by the time I noticed him, I was *way* too drunk already."

"We?" Shondra interjected, irritation creeping into her voice. "Oh. Right. You and *Mariska*? Did she take you to one of those... those strange goth clubs she likes so much? With all the weird, super loud music where everyone squeaks with all that vinyl and stuff?"

"Oh, c'mon. She likes good music, too. We all went to that punk show last month that was good, Shon'." Claire replied, trying to pretend that she hadn't noticed the obvious jealousy in her friend's voice.

It was a growing concern that the young woman had avoided thinking about for the last while. Shondra had been her best friend for years since art school; Mariska had only been a part of her life for a little while, but she also knew all about that otherwise hidden truth. It had been a source of regular stress to Claire that her two best friends didn't quite get along. They played nice and made perfunctory efforts, but it was exceedingly rare that she would make plans for them all, choosing the safer option of keeping the two diametrically-opposed women at arm's length.

"Well, I mean, we will have to agree to disagree on 'good music', Claire." Shondra scoffed with an awkward and slightly forced chuckle. "But seriously, what was his name? What happened?"

"His name was…." she paused, blanching and swallowing with embarrassment, hoping that Shondra wouldn't notice the pregnant pause while she sent more files across as a distraction. "You should have the files now. Charlie, his name was Charlie."

"You sure?" Shondra said, clearly having caught her hesitation. "Claire, you totally need to slow down a little. I know you're in near-perpetual recovery mode since… y'know... *he who shall not be named*, but…"

This time, Claire cut her friend off slightly, hoping to push the topic to its natural conclusion. "I know, I know. I just got a little…

carried away. But I had a great night and he was nice. We danced, had a few drinks, and had fun. Fun is *good*, Shondra. Remember *fun*?"

"Uh-huh." She replied, allowing some rare sarcasm out. It sounded oddly artificial. "Isn't fun better when you can… remember it? Anyway, uh, did you two, y'know…"

"Really, Miss. Gribbald. Put the poor woman out of her misery." Marcia strolled out of the small conference room, holding an empty box where they kept the meeting supplies; Post-its, Sharpies, pens, notepads, and the like. She had evidently been setting them out for the meeting with clients that Claire JUST remembered was in an hour. "You're going to give her an aneurysm, and if she dies before the meeting, I'M going to have to explain both her work AND yours, and I would like to not have to do that by myself. So let the woman breathe."

"O. M. G., Ms. Bryce!" Shondra said, mock-groaning to the woman for whom the authoritarian mannerisms did not actually run all that deep. "I don't… I'm not. Uh… do you need help with all that?"

"Indeed. I could use a hand with the setup in there." the boss said, gesturing for Shondra to help her out in the conference room. "Kirsten is out sick today, which means I am a bit short-handed concerning clerical matters. We'll have to send the phone to voicemail for the meeting, but the three of us should be able to manage well enough. Thank you."

As she got up, the caramel-skinned woman shot an anxious grin at Claire that underlined the lack of real communication between the two. Returning the smile, Claire gestured for Shondra to get going. It was a segue that gave Claire a moment to herself, and she let out a long sigh.

In truth, Claire was all but dying to tell Shondra about her night, but it was hard to tell only *parts* of a story, and she hated trying to dance around the facts, especially the particularly terrible way the evening had ended. She could remember that her interest in the man she was ninety-five percent sure *was* named Charlie had been piqued when she picked up on *his* interest from across the room. He was all but projecting his desire and that, along with a few too many drinks, had prompted her to lean into her more carnal desires.

How do you tell your friend that you could *smell* that someone was turned on from thirty-five feet away in a crowded room? How do you tell her that you've been a werewolf for the past year and that *that's* why you've been a bit more distant and a tad more private? And worse, how do you tell her that sometimes... you *like* it.

That was often the truth she found herself the most conflicted about. When she first learned what had happened to her, she was horrified. Broken. She spiraled into depression, desperation, and confusion that led to some utterly terrible life decisions. That early time had been a clusterfuck of epic proportions. Now, she was getting her life back on track; settling into the first full year of her new life with a slightly better outlook, more often than not. She was getting used to it.

Learning that most everything she had seen in horror movies was sprinkled with a heaping helping of utter bullshit helped. Yes, she transformed once a month on the full moon and could not avoid that. By all means, that change always made the days before and after a bit emotionally charged, but she had never lost her mind or become a ravening beast. She had run wild and hunted in the woods. She had howled at the moon and transformed into a creature that was neither wolf nor woman. More than a few of her tastes... particularly where *food* was concerned... had changed. She had been forced to give up on her half-hearted attempts at being a vegetarian, for example, but throughout all of it, she had always remained Claire Gribbald.

Less inhibited, and more emotionally charged at times, but she was still herself.

As the time for the meeting came around, the clients arrived, and everyone else assembled in the conference room. Claire collected her notes and the PDF file of her presentation on a thumb drive as some of the other advantages of her situation ran through her mind. Marcia was talking to three clients from the local chamber of commerce. They were there to review a presentation of proposed social media graphics that Claire had been designing for a countywide PSA. It wasn't the kind of thing that usually required an in-person meeting, but Marcia was taking them to lunch, as they had access to several other potential clients and she wanted the company to make a good impression.

A year ago, Claire despised these kinds of presentations. She hated trying to read the expressions on the faces of customers and she was a nervous wreck worrying that if she screwed up, it could cost the company work. These days, she simply smiled as she adjusted her blouse. From a room away, through the door, she could smell each client. She could hear their heartbeats and tell that one was drowsy, one had drunk way too much coffee, and one simply had to go to the bathroom. Enhanced senses also gave her an advantage over normal people when it came to reading faces and intentions.

She could tell when they were bored or interested; in which concepts excited them. She could tell when they lied. She seriously enjoyed having that basic edge in interactions that she had never had before. It more than made up for the downsides.

Before the door opened, she knew Marcia was coming, and sat back down at her desk for a moment so as to not look like she had been eavesdropping. At the door, her silver-haired employer nodded and raised an eyebrow. "Are you ready? We really need to wow them."

"I'll do my best, Marcia." Claire smiled as she stepped into the room where she already knew what to expect.

Chapter Three
-◝⟩●⟨◜-

"When ye git hungry, take my advice an' EAT. Maybe ye think yuir gonna watch yuir figure an' live on broccoli and tofu, but let me tell ya', girl, that shite ain't gonna fly. Th' wolf won't let it." The voice of the red-haired woman who had given Claire most of her basic werewolf knowledge was strong in her memory today. It wasn't entirely unexpected, all things considered, even if it was a bit annoying as Claire pulled her car into the drive-thru line.

"If yuir feelin' that pang in yuir stomach, listen to it. Cuz I c'n tell ye right now that if ye try an' ignore it f'r too long, tha's the right quickest way there is to find yuirself hairy an' grumpy when it's only th' tenth a' th' month an' there ain't a full moon f'r weeks." It was one of the more important lessons and was definitely relevant at the moment.

"Can I take your order?" The voice through the speaker box outside of her window kicked her out of her memory and Claire shook off the distraction.

"Uh… can I get… two double Whoppers? Cheese, bacon, ketchup, and no pickles or mustard." Claire said, leaning out the window of her car, as she talked a little louder than normal to the speaker.

"Is that it?" Came the disinterested, static-charged reply.

"No. Can I also geeettttt...." She said, looking at the menu with a pursed expression, "Two orders of the nine-count Chicken Fries…"

"Is that it?" the voice repeated, like nails on a chalkboard. Claire's irritation at being rushed started to set in, exacerbated by her hunger.

"NO. Can I also get a large Dr. Pepper and…" She was abruptly interrupted.

"Coke products only, Ma'am."

"Seriously? Since when…? Whatever. Cherry Coke?"

"No."

"Uh… just a frickin' Coke, then. Large, and *that* will be it." Claire snapped as her stomach rumbled loudly. Her hazel eyes flashed just a bit more amber in the moment. She was hungry and irritated and the two were not an ideal combination.

"Pull around to the second window." The voice said flatly as the speaker cut off. Gripping the wheel of her fifteen-year-old Pontiac Aztek, the faux leather covering creaked loudly in protest as she threatened to strip it clean off.

Taking a moment to breathe, Claire tried to calm down, muttering to herself. "Okay, I'm gonna feed you. Calm your tits. And hey, we have options. Cheeseburgers, or *that* asshole, so, y'know. Have it your way."

Pulling up to the window, the amber receded from Claire's eyes and she forced a tight-lipped smile as she held out her bank card to the disaffected teenager in the window. Barely looking at her, he took the card and closed the window.

Despite the glass between them, she could hear his droning voice begin to complain, "Yeah, I dunno. Some fat bitch who…"

Instantly, she rolled up her own window and smacked the power button on the radio to drown out the sound, talking to herself to add to the chaos that… with some work… eventually overwhelmed her hypersensitive ears. "Yeah, some brain-dead asshole sixteen-year-old who is seriously making me reconsider fucking eating people. Oh, yeah, I could yank his pimple-ass head out of the frickin' window and chuck it across the street, easy."

When she finally heard him yelling for her attention on the other side of the closed window, she glanced in the rearview mirror and winced a bit at the sight of herself. Her eyes were now a solid amber and she was fairly certain her teeth were starting to grow.

Scrambling for a pair of sunglasses, she slipped them on, rolled down the window without adjusting the radio in the slightest, and snatched the card out of his hand without a word. Then, as the sound of Led Zeppelin's IMMIGRANT SONG blared out of the car, she held out her hand again as he all but shoved the bag of food with her drink into it.

Shutting the window and pulling away a little too quickly, she was back on the road and heading home after just a few moments. She had already eaten an entire burger. Overwhelming hunger was, as it turned out, one of the occasional downsides to her situation.

As she tore into it, doing her level best to satisfy her craving, not crash into anything, and not get ketchup on her blouse, Claire worked to calm herself down. Her meeting at work had run long, and she had ended up only having a snack bar at lunchtime. At the time, she'd known it was a massive mistake, considering she was already stressed out from the night before and how it had ended, which was a surefire recipe for letting herself get overly worked up.

Since being turned, she found that she was much quicker to get angry, but it hadn't yet proven uncontrollable, in spite of her persistent fear of exactly that. The anger was manageable. Being hungry at the same time, however, was a combination she quite disliked. It made the anger feel twice as intense; twice as hard to contain. Still, to this day, the worst that had happened in public were a couple of audible growls.

On at least one occasion, it had actually sounded kind of like a fart, and she had been more than willing to lean into the misunderstanding in a rare case where a potential fart was much more acceptable.

Thanks to the typical afternoon rush hour traffic on I-275, she pulled into the parking lot outside of her apartment building two hours after she had left work, even though her office was only a few miles away. The old joke that she could have gotten out of the car and run home faster was quite true in her case. Somehow, though, that made it LESS funny to her as she collected the trash from the empty fast-food bags and tossed it all into the dumpster on the side of the building.

The apartment was enough of a mess at the moment; it didn't

need any help.

The two-story apartment complex was your standard, cookie-cutter Florida bank of buildings. Beige stucco exteriors were virtually everywhere and, like so many others, this one peppered arch shapes into the openings of the stairwells which, along with the three-deep run of faded red tiles along the roofline, allowed the owners the continued delusion of their prefab buildings being 'Spanish Colonial'.

Regardless, Claire liked her cozy little one-bedroom apartment. The fixtures were old enough to have a stylish, vintage feel, and she had put a lot of effort into making the place a home over the last couple of years. She had gotten some cute pieces of furniture and there was some art on the walls she had picked up from local artists. Regardless of the clutter, it was home.

What she didn't like, as she opened up the door and stepped into the mid-sized living room, were the piles of fur still scattered all over the living room, and the small bloody stain on her favorite throw rug.

Okay… she thought, walking around the rug to put her purse and her keys on the counter. *All you did was scare him. It's not like you frickin' ATE him. You wouldn't be that hungry today if you had. Plus… you don't DO shit like that, Claire. On your worst day, you haven't. You don't lose control like… You aren't like that. This wasn't that.*

Leaning down, she sniffed the air above the rug and knitted her brows. *Mariska's note said she took care of it, and it's not like the cops or fucking ANIMAL CONTROL were outside waiting when you woke up. Her scent is all over the room, so it's okay.*

Placing her fingers on the bridge of her nose, Claire pressed them together and groaned as she looked around. *What you DID do was make it to the living room and turn back to normal here, instead of outside somewhere or in the shower with a tarp down, like normal. Fucking fur is everywhere.*

The movies, she had long ago discovered, made a lot of things up. Oftentimes, those inventions were due to the technical limitations of special effects to make werewolves for the silver screen that had evolved into lore, but the reality was just a smidge messier in a couple of ways. Heading into the kitchen, she grabbed a white plastic trash bag from the box under the sink, along with a roll of heavy-duty cling wrap.

In the movies, werewolves would usually grow fur, then at the end of the evening that fur would either VANISH thanks to a basic dissolve shot or would literally grow BACK into the skin, thanks to the power of editors reversing film. Over the last year, she'd learned that was not the case. Instead, the nearly two-inch-long fur that sprouted all over her would simply SHED off when she transformed back. Everything would come off, except the hair atop her head, which would generally be a couple of inches longer after a change, her eyebrows, and any places she normally had body hair. It was a cycle that left a LOT of fur behind AND blew out her haircuts every time.

Looking down at the mess in front of her, Claire rolled her eyes and sighed. "Oh, fuck this. I need wine first."

Tossing the bags onto the bar next to her purse, she went back into the kitchen and poured herself a glass of wine, taking a moment, lamenting a bit more than necessary before getting back to it. By now, as she tended to transform more than once a month, she had the clean-up down, but it didn't make the process any more pleasant as she picked up the clumps of fur to stuff in the trash bag.

Really? She thought to herself, as she took a look at one of the handfuls of hair. *Wait, is that...? Shit, those are gray hairs. Ugh. Is my fur really going GRAY? I can't believe I'm having a vanity issue about my fucking WEREWOLF fur.*

On her knees, she worked her way across the room, which looked as if she had been wantonly rolling around across every piece of furniture as she transformed back to her normal form. There was somehow fur UNDER the coffee table and behind the old TV stand. *Okay, that's it. I either have to stop drinking or stop getting horny when I drink, because this is ridiculous.*

Twenty minutes later, the bag was mostly full and she pondered why she had to, on top of everything ELSE, be as tall as she was, as it simply gave her more surface area for fur to grow when she transformed. Putting the bag in the corner, she went to work folding up the blankets she kept over the couch and armchair for just such an occasion. They were cute, patterned blankets that she and Shondra found at a Ren Faire a couple of years ago that tended to stay folded up in the closet except when it got cold. These days, though, they served double duty to help reduce the amount of stray fur on the furniture when she transformed at home.

Cracking open her apartment door, Claire peeked out onto the second-floor landing of the stairwell to see if anyone else was out there, and as soon as she confirmed what her hearing had already told her, she stepped out with the two large blankets and the folded-up throw rug. The stairwell was an external one that, while covered, was open at the front and back, and since the rear of her apartment complex overlooked a small, wooded area, it was generally a good place to shake out the excess fur.

Holding the first blanket over the railing, Claire looked around again to make sure she was alone before beginning to shake it out. There wasn't all that much wind, so the remaining hairs that clung to the blankets drifted gently out into the air and down to the woods below the ledge like a weird, dark brown snow. *Dark brown with bits of gray*, Claire bemoaned, still fixating on that inane detail.

By the time she had finished the bloody throw rug, which she was hoping she could recover with OxiClean and a good scrubbing, she heard the sound of a door on the first level open up. Instinctively, she winced a bit and the hairs on the back of her neck stood up.

"Miss Gribbald? Is that you?" Came the voice of an older man calling up to her. The elderly Cuban landlord who lived downstairs with his wife and granddaughter was sweet and rarely gave her a hard time about anything, except breaking the building rules, which forbade pets.

"Yeah, it's me, Mister Álvarez. Everything okay?" Claire replied as she quickly tried to fold up the blankets, hoping that her actions hadn't been noticed.

"Oh, everything is okay. I'm just heading over to check the mail and… Que esto?" He replied, causing Claire to freeze. From inside the apartment, she could hear his wife call out to him, but there was also a TV on particularly loud inside, and even with her hearing, from that far away, she couldn't quite make out what was being said.

"Hay un montón de pelo en el piso. Parece ser de un perro." He called back in, far louder than seemed necessary, leading to another series of hard-to-decipher mumbles and his next response. Like the first comment, it was in Spanish, leaving Claire to wonder if they were talking about HER. "Na, ella no tiene perro. Okey yo le pregunto…"

"Is there any hair up there on your landing, dear? I know you don't have a dog, but there's a lot of… it looks like dog fur… all over the place down here," He asked. Looking around, Claire bit her bottom lip a little, grateful that MOST of the fur had floated well away from her as she grabbed the blankets up.

"No, it's pretty clear up here, Mister Álvarez." Thankfully, it wasn't a direct lie. She waited anxiously for the reply. Instead, there was a bit more back-and-forth, and she listened along to see if she would have to further explain what she was doing. There were times when living above the landlords was difficult, to say the least.

What came was a litany of Spanish that she, despite 4 years of it in high school, was unable to decrypt.

"No mami, ella dice que no hay nada allá 'riba. Si, se que el pelo está cayendo de arriba, pero ella dice que no tiene un perro…"

"No mami no voy a revisar el apartamento. ¿Tu se lo quieres revisar? Pienso que no…"

"Como?! No la estoy mimando. Por Dios mujer no dije que esta buena, tu esta loca!"

"Acabe de ver la novela y no me jodas mas." He shouted at the end of a string of comments, of which Claire recognized maybe three or four words. He finished up in English. "Okay, well have a good day, dear."

"A si...esta mujer está loca...todas las jevitas de 20 años se quieren acostar conmigo...ya quisiera por un día de fiesta." He shouted again before heading back inside and slamming the door. Taking the moment to be grateful she hadn't quite been caught, Claire rushed back inside her own apartment with a relieved sigh.

She quickly did what she could to get the rest of the finer hairs up, first pulling out a long sheet of the cling wrap and rolling it along the floor like an enormous lint roller. Experience had taught her to get as MUCH of the hair up as possible BEFORE unleashing the vacuum cleaner, lest she break another belt or clog it up again. It was, as always, a chore and a half, but after another half hour, she was settled onto the couch, wine in hand, victorious.

Shit… She thought, taking a sip. *I'm fucking hungry again.*

Chapter Four

"AHHH! There she is. There is my wild woman!" Mariska called out across the small, mostly empty ramen bar as she caught sight of Claire from the kitchen window.

A lean, predictably pale pixie of a woman, Mariska's smile was wide and happy as she leaned back to yell to the restaurant manager. " David!! Take over for a bit, I shall be right back. I am taking a break."

"What? You've got two bowls to finish, I need you in the kitchen. C'mon!" came the reply from the flustered-sounding man. At that, she looked over to Claire, flumped her shoulders, and rolled her eyes.

Looking back at the man in the kitchen with her, Mariska's voice dipped and got just a TINGE flatter. "No, you want to cook up those dishes and give me a break, because I have been working ever so hard this evening."

With a wry smirk, Mariska held up three fingers, pulling each down one by one as a silent countdown before David's voice came back, "You're overdue for a break. Why don't you go relax? I can take care of these orders for a few minutes."

"Ah. You have my eternal thanks, David. You are... exceedingly sweet." She said, biting her bottom lip mischievously as she vanished from the window. A few seconds later, the whisper-thin woman came out of the rear door to the kitchen, untying the back of her fairly pristine-looking white apron that looked even crisper on top of the almost cliché, black-on-black outfit she had on.

Her slightly wide face was set with large, round eyes and pale skin framed by bright, platinum-blonde hair that went halfway down her back, parting in the middle while sweeping around the sides. She looked to be in her early twenties at the MOST but was a good bit older than she looked, being a vampire.

27

Beyond that, she had also become quite a close friend over the past year that they had known each other, with Mariska fulfilling a unique role of both the bad and calming influences in Claire's unbalanced life. She encouraged Claire to come out of her shell to embrace a less inhibited lifestyle, being a well-established 'party girl' across a few decades now, while also working to help the anxious werewolf to try and accept that newer aspect of her existence as a good thing. It was a strategy that sometimes helped but sometimes blew up in their faces, as it had the night before.

The ramen bar, called *'Art of the Noodle'*, was a narrow little place lined with art along the walls from local artists, Claire among them. The ceiling was black and lit up by strings of yellow-white Edison bulbs to give it an 'outdoor' feeling. By the front was a café-style countertop bar with two patrons on stools who Mariska ignored as she grabbed a bottle of wine from the cooler, a single glass, and bounced to the high-backed booth in the rear that Claire tended to prefer.

"There she is, and looking far less ragged now than when last I saw her. When she ditched me. How goes it, *volchonok*?" Mariska said, as she slid into the booth next to Claire, bumping up against the much taller woman's hip. Without a hint of an accent otherwise noticeable, she slipped in the little affectation that translated into 'wolf cub' in the woman's native Russian.

"Oh, I'm fan*tas*tic. I'm *calm*. See, this is my *calm* face, 'Riska." Claire said, leaning in to only partially whisper with a clearly exaggerated, fake smile sarcastically on display. "C'mon, how do you think it's frickin' going? I've been stressing myself out all day over what happened."

Looking over to notice the two people at the bar gazing at them with curious expressions, the anxious brunette leaned over a bit further and lowered her voice. "He SAW, 'Riska. We... I got turned on, we started making *out* and I... we almost slept together before..."

"Please, you are panicking for nothing. I got your drunk-text and you saw my Post-It, correct? I said I took care of it, so it is, in point of fact, quite taken care of." Mariska shrugged nonchalantly, replying with a casual tone that didn't have the intended effect of calming her friend down as she poured a glass of wine and slid it over to Clare. "I am glad I actually checked my phone for a change, though, because that was quite the mess."

Taking a large swig of the offered wine, Claire groaned and slumped back in the booth. "What did you do?"

Leaning over the chair on her folded arms, Mariska's expression shifted to a faux-guilty one while her voice lowered so that their conversation wouldn't carry to the other customers. "Welllll, thankfully, you had given me a spare key in case of emergencies."

Changing course, Mariska straightened up and relaxed her tone. "I was a touch... concerned about how you took off at the club, so I… may have been out in the parking lot outside your apartment pacing nervously when you messaged me. My apologies, but I am still glad I did. By the time I showed up, I listened to make sure I wasn't going to be bursting in on a *GOOD* time, but all I heard was two sets of snores coming from the wrong room. So I decided to check JUST in case. You were already curled up on the couch sleeping off your... enboozening… and he was out cold on the floor with a bloody nose."

"Ugh… I remember everything up until right after the bloody nose." Claire groaned.

"Well, you were GONE. I saw from the fur that you had transformed, then changed back again, I suppose, maybe after you had passed out. I carried you to your bed and got you settled, which was adorable, by the way." Mariska leaned her head down to try to put her face into Claire's line of sight. "Seriously… you make this little… well, not a PURR, because you are not a wereCAT, but not unlike a little humming. Like a happy little engine. It is quite endearing, really."

Claire snickered in spite of herself and looked over at Mariska again, who continued. "I woke up loverboy, who immediately started freaking out. I nipped that in the proverbial bud and…

calmed him down quickly." As she retold the tale, she waggled her fingers in the air, mimicking an old-timey movie hypnotist.

"I used my little… what do you call it, the Jedi mind trick... to talk him into giving up the details, figuring if you were THAT drunk, you might need them too. He said that you brought him to the bedroom, completely inebriated, and started to make out. But you were so far gone that once you got… appropriately worked up, you transformed." Mariska related the story, smirking a bit as she did, "He turned and ran and, I still cannot believe it, missed your front door, running face-first into the wall."

"He knocked HIMSELF out, Claire. Praise be to the power of my influence that he actually told me that. The visual will keep my cold little heart warm for days." Mariska chuckled. "So... I cleaned him up and told him *firmly* to forget he had even been there. Oh, and to start walking his posterior home."

"And as you know, I am exceedingly persuasive. So… no harm, no foul. I *promise*. He does not remember a *thing*." She held up two fingers in a mock, scout's honor gesture. Taking another swig of her wine, Claire just sighed again and rolled her eyes.

"Thanks." She muttered, avoiding eye contact, clearly embarrassed. "I remember most of it. I remember changing and him losing his shit. I remember... running out to the living room to try and stop him to explain, which just freaked him out more. I was able to calm down enough to change back, but he still bolted, and missed the door."

"He passed out, I cried, and I think that's when *I* crashed, too. Well, after I drunk-texted you. Shit… he was bleeding. Sorry about you having to deal with that. I know it's a bitch for you to have to smell that." Claire said contritely.

"Meh," Mariska scoffed, leaning back a bit and waving the comment off dismissively. "I am a vampire, not a junkie. Besides, I had a pint before we went out and you keep a few cans in your refrigerator for me, so it was fine. Again, on my word."

Claire seemed to be working overtime to not feel better about the entire evening. Curling her lips a bit, Mariska sighed and employed a different strategy. "Really, I wish my little mind trick worked on wolves so I could just nudge you out of your depression, here; however, that is not in my power. I do have other means to soothe what ails you. Let us get some food in you, because I can see that gorgeous-but-telling gold creeping up in your eyes." Mariska raised an eyebrow and grinned. "Sooo, steak and broccoli bowl with gochujang sauce?"

"Extra steak, and no gochujang sauce. Garlic sauce, tonight." Claire stated, which prompted an exaggerated reaction as Mariska reared back, putting her arms in front of her face in a mock defensive posture.

"GAAARRRlic!!! HISSSSS!!!" she exclaimed before both women giggled, as that particular ingredient had no real effect on vampires. "Very well. I shall be right back and we can fill each other in on everything we missed last night. Rest, *volchonok*."

Getting up, the ethereal blonde skipped using the door and instead hopped up to slide into the kitchen through the service window, which elicited a look of shock from the two patrons at the counter. Looking back at them, Claire could now see that familiar twinge of crimson in Mariska's normally-black eyes as she spoke in that same, slightly flat tone she did when she insisted on being paid attention to. "Mind your business. Eat your food."

Without missing a beat, while Mariska waggled her eyebrows over at Claire, the two customers did as they were told.

About an hour later, dinner had been eaten, and with Mariska's shift over, the two found themselves walking the old, brick-lined streets of Ybor City as a warm breeze carried the sounds of the bustling nightlife not too far from them. As more patrons kept piling into the café, a little privacy had been needed and a walk seemed to be the answer.

One of the more unique elements of the old city founded on cigar factories was the presence of a moderately large population of wild chickens that wandered the streets with impunity. It was something the locals were used to and that tourists adored.

Tonight, it was a minor distraction as a small line of birds crossed in front of the two women.

Smirking slightly, Claire allowed herself a brief moment of indulgence since nobody was in earshot, and she let out a loud, moderately throaty growl towards the avian jaywalkers. With a flutter of feathers and squawking, the wild poultry ran away from the brunette werewolf and the vampire walking with her.

Mariska giggled at Claire's little display. "Okay, you CANNOT still be hungry after that, *volchonok*?"

"Oh, hell no. That bowl was like how sex used to feel back in the day." Claire shook her head, chuckling to herself as she beamed. "As always, you seriously killed it, Riska."

"I may not be able to EAT what I cook anymore, but I have been cooking for the better part of a century. I SHOULD be fairly good at it by this point." Mariska said, as she spun around to face Claire, walking backward now. This was made doubly impressive by the chonky, 2-inch-heeled black leather boots she was wearing.

Knitting her brows a bit and blushing, Claire replied contritely. "I'm sorry. I know you can't really eat, like, FOOD food. I don't need to be going on about it."

"Firstly, stop apologizing for everything. Two, I LIKE cooking. It relaxes me and I love the play of aromas. I love surprising people and I can still TASTE what I make, I just can't swallow it. Yes, you can laugh at that. And C, I LIKE cooking for you. You eat it all with intense passion and that pleases me." Mariska listed out her points with a grin, counting them off with her fingers as she did. "Again... that came off as perverse, but I stand by any interpretation you wish to apply. So, calm down. You are allowed to like my cooking. I'm GLAD you like my cooking."

The embarrassment started to fade, along with the anxiety she had been carrying all day after her disastrous evening last night. But the events of it all were still prominent in her mind, and now that there was nobody in earshot, Claire could talk about it as they walked.

"I would break my frickin' neck if I tried that," she commented on Mariska's casual, backward strutting as her very coordinated friend scoffed dismissively.

"Well, I'm fairly certain that you can heal from a broken neck, which reduces the sting of that particular bit of hyperbole. As for the other side of that coin, these aren't even the biggest heels I own by half. It just takes practice, not any kind of preternatural skill." The graceful woman explained. "Which is a long way around saying we need to take you shoe shopping and get you out of the sneakers more often."

"So… I really freaked him out, didn't I?" Claire asked, somewhat sheepishly, changing the subject back around.

As they walked, they came upon a waist-level wall that separated the sidewalk from the mostly-empty parking lot next to them. Still walking backward, Mariska hopped up onto the wall as she replied. "I mean, yes. I do not want you beating yourself up over it all night. But I am guessing you did not exactly warn the young man?"

Letting out a sigh, Claire nodded as she muttered to herself. "Yeah, obviously not."

"So, yes. He 'freaked out' and panicked. But no other harm was done." Mariska said, hopping off the wall to look up at Claire's downcast eyes. "And… as you said, you did not give him a warning. It is not as if he was the one you are going to show one day who *will* understand."

Looking down at the significantly shorter woman, Claire smiled awkwardly as Mariska continued. "Look. You would think I would be better at this kind of… pep talking… after all this time… but just bear with me and I will… get this all out."

With that, the whisper-thin woman clad in black stopped and did her best to finish her thought. "I shall hop aboard the self-recrimination express with you if you want. We can ride the rails together. That was, by the way, actually a thing people did when I was younger. But… a part of this is on me, Claire."

"This isn't YOUR fault, 'Riska. I was…" She put a finger over Claire's lips.

"Shhh. Momma Vampire is talking," she said, with a grin that showed more affection than it did any real sarcasm as she kept going. "I was turned during the Great Depression. By and large, my life has only improved exponentially. But sometimes even I forget just how bleak and horrible those first few years were for me. I was largely on my own. My maker simply abandoned me to suss it all out on my own and the rest of my life was basically gone. I *know*."

"I did not have someone to tell me that this new life could be exactly as amazing as I wanted it to be. I did not have a... friend that knew the hurdles. So... when I saw you with that asshat in that club last year and realized how raw and broken he had left you, I had to be for you what I didn't have." Mariska said frankly and honestly while Claire listened.

"And last night I... to use the parlance... fucked up. I... thought I could take you out on the town and show you the most exceptional night ever on the first anniversary of your turning. Show you that your life could be just as amazing as you want it to be. That you didn't have to wallow or focus on the bad times." the little vampire admitted, looking a bit sheepish, which looked in no way natural on her.

"I thought I could defeat your feelings with... volume, and just... powering through your harder memories. Maybe we should have gone to your place and streamed a bunch of teary movies and ordered a pizza for you. Maybe I should have taken you out to go running with wild abandon. I... I do not know. I just knew I didn't want you looking back on something I tend to think of as *exceptional* with... agony." She finished, looking legitimately sad for her friend, her black-lined lips pursed a bit.

"Exceptional?" Claire said, confused by Mariska's choice of words in describing her state of being.

"Yes..." Mariska replied with a dismissive shrug, trying to deflate the emotion of the moment. It was a hollow attempt betrayed by her words. "We weren't *friends* before."

The two stood there in silence for a moment, as the tiny,

century-old vampire looked up at the still fairly new werewolf who had marked the first year since her transformation only the night before. As she did, she leaned in and a mischievous grin crept onto her pale cheeks. "I may not be able to mesmerize you, hairy woman, but I can MAKE you laugh if you keep fighting me. Come, now, do not make me. You are strong, but I am far stronger, and you, my little wolf, are aggressively ticklish."

Pointing a finger sternly at Mariska, Claire pouted petulantly. "Don't you EVEN dare. I will…"

"What, kick your leg at five-hundred RPMs if I find your sweet spot? Give it up, *volchonok*. I have you! You are defeated. Smile, or I *am* going in for tickly scritches." Mariska smirked maniacally, raising her painted black nails in a mock attack. It was ridiculous and over the top and induced the desired result as Claire held her hands up in defeat and laughed authentically.

"I frickin' yield, okay?" Claire laughed a bit more as Mariska folded her arms behind her back and stood smugly in her victory.

"Obviously, being a wise enough woman, you do. I am INVINCIBLE! Now… the night is young, and so are we." Mariska declared, holding her arms up dramatically. "Well… metaphorically, and spiritually in my case."

Claire shook her head and smirked slightly as they continued walking. "Riska, I am not even KIND of wanting to do anything resembling a club or a bar after last…"

"As always, I am fervently ahead of you." Mariska winked and spun around. "Which is why I have a selection of some movies I know you like, a pint of cookies and cream, and a box of Riesling in the fridge back at my house."

"What say you? Monster girls' night in?"

Claire chuckled in spite of herself and nodded. "That sounds much more my speed right now."

Chapter Five
⊰ ⟩ ☾ ☉ ☽ ⟨ ⊱

It was a sunny Saturday and Claire sat in her cozy apartment, the windows open so she could hear the sounds of the birds outside and taste the scents off of the breeze from all the way across the bay. There was a cruise ship in dock and she was getting the occasional whiff of people coming aboard from a variety of states. It made for an interesting blend of seasonal aromas that all told the young werewolf a story. It was, all in all, an ideal day so far…

… Except for the blank canvas staring at her. "Shit, what's wrong with me?" she muttered to herself as she slumped back in her chair and scowled.

After spending the morning cleaning up her cluttered abode, Claire had moved the laundry draped over her easel in the corner of her bedroom and pulled out her acrylics to try and get some work done. It had been months since the last time she put brush to canvas to simply try and express her creativity, and she found herself missing that release.

In truth, it had been a full year. She had tried to paint a few times, making perfunctory attempts that hadn't yielded any real results, and a part of her was uncomfortable even trying. It felt like something had been lost when she was changed, and Claire was afraid it might never come back.

Sitting there in the sun-dappled room by herself, nothing seemed to come to her. All morning, she had worked up ideas of things she could paint to try and knock off the proverbial dust, but it seemed that here in the moment, the creative muse had abandoned her.

In school, her teachers considered her prolific. If an assignment called for one painting on a subject, Claire would frequently create two or three, examining the subject in multiple styles or from different angles, expressing her feelings through the skills she had spent years cultivating. She tended to prefer expressionism and neo-expressionism with leanings toward more representational art.

That, however, seemed to take a back seat to everything else for the past year. A year ago, she had met him and begun a whirlwind relationship that ended in both heartbreak and the establishment of a new status quo in her life. As it turned out, becoming a werewolf had taken up significant real estate in her mind.

This wasn't unexpected over the first few months, where it was trial and error combined with what little Mariska could piece together about her new state of being. Now, well into her first full year, Claire was hoping that she had become settled enough to get back to the things that she loved.

Staring into the abyss of white as it practically mocked her, however, was proving that she was still struggling more than she would like. Putting the brush in her hand down on the canvas, she leaned back and let out a heavy sigh. This was not making for a productive day off.

Pulling away from the vexing canvas, Claire looked over at her laptop, which was open on the dresser to her right so she could research any reference images she might need; however, she found herself surfing social media more than anything else at the moment. Most of it was inane nonsense to serve as a time-wasting distraction, at least until a message popped up in the corner.

"Hey, Claire. Long time no see? Are you around?"

She rolled her eyes. The message was from her sister, Ellie, in Pennsylvania. The sister she had barely spoken with over the last year, making only the occasional and desultory messages and calls when it had been too long. Considering it was October, she was well overdue.

Pretending she hadn't seen the message, Claire closed the laptop and stepped away to find a different distraction.

Even before she was changed, she had been distant from her family. Moving fifteen hundred miles away to go to art school and eventually set up new roots in Florida was not by accident; she had pretty much always felt like the black sheep of the Gribbald clan. She was the introspective artist in a family of loud, judgmental schmoozers. Most of the people in her family worked in some capacity in the restaurant industry, and Ellie had taken over their family's little seafood restaurant with her husband after they had their kid. She was the doting daughter carrying on the tradition Claire didn't honestly care much about.

In the kitchen, she considered picking up a bit and putting the dishes in the strainer tray away. In the living room, she thought about rearranging the furniture; anything to occupy her mind and help her avoid having to make an awkward phone call, especially since it was clear that her brain wasn't going to let her paint.

Mulling over her options, Claire's eyes drifted to the closet by the door, where she kept her rarely-used jogging shoes. It was a particularly nice day; perhaps getting out of the house and going for a run might help shake off some of the rust she was feeling. Running, however, like painting, was an activity fundamentally affected by her situation. Where once she found jogging relaxing, she now found it constricting and frustrating.

It was hard to jog for fun when, if she allowed herself the freedom, she could run TRANSFORMED. There was nothing quite as exhilarating as running in wolf form. Putting on off-brand Nikes and leisurely jogging around the bay didn't even come close.

In the bedroom, a large basket of clean laundry needed to be hung up and put away, so she walked back that way to take care of it. Hopefully, it would help to clear her mind.

Twenty minutes into the task, her phone buzzed once from on the nightstand next to the bed, and before she even looked, Claire knew what it was.

She sighed as she glanced over to see a second message from Ellie.

"Need to talk. Could you give me a call? Thanks."

What's so important that she needs me to call today? Claire thought, complaining to herself as she finished the last of the reasonable distraction activities she could manage.

It seemed there was no way around it; if she didn't call back eventually, her sister would just call her. Resigning herself to the awkward task, Claire flumped back onto her bed with the phone and dialed.

Seriously… you've been bugging me all morning and it's still ringing. Pick up the frickin' PHONE, Ellie. The phone continued to ring, and she stared at the ceiling, sighing.

Just as Claire was about to hang up and try restarting her day, her young nephew's voice piped up. "Hi, Aunt Claire!"

The energetic 5-year-old was all but screaming into the phone, which would have been obnoxious for anyone, let alone a woman with preternaturally-enhanced hearing. "Ahh. Uh, hi, Grant. Is your mommy there?"

"Guess what, Aunt Claire? Guess what?" The overly animated, slightly unruly child bellowed into the phone. Claire had turned the volume down and set it down on her belly to compensate for his volume and intensity.

"What, kiddo?" She replied, rolling her eyes at what bit of random toddler-logic she was about to hear.

"Inna… Innarupting cow!" He shouted, clearly trying to repeat a joke he had heard while confusing the specifics of the setup by skipping through it, as children tended to do.

"No, honey. It's 'knock knock'." the slightly nasal voice of her sister gently chided him as she took the phone from her son. "Give Mommy the phone, Granty. Okay, can you give Mommy the phone?"

Rolling her eyes again, Claire interjected. "Hello, Ellie."

"Hey, Claire. Sorry about that. Grant was running around the house with my phone thinking he was just *hilarious*. Right, Grant? Were you being funny?" Ellie said.

"MOOOOO!" The child shouted, now a good distance from the actual phone as Ellie had clearly re-secured it.

"Yes, honey. That's it. Okay, let Mommy talk to your Aunt Claire, okay? Okay." Ellie said, sounding a bit flustered before turning her attention back to Claire, who was a bit irritated at having to wait for a conversation she wasn't looking forward to in the first place. "Sorry, again. It's crazy around here. I am trying to get a bunch of food orders ready for the holidays so we can be well-stocked, and he's just been a terror lately."

"It's fine," Claire said, sounding anything but fine as she replied. "What's up?"

"Well… the holidays were what I was calling about. Aside from the restaurant, I'm also trying to make plans for Thanksgiving and Christmas." Ellie said, her tone becoming far more leading as she did.

"Okay," Claire said, hoping she'd get to the point.

"I wanted to know if we could add you to the count for both? Or, y'know, at least one of them." Ellie said, finally asking. On her end, Claire made only the most perfunctory effort to hold in a sigh, but the moment of silence told the story nonetheless.

"Honestly, I don't know. I don't have a lot of vacation time available this year, Ellie." Claire said, leaning on something that was only half-true, hoping it would placate her sister. It didn't quite work.

"Really, Claire? You used that excuse last year." Ellie said, her tone shifting from agreeable to a more judgmental one that Claire couldn't stand. "Grant hasn't seen you in a year and a half, since the funeral. The least you could do is make it out for Christmas."

"It's not an excuse, I have an actual job. I know you and Mom don't think it's a real job, but it is." Claire snapped back, having worked herself up for an expected conflict. Her sister bringing up their parents' passing in a car accident years earlier didn't help. However, instead of a snapback, she heard a sigh that cut into her stomach.

"Claire, I know you have a job. But… I also know you're avoiding us. I… don't know what's going on with you, but I'd like to. I… I miss you. Mom missed you too, before the accident. Grant is growing up so fast that you're not going to recognize him the next time you see him." Ellie said, laying on the familial guilt as heavily as she could, then immediately denying it; "Look, I'm not trying to guilt you into coming. I just don't understand why you don't want to? I mean, after Mom and Dad died, we're the only family we each have."

Sitting there, looking up at her ceiling, Claire imagined what she wanted to say but couldn't. Her mind filled in her half of the imaginary conversation as she measured her response. *"Oh, good thing this ISN'T another guilt trip! Because this is NOTHING like the lectures I had to listen to all my life! This is nothing like the spiel you gave me about applying to art school or the rant about going out of state to study! This is completely UNIQUE compared to the first Christmas back after I moved down here, where you sat at the foot of my bed and told me how I broke Mom's heart by leaving and not joining you at the FUCKIN' restaurant! Thank GOODNESS this isn't THAT, El!"*

"But hey, you want me there for Christmas, sure thing! Hope you don't mind if I bring my special friend! She's just like me, but half a foot taller, and covered in FUCKING FUR! Sure you want to trust me with Grant THEN!?!" Claire finished the rant in her mind before finally answering for real.

"Really? *MOM* missed me? Seriously? She cut *me* off, Ellie!" Claire hissed through the phone. "You know as well as anyone that she never actually wanted to talk *to* me, just *at* me? She cut me out of her life over my career choices, Ellie. That was all frickin' her. I'm sorry about what happened, but that didn't change what they did."

"This again? Come on, Claire. You need to get over it. You're holding on to drama from a decade ago and nobody cares but you." Ellie countered with a smug dismissiveness that rattled Claire. Biting her bottom lip, she could feel her blood pressure start to ramp up a bit, and immediately that fresh fear kicked in.

Calm down, Claire. Just… let it go. She thought to herself, taking long and slow breaths. *Don't… wolf out over the phone with your sister, for shit's sake.*

The follow-up that came was of a decidedly different and forced tone that she struggled to maintain. "Look, El. I'm... not avoiding you. I can talk to my boss and… I dunno... see if I can get some time, okay?"

"Really, Claire? That would just be wonderful." Ellie said, and Claire could hear her smile over the phone. It just made her feel that much worse, particularly after it was clear that the woman didn't care about Claire's discomfort with the topic of their departed mother.

"Well, let me actually find out first, okay? Just, I'll give you a call as soon as I find out if I can get the time." Claire replied, desperately hoping to just end the awkwardness of the conversation and placate her sister.

"Okay, just let me know as soon as you know so I can make sure we're prepared. This is great, Claire. So, otherwise, how have you been doing?" Ellie replied, insisting on keeping the conversation going, which caused Claire to stifle a groan as she answered as vaguely as possible. After all, she had reasons for keeping most of the details of her life to herself, and she had no desire to share with her judgmental family.

She could only imagine how her mother would have criticized her werewolfing were she still alive. *'Really, Claire? THAT'S how you hunt deer? I'm surprised that you're not skinnier at this point. And on that note, what are you eating, whole cows? Really, you should werewolf more like your sister.'*

Again, her actual response was muted. "Good. Things are busy at work, as usual. But you know me, keeping busy."

"Oh, are you still doing the… art thing? How is that going?" Ellie asked, finding the most dismissive way to encapsulate the interest Claire was struggling to reignite her passion for. Thankfully, or not, as the case may be, Ellie didn't give her sister a moment to respond as she started talking AT her instead of with her. "Grant has really taken an interest in art. He just loves seeing his Auntie Claire's paintings on Facebook, so we got him one of those kid's art kits and he just loves it. I think it may run in the family. I can tag you in his pictures the next time I post some, but I think you'll love it…"

The general tone of the conversation persisted as Claire's sister continued to talk over anything she had to say. It was a perpetually infuriating aspect of her family that contributed to not missing them all that much.

She zoned her out as best as possible as she started planning her evening. *Ugh. I need to call and see what Mariska's doing. Hopefully, it's something involving alcohol.*

Chapter Six
·)⟩●(⟨·

One would have thought that after putting her laundry away like a normal person earlier in the day, it would have been easier for Claire to assemble an outfit for the evening. However, going through her closet proved to be the standard exercise in frustration; a never-ending war between her desire to look nice and her inclination to blend in.

Nevertheless, after nearly forty-five minutes of hemming and hawing over multiple options, her bed was strewn with the corpses of discarded ensembles, and she felt fairly well put together.

Pulling up to the little dive bar that she and Mariska frequented, Claire looked at herself in the rearview mirror and adjusted her hair. As always, in spite of her well-earned skill at trimming them, the anxious, plain-clothes werewolf still struggled with her frizzy curls. Tonight, a decent amount of product seemed to have collected on one side, leaving her head a little unbalanced with nice, tight ringlets on the left and drier, frizzy waves on the right. Glancing at it again, she did her level best to relax and not worry about it. As much as she stressed over such things, nobody else ever seemed to notice, one way or another.

That being said, she no longer felt invisible, as she used to when going out; in fact, she felt quite the opposite since her transformation. Mariska attributed this to Claire putting out much more intense pheromones on a regular basis. Alas, impressing a member of *any* sex was not on her agenda tonight; she just wanted to have a few drinks, relax, and hang out with a friend.

Stepping out of her car, Claire slung her cross-shoulder-strapped purse over her head and adjusted the cute but casual-looking three-quarter-sleeve top she was wearing. It was dark blue with light blue swirls across the front and was snug enough to show off her curves, but not so tight as to make her overly self-conscious about her slightly thicker build. A low, wide collar showed off some measure of cleavage and made her feel better as she made her way inside to see if Mariska had already arrived.

The bar was just off the main strip of Ybor City and, whenever feasible, Mariska would just walk there. She liked the night air and generally hated cars; plus, as a vampire, she wasn't in any kind of real danger, despite barely touching five feet in height. As expected, the platinum-blonde woman was already inside and leaning against the bar, in mid-conversation with the bartender.

Both turned to look as Claire stepped in, and Mariska waved enthusiastically. "*Volchonok*!! It is about time you got here. Ahh, and wearing those nice, tight jeans we got last week, along with the Doc Martins. Not bad, not bad. Very lesbian chic, though you are playing for the other team."

"Doesn't she look lovely tonight, Samuel?" Mariska leaned over the bar with a sly grin, talking to the bartender. He was a young man with dirty-blonde hair in a short, caesar cut, and a round baby face peppered with blonde fuzz acting as a beard. He was slightly on the chunky side, a smidge taller than Claire's six feet, and seemed a bit embarrassed by the attention.

In truth, he was kind of cute, but Claire wasn't trawling for dates in any capacity, and she came over to put the young bartender out of his misery by picking up the thread before he had to answer. "I look okay. You have taught me well, 'Riska. That said, I'm loving your outfit as well."

"Pitcher and two glasses, please," Claire said with two fingers as Mariska interjected. "It is on my tab tonight, Samuel."

As the bartender got to work, the bar itself was starting to fill up, though there were still plenty of tables available; in particular, Claire's favorite: a little half-booth near the rear. The old, pitted bench was peppered with dozens of band stickers and was just isolated enough for her to talk with impunity, especially once it got louder. A couple of seconds later, the young man returned, and Claire took the large pitcher of beer and the glasses, smiling in a way that she hoped was polite and not misleading as she started towards her preferred booth.

On the way, she deftly avoided an already-drunk young man who was stumbling across the way. One of the perks of her condition was extremely sharp reflexes, for which she was regularly grateful. It took being turned into a werewolf to get past her years of being a klutz.

At the booth, Claire held the pitcher up, knowing Mariska well enough to predict what was next, as the tiny woman, clad head to toe in black, hopped effortlessly as a cat onto the tabletop before swirling like a ballerina in her chonky black leather boots.

Showing off her ensemble, Mariska wore tight, black leather pants with a string of chromed studs going up the left leg that led the eye up to the long-sleeved, tight fishnet top covering only a black, lace bra. A small black backpack-style purse rested over her back, and Claire knew it held little more than a flask of blood. Holding her arms out at her sides, Mariska put on a 'ta-da' pose as multiple bracelets on each wrist jangled, before plopping back off the table to sit in the rear of the booth.

"If I didn't already know better, I'd think you were trying to get us kicked out of every place we go with shit like that, 'Riska." Claire expressed with a sarcastic grin as she sat down and poured both glasses, knowing full well that Mariska could only nurse hers, pretending to drink. One of the bigger drawbacks for her was being unable to stomach most all normal food and drink.

"Nobody complains. And when they do, they rarely remember the reason." Mariska said, grinning, as her eyes flashed red for just a moment. The platinum-haired vampire particularly enjoyed her ability to influence the minds of others as needed and took liberal advantage of it to get away with all kinds of things.

"So… he is cute, is he not?" She said, leaning on her elbows and raising her eyebrows suggestively towards the bartender, who was too busy to notice them on the other side of the small space. "And I am fairly certain he is interested. I was building you up for a bit before your arrival."

"C'mon, 'Riska. I hate when you do that." Claire said,

protesting weakly, as she usually did. There was no real weight behind it, which generally resulted in Mariska plowing ahead with her plans.

"Look, I know our last night out... did not end well. Regardless, I was so proud of you, *volchonok*." Mariska replied, nudging Claire in the arm a bit with that same Cheshire grin. "I mean... I have tried hooking you up a considerable amount over the last few months, and it was wonderful to see you actually TRYING with someone at long last. My dear, I dare say you need to shake the rust off."

"Look, I was drunk and lonely and...well, you know how it goes. Sure... I could tell he was interested, but I don't know if that was real interest or just him reacting to the... y'know... the pheromones I pump out when I'm horny. It makes them... throw themselves at me sometimes. It makes them stupid, and that's not real. I mean, how am I supposed to trust if someone's interest is real?" Claire became serious for just a moment.

"Look..." Mariska replied, matching her friend's tone and doing her best to help. "Yes, you have a bit of an advantage in the dating department, and I KNOW that you stress over that. After all, it was used against YOU at least once. But it did not make you NOT you. You can only get people horny who WANT to be horny. You can attract people who already want that, but it is like my little mind trick. It doesn't work on non-morons and it doesn't make people do things they ordinarily wouldn't. You can stoke interest, but your pheromones cannot KEEP them interested, long term."

"In truth, even I could tell that the man in the club the other night wanted to bed you. It was... inspirational to see you finally notice it yourself."

Shrugging dismissively, Claire took a swig of her beer before raising an eyebrow. "Waitafuckinminute... I ditched you at the club to talk to that... whatever his name was. What do you mean, you saw me hitting on him?"

"Oh, my poor, sad little wolf, you could not ditch me if you tried," Mariska smirked with a wide, proud grin. "And you, in fact, DID try. I was keeping an eye on you, and you were great, but you were also so inebriated, a monumental task with that metabolism of yours, that you did not pick up on my scent in so calamitous a room."

"You just…" Mariska continued, shrugging dismissively to try and declaw the disaster of the earlier night out. "Well… you will get there. Baby steps. And LOOK at that babyface over there. He likes you, I can tell."

"I know you can tell. I can fucking tell, *too*." Claire said, rolling her eyes and taking another, much larger swig. One of the particularly useful parts of having the senses of a wolf was being able to smell the young bartender's interest. Feeling his pulse quicken as she walked in. Hearing his blood pump faster. On one hand, it took a good degree of the guesswork out of dating, but she also wasn't entirely comfortable taking advantage of it. "It doesn't… I don't need a boyfriend, 'Riska! The other night was…"

"Wassss… fun? Liberating? Exciting?" Mariska interjected with a raised brow. "Finale notwithstanding, you WERE enjoying yourself. For just a little while, you let yourself forget what… well… THAT. And that was GOOD."

"You do not need to find… 'THE ONE'. I doubt that's going to happen in a karaoke bar, anyways. But you are allowed to relax and want something for yourself. Even if it IS that willing young man's cock."

Almost spitting out her beer, Claire snorted out a laugh. "Holy shit, 'Riska!! Ha!"

"Clearly, you agree with my brilliance. Listen to your elders, *volchonok*." Mariska declared with an aura of faux pretense as she opened up her purse and pulled out her little travel flask. Taking a sip, she tucked it back in, unseen by everyone but Claire. "All kidding aside… you are under no obligation to… punish yourself with a vow of celibacy."

Flopping her head back against the back of the booth, Claire sank into the seat and groaned, "Shit. I am so goddamn horny, 'Riska."

"Of course you are. You've been keeping yourself from doing ANYTHING even remotely sexual for a year." Mariska replied, shaking her head and gesticulating a bit with her hands. "And… like it or not… this body of yours is not a fan of that decision. It is…"

"C'mon. Don't frickin' tell me it's a biological imperative." Claire moaned.

"Well, it IS. And I'm not just talking about you being a woman on the cusp of her sexual prime, Claire. I mean… what *else* you are. That part of you is… well…"

"If you say, 'an animal', I AM going to punch you." Claire protested, shooting her friend a pouty side-eye as Mariska took out her flask and took another drink.

"Then, it is good you said it for me, is it not?" came the snarky comeback as the pale woman shrugged. "Again, what you are doesn't control you, obviously, if you've kept your legs together for over a year now. But that IS a part of you and that part of you… she wants to FUCK, Claire. Badly."

"I want to *leeeettttt heeeeerrrr.*" Claire moaned in mock-protest, leaning her head back dramatically.

"Well then, we need to get you OUT of this corner booth and back into the proverbial GAME, *volchonok*." Mariska stood up on the bench dramatically. "And that means tonight, we dance and sing, and YOU let the world know that you are a woman on a mission."

Doing her best to keep Claire inebriated, Mariska was committed to the night out being a fun one after their last sojourn. Whenever possible, the tiny vampire would call the curious bartender over to deliver their drinks as an excuse to force as much interaction as possible between the two. For her part, Claire was doing her own level best to be receptive, which was easier said than done.

Growing up, she was used to being largely ignored. Pushing six feet by age fourteen put her off of the radar of most everyone she had ever been interested in. Nowadays, of course, she had a way about her that tended to attract the exact kind of attention she once craved. Sometimes, with just the right kind of prompting, she liked it.

"So, would you like another drink?" Sam said, walking over to collect the now-empty pitcher. Claire was momentarily by herself while Mariska was up at the small stage at the front of the bar, flipping through the karaoke catalog. Normally, the little stage hosted local bands and the like, but once a week, it was karaoke night. Mariska adored karaoke.

"Um… yeah. Actually. Yeah." Claire replied, smiling at him. While she could get drunk with a good degree of effort these days, one pitcher had done very little. Or, more accurately, it did just enough to relax her. "Thanks."

"Hey, not a problem. Same thing, ooorrr… would you like something different?" Sam asked, a telling smile on his face that Claire couldn't help but notice. "You… like rum and coke, right?"

"I do. Am I that predictable?" Claire asked with a raised eyebrow. It felt like cheating for her, like in her meetings with clients. She could hear the beating of his heart and even in the smoky bar, she could smell his interest. The young, soft-faced man liked her, and Claire knew it.

"Well, you two are in here almost every week, and I like to think I'm pretty good at this. So, y'know, I do pay attention. " Sam said with a little air of confidence as he gestured back to the bar. "I'll be right back with that drink."

"I'll be here," Claire replied, nodding and smiling a bit as the young man turned back towards the bar.

Walking back over with the three-ring binder of songs, Mariska hopped up, skipping over the table to sit on the bench next to Claire. "Welllll, look at you. It was subtle, but you were actually letting someone hit on you. Consider me impressed, *volchonok*."

"He wasn't HITTING on me." Claire protested weakly. "He's getting me a drink."

"A drink he knew you liked, because he pays attention to you. When a cute boy brings you a drink, he's hitting on you." Mariska said, flipping through the book.

"Unless that's, y'know, literally his frickin' job, 'Riska." came the reply with an exaggerated moan just before the young, blonde man came back with the requested drink, primping his hair and looking a bit anxious.

"So… here you go," Sam said, setting the drink down with a nervous half-smile. "If you need anything else, just let me know, uh, Claire."

Taking the drink, Claire took a sip, while Mariska smirked with that Cheshire grin of hers, still flipping through the book. Nodding, she replied with a pleasant enough smile. "Thanks. I will, Sam."

"And that's… on the house, by the way," Sam said, scratching the back of his neck as he turned to head back to the bar.

After a moment, Claire pursed her lips, rolling her eyes. "Okay, fine. Maybe he was hitting on me."

"Thank you," Mariska said as she found a song she was considering. Leaning over, she pointed to the selection. "So, what do you think? I mean… it's not my STYLE, per se, but if you can finally acknowledge that someone is actually interested in you, then anything is possible.

"Really? 'Don't Stop Believing'?" Claire said with a raised brow.

"You talk to him again, and I'll sing the most 'on-the-nose' song I could find. Deal? It's that or 'Werewolves of London', just to irritate you."

Chapter Seven
⊰)⊙(⊱

"SQUEEEE!" Shondra squealed from her little cubicle, which was adorned with tiny ceramic dragons, various action figures, little plastic jack-o'lanterns, and a veritable hoard of spooky things.

Halloween was right around the corner and it was the horror-movie junkie's all-time favorite part of the year. She adored the imagery, the music, and the overall spookiness. Up until last year, Claire did as well, although, for obvious reasons, she was feeling a smidge torn on the whole affair this time.

Leaning back from her chair, the brunette graphic designer and secret werewolf smiled across at the much shorter, rounder young woman who had been her best friend since they both attended art school together. "That sounded... 'excited' seems like too small a word. What's up, Shondra?"

"The Halloween store over by the mall is having a huge sale this weekend, and I still need to get a costume for the... y'know... the office party. That and whatever we're going to... um... do." Shondra said, looking at what Claire assumed was this information on her friend's computer screen. "Have you picked out your costume yet? We should run over on Saturday and see what's out."

Shiiiiittt... Claire thought, wincing a little, tucking herself closer to the left of her desk, out of sight, as she did.

Since the beginning, back when they were roommates in school, the two fast friends made elaborate plans for Halloween; themed, often matching costumes, big parties. They went all out. Halloween was Shondra's favorite holiday and one of the only times the stout woman felt even half-comfortable going to parties. That had all changed a year ago when Halloween had been interrupted by Claire having just been bitten and changed. As it turned out, discovering that she was a werewolf two weeks before Halloween hampered her ability to do anything particularly celebratory that year.

While Shondra knew precious little of that period, Claire had all but abandoned her life as it was in that early time of confusion, depression, anger, and grief. The distraught woman had almost allowed it to destroy her life entirely. Eventually, she got a handle on the situation, although it took a good amount of doing to keep her apartment and job after vanishing for weeks. All Shondra knew of the month she had gone missing was that it had something to do with Claire's now EX-boyfriend, and that the anxious brunette did NOT want to talk about it.

Ever.

It was the first rift in what had once been an extremely close friendship. A rift that had continued with Claire desperately trying to keep her biggest secret from her once-closest friend.

"Claire?" Shondra said, snapping the young woman out of her reverie, "C'mon. You said a few weeks ago that we could do something for Halloween again after… y'know."

With the topic orbiting a little too close to the subject Shondra knew was verboten, she got a bit sheepish and quieter as she spoke. "Did you… still want to?"

In truth, the answer was complicated. Claire missed the closeness of her friendship with Shondra and did want to. But the gap that had grown due to the weight of the secret between them had turned many of their interactions into far more awkward affairs, with Claire being regularly nervous about what she could and couldn't say.

Not wanting to disappoint her friend, she thought of many of the best times the two had spent on nights just like the one being planned. She missed those nights and she missed Shondra. Claire decided to push past the roadblocks she had been putting up and try a little harder.

"Uh, yeah. *Yeah*, we can run by on Saturday and check it out, for sure." Claire said, putting aside her anxiety to be as enthusiastic as she could muster under the unusual circumstances. To her surprise, it wasn't entirely forced, and she hoped that she could maintain the energy.

"Awesome! SQUEE! I am sooooo excited. I still don't know what I want to go as, but still, we should be able to stock up on lots of cool stuff for the ren faire in December. Some new weapons and stuff." Shondra said, immediately doubling down on the activities she was looking forward to, clearly hoping to try and restore some of what had been lost as well. "Did you have any ideas, yet?"

"Not really. I haven't thought too much about it, yet. Plus, it's not like there are a lot of great options for my height." Claire replied. This had been true well prior to becoming a werewolf, as pickings of pre-made suits were slim for women over six feet in height.

"Hence… an expedition of adventure and exploration," Shondra replied, working up her confidence. Neither woman was slim, but at a much shorter height and much wider middle, Shondra was no stranger to working hard to find cute costumes. "And, worst-case scenario, we can adapt some bits and pieces to make something awesome."

"Now, there's the OFFICE party on Friday first, so we need something that's easy to function in for work, so maybe two costumes, or a costume that is… like… half-removable. I dunno, something cool." Shondra continued talking as she clicked away at her computer, appearing to look up options on the store's website. "Then, there's next Saturday night."

Over the years, the pair had found a variety of different ways to spend the holiday together in whatever regalia they had come up with, but it was clear from the slight dip in Shondra's voice that she was still treading lightly. "What do you think? What did you want to do?"

A promise HAD been made that this year they would resume their celebration, and Claire was desperate to not disappoint. Taking a sip of her mostly cold coffee, she used the moment to look thoughtful, which served to help her collect her thoughts. "I dunno. I mean, we don't have any friends with tiny humans to drag trick or treating, or anything, so that's not an option. I THINK that they're doing some kind of... pub crawl thing in Ybor. I'd have to check, but..."

"They ARE! Heh. AND there's totally a costume contest at the *Bastion*, too." Shondra interjected, leaning over and smiling a bit over-enthusiastically. The Bastion was the goth club where Claire and Mariska had met, and thanks to the tension between Claire's dueling best friends, Shondra never actively recommended the place for ANYTHING.

"Are you seriously recommending an evening at the Bastion? Who are you and what have you done with Shondra?" Claire joked, though the expression on her friend's face seemed to scream the unspoken reply of *'I could ask you the same.'*

Instead, Shondra bit her tongue at the statement, choosing not to be sarcastic in the moment as she pressed forward. "Well.. okay. Yeah, it's... um... totally not my favorite place... But the party is being advertised as HUGE and... y'know... will also be spreading out to the streets, which should be a LOT of fun. TONS of costumes everywhere."

"And... y'know... if *Mariska* wanted to come, then... um... uh... we could *all* hang out." Shondra finished, skittishly, laying out the idea she had been struggling with presenting. Claire was slightly taken aback at the suggestion.

It was clear that Shondra wanted to make an effort to bridge the gap that had sprung between them, exacerbated by how close Claire and Mariska had become. To the curly-haired, caramel-skinned young woman, Mariska was an unknown quantity; a woman who she had never met or heard of until after Claire had vanished for a month because of her ex. To this day, all she knew is that Mariska had known Claire's ex and his band, and as a result, seemed to put herself at the center of Claire's life over the last year.

What Shondra didn't know was that Mariska was a vampire. Or that she had put herself out there to help Claire get through the hardest parts of her early days as a werewolf. It wasn't that Claire didn't want her friends to BE friends with each other, but each woman represented a foot in a different world to her, and she couldn't see how to reconcile that.

Not without telling Shondra the truth, and there were few things that terrified her quite so much as the idea of losing Shondra that way. In all reality, she had an easier time lying to her family. It had always been a distant relationship and keeping that at arm's length worked out just fine with her.

But Shondra was different. She had been like the better sister she had always imagined, and many a night Claire had sat in bed imagining every worst-case scenario that could occur if she dared tell her friend the truth that couldn't ever be taken back. She imagined seeing that horror on Shondra's face. She missed the closeness the two once shared, but cherished what they DID have too much to risk it.

"Really?" Claire replied, seriously moved by the gesture. "You… wouldn't mind?"

In truth, Claire had become VERY nervous going out without Mariska, who was far more gregarious and uninhibited. Shondra didn't understand it, but the whisper-thin, Russian vampire also intercepted potential drama and often acted as a kind of force field from things that would add to Claire's stress.

"We… don't always get along, and maybe that's my fault, Claire. But she's your friend too, and I don't want… I don't want to be… mean... about you having another friend." Shondra said. "I mean, I have other friends, too. Sure… it's all online stuff. Gaming friends and stuff, but you don't ever get jealous with *me* about it, and I figure… you have a lot of fun with her. Maybe I can give it a try on a night when I'm a little more… empowered. y'know. In a costume and feeling a little… safer."

"I can ask her, sure. I think she'll come, too. I mean… she doesn't ever turn down a frickin' party." Claire said, smiling broadly at the idea, wondering what Mariska would think about it. In the moment, the idea made her feel good and just a little lighter in her heart. "Yeah. Okay. I'll talk to her later tonight."

"OOOH! Yay! Then on Saturn's day, we shall go forth and

conquer the Halloween shop!" Shondra exclaimed happily as both women got back to their respective assignments. At her desk, Claire pondered that Mariska would likely not give her a hard time about the idea, and that it might just be a fun time. After all, as Shondra said, there was something empowering about being in a costume that reduced inhibitions, and she was hoping to feel like she used to when they went out.

Shondra let out a high-pitched squeak of excitement. "Eee!! O, M, G, Claire! I know it's, like, a week away, but I went online to check the expected forecast to check for rain, and this is kinda cool."

Grinning with a light chuckle, Claire leaned back again. "Well, give. What's the big discovery?"

"This Halloween's gonna be a FULL MOON, Claire! That is soooo cool." Shondra said, biting her bottom lip and smiling at her screen. "I can't WAIT!"

Across the small aisle between their desks, Claire leaned in close to her screen, praying that Shondra couldn't see the color wash completely out of her face while her eyes went as wide as platters at the revelation. She had forgotten to check the calendar. She had forgotten what day the full moon was.

Oh FUUUUCCCCKKKKK! Claire thought, clenching her fists at her desk, resisting the urge to bash her head against her keyboard for overlooking such a key detail.

"Uh… Claire? Are you… excited? Is it okay?" Shondra asked a little sheepishly, leaning over after picking up on the obvious lack of a response to the news she thought was cool.

Gulping, Claire leaned back with a massive and aggressively forced smile she was doing her level best to sell. "Oh… Yeah. I'm… super frickin' excited. This is… this is gonna be a… a BIG night for sure. Heh. Yeah."

Chapter Eight
⤙☽◉☾⤚

"Who are ye gonna tell, girl? Yer mum? Your best friend? Do ye honestly think that they're gonna talk t' ye again after ye tell 'em yuir the THING tha' they've watched eatin' people in movies since forever? If yuir LUCKY, they'll jus' disown ye. Never speak t' ye again. If ye AIN'T lucky, you'll end up hunted an' dead. If ye REALLY ain't lucky, you'll get me an' mine killed too fr yuir efforts." That voice of both reason and doom was echoing in her head.

The memory of the seemingly apathetic redhead tossing out that string of advice a year ago felt specifically relevant as her put-upon, Scottish lilt replayed for Claire. "Nay. Ye do THAT, an' what you'll see is utter horror in their faces. Horror you'll never be able t' forget fr as long as ye live. Is tha' the memory ye really want of those ye care th' most about? Do yuirself a favor, girl. End it. Cut those ties and move the fuck on, because ye cannae jus' go back t' how things were."

"Ye dinnae belong wi' them anymore. Ye belong with us. Yuir own kind. He may be an asshole. He may have done this, but the idiot cares about ye. Think about it, but know that ye simply cannae tell THEM."

The message had been a clear one and was obviously an influence on Claire's interactions with her family and friends. It was also a message that Mariska currently very clearly disagreed with.

"Oh, for fuck's sake, Claire. You should just TELL her, already, and stop giving yourself an aneurysm." Mariska said, her legs folded as she sat on the loveseat next to Claire's couch. In her hands, she was swirling around a glass of what was decidedly NOT wine.

In the center of the living room, Claire was pacing nervously, and for good reason. "Are you INSANE, Riska? Wait, this is YOU! What am I talking about? Of course, you're insane!"

"I can't just TELL Shondra that I'm a frickin' werewolf! There's no way! I can't believe I agreed to go to a Halloween party without checking to see if it was a full MOON night! What am I gonna DO, Riska!?" Claire grabbed her own glass from the narrow entertainment center and took a swig. Hers WAS wine.

"Dooooo… you want my answer again, or would you prefer to keep spiraling into the pit of despair? Because if you are enjoying this, I can just let it ride." The ethereal, blonde vampire in a loose-fitting t-shirt with a logo for a band called *'Pinched Nerve'* and torn jeans replied as she took a sip. The sarcastic bluntness had the desired effect of stopping the anxious brunette, who had been wearing a hole in her carpet as she paced.

"That's easy for you to say. You don't sprout fur all over once a month. She'll…" Claire tried protesting, but the tiny dynamo hopped up to her bare feet on the couch so that she would match Claire's impressive six-foot height. As she did, Mariska cricked an eyebrow and cut her friend off.

"She'll what, Claire? Do you honestly, really, deeply believe that SHONDRA… who has never once pressed you about why you up and vanished for a month because you ASKED her not to go there… would, what? Run screaming into the night and hide from you forever? Hate you? Give you up?"

Nodding exaggeratedly, Claire's eyes were wide as she replied. "YES! All of that, yes. That's exactly what I'm afraid of. Normal people think I'm… shit, *both* of us… are *monsters*. LITERALLY. Movie crap that… terrifies them. Is ANY of that soooo far-fetched?"

"For Shondra? For the woman you've described to me many a time? Yes. It is ALL far-fetched." Mariska said, putting her glass down on the coffee table and propping herself into a crouch, leaning against the wall.

"Claire, that woman is… she is your best friend. She has been for a decade. She trusts you. She loves you. She's like your sister, but… y'know… not a judgmental prig like your *actual* sister."

The lithe vampire had never met Claire's sister, only eavesdropped on phone calls. That had been enough to formulate a strong, decidedly negative opinion of the woman, to which she held quite firmly. But it was evident that she had a similarly clear read on Shondra and wasn't shy about expressing it. "Plus… seriously. She goes to ren faires, reads all kinds of fantasy fiction, and LOVES horror movies and everything even remotely spooky."

"I would bet she would think you were even more interesting if she knew the truth," Mariska declared proudly, puffing her narrow chest out.

"That's… insane." Claire protested, though it was weaker now. As she did, she flumped onto the loveseat opposite Mariska and sighed.

"Isssss it, *volchonok*? Is it really?" The little Russian vampire replied with a wry smile. "Come now. Do you think so little of your best friend?"

"*ONE* of my best friends." Claire protested, wagging a finger in the air while her head fell back against the chair in a posture of mock defeat.

"Well, I will not argue with THAT distinction. But seriously, Claire. Think about it. About HER. I know she does not like me, but we've all been in the same room together enough for me to know that she cares about you. She is a legitimately sweet, caring, compassionate person. She… doesn't know *how* to hate you if she wanted to. And I just do not think she ever could."

"She doesn't dis*like* you, 'Riska," Claire said, her head picking back up with an opportunity to change the subject ever so slightly. "I mean, she is recommending that we go to the party at the Bastion. And she wanted me to ask if you wanted to come, too."

"She… wants *me* to go out with you both? Seriously?" Mariska said, clearly taken aback, as, in spite of talking the woman up, she wasn't expecting that. In truth, the century-old vampire was not accustomed to humans actually liking her, and had assumed that Shondra straight-up hated her. She assumed she was viewed as the interloper; the person who had, when Claire vanished for a month, returned with her as a new fixture in the once-broken woman's life.

"Well, clearly she has taste, too. Then it is settled, we shall party together." Mariska proclaimed, doing her level best to appear as though the revelation had not affected her emotionally while she took a nip of her drink. It was not as successful of a segue as she had hoped, and Claire tilted her head and crooked an eyebrow.

However, that didn't stop Mariska from using the revelation to try and buttress her point. "And see, she likes ME. Or… at least is willing to tolerate me. Soooo, I really do think she would take it better than you think."

"How many people… like, regular people… have you told that you're a vampire?" Claire asked, more sarcastically than she probably needed to, taking a drink of her wine. Leaning back, the question seemed to put Mariska on guard, and she pursed her lips slightly.

"I swear, I want to go back in time and kick Beverly's magnificent ass for filling your head with so much nonsense," Mariska muttered as she took a drink and a long breath, referring to that ginger font of occasionally-detrimental information in Claire's memory. "Look, when I was made, it was a different time. Literally. It was the '30s and I was virtually homeless out in New York, trying to make it. The only thing I knew about vampires came from the Lugosi 'Dracula' until my maker found me. My maker… he only told me two things."

The otherwise effervescent woman became more solemn for a moment, which affected her long-abandoned accent. "He said… 'Ahh… you taste like the old country'… in Russian, as he drank me near dry. Then, when he stopped and decided to turn me instead of letting me die… when he opened his own chest and fed me his own blood… he said, 'Our old home is but a shadow of what it was. Perhaps it is a good thing that we can both remember it forever, now.'"

"That was it. The pretentious ass left me in an alley in the city

61

where I turned, curled up in the corner alone." Mariska said, still angry about the nearly century-old event. "So… when the hunger hit and I tried eating whatever food I could to satisfy it, only to vomit it up, I figured out what to do by… mimicking what he did. I did… a lot of... bad things, for a time."

"That was 1931. The movie hit big a few months earlier and… honestly… I used those rules to try and figure myself out for a WHILE." She scoffed, rolling her eyes. "Seriously… I avoided the sun for almost a year before I figured out that it was a fictional rule."

Both women chuckled at that before Mariska continued.

"And… people were way more frightened by the idea of what they thought of as *monsters* back then. So I kept it to myself for a VERY long, very lonely time."

"But I did eventually tell my secret… at least once. Back in the '70s, there were a few people I got a little closer to. And yes, I kept my truth hidden from most. But not all of them. There was one I told… Or, at least, one who found out. We…" Mariska continued, leaning forward on her crossed legs to make her point. "No, she could not handle it, so I DO know what you're afraid of. But she knew me. And knew me well enough to know that in spite of what I did in those early days, I was more than that. We did not part ways because she was afraid of me or what I was."

"She… was a radical. A musician and a businesswoman in an era where such things were unheard of. Everything wonderful about that era wrapped up in one package. And… I told her… and she…" It was clear that the recollection wasn't the easiest thing in the world for her, but Mariska soldiered forward. "She was scared at first. She didn't understand at first. But she LISTENED. She gave me a chance to explain… and show her that I wasn't what the movies said I was. And through all of it, we stayed friends for a time."

The story seemed a little brief, but in the moment, Claire was more focused on her own concerns to fully pick up on what wasn't being said, and Mariska was secretly happy to avoid having to go into any further details.

"That was then and this is now, *volchonok*. Now, people are superstitious about different kinds of stupid things, but not so much about vampires or werewolves. Hell, THESE days we've got books and movies where we get to be the sexy… occasionally sparkly… heroes. Shondra loves all of that, so I can't see her just going to knee-jerk terror." the little vampire finished with a nod.

"I joke sometimes and call us the *'monster girls'*… but you're NOT a monster. Neither am I. We just are what we are. Believe it or not, you're a good person. And when you're transformed, you're STILL a good… albeit sexier... person."

"But…" Claire said, bringing her legs up to the chair and curling up as much as she could for her height, as she chose to completely stress over Mariska's other comments. "What if you're wrong? What… what if I tell her and she DOES hate me?"

The fear in her voice was palpable and tugged at Mariska's heartstrings, prompting the much smaller woman to get up and walk over to the chair. With hardly an effort, she sat on the arm of the chair, tucking herself up next to her friend. "Just a moment ago, I told you… in slightly vague terms… that I have blood on my hands, Claire."

It was rare for Mariska to not use her nickname for Claire, and she tended to use the woman's given name largely when she wanted to punctuate a point. "You did not blink. Because you know me well enough to know who I am. Who I truly am, and it is more than a single detail that hangs over my past. Correct?"

Nodding silently, Claire pursed her lips at the truth her friend was expressing as Mariska continued. "I doubt Shondra will see you any differently. And if I am wrong… then you still have me. You're stuck with me, *volchonok*."

The two sat there silently for a long moment before the silence became more than the energetic vampire was comfortable with. "Okay, enough! We're being needlessly maudlin when there's a PARTY to plan."

Hopping back up, she grabbed Claire's glass and went into the kitchen to refill it from the box in the fridge. "Now… what are we going to dress you up as? This is exciting. Like an economy-sized Halloween Barbie, I get to play with!"

"Seriously, Riska? I can't play dress-up! I'll be fully wolfed out. Claws, hair, fangs, a good bit taller, the whole nine yards. Even if Shondra DID know, it's not like I could just… walk around like it was normal!" Claire protested as she got up to follow Mariska into the kitchen.

Taking the offered glass, Mariska refilled her own from a thermos she had brought with her. In the modern world, there were a lot of ways to get your hands on blood that didn't involve stealing it or drinking it directly from the source.

"Well… we could just put you in a slinky dress and you could go as 'Sexy Werewolf'. I mean, I've seen 'Sexy Paper Clip' costumes, so anything is possible, really." Mariska chuckled. The joke caused Claire to roll her eyes as she took a sip of her wine.

As she did, she caught a whiff of Mariska's drink and arched an eyebrow. "Is that deer?"

"Ahh, there's that nose. Yeah." Mariska smiled as she put the thermos away and had a taste, a little excited. "So… my butcher out in Saint Pete had a run on venison last week and had more of this available than anything else. It's not bad. Want some?"

"No, no. Thanks." Claire said, wincing. She was still in a bad headspace concerning all things werewolf-related. And while she had certainly eaten EXTREMELY fresh deer, she wasn't in that particular mood at the moment. Leaning back against the counter, she brought the subject back around. "And I am NOT going as a 'Sexy Werewolf', Riska! That's insane! Nobody is going to look at me and say 'Wow, great make-up'."

"Well, your eyeliner game is on point, but you could use a better foundation," Mariska said with a wry grin as she hopped up to sit, cross-legged, on the counter.

"Ha. Ha." Claire mock-laughed, looking irritated. "I can't DO this! I can't be fully transformed and… go OUT. What am I going to do, put a sheet over my head as a Charlie frickin' Brown ghost?

I don't want to have to cancel, it will just devastate Shondra, but I don't know what I'm going to do."

Sighing in a slightly exaggerated fashion, Mariska shook her head. "We'll figure something out, okay? Calm down, or you're going to end up wolfing out again tonight, and I don't think you want to clean up all that hair AGAIN."

Claire's eyes WERE, in fact, solidly amber-colored now. Flumping her head against the wall next to the counter, she groaned. "Okay... Okay. This is me calming down."

Then she took another very long swig of her glass. "This is wine, helping me calm down. You actually think we can pull this off? Be fully transformed all night in a costume? With Shondra not finding out?"

"Well... it would be easier if you talked to her first, but yeah. We can totally do it." Mariska said with a smile, reinforcing her opinion that Claire needed to come clean with her long-time friend. "You're going shopping tomorrow for a costume, right?"

"Yessssss?" Claire answered, a lingering but unasked question on her lips.

"Well then, so am I. I'll go with you. We shall teamwork this shit, *volchonok*!" Mariska proclaimed, holding up her glass in a mock-victory posture before taking another swig. "A toast to our impending Halloween victory! Are you sure you do not want some? This is a high-quality vintage."

"Yeeeeaaahh, no." Claire grimaced, taking a large gulp of her wine. "I'll need to restock on this, though, to keep me from freaking the frickin' hell out."

"Well... if not THE spirit, it is, at least A spirit," Mariska said, patting Claire on her arm supportively.

Chapter Nine – One Year Ago
·)）◐（（·

The motel was a roadside hole in the wall just north of Destin, Florida. It looked very much like the kind of place that most people used by the hour more so than by the night. A call to the managers of the hotel in the panhandle confirmed what Mariska Baranov had been told by Beverly McLeish: that the woman she was looking for would be there.

This was compounded by the sight of the old, yellow Pontiac Aztec in the parking lot that she recognized from the couple of times she had met the woman she was currently seeking.

As they pulled into the parking lot, Mariska pointed the driver to the Aztec and asked to be dropped off. She was riding in a late model, black SUV with very tinted windows that made the experience far more comfortable. Sunlight wasn't exactly the problem movies had made it seem for her and hers, but it wasn't pleasant. It had been as enjoyable a ride from Tampa as was possible. The situation was aided by a fading rainstorm that obscured the sunlight that much more.

He was a balding, middle-aged man with a slightly dopey expression on his face. "Here we are. Now what?"

The tone in his voice indicated that he wanted something the young-looking woman had no intention of giving. As she dipped her dark glasses and looked him in the face, her nearly-black eyes took on a tint of red. "Now I get out and you continue on your way. Georgia, was it? A trade convention in... Atlanta?"

Staring at him deeply, he seemed to falter, carnal urges overwhelming sense for just a moment. Mariska repeated her intentions as her eyes almost glowed crimson in the dim cabin. "You're tired and just want to keep going before it gets dark. And frankly, you *are* somewhat sick of my blather, I think."

After a second, his expression seemed to soften as he replied. "Well, I want to get going. Cross into Georgia before night falls.

Have a good trip."

"Aw, indeed. You must be exhausted. You've been quite sweet." Mariska said, pushing her big sunglasses back on her head as she raised her hood and stepped out of the door. "Don't speed, now. Thanks again."

Without missing a beat, she closed the door behind her and slung the small duffle bag over her back as the SUV drove off. Looking at the hotel, she knew the woman inside couldn't be so easily convinced to listen.

Werewolves... even brand new ones who had no idea what they were... were immune to her ability to influence minds.

Dressed in knee-high black combat boots, slightly torn skinny jeans, a t-shirt with a logo for a band called *'Sciatica'*, and a black hoodie, Mariska looked intently at the hotel until she could sense what she was searching for. She could pick up a werewolf easily enough. Everything about them gave off cues that she could feel. The smell, the warmth of their blood, their aura. They were a beacon for her senses.

The room was on the first floor near the car, and Mariska walked up to knock.

This is crazy, Mariska. Why are you doing this? She thought to herself, as her hand hovered in front of the door. *You've met her, what, once? Twice? You hung out with her and that useless boyfriend of hers after one of his gigs at the Bastion. You don't know her. You don't owe her anything because of BEVERLY, the woman who keeps blowing you off for that asshole? You can still keep yourself out of it and just... turn around.*

Before she could make a decision, a hoarse, cracked voice came from inside the room. "I'm paid up through the end of the frickin' weekend. Go AWAY."

"*Ay, blyat'!*" Mariska muttered a curse in Russian, realizing that as surely as she could sense the nascent werewolf, so too could the woman smell her coming. She also realized that being able to do so was likely causing the woman on the other side of the door to panic that much more. It also meant that those keen ears heard the mumbled expletive.

"So, your name is Claire, correct? Claire Gribbald?" Mariska called in, speaking softly and calmly as she did. "I don't know if you remember me. My name is Mariska. We met during the after-party for your boyfriend's band the other night. At the club, remember?"

"HE'S NOT MY FUCKING BOYFRIEND!!! GO THE FUCK AWAY!!!!" Claire literally growled through the door, and Mariska could hear the woman inside gasp and slap her hands over her mouth in shock at the sound. The sun would go down in a few hours and what was coming couldn't be stopped for her. The earliest of those changes had already begun.

"Sorry. Poor choice of words. I know Liam. He is a complete ass, I know. And… I know what happened. I know what's happen*ing*. Can I please come in?" Mariska asked, as calmly as she could, though she was starting to tense up. She had known it would be like this, and she had come anyway.

How could she not, knowing what Liam Docherty was, and what he did? Knowing that the woman inside the room would be facing this night alone, otherwise. She didn't know Claire, but she refused to allow that to happen.

"Please… please just go away. You don't… you can't know. Just please… please leave me alone." Claire all but whimpered, her voice coming low to the ground and cracking again. Through the door, Mariska could smell the salt of her tears.

"I know Liam. Me and his drummer, Beverly, we... hook up every now and again. That is how I know what is going on. I was... with Bev, and she told me what happened. She told me they were going to just head out of town before tonight… and that they had left you up here in Naples… hiding. I know what they ALL are in that sad little band of his. And I know he attacked you. Hurt you." Mariska said, placing her hand on the door where the lock was located. "So, I know what's happening to you. I have seen it before."

"I can push the door in so we can talk, but then the motel owner will have a fit and bill you. I just want to talk. Please… just open the door." Mariska nodded to nobody but herself as she bit her bottom lip. The lock on the door would offer her little to no resistance if she pushed on it even slightly, but that would only freak Claire out more, and she was there to try and make this easier, not harder. "I only… I would like to help."

There was a long moment of silence as Mariska listened at the door. On the inside, the relative stranger's heartbeat was going a mile a minute and the stress pheromones were being pushed out so hard they were almost stifling, but she waited in spite of herself. After about a minute, there was a shuffling sound, and the door unlocked. Slowly opening it, Mariska saw the woman inside.

At a solid 6 plus feet, Claire Gribbald was more than a foot taller than the wisp of a woman standing outside. Her face was puffy and red from crying, her hair was a brown, frizzy mess pulled into a sloppy ponytail with a pink scrunchie, and she was wearing what looked to be a pair of jeans and a t-shirt she likely had been in for at least three days. A light whiff confirmed that, and Mariska assumed the smell must be even worse for the tall woman wearing it, who could, no doubt, smell things at a level she was very uncomfortable with currently.

Not a good sign.

Saying nothing, Claire rubbed her nose on a tissue she had scrunched up in her hand, turned around, and stepped back into the small, cluttered room. Not waiting for anything as pedestrian as an invitation, Mariska stepped in and closed the door behind her.

"Been here a few days?" She asked, knowing the answer, but trying to get the broken woman to talk.

"Long enough. What the fuck do you want from me?" Claire replied, as she flumped down onto the floor in the rear corner with a fairly moderate thud. Looking around the room, Mariska was able to formulate much of the woman's week. There was a single small bag on the bed with clothes strewn about. There were also 6 empty pizza boxes, 3 bags of empty Chinese food take-out containers, and an assortment of other food wrappers. It was almost her time, and Mariska could see all the cues. "You wanna help me? You frickin' can't."

"You've been hungry all week, haven't you? Impossibly hungry… like you've never been before. Like all you want to do in the world is eat and you feel like you're going to just starve if you don't, right?" Mariska asked, sitting on the edge of the two small beds nearest where Claire had planted herself.

As Mariska spoke, she watched as Claire began sizing her up with her newfound senses. The brunette's head tilted to the side and her eyes narrowed. Her nostrils flared and she involuntarily sniffed. It wasn't conscious; rather, instinct that was working to rewire the woman's mind and body.

Clearly not having paid any attention to what Mariska had said, Claire's mouth opened and her quizzical expression tightened as she struggled to reconcile what her senses were telling her. "What… who are you?"

"No… go with your instinct. Listen to your senses. Ask your *first* question again, the one you stopped yourself from asking. You are *not* wrong." Mariska said, taking off her sunglasses and tucking them on the front neck of her shirt, her marble-black eyes now clearly visible.

Confused by everything, Claire scooched back just a bit, her nose twitching a bit as she sniffed again. Looking, Mariska could see the woman's hazel eyes start to turn yellow. "What are you? Something… Something's… wrong. I don't know what, but something's… different. You're not like *them*… like… his band. But… you're *not*... What are you?"

"That is the question. Those senses of yours, they're scaring you, aren't they? You can HEAR when someone lies. You can SMELL when they're scared or angry or horny. And now… you can smell it and hear it and SEE it… when the woman talking to you isn't quite... human." Mariska said, standing up and stepping a few feet back to give Claire a little more space. "You can feel it from there, right? I'm colder than I should be. My heart beats, but does so too slowly. My breath smells a little too salty. What do you think I am? It's an instinctual memory. It's in you now… carried across generations that are all in there now, just learning to talk to you."

Pointing to her head to emphasize her point, Mariska was speaking calmly and slowly. For the generally excitable woman, it was a bit of an effort. "Just… listen to that. That will never lead you astray."

Standing up again, Claire looked across the room through narrowed eyes. "No. That… that's not… what? No. This is *crazy!*"

"As crazy as what already happened? She told me what he did. Liam. Transforming in anger right in front of you? Sprouting fur and fangs and claws and taking a chunk out of you? That same shoulder and chest that don't even have the hint of a scar on them just... a few days later?" Mariska said, tilting her head and putting her hands on her hips. "Just say it. Say what you KNOW I am. I am going to say yes when you do, but it's better if you say it first."

"You're… a *vampire?*" Claire said, sounding as shocked to be saying it as one could be.

"Yes." Mariska replied, matter of factly, with a bouncy nod and a smile. "See. Not that crazy, right?"

"YES! It's crazy!! What the hell are you… What the FUCK IS GOING ON!?!" Claire exclaimed, balling her hands into fists and shaking as she screamed. Her voice was a full octave deeper and came out with a growl that resonated through the walls. Her eyes were fully yellow now, but Mariska knew it was too soon. It wasn't time yet, and while eventually she would be able to do what her body wanted to do at will, until that first full moon came, she would only stress her system out this way.

As Claire pushed herself back against the wall, panic in her eyes, Mariska bit her bottom lip and shook her head. "I know. I know this feels just… insane and impossible. But I promise you, I AM just here to help. I am not going to hurt you. I promise!"

Raising her voice just a bit, the tiny woman stepped forward and spoke more forcefully. "Claire, listen to me. You're going to hurt *yourself* if you don't calm down. Now… listen to my voice and look at me, please."

Begrudgingly, Claire looked up at the smaller woman, with obvious fear in her eyes and sweat on her brow.

"I'm just here to help you." Mariska raised her eyebrows and held her hands out, open. "I'm not lying... and you *know* that. Like I said, your senses would tell you if I was lying. Just please... calm..."

Before she could finish the sentiment, the sound of loud banging came from the room on the other side of the wall, as a muffled voice shouted. **"Shut the fuck up over there!"**

"Oh, I do NOT *think* so..." Mariska muttered as she held up her hands, a hint of her original Russian accent leaking out. "Claire... just... take a breath. Calm down. I'll be right back. Everything will be fine, I promise."

"Wait... don't..." Claire protested weakly as Mariska started out of the room. "Fear not. With that rain and the clouds, my... gifts... are unobstructed."

As Mariska closed the door behind her, the anxious woman still inside the hotel room could hear everything.

Stomping over to the next room, Mariska was chastising herself. *What are you doing, you dumb fuck? You don't know this girl. Her problems are NOT your problems. You should just tell her to fuck off and go home and let her deal with this nonsense on her own. YOU did it by yourself when you were changed and you survived; she can, too.*

Stopping in front of the door, the tiny vampire bit her lip and centered herself. That was *exactly* why she was there; to stop what had happened to her from happening to an innocent woman. Calming down a bit, she knocked on the door, as Claire made her way to the window and peeked out of the thick curtains to see what was happening.

"Fuck off, bitch! Fuck off and shut up! Don't make me come out there!" came the voice of the man on the other side of the door. From a room away, Claire could smell the sex on him and the anxiety of the woman in the bed over there. She didn't understand

WHY she could smell it. She didn't WANT to know, either; she just wanted it all to go away.

It wasn't, however. And she could still hear it all, as much as she could hear that the vampire was telling the truth. She could almost see the other room without using her eyes, which only served to frighten her more.

"Yeah, no. I am done." Mariska said, pushing ever so slightly on the door to the other room. Effortlessly, it flew inwards, and Claire could hear the lock shatter as the man screamed in anger.

"Bitch! What the fucking hell do you…" he said, then Claire heard a gasping, gurgling sound that made her blood run cold. What was happening?

"Shhh. The adult is talking." Mariska said, her hand on the man's throat in what looked like an almost gentle gesture. "Now, look at me."

What Claire couldn't see was that same red glow filling her otherwise black eyes as she spoke. "The lady… you are done with her. And you are going to pay her with evvvvvverything in your wallet and then some, okay?"

The gurgling sound relented as Mariska let go. Gasping for a minute, the rageful man's voice was now disturbingly calm. "Yeah, sure. Absolutely."

"Then, you are both going to leave and go home." She continued, as both people nodded. "And when you do, you're going to forget this happened, right? You came here, did what you came here to do, paid the hotel for the door *you* accidentally broke, and left."

"Yeah." both said, nodding as Mariska turned and walked back to Claire's room with a fresh bounce in her step, not saying anything else.

Claire was watching from the window in mild shock. Stepping back in, Mariska closed the door behind her and smiled broadly. "Well, that was an asshole. Sorry about that. Uh… right, where were we?"

"What… what did you DO? What… what was that?" Claire

73

asked, clearly confused but a bit more calm.

"Oh, that was just… I suppose you may have seen that in a movie. I can… make suggestions. Influence those susceptible… AKA morons… into doing what I tell them." Mariska said, as she walked over to the corner of the bed and plopped down on it, crossing her legs casually.

Processing everything, Claire closed the curtains and collapsed into the chair by the window, rubbing her forehead a moment, looking a little scared. "I don't… understand. You can… make people… DO things?"

"Some people." Mariska shrugged a bit, dismissing the importance of the ability, trying to calm the concern. "As I said, idiots and the like. However, it cannot affect you. It doesn't work for those who are like you."

"What do… what do you mean, like me? I'm not… I'm…" Pausing, the word was hung up in Claire's cracked throat, as saying it would mean she was beginning to believe it was true. "It doesn't work on… on…"

Mariska leaned slightly towards her and raised her eyebrows. "You have to say the word. I know it's terrifying. I know you don't want to. But you have to say it. You have to let it be real."

"*Werewolves.*" Claire all but whispered, her head hanging low as she brought her legs up tight and began to shake slightly. As she did, tears began to flow freely and the broken woman began to sob.

Watching, Mariska froze. She remembered how lost and alone she had been all those decades ago when she had been made and abandoned like this. How terrifying it was and how confused she had been. She wanted to make sure that this woman she had only just met wouldn't have to deal with the situation alone, but she didn't know what to do when it came to tears.

Tears were something she had learned to keep locked inside. Tears let others know that you cared, and that was a weapon to be used against you. Mariska Baranov *did not cry.* As such, she was ill-equipped to process Claire Gribbald's tears as she sat there. All she knew was that watching the vulnerable woman release her pain caused her own stomach to tighten up into a ball. It was uncomfortable, and she didn't like it.

"It's... it's... you're going to be okay." Mariska said, her own voice cracking slightly, to her own surprise. "I understand how scared you are. I truly do."

With that, something happened that the pale woman had perhaps expected, though she still found herself completely unprepared as Claire leaned forward in her chair and wrapped her arms tightly around her.

Tears turned into racking sobs of anguish as Claire clung to Mariska like a desperate child mourning the loss of everything they thought they knew. Standing there, Mariska remembered that night, so long ago, in a cold and empty alleyway in New York where she had been abandoned. She had died and been reborn in that dirty, trash-strewn place.

It was the single most painful memory of her long life, and the one that had prompted her to come all this way for a woman she barely knew. It lived strongly in her mind, all of the fear and pain she had felt all those decades ago, as Mariska returned the hug, and to her surprise, let her own tears out, for the first time in a very, very long time.

Chapter Ten
-)ᗝ♦(C-

An hour and a half later, the sun was kissing the horizon of the Eglin Air Force Base Reserve in the panhandle of Florida. The two women walked across the expanse of a long, grassy plain and through the underbrush of the dry Florida thicket until they were far from where they had parked Claire's car.

It was still light, and the air had that smell of the coming night carried upon a warm breeze, but for Claire, it carried so much more. Her senses had never been more alive as she was flooded with stimuli that filled her brain with images of what was spread out before her in that unknown wilderness. There was a combination of terror and excitement in conflict with her lingering denial.

Still wearing the same ratty jeans and t-shirt, Claire's face was still a bit puffy and red from the tears she had let explode back at the motel before the woman at her side told her that it was time to leave for the night.

"Are… you sure it's… it's safe here?" Claire asked through a clenched jaw and tight lips, feeling a tingle across her skin as her adrenaline began to rise ever so slightly.

Next to her, Mariska nodded and smiled. "It is. Hunting season here isn't for a couple of months when the deer start mating. Right now, the park is empty. You can smell it as well as I can sense it, I'm sure, but there's not another person for miles. Nothing I can pick up at all. We're as alone out here as is possible."

"This is a good place for you." She continued, setting down her own small shoulder bag packed with some provisions for herself and a change of clothes for Claire they had taken from the motel room. "And… I won't ever be too far. Okay?"

"I'm… I'm really scared." Claire said, her voice shaky as she threatened to cry again. Standing there, to Mariska's senses, her body appeared like a thing on fire. The sun was riding the horizon now, halfway gone as the sky turned a deep orange-pink above them. Internally, the change was already in process for Claire.

With her nigh-immortal eyes, the 'young' vampire could see an aura of stunning golds that was getting brighter, along with the blood rushing like a flood through Claire's veins. It was running hot and pulsing as if to burst. Her skin was giving off excessive heat, and she was actively sweating now. Every pore was opened and pumping out pheromones that were almost dizzying to the pansexual blonde, who had to work to keep herself calm.

Listening, Claire's breath was shallow and a little raspy and there was the faintest of creaking sounds that Mariska knew were the fine hairs on the woman's body about to kick into overdrive. It was only minutes away. Mariska could sense it, and Claire could feel it.

"It's… it's really real. It's… it's happening, isn't it? I can feel..." She muttered, her voice almost a whisper. It sounded noticeably deeper, and as she heard herself, Claire stopped and bit her lip nervously.

Turning, Mariska put her hand upon the taller woman's shoulder and nodded with the most calming smile she could muster. "Indeed. Any minute now, Claire."

Almost flinching at the touch, Claire's mind was racing a mile a minute as nothing but her fears were being heard. Mariska just kept talking. "It is okay. Just try and be as calm as you can. I don't know exactly what you're feeling, but I am here. It's really okay. I know it feels like the end of the world, but… it's really just a different sort of beginning. I promise, you will be okay."

A muscle spasm ran like a shot of lightning through Claire's entire body, from head to toe. As the wind rushed out of her, she tucked in tight for just a second in anticipation of the pain she imagined would come, but didn't. "AAAGH!!! Mariska… Mariska, I'm scared! Will it… will it hurt?"

"Shhh, shhh. No. No, it won't hurt. I've never seen it hurt anyone who has let it happen. It can be hard if you try and fight it, though." Mariska said, concerned for the woman who was clearly no longer a stranger to her. "You need to breathe, and just let it wash over you. Just… let it out."

"Also… I know this will be… kind of embarrassing. But… those jeans? Those WILL hurt if you grow while wearing them. Same with the sneakers." Mariska smiled a bit and nodded. "Sorry. But… ripping out of denim isn't as easy as it looks in the movies, and you are going to get a good degree... thicker. A little bigger all around, really. You should… uh… well. You should likely remove all of that. Sorry."

"Shiiiit." Claire said, looking down at herself. She hadn't even thought about her clothes, and she blushed. In spite of what was happening, she was still self-conscious and embarrassed. She was tall, thick, and lumpy, and standing in front of a woman she knew liked women. Reluctantly, she pulled her clothes off a piece at a time, letting it all just lay in a pile on the ground.

Still clearly straining to remain what she had been, Claire's skin was flushed red, but it was too late. The change was beginning in earnest. When she looked down at Mariska, the formerly hazel eyes of the now naked woman were massive and a stunning shade of amber that took Mariska's breath away.

"You… you and Beverly both said… said that I'd still be ME… but what if… what if I'm like HIM? Like Liam? He went wild when… he… he attacked me…" Claire said, the fear that had been gripping her heart exposing itself. "She also said that he lost control. What… What is I… I don't want to be a *monster!*"

Cupping the face of the taller woman, Mariska could feel hair beneath her hands beginning to press out. "He attacked you because he's a frightened, angry CHILD. The wolf was his EXCUSE, Claire. The wolf only makes you more of what you already are, and I don't believe you're anything but a good person. And in a minute, you'll still be a good person."

"You will be changed. Your emotions… closer to the surface. You will feel urges to be what you are, and that may frighten you. But… you will still be you. All of the things you have read and seen in films are… nonsense." Letting go of Claire's face, they both turned to watch the sun vanish completely. On the other side of the sky, the moon was low and already fully visible as tears streaked her cheeks. Looking up at her, Mariska stepped back to give Claire some space. "It's time. Breathe out. Let it happen."

Still hunched over, trying to cover her body, the moonlight washed over her and she nodded to Mariska. Closing her eyes, she let out a long breath and let her arms fall to her sides. The knot she had been holding onto in her stomach became too much to manage as it began.

It was not the first time the lithe vampire had seen a werewolf transform, but it was the first time she had seen one do so for the first time. Swallowing, Mariska was far more anxious for Claire than she would have thought possible as she watched.

Slowly, Claire's shoulders began to widen, as her feet and hands began to lengthen. The fine hairs on her body stood on end and began to grow longer and darker, the same soft brown as the hair atop her head.

Claire bared teeth that were now much longer, with pronounced canines visible by the light of the still-purple sky above her. She let out a whimper as her arms grew longer and a fair bit denser, her musculature becoming more defined. Wincing, she felt a momentary flash of numbness that shot down her spine as a tail began to form over her rear.

Another burst of growth caused her to shoot up and forward as her legs finished reforming to a quadrupedal configuration. Slightly off-balance from the change and the newly-formed tail, Claire lurched, threatening to fall over, only to find Mariska in front of her.

Catching her easily, the whisper-thin woman effortlessly held the much larger woman upright, nearly fully transformed. Claire rested her now-massive hands on Mariska's narrow shoulders and stared at the long fingers that ended in curved, black claws. As she did, the little blonde vampire put her own hands on Claire's forearms to help stabilize her.

Chuckling, Mariska nodded, looking up at Claire's

still-morphing face. "I have you. It is fine. I forgot to warn you about the tail, but it's looking good. You're doing good and it's almost complete. Once it is… you'll know what to do. You'll know how to walk. This… what you are… it comes with instincts, remember? Built-in muscle memory is carried down from every generation in that bloodline."

"Those instincts… they will guide you tonight, if you let them. But they will NEVER make you do something that is NOT who you are at your core. You need to believe that." Mariska said, doing her best with her admittedly second-hand information.

"There… you can do it. Just stand up." Mariska said, gently taking her hands away from Claire's now fur-covered arms as she wobbled back. She watched Claire's increasingly striking face as her cheekbones raised higher and her eyes grew a bit larger still. Her nose widened as the end turned black and the same fur that covered the rest of her now spread out across her more diamond-shaped face. Those stunning, amber eyes blinked wide, seeing things in a way they never had before.

It had, in truth, taken less than half a minute in total, but there in the moonlight, the once-panicked woman stood transformed. She was covered from head to toe in a silky, thick brown fur that shimmered as she moved. Her long ears and tail twitched with every new sound and sensation while her eyes took in the new form that Claire was shocked to realize felt perfectly natural to her. The aforementioned instinctive muscle memory was settling in.

Most importantly, Claire was processing it all in her *mind*. It was like Beverly had told her a few days ago, when the woman had tried to help her understand what was happening to her before leaving: '*Yuir never NOT the wolf, but th' wolf is never not you, either.*' She was still herself, just more, now.

In spite of the astonishing change that had just occurred, Claire stood there, thinking clearly and calmly; in truth, far more clearly and calmly than she had before, as she bit her lip and almost smiled. It was strange and new, but like Mariska had said, also familiar. Nothing about her body felt alien to her in spite of what had just occurred. Those generational instincts were kicking in to bring an unexpected comfort to the newborn werewolf.

The werewolf... in a pink scrunchie.

Looking down, she swallowed as she could suddenly hear even better than before. Every crack and breath of every living thing in the woods just on the other side of the field called to her. The scent of the deer and squirrels in the forest filled her nose. She could clearly make out every chirping bird and crawling bug, and she wanted nothing more than to indulge those senses, to release the pent-up energy inside her that earlier had threatened to devour her.

In spite of her best efforts to put on a calm facade, Mariska was literally beaming. She hadn't planned to care about the confused woman, but here she stood, relieved and happy for her. This was no curse. This was a woman freed and made more than who she was, but still, the woman she had always been.

Looking down, Claire was twitchy, glancing towards the woods with anticipation that threatened to burst forth as she tested the one thing she hadn't yet, and spoke. It was a single word uttered in a deep, throaty, and resonant way that the tiny, pale vampire could feel in her chest.

"Mariska?" Was all she said, but the single word's meaning was clear. Claire was ready. She was finding herself in a new skin, with new experiences, and an overwhelming urge to test them all. Fear had been replaced with childlike excitement, like a kid on Christmas waiting for their parents to give them the go-ahead to start unwrapping presents.

So happy for her newfound friend, Mariska nodded and smiled broadly, answering with just a few simple words.

"Go... run. For the first time in your life, be free."

Chapter Eleven
-꒰●꒱-

"Ugh, I wish I could actually drink coffee. It is unnatural for anyone to be up this early, much less a *vampire*." Mariska groaned, flumped lazily in the passenger seat of Claire's yellow Pontiac Aztek as they pulled up to the Halloween store. "At least I had a particularly hopped-up barista before you picked me up, so…caffeine by proxy, right?"

Shooting her a sarcastic glare that betrayed how anxious she was, Claire replied, "Really?"

"Oh, it was a joke. *I am kidding.* This is my *kidding* face, *volchonok.*" Mariska replied, rolling her eyes behind the enormous sunglasses she was wearing. "Besides. I'm trying to get all the gallows humor out of my system before we meet up with Shondra."

"Where is she, anyway? Are we waiting in the car or meeting her inside?" Mariska said, looking around the half-full parking lot outside of what clearly used to be an entirely different store with a large, vinyl banner stretched over the top that said *'BOO TOWN.'*

"I dunno. We can go check it out in advance and send her a text that we're in there." Claire said, finding a good spot under a tree close to the main entrance. While sunlight didn't exactly cause vampires to burst into flame, they did burn fairly easily, and could get very, very sick from being under direct sun for too long. For her part, Mariska was wearing a long-sleeved black blouse, a large brim black cowboy hat, and her oversized sunglasses. She looked as much like a goth cowgirl as she did a vampire; a goth cowgirl who was a bit more surly than her usual effervescent self, as she was far more accustomed to being up and functioning late and sleeping most of the day.

It was eleven in the morning, and Mariska was proving to be the opposite of a morning person, which Claire couldn't help but find entertaining. Usually, she was the more crotchety of the two, and she was secretly amused to have that dynamic flipped.

With a text sent, the two women exited the car and made their way into the cavernous Halloween store to begin looking around. Stepping inside the doors, they were both hit with the air conditioning wafting a bouquet of scents their way. Of the two, Claire's nose was the more sensitive, and the mix of teenage hormones from the young staff crewing the seasonal pop-up, chemicals from the smoke machines, and a variety of latex and plastics from the cornucopia of masks, was noticeable but nowhere near as overwhelming as it would be if the store wasn't mostly empty of people.

About fifteen feet in was a fairly large display of animatronic creatures of every type; writhing zombies, a jabbing serial killer in a Michael Myers mask, a creepy little ghoul girl on an automated swing hanging from a fake tree, a ghostly pirate, and of course, a werewolf.

"Ooh! Look, *volchonok*! It's your ex. We could get this just so you can blow it up, right?" Mariska said, excitingly walking over to the mechanical, five-foot-tall creature and pointing at it with a grin.

"C'mon, 'Riska. Ixnay on the nickname." Claire groaned through a slight grin as she walked over to the creature that was the most accepted representation of what she actually was, a chagrined expression on her face. "I don't want to have to try and come up with some... weird frickin' reason to try and explain to Shondra why you call me 'little wolf' all the time."

"Technically, *'wolf cub'*, but *'volchonok'* sounds much cuter than *'malen'kiy volk'*. Wait, she knows Russian?" Mariska asked with a raised brow, looking genuinely curious. "My opinion of her continues to rise."

"No, but she has Google Translate on her phone and if she hears it she WILL look it up out of curiosity. She is just... super curious. It's..." Bending down to look at the machine that was moving with a series of loud clicks and whirrs, Claire knitted her brows. "Ugh... see, this is the shit I have to worry about her thinking I am. This is…"

"NOT you, *volchonok*… AGH, sorry. Claire." Mariska said, making the universal *'my lips are sealed'* gesture across her face as she caught herself. "But, no. This is an awful horror movie cliché, not who or what you are. She would understand that, from everything you've said of her."

"Shondra loves shitty horror movies. Hell, I used to love shitty horror movies." Claire bemoaned, turning away from the machine she was, in fact, tempted to destroy just for shits and giggles. "Now I can't enjoy them without nitpicking them for technical errors. Last month, we did a movie night. Streamed a bunch of movies and I had to bite my tongue every time a movie werewolf did something stupid. It's…"

Interrupted mid-sentence as the store's automatic double doors opened again to show Shondra McKay, Claire stopped herself and turned towards her friend. The stout woman's hair was pulled back into a wild, poofy ponytail, and she was wearing a pair of black leggings, lavender Converse sneakers, and a navy t-shirt with a print of a wolf howling at that moon on it.

As she walked over, Claire whispered through gritted teeth, too quietly for anyone but Mariska to hear, "Oh, come the fuck on. Really? Please, 'Riska…"

But it was entirely too late as Mariska was positively beaming at the sight, a mischievous grin on her face. "Shondra! Good morning! I love your t-shirt. Aren't wolves just the best?"

Stifling the overwhelming urge to audibly groan, Claire instead bit her tongue and smiled as Shondra made it over and gave Claire a hug. "G'morning."

Turning towards the shorter, whisper-thin blonde, the rotund woman had an authentic and enthusiastic smile as she ran her hands down the front of her shirt. "Yeah, I… um... got this at the Bay Area Ren Faire they had at the science center last summer. I love it, and yeah. They are just soooo beautiful."

Opening her arms, Shondra hesitated, but she was making a concerted effort to close some of the distance between the two of them. For just a moment, the little Russian vampire didn't quite know how to react, before she committed and leaned into the hug.

Mid-hug, Mariska tilted her head towards Claire to respond. Instead of snark, the reply was more sincere as she spoke. "Oh, absolutely. Very much so." As she said it, she opened her eyes wide as if to try and buttress her point that Shondra would accept Claire's secret.

For her part, however, the literal werewolf in the room was in no way convinced. Changing the subject, Claire hiked her purse up on her shoulder and interjected as her two best friends stepped back apart. "Soooo... I *know* you've been thinking of ideas, Shondra. Let's hear it."

Clapping her hands together excitedly, Shondra giggled. "Yeah, yeah! Okay... so, yeah. I have a FEW ideas. Especially since... y'know... the three of us will be going together. I mean... I don't know if you're up for a... group costume?"

Mariska's head jerked slightly at the concept she hadn't considered. The prospect of the impending evening suddenly became less exciting for Mariska and her brows knitted "Wait, what? Group costume? Like... all three of us wear the same thing?"

"Yeah, sorta. Well, at least the same, y'know, theme. It'll be fun!" Shondra said excitedly as she looked around the store. "Claire and I have done it a bunch of times. We could do, like, zombies? Or, something like the Sanderson Sisters from 'Hocus Pocus'? We should look around and see if we get any ideas."

"Yeah, that works." Claire said, nodding and smiling more now that Mariska was a little uncomfortable in the moment. Still, she was purposefully standing between Shondra and the obnoxious, animatronic werewolf as she gestured towards the other side of the store to get them away from the ugly thing. "Lead the way."

Going through the aisles, the three women began their search, with Claire and Mariska both loosening up as they went, easily getting caught up in Shondra's unbridled enthusiasm. Starting at the front of the store, they zig-zagged their way through the colorful assortment of masks, props, and more. Picking up almost every mask that could be interpreted as even a little sexy, Mariska began having more fun than she had expected.

With a plastic, faux-Parisian masquerade mask on a stick, the tiny blonde in black twirled around in an exaggerated, balletic dance move that she was surprisingly good at. "Ooh, we COULD do something like a 'Phantom of the Opera' theme. I could be the brilliant ingénue to your scarred and tortured Phantom, Claire. Then there's Carlotta or a gender-bent Raoul or literally anyone in a foppish masquerade costume for Shondra."

Modeling the mask with a grin, Mariska froze in a melodramatic pose. "Très classy."

Holding her hand up over her face where the Phantom's mask generally sat, Claire knitted her brows and shrugged her shoulders. "Yeaaaah, that mask is kind of small. Not exactly great coverage, 'Riska." The intention was clear, though confusing to Shondra, who didn't understand why full-face coverage seemed to be a must.

"Hmmm. That would be super classy, but…" Shondra broke into an impromptu, off-key, sing-song voice as she continued her sentence. "...I cannot sing to SAVE my LIIIIFFFEEE, and I would feel compelled to dooo soooo all NIIIGGGHHHTTT!"

Mariska couldn't resist chuckling, not AT Shondra, but WITH her, as she replied with an improvised song of her own, which sounded significantly better. "There are some tips I could teach you… had we the tiiimmmmeeeee."

"Another point, Riska. YOU'RE the only one of us who can actually sing." Claire said, holding up and dismissing a 'Phantom' mask, her lips pursed, as the idea would have been fun had Halloween been on any other night that week.

"Exactly. Hence, the ingénue." Mariska said, putting the mask back and pointing a finger up in the air.

"Wow… you have an amazing voice, Mariska. That was totally awesome." Shondra said, genuinely impressed, if mildly embarrassed by the comparison to her own efforts.

"Why, thank you. I've wanted to be a singer most of my life. Alas, it... it never quite came together." Mariska said with a dismissive shrug as they kept walking to the next aisle. "Still, I do drag Claire here to karaoke as often as possible. You should come out sometime. I was not kidding, I can give you some pointers. Plus, with enough alcohol involved, anything is possible."

There was a hint of melancholy on the woman's voice during the earliest admission, as she had once dreamed of stardom on the stage during the roaring twenties and the thirties. She had worked occasionally in old clubs before being turned, and had chosen, over the years, to step away from many opportunities for fear of being discovered. After all, for someone who fundamentally looked the same as she did a century ago, musical fame was a potential problem no matter how much she tried to change her aesthetic over the years.

Shondra's attention was immediately piqued by the revelation. "O, M, G, Claire. You sing... like... karaoke!? You are kidding me! Okay, we have GOT to make this happen! How could you have never mentioned this!?"

Stopping in front of a long wall of full-face latex masks, Claire fidgeted anxiously. She had been reluctant to let the two sides of her life overlap much for fear of something cuing Shondra in on the truth of what she had become.

"I dunno. I... just didn't think you'd be into it. I know you're not much for... clubs, or smoky bars, or anything." Claire said, which was at least partially true. "Plus... I really am god-awful at it. I can't get drunk enough to ignore how bad I am."

"Oh, nonsense, *volchonok*." Mariska said, immediately catching that she had slipped up and used the nickname. Quickly, she pressed forward, hoping she could get Shondra to ignore the term. "You do a great job. You have a layered, raspy 'Bonnie Tyler/Joan Jett' thing going and can take on songs I cannot pull off. Plus, you have considerable power from those big lungs. On hard rock, you kick much proverbial ass, and I'll hear no more self-effacing whining on the subject, thank you very much."

"Oh, I SOOOO need to witness this, Claire!" Shondra said, at the moment seeming to have missed the blunder, much to both Mariska and Claire's relief.

It was a short-lived relief, however, as Shondra raised an eyebrow. "But... uh... what's *'volchonok'?* That sounds really pretty. What is it, Eastern European? Russian?"

Claire froze, turning white, as Mariska, already as white as was possible, pursed her lips and tried to think of something to say. "Ahh... it's just a silly little nickname I call Claire. I really popped her 'club' cherry, so it's kind of... uh... a term for a... *newbie.*"

The lies seemed painfully transparent even without Claire's senses to reveal such things as Mariska continued, hoping to bury the issue with more information. "And yes, it is Russian. I was actually born there, what feels like AGES ago."

"Oh, wow! That's totally awesome. I, uh, had no idea." Shondra said, legitimately impressed and seemingly appeased, or at least sufficiently distracted. "I mean... I'm from Santa Barbara, originally. Which is, y'know, totally boring, I know."

"Also, I can't believe you never made it as a singer. You're amazing. Still, you're so young there's no reason not to keep at it, really. I bet you would, y'know, totally do great." Shondra said, bringing the subject back around while looking at masks. While the two women were talking, Claire's eyes had been drawn to a particular mask that made her stomach tighten. It was a hairy, latex werewolf mask that, like the animatronic, was everything she was afraid that Shondra would see her as: a slavering beast. Like before, she did her best to position her own body between her friend and the faux werewolf.

This time, however, it didn't work quite the same way. She was blocking Shondra just fine, and she was busy looking at a large skull mask made of chromed plastic, but Mariska could see what she was doing, and with a slightly irritated expression, decided to point it out.

"Oooh, what's that? Looks like a werewolf." she said enthusiastically, causing Claire to become even whiter as her eyes practically bugged out and began to show hints of telltale yellow as her anxiety started to rise.

As Mariska spoke, Shondra turned towards Claire to look at what was being pointed out with an excited smile. Claire turned away quickly, but for just a second, both women looked each other in the eye. She couldn't tell if the momentary confusion on her friend's face was due to how obviously anxious she was, or if Shondra had seen the color change. Nevertheless, as she turned towards Mariska, Claire was *not* pleased.

Shooting her other friend an angry glare, Mariska had a less-than-happy expression on her own face that Claire couldn't quite read. The two women were no strangers to arguments, but there was something else there behind Mariska's black eyes that Claire wasn't used to seeing either: hurt.

What are you doing? Claire mouthed, her anger being replaced by a more plaintive expression.

HELPING. Mariska replied, equally as silently, as she gestured back to Shondra, who seemed excited.

Turning back, Claire took a breath and calmed down enough for her eyes to change to normal as Shondra picked the mask up off the rack and realized it also had what looked like a floral bonnet built into it. "Oooh, it's supposed to be the wolf from Red Riding Hood. I get it."

"Okay… we could totally do, like, a Red Riding Hood, Big Bad Wolf, Huntsman thing, maybe?" Shondra said, looking them all over to imagine the scenario in her head.

"Well, only if I get to be a *sexy* huntsman." Mariska said flippantly, with a grin. It was clear to Claire that she was upset about something and taking the moment to lash out just a little by pushing the idea further.

Being the tallest of the three by far, Claire knew where this was going, and rolled her eyes as she took the mask and looked at it. "And I'm supposed to be the frickin' wolf, I guess?"

Listening to their tones, Shondra could tell something was wrong, and she raised an eyebrow quizzically. She might not have known her best friend's secret, but she was in no way stupid and knew things hadn't been right for a while now. The tension was starting to get to her, and that was showing as her face sunk a little. "Yeah, no. I… I'm sorry. I… uh… I don't think this is a good idea. I mean, it's obvious that you don't want to do any of this, Claire. We should probably just go."

The words hit like a knot in the woman's stomach that doubled down and tightened to the point of pain. Closing her eyes, Claire took a long breath and let out a sigh. She didn't know what to do. She couldn't tell Shondra the truth of why she was upset without telling her that she had become a werewolf, and Mariska seemed hell-bent on pushing Claire to come clean one way or another. She felt impossibly trapped and struggled to find a way out.

"No, no." Claire protested, trying to salvage the scenario that had spiraled out of control so quickly. "I *want* to go out for Halloween, I do. We both do. I'm sorry. I'm not trying to be a pain, honest."

"And hey, maybe this could work. I mean, it's a full head mask and it's…" Claire was embarrassed and desperate to make Shondra feel better. So much so that she pulled the mask over her head to show it off. "See? Not bad, right?"

Putting her hand over her mouth, Mariska stifled a chuckle in spite of herself at the awkward display. Replying, Mariska spoke honestly on an entirely different level that didn't go as far over Shondra's head as the vampire would have expected. "I think you'd look amazing."

"I'm sorry. This is kind of my fault. I've been surly all morning with our Claire. I work late nights, and mornings are NOT my friend. Since she picked me up from my house, I have been griping and complaining." Mariska admitted. This was technically not inaccurate. She picked up a rigid, foam sword from a barrel of mock-medieval weapons and shook it to test its weight.

Watching as Mariska swung the fake sword with surprising skill, Shondra pondered their words with a sigh. "Yeah, I just... I thought it would be fun. I wanted to try and… y'know… get back something that we used to do, Claire. But it just feels like I'm pulling teeth, and I don't know what I'm doing wrong."

"Nothing. You're not doing *anything* wrong." Claire protested, still wearing the mask for a second, which made the moment seem inappropriately ridiculous. Frustrated, she tugged the mask off her head, which tore the latex opening in the back as she did. Looking at the minor damage, she winced and bit her bottom lip. "Aw, shit."

Holding the mask at her side, Claire sheepishly ran her hand across her neck. "Look, I know you're tired of hearing that I'm… just still in a weird place. I know it's got to drive you nuts, but…"

To Claire's shock, the usually non-confrontational Shondra cut her off, shaking her head. "No! It… it drives me nuts that you won't let me in, weird place or not, Claire. I mean… you used to tell me everything, but you won't say anything about HIM. That… jerk who we all know messed you up so hard that you barely… you never really talk to me anymore. You obviously talk to Mariska, and I'm glad at least you have *someone* to talk to, but for me, it's n… nothing. It… it *hurts*, Claire."

Mariska wanted to interject, but found herself at a rare loss for words as she looked at Shondra. There was a deep sadness in the woman's eyes as she shook her head and hiked her purse up on her shoulder. "I'm sorry. This was… this was a stupid idea. I'm… I'm gonna just go home. I'm sorry. I should have known better. You just don't… I'm sorry."

Turning back to the door, Shondra moved to leave as Claire dropped the mask to reach out to her friend, only to pull her hand back like it was poisonous. In her mind, all she could imagine was what it would look like on Halloween, during the full moon. All the pent-up revulsion and fear she felt that Shondra would hate her more reared back up and she bit her lip again. "Please…"

Stopping, Shondra turned halfway back. "Please,'what', Claire? I'm… I'm sorry. But… this is just too much. I can't keep being the only one of the two of us who's... TRYING to be friends anymore."

Shondra spun around and kept walking until she had left the store, leaving both women standing next to the wall of masks. Claire's eyes were shimmering and her hands were shaking. She couldn't believe how badly it had gone.

Swallowing, Mariska realized that she had screwed up, and was equally speechless.

Her eyes still transfixed on the now-closed doors, Claire wiped her eyes to catch any errant tears before they escaped, sniffling. In a gravelly voice, she whispered.

"That... was helping?"

Chapter Twelve

Wallowing in self-pity sucked.

Claire came to that conclusion while nursing a mostly empty glass of wine. Only a day left to go before Halloween…and 'glass' was an exaggeration; as the dishes were in serious need of washing, her wine was in a coffee mug emblazoned with an image of a dancing Snoopy.

In one fell swoop, thanks to a half-hearted effort to fulfill a promise, Claire had stepped in it with both of her best friends. Since the incident at the Halloween store, she hadn't spoken to either woman. As a result, she was well and truly miserable and didn't know what to do.

Sitting like a lump on her couch, she looked at the bag from the store that had been sitting on the chair for the last few days. She had accidentally torn the ridiculous 'big bad wolf' mask she had tried on in the store, and already feeling like she had ruined everything else, decided to buy it. As such, there lay an adult-sized 'Granny Wolf' costume that had cost her 60 dollars, when all was said and done.

She also had no intention of wearing it, seeing as how on the full moon fell on Halloween night, she would not exactly need *that* to look like a wolf.

Claire still didn't know why Mariska had insisted on prodding her at the store and pointing out the stupid wolf mask. Her pressure to reveal her secret to Shondra had caused things to blow up; yet, for some reason, Mariska was also angry at Claire.

She had no idea why that was, but what she did know was that after days of silence, she was starting to crack.

The full moon was a day away. Today had been Claire's office Halloween party, and she had seriously considered just not showing up. The last week had been extremely painful, with Shondra barely saying two words in a row at any point to Claire.

The silence had become deafening, as the saying goes. Neither woman spoke to the other outside of work requirements, and neither had dressed up, making the tension at the office palpable.

Flipping through the streaming channels, she noticed there was nothing but horror movies and other spooky shows available. All Claire wanted was a distraction from the holiday, not a slew of reminders of just how much fun she and Shondra used to have at Halloween.

Taking a sip of wine, she saw that was clearly not going to be an option. The movies were ALL films she had watched with her long-time friend, either on TV or in the theaters. The first one in the queue was '*Halloween*' itself, which Claire had never seen until meeting Shondra. The bubbly and outgoing young designer had an affinity for horror, sci-fi, and particularly fantasy, and loved sharing it with Claire.

They weren't something that Claire had really sought out on her own to anywhere NEAR the same level of intensity as Shondra, but she shared enough interest for it to be something the two women bonded over back when they were roommates at art school in Orlando. Claire's mind drifted back, bouncing through her memories as if to torture her.

"O. M. G! I still can't believe you've never seen 'HALLOWEEN'!? You have been so sheltered from greatness." Shondra said, in the cramped and cluttered apartment the two had shared.

The furniture there had been a broken futon with an assortment of throw pillows in the living room, as well as a small TV set up on some old apple crates Claire had brought home with every intention of repurposing for an art project. In the corner, the tall brunette's easel had a half-finished canvas sitting on it, her supplies all strewn out on the TV tray next to it. On the canvas was an attempt at a Van Gogh-inspired night sky that she had abandoned in frustration.

"I wasn't sheltered, I just never got into slasher flicks. I like psychological thrillers and ghost movies and shit like that when I want to be creeped out." Claire said, placing the box of pizza they had ordered on the hand-me-down nightstand she had brought from home with much of her bedroom set when the young artist had moved from Pennsylvania to Florida for school. "I mean, isn't the cliche of the 'dumb horror movie teenagers' all kind of based on this one?"

"INSPIRED from! C'mon… there's a difference, Claire!" Shondra said with a massive smile, grabbing some glasses and a bottle of Dr. Pepper from the small fridge in their tiny kitchen. As she was now, this memory of a younger Shondra was just as short, though maybe just a bit less round in the middle, but with even more unruly hair in a mop of curls upon her head. "This… and a few other films like… uh... Black Christmas and the Texas Chainsaw Massacre set up a lot of the sub-genre. But this was the movie that kind of codified and, y'know, perfected the style moving forward. *This* was the movie that set up the standard that all the kind of lame knock-offs perpetuated. But it's really good! Honest."

That night, what seemed like forever ago, had been their first Halloween together. They had only known each other for two months after meeting in a shared class on color theory, and found that they got along well enough to help solve their mutual problem of needing a roommate. They ended up watching four of the films in the series, pointing out the plot holes and obvious California palm trees in what was supposed to be Illinois, laughing, and enjoying the otherwise quiet evening in.

Clicking through the options on her TV, Claire's mind just couldn't focus on anything but how badly she had ruined her longest friendship AND her newest in one fell swoop.

On the chair across from her, that stupid werewolf mask in the granny bonnet was staring at her from the inside of the transparent bag, prompting her to toss a pillow at the chair to cover it up.

The second Halloween they spent together, still at school, was a wildly different affair. They had been much more settled, and the little off-campus apartment they had still been living in looked far less like teenagers lived there. The campus of the now-defunct 'Orlando Academy of Creative and Entertainment Design' was located in a series of connected suites of a business park not far from the center of the city, and there was a party being held there for the students that year.

The TV show, *Game of Thrones*, was still very new and very popular, and both women enjoyed watching it enough to be inspired to show up dressed in themed costumes. The portly Shondra was wearing a homemade dress, white wig, and puppet dragon on her shoulder, while the 6-foot-tall Claire had her fairly short brown hair slicked back and sprayed with a temporary blonde color, with foam sculpted and painted to look like a knight's armor.

Seeing the show in her queue on the online streaming options had recalled the evening in Claire's mind. She wondered if every bit of popular culture was going to prompt SOME kind of obnoxious memory.

"Claire…" Shondra had said that night, fidgeting with the little puppet of a dragon that was perched on her shoulder. "He's… um… he's totally falling off again, I think. Could you check the clip, please? I don't want it falling apart inside, y'know?"

With a smile, Claire tucked the large foam sword she was carrying as a part of her 'Brienne of Tarth' costume under her arm, as the suit she had constructed didn't have a sheath to speak of, and re-adjusted the clip on the shoulder of Shondra's 'Daenerys Targaryen' costume. "Nah, it's fine. It's meant to be able to move a little or you'll crimp the little wire that lets you move his head. You made it that way because you know your shit. It's all good, Shondra. Promise."

"O… okay. I just… I just want to make sure it looks good." she said, the nervousness in her voice showing through. Of the two, the squat, overweight young designer was even more introverted and uncomfortable in crowds and parties. Both young women were reserved in their own ways, but together, Shondra made Claire look positively confident. Growing up in a small, fairly isolated Pennsylvania town, Claire was at least a little better at faking social skills, and had spent enough time as a teenager sneaking out to find different ways to get into trouble.

For her part, Shondra replaced misspent teen years accruing skills such as learning how to design, build, and sew her own costumes for cosplay at conventions, ren fairs, and events like tonight. Both women were in costumes that the darker-skinned young creator had handmade with moldable foam and a significant amount of hand-sewn fabrics. While Claire fancied herself a painter who was good at graphic design, Shondra was a graphic designer who was good at fabrication. They worked well together in school and complemented each other socially.

"It's okay, Shondra. Shit, we're not in there yet, so just take a breath and relax." Claire said, knowing full well that her friend's concerns about the costume were, in fact, her nerves surfacing about the impending social interaction.

Biting her lower lip, Shondra knitted her brows and chuckled nervously for a second as she looked up at Claire. "I know, I know. I'm being goofy and worrying over nothing. I know. It's… I know, like, everyone in there. We go to all the same classes."

"It's just…" Shondra paused for a moment, fidgeting as she worked out what she wanted to say.

"What is it? You can talk to me. We can always talk, Shondra." Claire said, tilting her head. She knew that her friend had a hard time admitting emotions. Her vulnerabilities had been used as a weapon against her far too often and Claire knew it. As such, she often held her friend by the hand to help where she could.

"It's… my mom always told me that when I went to art school, I'd FINALLY meet people that were… y'know… more like ME. Where I wouldn't feel like so much of an outsider." Shondra admitted with a mix of pain and relief in her voice. "But… it feels so… so much like just… an extension of high school, y'know. Cliques and bullies and I still get made fun of for the stuff I like… it's the same as it ever was and I still don't fit in. I just... don't want to go in there and feel like that."

"Hey, you DO fit in. You fit in with me. As for them, honestly, I can't remember half of their names and I'm in the same classes. You look amazing, WE are rocking these outfits, and if anyone gives you shit, I DO have a big foam sword and an in-character justification to kick ass." Claire replied with a warm smile, working to try and build up Shondra's confidence, as she brandished the costume sword.

"Look at you. You're the QUEEN. Walk in there like the queen of fucking dragons and own it. You've got this, Shondra." Claire said, as her friend's shoulders straightened up. The words seemed to have a positive effect as they resolved to own the night.

And own it they did.

Slouching further into the couch, Claire sniffled as the memory played out for her. Here she was, pulling away from Shondra because of her own insecurities; her own fears focused on no longer fitting in. In a strange way, becoming a werewolf caused their roles to be reversed and it was CLAIRE who feared rejection. It was a fear that was now manifesting as reality due to her own actions; actions that had left Shondra AND Mariska hurt. Actions that had left Claire utterly alone.

"What the fuck are you looking at?" Claire grumbled, the corner of the werewolf mask peeking out under the pillow. It was just the tip of the snout, but it was enough to elicit the flippant comment. Pulling herself up, Claire went into the kitchen to refill her makeshift glass with some more wine before realizing that the box in the fridge was empty.

"Yeah, yeah. I know. This is a sign I need to stop drinking, right? Claire said, now actively talking to the empty room. Turning back around, she grabbed the latex mask from under the pillow and pulled it out by the end of the nose.

The woman was a wreck, standing in her living room in a pair of pink cotton pajama bottoms with little white hearts on them and a baggy, oversized white t-shirt from one of the marketing companies' clients that had a couple of old wine stains on it. The collar was cut off to make it comfier for a 'hang around the house' shirt and had a logo for 'Brekken Printing' on the front.

Putting her right hand up the open bottom of the mask, she looked at the thing in the eyes. It was the exact image she most hated when it came to werewolves. A long, gnarled snout with lips peeled back to show a mouth with way too many teeth that were way too big. The sculpted face came with a tongue that looked more Lovecraftian than lupine.

The faux-gray fur on the mask was cheap and disheveled-looking with overly pointy ears and bloodshot eyes sculpted just around the narrow eye slits. It was the monster she knew people thought of when they thought 'werewolf'. It was what she was still afraid she was, in spite of a year of living a very different reality.

After that night where Mariska had taken her to the woods to run and experience the change for the first time, she had stood there, in front of Mariska. The sun was just a few minutes away from cresting the horizon again and she was still transformed. The two women walked carefully back to the secluded side road where they had parked the car and left Claire's bag, with a fresh change of clothes she would be needing in just a few minutes.

As the endorphins were wearing off, the excitement of that first night turned back into anxiety. But Mariska put her hand on Claire's fur-covered face and turned it to the black, tinted window that was as clear as a mirror in the pre-dawn light. Claire could hear her friend's reassuring words. "See? You are not a monster. You never lost control or went crazy. You ran and you howled and yes, you *hunted*. That is just a part of what you are now. But you aren't some kind of beast. Look."

In that reflection, she looked upon her changed form for the first time, while Mariska told her what she saw. "This is a part of you now and forever. But it's not a curse. It's elegant. It's beautiful. Look. Really look."

Looking now at the horror show of a mask, it was nothing like what she became. Yes, the broad strokes were the same, but in the details was all the difference in the world. Where its teeth were jagged and deformed, hers were sharp, but curved naturally; pronounced, but not monstrous. When she transformed, her fur was smooth and silky; plush and soft, not ragged or matted. And her eyes were tapered along the lines of her cheeks that lead to her long ears. Not bloodshot, beady things but deep, shining pools of rich amber, rimmed in a black that made the color that much more intense.

Standing there in her living room, she tilted the mask she was wearing on her hand like a puppet and worked the mouth with her hand. "You probably should. This isn't helping, is it? Moping here like an angry little kid, trying to get drunk, so you don't have to think about how you screwed up."

As she spoke, she put on a mock, 'monster' voice, affecting a fake growl only to reply with her own normal voice. "What the hell am I supposed to do? Mariska just… doesn't seem to get it. I can't tell Shondra the truth. I'd lose her forever, and I can't deal with that."

"You and her aren't talking, anyway. So, you're losing her and she doesn't even know why." She replied, speaking through the mask to verbalize her own internal fears. "She probably thinks it's something she did. Or worse, she's internalizing it as an inherent problem with who she is."

"She trusts you, Claire. You're pissing on that because you're a scared little puppy." She finished, pulling the mask off her hand and tossing it back on the chair. With a sigh, she stepped over to the window and looked out into the night. The moon was almost full, but not quite enough to force a change against her will. That would be tomorrow.

Tonight, however, was different. Tonight she could do something, and at least try to fix what she had broken.

Chapter Thirteen
⊰ ☽ ☉ ☾ ⊱

Sitting in what would ordinarily be her dining room, Shondra McKay was engrossed in a particular activity that helped her relax when she was stressed out. Across from the window was a long, L-shaped desk with two computers on it and an assortment of bric-a-brac strewn about next to a mostly empty can of Cherry Coke Zero.

One computer was a fairly clean looking, silver-skinned iMac that had its screensaver running, flowing lines of color streaming across in a hypnotic spiral. The other was a large black tower with glowing green LED lights. Shondra sat in front of it with headphones on. On the screen, digital chaos was erupting as she tried to lose herself in an online game.

Near her feet in a plush, red doggy bed, sat a chocolate-furred poodle, coat untrimmed and allowed to curl up naturally. While she tapped away at the glowing keys of her gaming computer, staring intently at the screen, her little dog snoozed with his head next to the fuzzy purple unicorn slippers she had on.

But her mind wasn't quite as focused on the game as it should have been. She couldn't understand why, but it had become clear over the last few months that Claire Gribbald, who had been her best friend for about a decade, just didn't care about her anymore. It had been building for a year, ever since the tall brunette had vanished for nearly a month with no explanation.

With her memories swirling in on themselves, Shondra couldn't figure out what had gone wrong. Claire had begun dating someone she had met in downtown Ybor. Shondra herself had never met the man; all she knew was that he was Scottish and played the bass guitar. Her best friend, the woman who helped her get through college, was actually dating 'a guy in a band', and the idea had made Shondra roll her eyes, even then.

For a few weeks, it was all Claire could talk about. "Liam's band is playing downtown tonight.", "Liam and I went to the beach for the weekend and it was so romantic.", "Liam wrote a song about me."

Frankly, it had gotten on Shondra's nerves. The two had been close friends for years, and roommates for half of the time they had known each other. They did a lot together, but hadn't been joined at the hip since art school at least. Looking back, Shondra couldn't help but realize that she had been jealous of her friend, and the boyfriend who had been occupying so much of her time.

They had a lot in common, like a mutual love of fantasy fiction and art, Ren faires, and dressing up for Halloween. They enjoyed going thrift store hunting together. They didn't share all the same interests, but Claire liked to say that they spoke the same 'nerd base language'. What they liked, they both liked with the same kind of passion. Though, for a while, it seemed like the only thing Claire liked was *Liam*.

So, Shondra had been jealous; not so jealous that she had been blinded to the other early warning signs regarding the man, though. More and more, he dominated Claire's time. He talked her into spending her savings on equipment for his band. He talked her into paying for a lot of things, and seemed to try to keep her to himself. Whenever they had made plans, Liam would swoop in with alternate plans to keep Claire disconnected. It had concerned Shondra, and she had desperately wanted to say something.

Wanted to, but didn't. Not in time, at least, because all the rotund woman knew was that SOMETHING bad had happened. Months into her relationship, Claire was leaving to go on a mini-vacation for the weekend with Liam about a week and a half before Halloween. She had been super excited and talked about it for days.

As Saturday and Sunday passed, Shondra thought nothing of it. She wasn't expecting to hear much in spite of the fact that Claire had often snapped pics of their nights out to share with her. Monday came and went. Claire wasn't expected back until Tuesday from the trip, but when Tuesday came and Claire didn't show up or call into work…

Leaving half a dozen voicemails and trying to reach her on every social media platform had yielded no responses, and Shondra was officially scared. She had no mutual friends with anyone in the club scene where Claire and Liam had met, and she didn't want to go to the police. For all she knew, the overly-attached lovers had just lost track of the weekend and were still out there screwing like animals and having a grand time. Still, Shondra was concerned.

By Thursday, Claire finally resurfaced; at least, in a manner of speaking. Shondra had been a wreck, trying to focus on deliverables at work when Marcia said that Claire had called in that morning. The silver-haired owner relayed, with no small amount of concern in her voice, that Claire had a family emergency of some kind. It was something that would require her to be out of town for at least the next two weeks. As she had the vacation time accrued, Marcia granted it, begrudgingly, and wished her well.

However, Marcia also told Shondra that she didn't believe what Claire was saying. She said that Claire sounded frightened and weak. Something was wrong, but with no idea where she had gone, all Shondra could do was wait.

Wait, and do some investigating.

The young graphic designer was no slouch when it came to researching, and had spent more than a little time digging up whatever she could find on Liam Docherty. He was from a small village in the north of Scotland called *Arvenly* where he had founded a punk rock band called *'The Slaughtered Lamb'*. He and his bandmates were apparently here on an education visa, but it didn't look like any of them were still going to college there, or anywhere that she could find. As far as Shondra could tell, they were likely using Claire, and she was terrified that they had finally used her up.

More research revealed that there had been no deaths or major accidents in regards to any of the family members that she knew about, though she had resisted the urge to call Claire's sister to check.

Two weeks became three weeks, and Halloween came and went. By the beginning of the fourth week, Claire had called in to work. Shondra wasn't privy to the specifics, but she had told Marcia something about a family funeral that she had to attend back in Pennsylvania that Shondra knew could not have happened. Then, Claire finally called her.

It was, perhaps, the most painful conversation she had with her friend, as it was clear that SOMETHING horrible had happened. It was also clear that Claire wasn't going to say exactly what. All Shondra knew was that it had ended between her and Liam, and it had ended so badly that Claire had literally begged for her to not push the issue. She apologized profusely for vanishing, sounding like at any moment she would break down and cry, but no tears came. She was clearly putting forth a maximum amount of effort to restrain her emotions.

This state of being would seem to continue and become more consistent until the two finally had their overdue falling-out earlier in the week. Shondra was sick and tired of the excuses and the obvious put offs.

Also, she was tired of Mariska.

When Claire reappeared and tried sliding back into her life, she had a new friend who she would spend most of her free time with; the pencil-thin party goth who Shondra strove so hard not to resent; after all, she did seem nice. They were even getting along on Saturday in the store, much to her surprise.

While Shondra reminisced, the little brown dog at her feet began to growl. With her headphones on and the sounds of animated destruction filling her ears, however, she didn't hear anything. When there came a light, hesitant rap on the door of her little apartment, she also didn't hear it, at least until she was startled out of her trance by her little dog barking up a storm.

"AGGGHHH!!! Oh, heck. Poop, poop, poop! Clive, you scared the heck out of me. What is it, fuzzybutt?" She said, turning in her chair and pulling her headphones back as the dog stood defensively, growling at the door. Seconds later, she heard a familiar voice saying, "Knock, knock."

"Claire?" Shondra said, before letting out a sigh, typing 'AFK', and muting her microphone for privacy. Putting the headphones on the desk, she pushed up from the desk chair she used for both work and play, and walked over to the door. "Uh... um... What... What are you doing here?"

Scooching her little dog out of the way gently with her foot, Shondra put her hand on the doorknob, but stopped herself from unlocking it as she waited to hear what Claire had to say. "I... I wanted to talk. To apologize."

"To e... *explain?*" Shondra replied through the door, aggravation evident in her words as she had no interest in a hollow apology without something to let her know WHY Claire had been acting the way she had been for so long.

There was a long pause before Claire's voice came through the door, sounding smaller than before. "I'd... like to try. Please."

Sighing, Shondra rubbed the bridge of her nose between her thumb and forefinger before unlocking and opening the door. She wasn't prepared for the sight of Claire standing at the top of the steps, holding a pizza box in one hand and a two-liter of Dr. Pepper in the other. On her head was the ridiculous werewolf mask she had tried on in the Halloween store.

In spite of her anger, Shondra was clearly working overtime not to smile as she pursed her lips and nodded. "What's all this supposed to be? Uh... Some kind of, what, a... peace offering?"

"Uh... heh... basically, yeah. I... I really want to... damn it..." Claire said, her voice muffled before she put the soda bottle on top of the pizza box and pulled off the mask to continue. "I wanted to talk. I know I fucked up. I know I've just been a shitty friend for a while now and have been dismissing you and you don't deserve that. And... I don't know if you even want to forgive me, but... I at least want to tell you... y'know... why."

Saying the words, Claire's stomach tightened. Throwing on

some clothes and making the plan to come and talk to Shondra, she was a woman on a mission and that mission was… one way or another… to come clean.

It was one of her greatest fears, but she needed to face it, and hoped that the stupid mask might help diffuse not only the tension between them, but the tension tearing her insides out. The anxiety was so thick that she could feel the wolf just under the surface, pushing to come out a day early. "Please. I don't have any excuses. I know I don't. But please… let me at least give you a reason."

"Whatever." Shondra said, stomping into her apartment and leaving the door open, speaking more tersely than she was accustomed to. Standing in an attack posture at the door, her little dog's ears were back against his head and his teeth were bared at Claire, sensing her…nature as he let out a perpetual, low-level growl. "C'mon, Clive. Hush up. Be a good boy or mommy's gonna give you one of those little knock-you-out treats."

Begrudgingly, the tiny poodle backed off, gluing himself to his owner's feet as Claire came in and put the box down on the coffee table. "I… uh… forgot to grab napkins."

"Again… whatever. I'm not hungry, Claire." Shondra said, working hard to hold on to her anger and not let this be easy for her. "What do you want to say?"

She sat down hard in the middle of her couch with a raised eyebrow, not offering Claire a place to sit. The anger was still strong; strong enough to overpower the woman's usual stutter. Looking about, Claire fidgeted awkwardly, standing on the other side of the coffee table, feeling unwelcome in Shondra's apartment for the first time. It was a sensation that tightened the knot in her stomach, prompting her to close her eyes and breathe for a moment.

Of course, Claire wasn't angry, but as it was, ANY strong emotion could trigger an unplanned transformation at most, and her eyes turning a startling shade of amber at the least. As a point of fact, that was a big part of why she had distanced herself from Shondra so much. The occasional yellowing wasn't a problem if she got emotional with Mariska, but would be more than a little noticeable with the otherwise 'normal' woman.

Calming herself down, Claire's voice was cracked and tired sounding. She hadn't slept well all week and it showed. "I'm... I'm sorry. More than I know how to say, I'm sorry."

"I know how I've acted for... for almost a year now. I've been... distant and cold. I've kept you at arm's length and whenever you've asked why, I've dodged the questions or just... begged you not to ask." Claire said, rubbing the back of her neck as the muscles were tensing involuntarily. "Which... no matter what... you always did, even though you didn't want to, and that's not fair. I've been a shitty friend, and I deserve this. I know that."

At that, Shondra rolled her eyes. She wanted an explanation, not an attempt at getting pity, but she bit her tongue and let Claire continue. At her feet, little Clive was still standing in defense of his mistress.

"This week... is... hard. Halloween is... *really* hard. I thought I was getting better. Dealing with it. But it's just getting worse, and I don't know how to manage it." Claire said, talking almost at random in a stream of consciousness as she did.

Shondra sat forward and again rubbed the bridge of her nose. "Look... just sit down and tell me, okay? Please. All I want to know is WHY, Claire. I GET that something really bad happened to you. I KNOW that he hurt you somehow. But you won't TELL me, so how do you think that makes ME feel? We... we USED to tell each other everything."

Awkwardly, Claire sat in the offered easy chair to the side of the couch, hanging her head. "Like shit." She said, defeated.

"Like... yeah. Like that. Like all the years we were friends was some kind of stupid... lie. Some emotional long game you were playing to string along the fat little nerd you just hung around with to make yourself FEEL better. So yeah, it felt like... like that, Claire. So tell me, am I WRONG? Do you REALLY care about me, or is this just some... stupid attempt to absolve yourself of feeling guilty?" Shondra said, her voice raised and her eyes watering as she let her own feelings she had been bottling up for a while now finally pour out.

Biting her bottom lip, Claire just sat there and let Shondra continue.

"Because if you EVER knew me, you should know that I... I really care about you. You've been... like... like the sister I always wanted, Claire! And lately, it just... it feels like that was all just a big lie." Tears were beginning to flow, which prompted little Clive to leap up and try to lick Shondra's sadness away. "Get down, baby. Good boy... but get down."

Standing up, Shondra was now looking down at Claire, fully baring her soul. "So what happened? What did he do to... to break you like this, that you are SOOO afraid to tell me? That you'd do this to me for so long, because I can't pretend that everything is NORMAL, Claire!"

"I know he was bleeding you dry and that you were letting him, and I kept my mouth shut even though MARCIA could see he was emotionally abusing you. So what happened? What? Did he... oh my goodness... did he *rape* you?"

With that, the anger subsided enough for Claire to hear the genuine concern in Shondra's voice as the woman let out her own fears.

"N... no. He.. he didn't do that. Not... not *exactly*, at least. No." Claire responded, shaking her head and wiping her own wet eyes on the sleeve of her long-sleeved sweater. "He..."

Taking another breath, Claire kept her head down and her eyes closed, because even without looking, she could feel the amber flooding her irises as she spoke. "In the beginning, it was wonderful. He... was the kind of person I never thought would be interested in someone like me. He... was a musician. He seemed so smart, he had seen so much of the world, and he had... cool friends and did these super interesting things. He always seemed to know what I was thinking and feeling, and had all these wild stories. He was all of this, and he liked ME."

"He liked ME and I... couldn't believe it." Claire said,

admitting her own weaknesses. "I… really never knew what that was like, and it got into my head, hard. I mean, I… tried dating a couple times before, but I had never FELT like I did when I was with him. I mean… I don't know. You think I'm so much more confident than you, Shondra, but it's an act I learned to pull off, competing with my sister for attention growing up. It's… literally a mask."

"Yeah, I… I know, Claire," Shondra said, sitting back down, the anger beginning to fade in her voice. "I mean… y'know... I didn't think we got along so well because we didn't have anything in common. I knew you were totally a mess too, but you knew how to fake it better than me."

Nodding, Claire prayed her eyes were normal again as she looked up. If they were yellow, Shondra didn't react to it as she prompted Claire to continue.

"So… I ignored all the signs. I ignored how he would make me feel like… less than… when we were alone. Or like… property when we were out with his band. How he would expect me to pay for things and withhold or dole out affection based on my expectations of it. Looking back, I can't believe I couldn't see how textbook his bullshit behavior was. At least, until it all… exploded on that weekend we were going to go out of town."

"So, if he didn't… if that didn't happen, what DID? I mean… what could it have been that has you so messed up, Claire? Did he... clean out your bank account? Steal from your apartment? What, is he… some kind of… *werewolf* and he attacked you? What the heck was soooo bad? I don't understand?"

"*COUGH!!!* *COUGH!!!*" Claire choked on her own spit after what Shondra said with obvious sarcastic hyperbole. It was literally exactly what happened, but presented as what it sounded like: an impossible line of bullshit. Immediately, that ball of tension tightened in Claire's gut.

"Shit… shit, sorry." Claire said, getting the coughing under control. As she did, she let out an awkward chuckle, not knowing HOW to react to the idea, before calming herself back down.

A little frustrated, but also concerned, Shondra got up and walked into her tiny kitchen. "Hold on, hold on. Don't die."

Coming back, she brought out two small glasses with ice. The novelty glasses had images from the Lord of the Rings movies on them, well used and faded. Cracking open the bottle of soda Claire had brought, she poured two glasses and handed one to the woman who she still wanted as a friend. "Here you go. Just... please. Relax, okay? You don't have to be afraid that I won't understand, and I won't ever JUDGE you for what happened, okay? Please, Claire. I just... I need to understand."

Nodding, Claire took the glass and had a large sip as she struggled to believe what Shondra had said about judgment. Setting it back down, she dropped her head again, fidgeting in her seat for what felt like far too long while silence filled the air between the two women.

"He... hurt me." Claire said, her voice a weak, cracking thing.

"Honey, I know he did, but..." Shondra replied, seeming to miss the weight of the statement as Claire cut her off to reiterate the idea.

"No. He... hurt me *badly*, Shondra. He attacked me. He almost... *killed* me."

Chapter Fourteen

Shondra's face had gone cold and her eyes were wide. She had suspected so much when she had tried to imagine just how badly the breakup with her best friend Claire and her ex Liam had gone. She had imagined a multitude of scenarios but wasn't prepared for what she was hearing right then and there.

Talking, Claire stood back up, beginning to pace as she did when she was wildly uncomfortable; and in that moment, she absolutely was. After all, the story she was trying to finally tell ended with her as a werewolf.

"He... attacked you? Oh my goodness, Claire... how could... what happened?" Shondra avoided mentioning her own feelings of resentment that secrets had been kept for nearly a full year. Instead, she tried to focus and let her tell the story as she needed to.

Nervously, Claire turned away and continued. Her emotions were too high and she was fighting her body's natural defense mechanism. It WANTED to change to help her manage the stress. She had every intention of telling Shondra, but it needed to be on her own terms.

"We... things were going... okay, I want to say they were going well, but I wasn't a complete idiot." Claire begrudgingly admitted. "I mean, I was in love and it blinded me to a lot, but I could tell he was using me. I could tell he was gaslighting me, but when we were together, it was always like I was in a daze. It was so fucking stupid. So... I had the idea of driving out of town for a long weekend, just us, and trying to reconnect. He was getting weird and distant and I didn't know what was going on."

"Sounds familiar..." Shondra said almost instinctively before pursing her lips. "Sorry. Sorry."

Continuing, Claire nodded. "No, it's okay. I deserve that, I know."

"So, I went to pick him up at the shitty ass apartment he shared with his band. There were three of them: the drummer, Beverly, the lead singer, Quentin, and the lead guitarist, Duncan. The place was… always a disaster… and they always seemed to be part of the problem. At the time, I rationalized some of his weird behavior as him putting on a macho-ass routine to impress his little fucking... pack. His latch-ons. At least that's how I justified ignoring his bullshit for months."

"I had rented a room at this resort in Kissimmee for the weekend and… made all kinds of stupid plans," Claire said, her voice cracking, which made Shondra want to get up to hug the woman. She held back, however, and remained seated.

"I got there to help him pack the car, and the bandmates were being dicks as usual," Claire said, fidgeting, while keeping her back to Shondra. "And worse, Beverly was hanging off of Liam's arm. I tried to not let it get to me, the way she flirted with him, but it made me jealous. It was still early, and they had a gig that night at the Bastion. The plan was to leave the club and go straight to the hotel."

As she told the story, in her mind's eye, the memory began to play out for her.

"Awww, what're we s'possed t' do this weekend while yuir gone, love?" Beverly said, smirking smugly and shooting Claire the side-eye. Her words, tinted by a thick, Scottish accent, were dripping with false honey.

"You'll figure something out, I'm sure," Claire replied sarcastically, pursing her lips. The two were on the worn-out couch, Beverly sitting too close for Claire's comfort. The drummer had a shock of bright ginger curls in a short, punky haircut with a side fade. She was wearing tight jeans that hugged her extremely wide bottom and a band t-shirt over her otherwise smaller frame. Liam was nursing a beer and dressed just as casually.

"Exactly. Y'all don't need me t' tell ya' how to piss anymore, do ya'?" Liam said with a wide grin as he stood up from the couch, his accent pronounced, but not as thick as Beverly's. At a lean and somewhat lanky six foot four, he was taller even than Claire, though much trimmer. He had mid-length black hair that was slicked back into a ponytail and a two-day growth of beard that was almost perpetual. His eyes were a shade of blue that Claire found mesmerizing. Overall, he was an attractive young man.

By Claire's standards, he was gorgeous, and gave off an aura that she found herself inexplicably drawn to. Later on, of course, she would learn that this was a literal feature of what she had become, but at the time it only strengthened the feeling she thought was love.

On the couch, Beverly stretched out to fill out the space that Liam had just vacated, making a pronounced pout. "Well, poop."

"I think she's in heat again, Liam." Came the sound of Quentin from the kitchen, as he and Duncan came out with beers of their own. The two were Liam's younger brothers. Fraternal twins, they were almost always together whenever Claire was around, and had mops of shaggy brown hair. They weren't identical, but they were definitely brothers. Duncan finished Quentin's thought out loud. "Figure we should take her out on th' town tonight? Keep her busy?"

Claire was blushing with mild embarrassment as she commented. "Yeah, I know NOW how fucking obvious it was that she was probably sleeping with ALL of them, but at the time, I just... I guess I *LET* myself ignore it. I... didn't want to see it. I know... stupid."

Chuckling, Claire didn't comment on the other cues that hinted at what she had yet to discover about all four of them. All the thinly-veiled 'wolf' puns and 'dog' references they seemed to relish peppering in to mess with her. Or maybe just to groom her. Claire still wasn't quite sure.

"So... we loaded up my car with his luggage and I went home to get ready." Claire relayed the story of the evening as best as she could to Shondra. "I... I did myself up as nice as I could. I really wanted to look as good as I thought I could when I went to meet up with him backstage after the show. As for the show itself… it was even more fuel to the fire. It made me even… stupider."

With a rum and coke in hand, Claire pushed herself as close to the stage as she could get in the fairly crowded club. She had done her hair and was excited as the club owner came out and introduced the band to the waiting crowd. "All right, everyone! Here they are! Give it up for '*The Slaughtered Lamb*'!!"

The roar was enough to make Claire's ears start ringing as the band headed out on stage, which only served to make the experience more intense for the already-smitten woman. There, on stage nearest the side she was closest to, was Liam. Even now, remembering it, he seemed unreal to her. With the stage lights illuminating him like some kind of god, the world seemed to fall away as the band played and Claire allowed herself to fall with it.

Time seemed to be both too fast and too slow while they played. The set was a mix of their own music and popular punk rock covers that Claire loved, and she became as drawn into the moment as everyone else in the crowd. But she wasn't everyone else, and Liam made sure she knew it.

While most of the songs were sung by Quentin, near the end of the night, Liam stepped forward and to the center stage. He had told her he wrote most of their music, but he didn't generally sing. At that moment, though, he took the microphone from his younger brother and took charge.

Biting her lip, Claire knew the song he began to sing, his voice deeper and more gravelly than his brother's. It was one he had hummed to her many a late night together. The song he said he had written just for her. There was a resonant, breathy quality as he sang, finding her eyes in the crowd and locking on her as he continued.

Even now, in recalling the memory for Shondra, Claire found herself falling into the moment again in a way that was uncomfortable for both women. Clearing her throat, Claire shook her head and moved the story past the concert.

"So… ahem… yeah. The Bastion has a pretty decent-sized

dressing room for the bands, and I'd been back there before. When I showed up... the after-party had already started."

It was clear to Shondra that Claire was stalling, talking about the lead-up to avoid getting to the heart of what had happened, but at the moment, she didn't push her any further, letting her continue. All the while, her little dog, Clive, sat right next to her in a strange defensive posture.

"That's... actually where I met Mariska." Claire continued, turning back to sit down. Looking at Shondra, she was calm enough to keep her eyes their normal hazel for a bit longer. "She hung around the clubs all the time, but she knew them. The band. PARTICULARLY Beverly."

Smirking awkwardly, Claire chuckled. "At the time, it was actually a relief. They were all over each other, and it made me think that I had just misread the cues from Beverly or... y'know... that she was just a raging bitch who liked to fuck with me."

"Mariska's, what, bi? Pan?" Shondra asked, genuinely curious with regard to the woman she knew so little about.

"I think she might just be a lesbian. Mariska, at least. Beverly might be bi or pansexual, I guess. Whenever the band was in town, they would hook up for a while. It was... like a THING for them." Claire said, still seeming embarrassed as she recounted the night.

"Oh, is this your new friend, Liam?" Mariska said, her black lipstick smeared across her pale face, with sarcasm Claire hadn't been able to read in her voice. She would later learn that the pint-sized vampire couldn't stand Liam. "She seems... well, better than you, at least. Hopefully not just another piece of meat?"

It came off as playful, and Claire hadn't registered that when Mariska was looking her up and down, it was in noticing that she was one of the only humans in the room outside of the club owner and his boyfriend.

"Oh, aren't ye always a fuckin' comedian, Mariska. Who told you t' come back here, anyway?" Liam said with a smart-assed smirk, walking over to put an arm around a very out-of-her-element Claire.

"Call of... the wild. You know I can't keep my hands off of her when she's like this." Mariska said, running her fingers along the back of Beverly's neck, who shuddered at the sensation, grinning devilishly. "She's an animal."

The bluntness of it all was painfully obvious to Claire NOW, but at the time she had no idea. She shook her head and continued. "So... this isn't the point. The after-party went long and the club itself was already closed. The band went to pack up the van and Mariska even tried to warn me when we had the room to ourselves for a moment. I didn't know exactly what she meant, but she did try."

"So... it is... Claire, correct?" Mariska's voice echoed through her memory, "I know you think he hung the moon. He has that effect on people, but he is a user. He uses women up and tosses them away."

"She tried to warn me, but I protested, of course, and blew her off. I was... hopped up on hormones and stupidity, and I didn't listen. Mariska went home and I went out to the alley behind the club where they were parked." Claire said, biting her bottom lip and nodding, tension tightening her shoulders as she closed her eyes. "The gear was still on the street behind the rear of the van. Duncan and Quentin were gone, but I could hear what was happening. She tried to warn me but I had to see it for myself."

"I... opened the van doors, and there they were. Beverly was riding Liam like he was a fucking horse. I... could NOT believe it. I didn't WANT to believe it." Claire said, putting her face in her palms as she took another breath, trying to calm down and keep herself from succumbing to what she was feeling.

"Oh, no..." Shondra said, licking her lips anxiously. She knew at least part of where this was going to lead, but still was unprepared.

"She turned to me with a smirk, like she knew I was coming. And she grinned at me and said, 'Jes' warmin' him up f'r ya', girly.' Like that made it okay." Claire clenched her fists in her lap,

116

taking a moment to catch her breath. "I was furious. I KNEW shit like this was happening, but he didn't even look all that upset. I... screamed at him. Raged and shouted. I told him it was over. I told him to stay the fuck out of my life. THAT was when he got pissed off."

Instinctively, Shondra stood up to go over to Claire, but was unprepared for her friend to virtually leap back out of the chair and out of reach. Quickly, Claire turned her back to Shondra, visibly trembling with an effort her friend was oblivious to. "No! Please.. Just... I *need* to finish. Please."

Watching as Claire took a series of long, rapid breaths, Shondra didn't register that Claire's voice had momentarily dropped half an octave as she continued. "He said... 'Fuck you! You don't leave me! You're MY bitch, and...'"

"What?!" Shondra said in disbelief, muttering to herself as Claire continued.

"He said I was his bitch. That I was his. HIS property and he would fuck whoever he wanted and I'd deal or not, but that wasn't his problem. He screamed at me in that alleyway. It was so loud, I'm still shocked nobody came back out." Claire nodded, half-looking over her shoulder. "I told him to fuck off and started to walk away. He... roared at me."

"When I turned around, he... wasn't Liam anymore. It was terrifying." Claire said, glossing over the details of his transformation out of that lingering fear. But the image was burned into her memory for all time. In the alley, he ran at her, growling. In less time than it took to tell, he was no longer human. Covered in deep, black fur, his blue eyes growing larger and even more vivid in color.

"Ah, SHITE! Rein it the fook IN, you twat!" Beverly yelled in protest, far too calm for the moment as Claire was frozen in utter terror. The last thing she remembered was the cold sensation in her shoulder as he bit down hard, and the sound of his voice, a jagged and terrifying thing in the night, as blackness enveloped her. "Yuir fuckin' MINE, bitch!"

She spoke again. "It hurt. It hurt more than anything I ever felt before. It hurt so bad that I blacked out in the alley. I... woke up in a shitty ass hotel room up in Destin. Liam wasn't there and I was in so much pain. Everything was just... agony. I had bandages all over and I was almost too sore to cry. I looked around, and of all fucking people, Beverly was there."

"Wait, what? Please tell me... tell me you're kidding me?" Shondra said in a mix of anger and disbelief. "Oh my goodness, I... I can't... I swear If I ever meet..."

"NO!" Claire shouted, her voice low and gravelly as she did, with clear desperation in her voice. On the couch, little Clive began barking at her. "No... She's... dangerous. They're all..."

"Hush Clive! Hush your face!" Shondra snapped, a twinge of fear beginning to work its way into her heart as the story continued to unfold. Slowly and carefully, Claire told her the broad strokes. In her mind, however, the moment was crystal clear.

"Calm yuir shit down, girl. I know yuir freakin' out and ye think I'm th' last bitch ye ever wan t'see agin. But ye need t' listen t' me." Beverly said, sighing, with a put-upon demeanor that didn't match at all with the terror Claire was feeling.

"Ye know what he is, now." Beverly said, sitting on the end of Claire's hotel bed. Fearfully, Claire scooched back up and winced in pain as her shoulder protested. The senses that were only beginning to come alive were telling her that Beverly was different as well, and put her body on alert. "Don' worry. That shite will be healed up by th' mornin' like it never happened."

"That's... not possible." Claire said, weakly. "None of this is possible."

"It is f'r *us*, girl." Beverly said, her tone less threatening than it had been a moment ago. "N' yes, I said *us*. ye know what ye saw. What he IS. An' yui've seen enough fuckin' movies t'know what that means f'r YOU."

"No..." Claire whispered, meekly.

"I pulled his dumb, drunk ass offa ye, an' I calmed him down.

He lost control, like a fuckin' child. An' he'll leave ye be f'r as long as ye need to figure yuir shite out. But he won't wait forever." At that, Beverly's voice got colder again as she shook her head. "We're a *pack*, y'see. An' asshole 'r no, he's in charge. An' he tends t' get what he wants. And right now, that's you, big girl. So, welcome t' the family."

Shaking her head, Claire remembered just how much those words filled her heart with panic; panic that Beverly had just waved away as she scoffed.

"Shut it, girl. I ain't got time t' hand hold y'here. Th' van's waitin'. Th' moon is comin' next week an' we're gettin' outta town f'r a bit. This place… nobody'll give a fuck if you wreck, but I'm takin' off." Beverly said, leaning in. "For what it's worth, I'm sorry ye found out th' way ye did. It was right fucked up, and he'll be hearin' it from me, ye can be sure. I drove ye up here in yuir car, so it's sittin' in the lot. It'll need a good cleanin' as ye kinda bled all over it."

"That all said, ye need t' pay attention, because ye need t' know what t' expect." Beverly said, shaking her head.

"Yuir first change will be here with th' moon. Jus' a few days off, now. Once that's happened and you've popped yuir cherry, if ye wanna change, ye jus' do it. There's no rule tha' says ye gotta wait f'r a full moon t' change. Once ye do, you'll fuckin' love it. Th' wolf is freedom. Contentment. All this shite runnin' in yuir head makin' ye doubt everything? That goes away an' ye c'n just be yuirself. The most free, most YOU version a' you there'll ever be."

"But when the moon DOES come… ye WILL change. Tha's the one day outta each and every 28 days where we dinnae have a choice. That's when the wolf INSISTS of comin' out t' play, th' second th' sun is gone, no matter if ye can see it 'r not. From sundown t' sunup, you'll be th' wolf. Jus' like me. Jus' like HIM."

Terrified, Claire could do nothing except nod as delicately as possible as Beverly continued, going into an all too brief dissertation of the most basic rules of what Claire could expect to come. It was all told in a disconnected, blunt fashion before the callous ginger got up and unceremoniously went over to the door. "Look… Like it 'r no', he'll come back f'r ye. So make yer peace wit' what ye thought was yuir life, big girl. I'll be seein' ye."

As Beverly left, Claire wept as she could hear the van take off, leaving her alone in the room to contemplate her fate, and the threat that Liam would be coming back to eventually claim her. Fear of this had lingered in the back of her mind for the last year, in spite of Mariska's insistence that he was nothing to worry about anymore. This fear had permeated all of her interactions; a fear that, no matter what Mariska said, that she might be like him. That she might lose control. Or worse, that whatever power he had once held over her might make her want him when he did return.

It was those fears that led to Claire telling only the more sanitized version of the events, skipping any references to his transformation. Any references to werewolves.

Listening, Shondra was virtually in shock as tears flowed from her face. "Oh my god, Claire. How… how could you not tell me? I'm so sorry."

"What, do you think he'll come back? This is crazy. Did you call the cops?" She said, trying to work through all the most sensible ideas.

"No. I couldn't. I couldn't tell… anyone." Claire whispered, her back still to Shondra.

"Except Mariska?" Shondra asked, not with jealousy or scorn, but instead with a twinge of disappointment and sadness.

"She… found me at the hotel, Shondra. She… she already knew everything. She knew." Claire said, turning, but keeping her head down and her eyes closed. "A couple of days later, she showed up at the door. Beverly told her where I was and… and what Liam did. I guess… on some level… she didn't want to just leave me there, either. I think… maybe… he might have hurt her once, too."

"And Mariska… she didn't have to… but she stayed with me until I was… able to come home. I… I don't know if I would have been able to without her, Shondra." Claire's shoulders slumped. "And she's pissed at me now, too."

There was an impossibly long moment of silence in the room as Shondra considered everything Claire had just told her. With half-lidded eyes, it was clear that she had noticed the holes in the narrative as she went back to the couch and sat down. "I'm... not pissed at you Claire. I'm hurt. You should have called me. You should have told me, of all people, what had happened. I knew he had to have broken your heart, and I spent a year wondering what had happened and how I could help you, while you just kept pushing me away."

"I'm... sorry."

"I know you are, Claire. But... it's not enough for you to just be sorry. Because... Mariska, I understand. I get it now why you two are so close, I do. And if you're this close with her, she'll forgive you. Hell, I forgive you, I do. But I'm still hurt, Claire." Shondra said, closing her own eyes to try to get what she was feeling out through a cracked and broken voice, tears staining her cheeks again. "But there's still something you won't tell me. I know it. I can hear it in your voice. You aren't telling me the whole story, Claire."

A shudder went down Claire's spine. The full moon might have been a full day away, but the familiar sensation was growing stronger as she could barely contain it.

Turning around, Claire walked back to the middle of the room. Bending down, she picked up the ridiculous werewolf mask she had brought with her and looked down at it, her hair in her face enough to conceal her eyes from Shondra. "He didn't beat me or punch me. He... He... *cut* me. Deep. Mauled me. The bandages covered two-inch-deep slashes and a chunk... a chunk of me he took out of my chest. He did all of that in a few seconds... but he didn't have a knife."

Looking at the mask, then back up to Claire, Shondra looked confused as she knitted her eyebrows and her mind started making impossible connections. "Wait, what? How did he..."

As Shondra spoke, she trailed off and whispered the word she'd overheard in Russian only a few days ago.

'Volchonok… *wolf cub*."

"What?" Claire said, surprised as she kept her face away, stepping back.

"I have GOOGLE translate on my PHONE, Claire. Mariska… she calls you… *'wolf cub'* in Russian. That piece of shit's band is called *'the Slaughtered Lamb'*. You KNOW *'An American Werewolf in London"* is, like, one of my favorite films." Shondra said, standing up to look at Claire, the confusion being replaced with determination. "You have ghosted me every twenty-eight days… every full moon, like clockwork, and that's… that's tomorrow."

"That's… Halloween. Of course. Oh my goodness." Shondra's eyes were wide as saucers, "What… what are you trying to tell me, Claire? You can't be… you can't be serious."

"I… I wish I wasn't, Shondra. I wish it wasn't true. I wish I could have just figured out how to keep you as my friend and never… never say a…" Claire said, her voice now clearly at a lower, more raspy register and her back turned to Shondra.

"This… this can't be…" Shondra said, gulping as, to her surprise, she was beginning to believe what her mind was piecing together. "Turn around, please. Claire… look at me."

"I... can't. I came here to tell you the truth. But… But I can't… keep it… in." Claire said, visibly shuddering now as her emotions finally broke like a dam bursting. Whether or not she wanted it to, the change was happening. "I can't… I… Oh shit. No! Nonononono, not like this!"

"Ohmygod…" Shondra said, stumbling back into her couch in shock as she watched Claire's nails turn black and brown hair begin to grow and thicken over the backs of her hands. Through tear-stained eyes, she saw Claire's ears push back through her hair, sprouting fur as they did. She watched as the impossible unfolded in front of her.

Claire's senses were filled with Shondra's natural fear and

shock. Endorphins and the smells she knew she would perceive flooded the room as she slowly turned around. Looking up, Shondra gasped as Claire stood before her, her brown eyes locking on Claire's now much larger, almost-glowing amber eyes.

There was an agonizingly long pause as Claire stood there and struggled with what to say and Shondra tried processing the impossible, clutching her tiny little dog like a child would a stuffed animal. Swallowing, Claire brought her arm up to rub the back of her neck. The slight motion caused Shondra to flinch ever so slightly. It was clear she was still afraid, but she was also transfixed in the moment as she muttered, "C... C... Claire?"

"Uh... yeah." Claire replied, her deeper voice resonating through the small space as she looked down at her larger frame seriously stretching the clothes she was wearing. "I... am *really* glad I wore sweatpants and sandals."

As soon as she spoke, Shondra's calm cracked as she let out an ear-splitting scream. *"AAAAAAGGGHHH!!!! OHMYGOD, YOUCANTALK!?!"*

Claire instinctively pulled back, fear in her eyes that the worst case scenario had come to pass, while, in the moment of release, little Clive began barking wildly again and, in his own panic, nipped at his owner.

Letting out a shout of pain, Shondra pulled her hand away and Clive hit the ground to run at Claire. **"Ow!!! Bad Clive! NO!"**

But it was too late, as Claire panicked herself and bolted at full speed for the front door, tears in her eyes. Before Shondra could react, the front door was yanked open, pulling the hinges partially off the doorframe. Scrambling off the couch, she snatched up her tiny dog and ran after Claire. *"Fuckfuckfuck, no! NO, STOP!"*

She stopped at the door, looking out. Claire's yellow Aztek was still parked out front, but the woman herself was gone.

"Well..." Shondra muttered to herself under her breath as she gasped, letting out a nervous chuckle and clearly not terrified anymore. "That... explains... a lot."

Chapter Fifteen
⋅‍)‍)‍❂‍(‍(‍⋅

Officially, the little café called 'The Art of the Noodle' was closed. The front lights were off and the door was locked, but Mariska Baranov was still there, cleaning up for the night.

Back in the kitchen, the petite blonde vampire was scraping off the grill used to make the meat served in some of the specialty ramen dishes they were known for in town. It was clear from the energy she was putting behind her efforts that she wasn't in the best of headspaces.

Dressed in a simple black t-shirt with the company logo on the back, black skinny jeans, and a pair of bulky black leather work boots, she had a scowl on her face as she shoved the metal scraper across the surface of the grill, grumbling to herself. "You didn't do a damn thing wrong and you don't have anything to apologize for."

"She wasn't listening to you, and she was just going out of her way to be…" Mariska griped, as she pressed hard enough to bend the stainless steel handle of the scraper, which then screeched across the surface of the grill loudly. The sound echoed through the small kitchen as she winced. *"Ay, suka yobanaya!"*

Stepping back, Mariska tensed up. Looking at the scraper, she grabbed it with both hands and did her best to bend it back the way it had been. Clearly, her falling out with Claire over the weekend just wasn't going to let go of her attention. She put the mostly-repaired tool away and took a breath.

The week had gone fairly well; she had done a decent job not thinking about the fact that she and one of her only real friends in this world weren't speaking. She worked to stay distracted. Today, however, seemed like it was going to be the exception…probably thanks to the date.

It was the day before Halloween; the day before the full moon, and the day before she and Claire were going to go out and celebrate with Shondra. It was the day that Mariska knew her friend was terrified of, but the diminutive creature of the night had worked to convince Claire that a suitably-concealing costume could make such an evening possible, even though there was no way for Claire to NOT transform under a full moon. It was an audacious and admittedly over-the-top idea that Mariska had secretly hoped would prompt Claire to finally come clean.

In the past year, Mariska had barely spoken with Shondra, who had been Claire's bestie for a decade, but she was honestly excited to possibly be able to rectify this. To be able to do so without having to perpetually lie to protect Claire's secret would be a massive relief for all involved. At least, that was what Mariska had hoped. Instead, the shopping expedition ended in hurt feelings all around, ultimatums, and a week of silence.

Tonight, however, Mariska knew that the perpetually anxious young werewolf would be driving herself nuts about her impending transformation. It was generally a night that they spent together to assuage Claire's fears of losing control. She never had; not even close, but that fear was still crippling for her. The fact that Mariska was many times stronger than Claire even in full wolf form gave Claire a little comfort. It was essentially an emotional placebo, but it was one Mariska knew Claire would be needing in just shy of 24 hours.

"*Kak zhe vsyo zaebalo!*" Mariska exclaimed, again in the language she grew up speaking a full century ago. It came out the most when she was frustrated. Turning off the lights in the kitchen, she grabbed her purse and her keys and went to leave and lock up the restaurant for the night. She needed to deal with this, and if Claire wasn't going to pull the trigger to talk to her, then it was up to Mariska to be the grown-up.

Over a century old, and being the grown-up was still something she hated.

About three-quarters of a mile from the bustling nightlife of Ybor City where she worked and frequently partied, Mariska walked up to the yellow-brick, Spanish eclectic revival-style two-story house she called home. The tile roofline was tucked back behind a bank of fairly thick trees that wrapped around much of the house that she had lived in, on and off, for a couple of years now.

She had discovered the quaint house thanks to an internet search that showed that it had been built in 1931, which was the same year she had been turned. Since the deceptively young-looking woman liked synchronicity in such things, she took it as a sign to pounce on the property. Having no credit to speak of, with paperwork that was a flimsily constructed fabrication, like many vampires, she dealt mostly in cash and had collected more than enough of it over her life to avoid attention and live how she saw fit.

Stepping inside, Mariska snapped on the lights and sighed. In contrast with her fairly modern style of dress and mannerism, her home reflected a woman with a long history. The built-ins along the living room walls were filled with antiques and keepsakes from a life well-lived. In her case, it was a multitude of memorabilia from the decade where she first found herself enjoying her significantly extended life: the 1960's, and shelves filled with old vinyl records and concert posters lined the walls.

She walked past to the kitchen, dropping her purse and cell phone off on the counter nearest the door. At her feet, a gray and black cat snaked between her legs as she did, meowing aggressively. "Oh, have I neglected to fill your bowl, Tchernobog? How terrible of me."

Smirking down to the cat, she went to the pantry to grab a scoop of cat food for her little roommate. The plan was a quick shower and a change of clothes into something that didn't smell like ramen, then a trip over to check on Claire. Figuring she was on lockdown at home in anticipation of a bad night tomorrow, Mariska had begrudgingly decided to go and at least try and talk things out.

That was the plan, at least until her uniquely keen senses caught that something in her normally secure home was wrong. The smell was faint but familiar…TOO familiar, as Mariska narrowed her gaze and looked up towards the source of the aroma she knew well.

"*Nochnaja babochka…*" She whispered the none-too-pleasant Russian epithet to herself before beginning a sprint up the curved stairwell to her own bedroom. Unsure of just what her intruder's intentions were, Mariska stopped outside the door, working out the best way to enter defensively in spite of her virtual certainty of who was there. After all, while Claire did have a spare key, she wasn't the only one who knew how to get in.

From the crack under the door, she could see what looked like candlelight leaking out onto the old, wooden floor of the hall. From inside came a honey-sweet voice with a thick, Scottish accent. "Really, love. Are ye gonna keep me waitin' all night?"

Scowling, Mariska took a chance and opened the door. The room was lined with candles as the only light source, and in the center of the room, laid out across the black silk sheets of her bed, was Beverly McLeish.

Swallowing, Mariska's usually cool blood pumped just a bit warmer at the sight. Scooched up near the pillows, the ginger werewolf was fully transformed. The impressive curves of her ample rear were all but shimmering under the candlelight, which reflected off of her reddish-brown fur as she lounged there, striking as seductive a pose as she could.

But that was never the aspect of the woman that Mariska was most drawn to. For the tiny vampire, it was Beverly's eyes. They were an impossibly arresting green that glinted from across the room. It was those eyes that Mariska first fell in love with and, in spite of the woman's best efforts to appeal to her with carnal seduction, those eyes were enough.

Doing her level best to not automatically succumb to the sight, Mariska pouted slightly. "I don't remember giving you a key."

"Heh. Since when do I need a key t' go where I want t' be? An' I wanted t' be here. Wit' you, love. C'mon… I don't bite." Those amazing eyes sparkled as her mouth spread into a decidedly toothy grin. "Well… unless ye want me t'."

The lithe vampire's senses were flooded with the scent and sensation coming off of the woman transformed before her. Even her usually faint and slow heart seemed to beat harder in her ears; hard enough to drown out another sound.

Her cell phone, sitting next to her purse downstairs, began to vibrate. On the screen, the word "Volchonok" and a photo of Claire dressed in club clothes dancing with abandon popped up. It was a photo Mariska had taken on a wonderful evening a few months ago when her friend had finally cut loose and relaxed enough to dance. It was a memory Mariska cherished, but one entirely too far from her mind at the moment.

High above Claire, the moon was waxing especially gibbous in the sky. The next night it would be completely full, but tonight it was more than enough to fuel her legs as she ran at full speed through the underbrush.

Under that not-quite-full moon, her emotions felt like raw, exposed nerves that burned with each deep breath she took. The Hillsborough Wilderness Preserve wasn't too far from Shondra's apartment and she had made it there with relative ease in the night. Now she could truly cut loose.

It had been about two months since Claire had let herself open up like this, and she pushed 35 miles an hour. The drybrush and swamps of Florida were somewhat restrictive for running, and far too warm for someone covered in fur head to toe, but it still felt remarkably good at the moment, as it had for the past four and a half hours of intermittent running.

But her mind wasn't entirely focused on the run that usually felt like freedom. Instead, she felt trapped, caged in by a pain in her heart. She did not see the trees passing her in a blur, the moonlight upon the still waters on either side of the embankment, or the eyeshine of alligators watching her warily. What she saw was the wide eyes of Shondra McKay, frozen in fear as her friend had watched her transform for the first time.

As the warm Florida air felt like a freezing fire in her lungs, all she could see was the fear in Shondra's eyes. All she could hear was her friend's scream.

Claire stopped with a harsh skid, kicking up a massive cloud of sand and pine needles off of the ground. She stood now in the middle of a fairly wide clearing, while the moonlight bathed the area around her and shone off of her smooth, brown fur. She was still wearing the ratty sweatpants and old t-shirt she had worn earlier that night, but both were stretched tight, dirty and torn in multiple places. Falling to her knees, Claire's amber eyes were wet with tears. Her voice was deep, resonant, and raspy as she cried her pain out.

It was what she felt in her heart would happen, and now that it had, she couldn't see how she could ever go back. She couldn't imagine how she was supposed to go back to work or carry on with her life now that Shondra knew the truth.

Kneeling, with her clawed hands on her knees, Claire's thoughts wandered back to Mariska. The two of them were also not on speaking terms, which meant that she had nowhere to go. Spiraling into depression and anxiety, Claire couldn't think straight, and couldn't see a way out of the hole she imagined herself into.

The field she stood in, like most in the area, was riddled with ponds and water from the swamps so common to the so-called Sunshine State, and Claire looked into one as she stood back up. With her breathing beginning to slow, she gazed into that calm, clear reflection at her face. The face she had spent so long trying to become comfortable with. The face she had all but convinced herself wasn't that of a monster. But here, a monster was all she could see.

The blood didn't help. In a few small patches around the corner of her mouth were bits of blood from the deer she had relished hunting down an hour ago when hunger had become too strong and she could no longer see any reason to rein herself in.

Standing there, her ears twitched and tilted back on her head at the echo of a sound coming from the edge of the woods behind her. Turning, she instinctively went into a low crouch and opened her golden eyes wide towards the source of the sound.

The hair on her back stood on edge and she began a rumbling, low growl. Sniffing the air, the wind at her back kept any scent from carrying towards her, but the moonlight and her keen eyes showed her that she wasn't alone. As that growl grew deeper and stronger, Claire strained to see what was just inside the brush, beyond the edge of the treeline. A shape. A shadow that began to move.

Echoing across the clearing, she heard the faintest of sounds, a low and jagged-sounding voice in the night sky:

"Heh."

Eyes narrowing, Claire took off again at full speed towards the source of the sound and the shape that had been watching her. Pushing up to a forty-mile-an-hour sprint, she altered her posture to do something she rarely did, and ran quadrupedally. The hundred-and-twenty-yard gap closed quickly.

When she was twenty yards from the edge of the trees, the shape finally moved…and fast. Darting deeper into the woods, whatever it was she had seen was now running quicker than she could.

With a crash, Claire burst from the clearing into the brush, close behind the shape that had intruded on her solitude and anguish. It was becoming increasingly clear that it wasn't human, deer, or anything remotely normal.

In the darkness, as moonlight dappled through the canopy above her, the shape took a hard right, moving deeper into the woods. Behind it, Claire was laser-focused on her target. Those massive, amber eyes locked on the black shape that continued to cut in and out of the trees, which were becoming more densely packed together the deeper they went.

"UUUNGH!" Claire grunted as she got close enough to

shoulder-check one of the tall, thin pine trees. With a loud snap, the trunk nearly buckled from the impact. The force also pushed her further in the other direction and she hit another tree on the other side.

It was slowing her down, and the shape, more skilled at avoiding them, pulled ahead. With lungs threatening to burst, Claire changed tactics and cut a harder right turn to where the brush was thinner.

She was now parallel with the shape, and beginning to match its pace better through the lighter trees. Gradually, she weaved closer and closer, until the shape did the unexpected.

With a sharp turn and a burst of speed, it cut hard in a path directly towards her. A second later, she watched as, from the shadows, the black shape's eyes snapped open, an icy blue that Claire instantly recognized. With a throaty roar, the shape exploded into her with a powerful tackle that threw both of them out of the thick of the woods and into another clearing.

Rolling, Claire's rage was at full expression as she tried to dig her claws deep into the black fur of the creature on top of her. But as he twisted, grabbing her powerful wrists, he slammed her hard on her back onto the ground of the clearing, which was a narrow hiking trail that wound through the park, blissfully deserted at this hour.

Panting hard, Claire struggled against the iron grip that held her to the ground. She could feel the heat coming off of the form atop her as she looked up into the cold, azure eyes she had only ever seen once before. Rimmed in a galaxy of the darkest black fur, they were the eyes of her maker. With a voice that sounded like leather on asphalt, he spoke. "Miss me, beautiful?"

Claire's eyes narrowed as she growled back, venom on her tongue. "Liam."

Chapter Sixteen

⊰ ⟩ ◉ ⟨ ⊱

"GET THE FUCK OFF OF ME!!!" Claire roared into the night as she rolled back enough to plant her clawed feet into the stomach of the creature atop her, and kicked hard.

It forced him off of her, breaking his tight grip on her wrists. Tumbling into the dirt of the hiking trail behind them, he quickly leapt back up to his feet. Standing up to his full height, the moonlight glistened off of his jet black fur as his ice-blue eyes cut into Claire.

He was back. He had found her. Liam Docherty. Claire's ex-boyfriend, and the one who had turned her into a werewolf.

Getting back to her own feet, she scrambled backward a few steps, putting more distance between herself and the creature that had been stalking her that night. Her brown fur and tattered clothes were covered in dust and bramble from the woods of the nature preserve.

Casually, he brushed his shoulder-length black hair out of his face with that same half-smirk that once made her feel special and complete at his side. Now, it made her stomach churn.

Since the night he had first changed in front of her a year ago, she had not seen or heard a hint about him. On that night, she had only glimpsed the man she once loved in this form. Here, awash in the light of the nearly-full moon, she could take him in for the first time.

Lean, but tightly muscled, she watched his chest heave in the darkness. His narrow face was now more diamond-shaped while transformed, and his eyes were like pools of radiant ice. She stared at them, transfixed for a moment. Through the rage burning in her chest, as she looked at him, she felt something else. A feeling she hadn't had for the man since the night he brutally attacked her: passion.

The feeling was entirely uninvited. Still, his voice, like hers, was deeper and more resonant in this form. Harsh and sharp, it felt like good whisky going down, and she felt herself go warm at the sound. "Look at'ya! If I knew you'd be this magnificent... I never would'a waited this long ta' come back to ye."

"FUCK YOU!" Claire growled back at him, taking another step back as the sound of that Scottish lilt she reluctantly missed filled her senses again. "This is all your fault! You tried to fucking *kill* me! You turned me into *this!!!"*

"I didn't try t' *kill* ye, beautiful. I tried t' FREE ye. And look at ye! Standing out here, running like the wind. Huntin'. *Feedin'.* You know there ain't nothin' freer than this, don'cha?" Liam said, looking at the spot of dried blood on her cheek.

Gulping, Claire's eyes went wide. Wiping her face defensively with the back of her hand as she stood there, anxious and unsteady, she didn't know what to do. So, she did one of the only things left that her rational mind could think of. Turning quickly, she began to run again.

Her adrenaline took her as fast as it could down the trail as Liam stood and watched. Tilting his head, he grinned again. "Well... this is fun."

Following the path, it veered to the right, and Claire kept pushing. Having run for hours that night, however, had left her drained, and panic would only carry her so far as her pace began to slow. Before she could make it much further, and without warning, the woods to her right exploded again in a rush of black that knocked her off of her feet and sent her rolling to the ground.

"If yer gonna' make me chase ye all night, I cannae say I mind. It's good sport and I could use a bit'a fun." Liam said, standing over her as she tried to catch her breath in the darkness. "But I didn't come here t' fight, beautiful."

"S...STOP CALLING ME THAT!!!" Claire screamed at what he used to call her before that night. "You DON'T get to say that to me anymore!!"

As Claire scooted back across the path and slammed herself into one of the trees lining the woods, Liam crouched down to meet her eyes better. His voice was a bit smoother and calming.

"What else could I call ye that would do ye justice?"

Digging her claws into the warm earth beside the tree, panic gripped Claire's heart as confusion pushed in around the edges of her mind. She panted deeply, her lungs burning cold in the night air, and she felt light-headed as his scent permeated her senses. It was as if her entire world was him, in that moment, as he spoke.

"I know yuir angry wit' me, beautiful. I do, n' it's not like I don' know why," Liam said, raising a brow as he nodded. "I fucked up. I know I fucked up hard an' I hurt ya' bad. I hurt ya' so bad I couldn't stand to see ya' afterwards."

Knitting her brows, Claire scowled again. Anger was helping her clear her mind enough to reply. "What happened to, '*You're MINE, bitch!*'? Here you are, coming back to, what, reclaim your property like Beverly said you would, and I'm supposed to feel *bad* for you?"

"Look…" Liam said, standing up and stepping back so as to let Claire up and off the ground. "I was wasted. Piss drunk, that night. I got drunk an' I got horny an' I did… everything wrong. I know that an' I'm not trying to make excuses f'r it."

"Sure as shit sounds like you are. What do you fucking *WANT*, Liam?!" Claire said, standing back up and staring across at him with daggers in her eyes.

"I jus' want a chance t' talk t' ya." He said, holding his massive, black-furred hands up in an 'I surrender' posture. "I went t' yer apartment, but ye weren't there. So… I let th' nose do the work and tracked you out here. Thought… maybe this was perfect, y'know? Out here we c'n both be who we really are and speak our minds without the chains of that other shite holdin' us down."

"You sniffed me out from my apartment to HERE? Across half the city?" Claire said, her voice dripping with incredulity.

"A'course. I could find yuir scent a planet away. There ain't no scent that I know as well." Liam said, matter-of-factly. "I know this is gonna come out all wrong, but… like it 'r not, I DID make ye. That smell you have now… it's a part a' my own. It's a blood link, Claire."

It was the first time that night he spoke her name, and Claire found herself taken aback by it.

"A soul link, Claire…" he said again, taking advantage of her obvious reaction to double down on the moment, "I'm sorry. I fucked up royally, I did. I know it, and it's most all I've thought about this whole year. I… I was plannin' on tellin' ye that weekend at the resort. Ye planned such a perfect weekend, an' I knew I couldn't hide from ye through another moon, so I figured that I would have to tell ye the truth somehow."

"And I panicked. I was so…" Scowling slightly, he curled his lips back for a moment as he spat out the words, "I was afraid. I was so afraid that ye run in terror that I let myself get wasted. So drunk tha' I let myself do what I did with Beverly. So drunk tha' when you saw... and threatened to leave me… tha' the wolf jus'... came out. It came out all wrong."

Shaking her head, Claire muttered under her breath, "No. nononono. You don't get to do this. You don't get to make this about you."

"It's not an excuse, Claire. But it IS a reason. N' I figure… you deserve t' know." Liam said, a look of contrition on his face as Claire struggled to see past the scent still filling her being. "I know yuir better than that. But… I wasn't as strong as ye are, Claire. I was weak and drunk and angry and hurt and I lashed out at th' one person who always gave me a chance."

"C'n ye honestly tell me ye got NO idea wha' that feels like?" he finished, his words cutting into Claire as she thought about her unplanned transformation in front of Shondra earlier that evening. She remembered the look of fear in her best friend's eyes and the horror in her own heart as it all happened. The panic and fear that she had just destroyed something so important to her.

With her mind a flood of thoughts all fighting against each other, Claire stepped back against the tree again and slid to the ground. As she did, tears began to wet the fur of her cheeks. "There… you've talked to me. Happy?"

"I'd be happier if ye talked back t' me." Liam said,

condescension on the edges of his voice. Claire tried to lean into her anger; keep herself from feeling anything for the man but the rage she wanted to feel, in spite of what was beginning to feel like a betrayal from her own body and soul.

"*WHAT* do you want me to *SAY*, Liam? You *USED* me… you *LIED* to me… and when I caught you fucking cheating on me with Beverly… you almost *KILLED* me! What were you expecting tonight? That I was going to give you a big fucking HUG? Are you out of your mind?!" Claire snapped back, exhausted and trembling, but still angry enough to speak her mind. For his part, Liam simply sighed as he collected his thoughts.

"What was I supposed t' do, cut in on 'r first date and say, 'by th' way, ye should probably know I'm a werewolf. It's actually no' all tha' bad, an' kinda awesome sometimes, but I don' want ye t' freak out. Cool?'?" Liam said, leaning into the words to emphasize how ridiculous it sounded. "Did YOU tell yuir friends, once ye knew? Or did ye do everything ye could t' keep it as secret as ye could, hoping you'd find a way t' say it without them hatin' ye, and never quite findin' tha' way?"

The words cut deep as Claire again thought of the look of fear on Shondra's face that she could *smell*. In spite of her anger, she despised that his points were starting to make sense to her. In order to stay angry, she tried to double down.

There was, however, a weakness in her voice that Liam could pick up on as clearly as if it were a neon sign about Claire's head. "So, what? You think you can follow me around and, what, try and talk me into forgiving you? Forgetting what you did? You didn't just attack me, Liam. You fucking ABANDONED me afterward! Do you have any idea what that was like!?!"

Without missing a beat, Liam nodded. His face was serious and Claire's senses were still on overload, threatening to overwhelm her reason. "I… no. No' th' same way, I won' lie t' ye. I was born this way… bu'… it's no' always easy growin' up a wolf, either. I do know a wee bit about bein' abandoned, an' I know how it hurts t' jus' feel discarded. My mum discarded me. Pawned me off on my da' an'... well... I shoulda' been better wi' you." Liam said, shrugging. "I know I shoulda helped, an' in spite a' everything, I'm glad Beverly stepped in to help as much as she did. I won' lie t' ye, Claire. I was a coward."

"I knew ye were furious wit me. I knew anythin' I said woulda just made things worse. I was a coward, and I regret that more than anythin' else." Liam said, an admission Claire was fighting against believing as she felt her resolve weakening. Something didn't feel right and she couldn't think straight enough to work it through.

"And... w... w... what about Beverly telling me you were going to come back to CLAIM me? That I'm your *p... property?!* Is that what you think this fucking is? That I'm going to come running back to you thanks to some apology that's FAR too little and WAY too late?" Claire snapped back, her voice warbling as she did. The conviction behind her protestations was wavering.

"Look, Beverly is... she's a jealous, needy thing. She may be all over the place, and have a sweet heart sometimes, but she can be a bitch when she wants something." Liam said, shaking his head. "She was angry, too. Tha's why she came onto me so hard tha' night when she knew I was waverin' and scared. She wanted t' try and put th' lock on me n' push ye away. But I've had a year t' talk t' her an' tell her how things need t' be."

The words were spoken calmly and pleasantly, in spite of the natural gravel in his transformed voice. Nevertheless, the specific words made that pit in Claire's stomach tighten like a noose. "Need? Wh... what... what does that mean, Liam?"

"It means... ye need t' come home, Claire." Liam nodded, a matter-of-fact tone in his voice. He stood up to his full height again and Claire found herself momentarily transfixed by the sight of the moonlight dancing across his black fur.

The striking sight sent another shot of warmth through her body that terrified her as he continued. "You've had a year. C'n ye honesty tell me that ye jus went back t' yuir life like everythin' was fine? Can ye look me in the eyes and say life is great an' ye don' think about runnin' t' freedom most a' every day?"

"I know how strong th' call is, beautiful. We still have our lives amongst th' rest a' them. Th' regulars. Th' humans. But we'll never fit in tha' world. YOU'LL never fit in there. N' I think ye know that now." He said, his tone more declarative than it had been as he shifted back to her old nickname. "I think ye KNOW where ye really belong."

"N… no. You're… you're wrong. I don't belong with… with…" Claire said, terrified that a part of her wanted to believe what Liam was saying. That a part of her wanted to listen.

"With yuir own kind? With me?" Liam said, nodding again. "The full moon ain't until t'morrow, beautiful. I wen't lookin' f'r ye at yuir apartment, but I found ye here. Runnin'. Ragin' and cryin' against somethin'. Wha' happened?"

"None of your F… FUCKING business!" Claire roared back, angry, as the pain pushed its way out in spite of her best attempts at concealing it. Tears started running down her face.

"Someone hurt ye, didn't they? Or worse… ye hurt THEM." Liam said, piecing it together as he tilted his head to look down at Claire again. "Told 'em, didn't ye? Some a' the regulars? Tol' the truth an' it blew up in yuir face, didn't it?"

There was the flavor of compassion in his voice as Claire's body language betrayed her pain. Sitting against that tree, she curled up into a ball, wrapping her powerful fur-covered arms around her legs, her tail tucking in tight. Thick, heavy sobs burst out of her as she released it all. In spite of everything she had wanted, she had lost control again, and was crying in front of him.

A moment later, she felt a sensation like a bolt of electricity down her spine as he knelt down to her and put one of his own, massive hands on her left shoulder. She jerked up slightly, her eyes wide as she felt a stew of conflict threatening to boil over in her shattered heart.

"I know…" he said, a gentleness she remembered in his words.

"I felt all a' this an' more when I hurt ye. An' I cannae take it back. But I can try an' make it right. An'… I c'n try show ye that yuir not alone anymore."

138

Putting a hand on the side of her face, Claire shut her eyes tight and curled up further. Effortlessly, he pushed her cheek up and towards his own face. His voice was still rough and resonant, but it seemed to become softer and more delicate now. "We need each other, beautiful. We're all we've got, now. If ye let me... I c'n show ye all of it. I c'n show ye a home. A family."

In that moment, the pain of the now overwhelmed the pain of the past as Claire thought of everything that she had allowed to crumble. Her friendship with Shondra and Mariska. She thought of her sister's words on the phone and the distances she had allowed to grow unchecked between herself and those she loved. And she thought about his warm, soft hand that felt good on her cheek.

She thought about what he did, but framed against her own slips and mistakes, she found herself listening to his words, which felt like a light in the center of the darkness. It was the only light leading her to somewhere that promised safety from that kind of pain. Slowly, she opened her eyes and looked up.

In the warm night air, she could feel his hot breath against her face, he was so close. Her bright, amber eyes locked onto his brilliant, blue ones. Her muscles tightened as she felt herself growing hot and tingly in ways she had been so afraid to let herself feel over the last year.

Intimacy was dangerous; but, with others, she had to restrain her feelings, keep them under tight control for fear of letting the wolf out in a moment of unrestrained passion. Here, under the moonlight, the wolf was out, and that fear was replaced by a longing she hated. In spite of herself, she wanted to give in to those feelings. Feelings that didn't even seem possible.

Biting her bottom lip, Claire tried to pull away again. Tried to think straight and remember what he had done to her. At that moment, however, she couldn't. Her mind felt like it was in a fog and she couldn't block him out of her senses. His scent subsumed her. His voice surrounded her. His eyes devoured her.

Leaning in, Liam closed the already tight gap between the two for a kiss. She could feel his heat as her own wet lips met his and the sensation made every hair on her body stand on end. Squeezing her own legs in even tighter, she felt her claws digging into herself as her entire form shuddered with a wave of sensation that broke over her, threatening to drown her.

Then in her mind, came a flash of memory. Shondra and Mariska, smiling. Beverly sitting on the edge of her hotel bed, staring down at her judgmentally. Liam's own face, still human, with controlling hatred in his eyes as she watched him change for the first time to attack her.

"NO!!!!" She yelled, pushing him hard off of her, clear across the running path to the brush on the other side, where he rolled with a thud. Kicking up dust, his scent still filled her mind, but there was another smell now. A familiar and frightening one. Blood.

Looking down, her black claws were tipped with a bit of Liam's blood. She had scratched him deep when she'd shoved him. Across the way, he picked himself up, ran his black-furred hands across the gashes down his chest, and looked at his own blood. His face, soft and caring a moment ago, shifted into the face she remembered from that fateful day, as those ice blue eyes went cold again.

Pushing back against the tree, Claire's fur rose across her back and her ears flattened. The growl returned to her voice as the anger of her memories helped her mind clear. She still felt that passion inside of her. She still felt the wolf's lust wanting to find expression right then and there. But her mind was her own for at least this moment and she was fighting to hold onto it.

She had no words as she bore her teeth, pushing so hard against the tree at her back that it cracked. Looking back across at her, Liam took a long breath and shook his head. "Okay. I know ye need yuir space, beautiful. The sun'll be up in a couple'a hours. Th' van's not far from here, an' I c'n take ye home if tha's wha ye want."

Raising the tip of a finger, he tapped it to the side of his nose. "If ye want t' find me, ye know how. I'll wait f'r ye. Take yuir time n' think about it."

Holding his hands out, palms up, Liam nodded. His voice was calm but determined as he spoke for the last time. "We belong together, beautiful. We always have. I could see how magnificent ye could be from th' first time I laid eyes on ye. And no one will ever see tha' the way I do. We both know it, an' once you accept it, I'll be there f'r ye."

Calmly and slowly, he stepped back into the darkness of the trees and left her alone in the woods. Frozen in place, Claire waited until the only hint of him she could sense came from the blood on her hands.

Chapter Seventeen
⟨ ☽ ☉ ☾ ⟩

It had been a year since Mariska had seen Beverly McLeish, and at that moment, the diminutive vampire realized just how much she had missed her lover.

As Mariska softly stepped across the room to her own bed, the ginger werewolf reached over to place a single claw on the center of the pale woman's chest. Reaching down the front of Mariska's shirt, Beverly pulled her over to the bed with a rumbling growl.

She grinned, licking her lips as Mariska crawled onto the edge of the bed. "Ach, ye smell… amazing. Like ye always do, love."

For her part, Mariska had no words as she ran her fingers through the fur across Beverly's cheeks and pulled her in for a long, slow kiss. Pushing her back against the bed, the smaller but far stronger woman climbed on top.

"Still as stunning as I remember," Mariska whispered as she pulled back slightly, looking longingly into Bev's face.

"Ye missed all this?" Bev smirked up at Mariska seductively.

"All of this, yes." Mariska said, running her finger across Bev's cheek, framing the woman's emerald green eyes and looking deeply into them. The look of seduction melted slightly as Bev bit her bottom lip and chuckled.

"Silver-tongued devil, ye are. An' here I am… just waitin' t' be licked." Beverly arched her back, her pulse quickening and her blood pumping so hotly that it overwhelmed the already-enflamed passions of the blonde vampire.

As she smiled, Mariska's fangs extended, which made those crystal green eyes of Beverly's flash wild for an instant as she slid her claw down the front of Mariska's shirt, slicing it open. "Aye… there she is. There's m' sexy beast."

The candles had long ago burnt themselves down to nothing. Mariska opened her eyes. Contrary to popular opinion, she didn't burst into flames upon contact with sunlight. UV film on her windows and some stylish, burgundy black-out curtains did the job just fine.

Rubbing a hand to the side of her bed, it was empty but still warm from where Beverly had been. Looking up at her bedroom ceiling, the lithe vampire had a wide smile on her face as her memory filled with the events of the evening.

The year-long absence had been keenly felt as soon as the two reconnected, leading to a night of unbridled passion that made her otherwise cool blood feel warm again. Letting out the slightest of moans as she lay there naked, Mariska allowed her mind to drift back over the evening.

Her pent-up needs had boiled over when she saw Beverly waiting for her. Transformed, the ginger werewolf's confidence was intoxicating to Mariska. The Scottish drummer with the prodigious posterior was more than attractive in her normal form, but when she was fully transformed, it made her irresistible to Mariska.

Clearly, she had a type.

The specifics of the evening were now a lovely stew of memories, warming her as she could feel her fingers exploring the savage woman's enhanced form. The taste of her was a magnificent contradiction, like a garden of heather and a kick of whisky combined. It was a flavor that still lingered on Mariska's lips.

Sitting up, she reached out with the senses that gave her a unique view of the world. Strong and distinct, she picked up energy and the pulsing of life more than the individual scents and sensations of the world the way that Beverly or even Claire experienced things. She could feel the presence of her lover in the shower.

Stepping across the cool, hardwood floors of her home, she pushed open the old door and felt a rush of steam coming from the space, all of it carrying the essence of the woman inside. Through the sheer, frosted curtain, Mariska saw the now-fully-human Beverly rinsing off in a pose seductive enough to tell the tiny voyeur that those hyper-sensitive wolf senses had alerted her to her presence.

This suspicion was verified a moment later as the woman's Scottish lilt moaned out, "Mmmm, I was wonderin' if ye were gonna sleep all day 'r 'no. Though, after las' night, it was sorely temptin', I'd say."

Bending down, Beverly aimed a view of her bottom towards Mariska as she turned off the shower. Her ways had a habit of hitting Mariska right between the eyes every time. Smiling, the little blonde vampire grabbed a towel from the cabinet to the side of the door and held it up for Beverly to take. In spite of the knowledge that Mariska's passions were drawn to far more than the woman's physical attributes, Beverly flaunted them out of habit.

Pulling open the curtains with a mischievous grin, she did just that and began to towel off as slowly as she could. "Mmm, thank ye. Y'know, you could always help out here n' I've never objected t' yuir touch. Could make th' mornin' even more interestin'."

"After last night... I think I need some breakfast, first." Mariska said, nodding. "Sooo, did you clean up already, or is there a big pile of ginger hair behind a door somewhere waiting for me?"

Chuckling, Beverly stepped out of the shower and stood on the fuzzy throw rug as she dried off her short, curly red locks. "Nah. I made a right mess, but it ain't yuir mess, love. Jus' 'fore dawn, I listened 'round and there wasn't anyone around. So... it all went in tha' little river behind yuir backyard. No fuss, no muss. This ain't me first rodeo, after all."

The mischievous smile became wryer as she raised a brow to continue. "What, are ye used t' cleanin' up tha' kinda mess these days? You an' th' big girl?"

"Claire and I? No. We're not... like that." Mariska replied, slightly embarrassed, as she took a moment to pull her long, platinum blonde hair into a ponytail before turning back to Beverly.

Draping the towel around herself, Beverly sashayed past into the bedroom to start getting dressed. "Now… after last night, ye must be right famished, love. What say we head down t' tha' big ol'kitchen of yuirs. I crack up a couple'a eggs f'r me and a bottle a' something chilled an' red f'r you, an' we catch up a little?"

Downstairs, both women were refreshed and dressed again as Beverly worked her way around the familiar kitchen. Mariska's cat wove himself in between her legs. "Now, I know yuir a hell of a cook, but I interrupted yuir night… in as pleasant a way as possible… so ye can let me make up f'r it by serving ye, this mornin', aye?"

"Just don't leave me any dishes, and we have a deal." Mariska said, looking around for a moment as she sat at the kitchen counter. "Damn, where's my phone? What time IS it, anyway?"

"I reckon it's crazy early f'r YOU, love. It's about… nine-thirty, give 'r take." Beverly said, looking into the refrigerator, which was surprisingly well-stocked for belonging to a vampire who couldn't eat regular food. There was also a significant supply of small metal containers that looked kind of like flat soda cans.

On each was a small white square with what looked like dry erase marker notes denoting the source of the contents. C, S, L, P, and D… short for Cow, Sheep, Lamb, Pig, and Deer. Beverly surveyed her options. "What'r ye craving' this mornin', love?"

"Aside from another round?" Mariska replied playfully. "Just grab me one of the 'P' cans, please."

"Weeeelllll… that ship hasn't exactly *sailed*, but it'll have t' wait until I've fed th' beast." Beverly replied with a smirk, looking around at some of the posters on the walls of the adjacent room.

One in particular caught the woman's eye, and she smiled. "Holy shite. Is tha' from? Ay, it'tis. Ye got a poster from th' *'Glasgow Calling'* festival from way back then?"

"Do I have a poster from the music festival where I went and met a certain redheaded drummer with a truly wicked sense of humor who got so drunk between gigs that she fell asleep in my tent?" Mariska said with a wry half-grin. "I might, yes."

"And here I thought ye didnae care." As she continued to look at the kitchen, the ginger werewolf sniffed lightly. The food had a scent that was distinctly not Mariska's.

"Yuir friend, the big girl. She come here often?" Beverly asked, a hint of something unusual in her voice that gave Mariska a moment of pause.

Raising a brow, Mariska finally realized what she was getting at. "We're not a couple, if that's what you mean, Beverly. She's my friend. She's a GOOD friend, but that's it."

"Ye don' seem so sure a' that, love?" came the somewhat flat reply as Beverly leaned over the counter.

"Don't be jealous, I…" Something was off about her part-time lover that wasn't exactly jealousy. Or not *just* jealousy. "What's going on, Beverly? This is the second time you've brought up Claire. And what are you doing back in Tampa?"

"As I recall, ye did'na mind m' answer last night all tha' much. In fact, from the smell ye made twixt those adorable little legs when ye saw me, ye were happy as punch t' forget about such things, weren't ye?" her grin was betrayed by the cues Mariska could feel.

Standing there, prepping breakfast, grabbing a metal mixing bowl for the eggs, Beverly's posture and body language were still seductive, but Mariska could see much more. Her heart rate was too fast. Her blood was running too hot and her stomach was churning a bit. Outer appearances aside, she was suddenly very nervous.

Too nervous.

"We're here f'r some gigs. Th' band is playin' a few clubs here. One in Saint Pete, another in Orlando. Probably in town another… a few weeks at least, is all." Beverly said, fidgeting with the spatulas off of the hanging rack above the island. The tension was mounting.

146

"The BAND... *bud' ya proklyat*..." Mariska muttered to herself in Russian, a minor curse of shock. "You're telling me LIAM is in town, too?"

"It's HIS band, Risky. A'course he's here. We came in a couple a' nights ago an' were jus' gettin' settled." Beverly said, trying to act as nonchalant as possible, evoking a little pet name she had for the lean vampire. "I was bored an' I missed ye, so... I came over. Ye always said I could make m'self at home when I was here, didn't ye?"

"C'mon, love. That's it. I jus' wanted t' see ye again. We stayed away so tha' she..." Beverly said, speaking partial truths. The pause was enough for the vampire to pounce.

"What? This is about Claire? He's back for *Claire?*" Mariska said, getting up from the stool to look Beverly in the eyes.

"He's here for her, yeah! So what, he *made* her... we all gave her time t' git her shit together an' he wanted some alone time. But we're a *pack*, and like it 'r not, she's a part'a that pack now. She has been this whole year, even if she didn't wan'ta deal with it." Beverly said, anger in her voice as she snapped back. "But none a'that meant I didn't want t' be with ye, Risky. I'm no' lyin' t' ye. I missed ye. I've missed ye f'r months."

It was true, and as Mariska gripped the edge of the black, marble counter, her senses confirmed that. In truth, Mariska had missed the sensual redhead as well, but that was beside the point as she squeezed hard enough to crack the surface, clearly upset.

"This was, what, a... a *yebucheye* DISTRACTION!?!" Mariska shouted, anger and hurt feelings clear behind her big, black eyes as the accent that almost never came out began to leak into her words. "That... *HUY MORZHOVIY* sent you here to keep me busy and you DID it, Bev?! I... I..."

"Love..." Beverly said, taking a step forward to put a hand out towards Mariska. The tiny woman's black eyes went red with anger.

"NYET! I can't believe you would... how..." Mariska was furious as she looked around, trying to remember where she'd tossed her phone. Closing her eyes for a moment, she tried to calm down. "Where is he?"

"Wherever SHE is, I'd guess. Beyond that, I dinnae know. I swear t' you." Beverly said, nervously stepping back, no fear in her voice, but radiating a wave of shame.

"It doesn't matter, does it? Whatever you feel for me will always take a back seat to your little master's wishes, won't it?" Mariska hissed, venom on her tongue as Beverly's lips trembled.

"Y… ye don' understand. I *cannae…*" Beverly protested meekly.

"He might as well put a *leash* on you. I can't believe you would do this. Use me like this." Mariska said, the rage in her voice now replaced with genuine pain at the betrayal. "Just… get out."

There was a pregnant pause between the two that was only broken when the woman barely licking five feet in height slammed her hand down onto the marble countertop hard enough to send a long crack down the entire length of it. The sound echoed like a thunderclap as tears welled up in the ginger werewolf's eyes.

Nodding, Beverly stepped back, and without a word, ran out to the front door, slamming it as she left. In the kitchen, Mariska was shaking with a cyclone of emotions ranging from raw anger to blinding pain and rejection.

No longer caring about their petty misunderstanding, she realized she had to find her friend. Stomping over to the closet, she grabbed the clothes she kept handy for daytime travel. Slipping on her black hoodie, she picked up a pair of thin, black gloves and looked around for her sunglasses when she finally saw her phone.

Her heart froze as she looked at the screen. "Oh, no. No. Sixteen missed calls?"

Scrolling through them, they were all from Claire, as were the messages that had clearly maxed out her voicemail. She was particularly frustrated now, and it was all she could do to not crush the phone as she entered the codes and waited through the lengthy computerized woman's voice telling her every detail about the calls.

'You have reached the voice mailbox of... Mariska Baranov."

"I fucking KNOW who I am!" Mariska muttered through gritted teeth that were becoming decidedly pointy.

"You have... nine unheard messages. Three saved messages. Would you like to..."

"Yes!!! Now!" Mariska shouted, pressing ONE multiple times.

"You have pressed an incorrect key. If you would like to hear your messages, press STAR."

With a more measured push, the phone chimed in response.

"First message... sent... yesterday... at twelve... forty-seven... am..."

"Play the *yebucheye* message, you *zalupa konSKAya*!" Mariska shouted, slipping back and forth into Russian through an ever-thickening accent.

"Message from... phone number... eight... one... three... eight... six... seven..."

"RRRR!!!! ***Shtob tebe deti v sup srali!!!*"** She screamed over the voice, clenching her free hand tightly.

"Duration, one minute and thirteen seconds."

"Zhopu porvu margala vikolyu!!! Okay... okay... calm down. Calm down..." Biting her tongue, Mariska took another breath, relaxing just enough to listen to the first message. Surprisingly, the voice coming over the phone wasn't Claire's.

"Uh... Mariska? Hi... uh... This is... um... Shondra. Uh... Something's wrong. Like... really, really wrong...."

Chapter Eighteen
⋅)⊃◉((⋅

It had been an exceedingly long night for Shondra McKay.

When Claire had shown up the previous evening unannounced, she hadn't been sure what was going on. As the two hadn't been speaking all week due to the Halloween blow-up, Shondra was not expecting what had unfolded. Of course, there was no reasonable way anyone could have predicted that her best friend for the better part of a decade would end the conversation by revealing herself to be a werewolf.

In a thousand years, no rational person would have looked at the clues over the last year and thought "werewolf", but as the rotund young woman had spent long hours thinking about it, now, it all made a strange kind of sense.

For the past year, Claire had been strangely distant, since the break-up between her and Liam Docherty. Every 28 days like clockwork, she vanished for at least a day, which Shondra had simply been assuming was her 'time of the month'. Now, she knew that it WAS a very specific time of the month…just not quite what she had expected.

There were other factors; Claire's ratty hair after every full moon. Her reluctance to say ANYTHING about the breakup. Her new tight-lipped friend, Mariska. Claire freaking out over the werewolf mask in the Halloween store made a LOT more sense now.

All of this was running like crazy through Shondra's head as she drove across Saturday morning traffic to Claire's place.

The night had been long and stressful after Claire's impossible transformation when she stormed out of Shondra's apartment and ran off into the night, but it had given the frightened and confused young woman ample time to think.

Shondra had spent the first hour sitting at her desk chair, looking at her damaged front door, wondering if Claire would come back, and what she would look like if she did. Of course, she had been frightened, because who wouldn't be under the circumstances?

But…she was still her friend, albeit covered head to toe in brown fur, with massive claws and golden eyes, and instead of raging or roaring at her, Claire had glanced down and made a joke about being glad she wore SWEATPANTS.

Despite freaking out after hearing the resonating voice coming out of this crazy new form, her mind kept going back to that silly joke. Whatever else, that silly joke was one hundred percent Claire Gribbald. She was still the woman Shondra had known for a decade.

Calming herself down, Shondra had looked around her apartment and noticed that Claire had run off in such a panic that she'd left her car keys and phone with the pizza on the coffee table of Shondra's living room. She realized the phone contained Mariska's number.

From what Claire had told her, Mariska knew everything, and if that was the case, then maybe she could help. However, the enigmatic, pale woman who was never up during the day wasn't answering.

"Okay, you don't have to think about that, Shondra." She said to herself in the otherwise empty car as she pulled off the interstate at her exit. "Nope. Your best friend is a werewolf, and her other friend works super late at night, has black eyes, never eats anything, dresses in head-to-toe black, is crazy pale, and hates the daytime. That does not mean ANYTHING at all and you are being crazy thinking otherwise. Yes. Just go… check on Claire and see if she came home, and… don't think about the ton of panicky voicemails you left for the woman who is absolutely and definitely NOT A VAMPIRE."

"Because that is a thing that does not exist. At all. Not even a little bit, Shondra." She repeated, talking faster as she did, clearly riding an anxiety high that was exacerbated by her having sat awake all night and through the morning waiting for some word from Mariska or Claire.

Pulling into the parking lot of the apartment complex, Shondra found herself hoping to find Claire's car in the lot, as if the entire night had simply been some kind of impossibly vivid fever-dream. Parking her own little Nissan Cube, she sat there, staring at the building. As she did, her mind wandered back to the first of the phone calls she had made to Mariska hours ago.

"Uh… Mariska? Hi… uh… This is… um… Shondra. Uh… Something's wrong. Like… really, really wrong. Look, I… I… I know we don't really know each other much, but you're her friend too, and something… uh… happened. Something that… uh… I think you know about, from what she told me? And then… kinda… SHOWED me. But it… I freaked out and my dog freaked out and then I think me freaking out made her freak out, and she… she's gone. She ran away and she's gone and… You know what I'm talking about, right? She said that you helped her when she kinda vanished before. When it… that thing I'm talking around but trying to be all super vague because I don't know if I'm crazy and you're gonna hear this and think I'm crazy, so I'm not saying any specific words, because I don't know if that's anything you're not supposed to leave voicemails about?? I don't know. I don't know, but I think she's… I think this is bad and I need help. I need to find her. Please call me back, I have her phone. Well, I have her car, too, but… please call me."

It was one of many long, rambling, and virtually incoherent messages Shondra had left for the woman after putting a significant amount of thought into whether she should call her or just hide and pretend nothing had happened. But the broken front door of her apartment, along with everything she had seen and heard, and the messages she had left, told her she couldn't do that.

Taking her keys out of the ignition, she put them at the bottom of her purse and pulled out Claire's keys. Claire's phone was plugged into the console of her car, as she had killed the battery and needed to recharge it, and since Claire HAD to get an iPhone, it meant that it couldn't just use a regular charger.

"Okay… you're overthinking everything, Shondra. Well, of course, you are. That's what you do, you overthink things and get so worked up that you forget to do things like check her car for a phone charger or just buy one at a CVS on the way over, because you're thinking so much you aren't really thinking." Shondra said, continuing to talk to herself as she worked up the nerve to get out of the car.

Finally, she opened the door and stepped out. Grabbing her purse and Claire's keys, she left the phone in the car to charge and started walking to the apartment across the lot. Once she was out of earshot, of course, the phone began to ring. The name on the display read 'Mariska Baranov'.

At the bottom landing of the two-story building, Shondra looked up and swallowed as she paused to take a breath. "You are being crazy. You're just checking to see if she came home and if she's okay. That's all. Nothing to be worried about. She was different, but she was talking like it was just a thing that she does. She's still Claire. You can…"

Before she could finish her little pep-talk, however, the door to the downstairs apartment opened up, "Oh, hello. You're Miss Gribbald's friend, right? Sharone?"

"Geeeee… ugh… heh…" Shondra squealed in shock as the building's landlord stepped out, adjusting his glasses. The elderly Cuban man was feeble-looking but clearly curious as she continued. "Uh… heh. Hi, yeah. No. Yeah. Yes, Mister Álvarez. It's Shondra. But, yeah. I'm Claire's friend, yeah. Yes."

There was a slightly awkward pause as Shondra grinned a bit too broadly. "Uh… how are you and your wife?"

"Meh. I'm not dead, that's a perk, right? Here to see Claire?" He asked, shrugging.

"Yeah… I mean… I guess." Shondra replied, shaking her head as if to say no, before switching to a nod, having no idea what to say.

"She woke me up a few hours ago, looking like she must have had a wild night out." Mister Álvarez said with a cartoonish wink.

"Lost her keys somewhere and needed me to let her in."

"Yeah, well, you know us. Kids these days and all, y'know? Anyway, Claire… uh… left her keys at my place. So… y'know… here I am." Shondra said, nodding too excitedly as she held up the keys, jiggling them. "D… Dropping them off. I'll… uh say you said hello."

"Okay, well you have yourself a nice day, Sharone. You might want to talk to her, though. She looked like hell. Like she wrestled an alligator. I know you kids party pretty hard these days, but I worry." Mister Álvarez said as he waved again and went back inside. Taking a moment to catch her breath, 'Sharone' calmed her freshly spiked nerves and started up the steps. She was surprised to find the keys shaking in her hands as she approached the door.

Doing her best to rationalize her way through the moment, her mind was having something of a war with itself. She hadn't slept at all through the evening and kept running through what had happened the night before. Claire was there, or at least had been there.

Impossibly, Claire was a werewolf. But Claire had been one for a year now, and aside from being distant, she never once gave Shondra cause for alarm. Today, however, was to be a full moon and she had no idea what that would mean. All she had were questions, but inherently, she trusted her friend. Claire would never hurt her.

Knocking gently, Shondra waited for a full minute before knocking again, louder this time. Another minute passed and the anxious young woman had no idea what to expect, but decided to press forward. *It's Claire. She's not going to hurt you. It's Claire.* She thought, working up her own courage.

At the door, her hands fumbled with the keys. She shook so badly that she dropped them to the concrete landing at her feet before forcing herself to calm down.

What are you doing, Shondra? She thought to herself, holding the keys. *Just… go in. You're just checking on her and it's broad daylight. So… she should still be the Claire you've known for years. You... You can totally do this. You can totally do this.*

Slowly, she slid the keys into the three locks and... taking a massive breath... carefully opened the door.

Looking inside, everything looked normal. There was little difference from the last time she had been over to her friend's house, aside from Claire obviously having rearranged the furniture in the living room. But that was just something of a Claire-ism; she was never quite happy with the layout of her apartment, and liked rethinking it. Seeing this familiar habit in action was comforting.

Stepping in, she closed and locked the door behind her and began hesitantly looking around, looking for cues and listening for Claire. The woman tended to snore, she remembered from their years as roommates, but the apartment was remarkably silent.

Maybe werewolves don't snore? You don't know. Maybe... I dunno... maybe that cleared it up, or something? It could be. Shondra thought to herself, trying to think of any excuse to keep stalling.

Working up the nerve with maximum effort, she half-whispered. "C... C... Claire? Are you here?"

Pausing to listen, she put the keys on the kitchen counter and repeated herself, with more confidence and a little more volume. "C... Claire? Claire, are you home? It's... It's just Shondra. You... you left your keys and stuff at my apartment. Are... are you... okay?"

The normally motor-mouthed woman was practically terse as she waited for a reply that didn't come. The silence did not prompt her to relax much as she began to look around. The apartment was largely the same. The sink was still a mess and needed cleaning. The fridge was still overstocked with meat as it had been the last few times she had visited. That hadn't registered as unusual, but now it seemed like a neon warning sign.

In the back were a handful of metal cans that looked kind of like flasks. They had little "M"s written on them in markers, and Shondra's stomach flipped as she imagined what could be inside.

Step-by-step, the anxious woman exploring a very brave new world made her way to her friend's bedroom to find the door closed. *Okay… Claire hears, like, everything. All year, no matter how low you've whispered, she's responded. If she was in there, she totally would have woken up or said something. Well… unless she's too exhausted from the night before, which is totally an option. You have no idea what that does to her. She could be in a super deep sleep.*

Putting a hand on the doorknob, a part of her mind wished she had grabbed a weapon of some sort. She chastised herself for the thought. *No! This is Claire. No matter what, this is Claire. She… she made a dumb joke after transforming. She was still herself. She is not dangerous. This is still Claire. She's… she's your friend.*

Slowly, she turned the knob, which clicked loudly enough to make her jump. Catching her breath, she pushed the door open just enough to peek in. Breathing a deep sigh, Shondra could see that the bed was empty.

She pushed the door the rest of the way open to reveal that she was, at least for the moment, alone in the apartment. The bed was disheveled, which wasn't a massive surprise to the woman who had been Claire's roommate for years, however, it was also peppered with bits and pieces of discarded clothes.

Worse was the sight on the floor in front of the door to Claire's bathroom, where Shondra saw the discarded, torn, and stained clothes she had been wearing when she had changed in front of her.

Before she had a chance to ponder the meaning of that discovery, however, she heard the front door handle jiggle, and a light knock echoed through the empty space.

Oh my goodness! Oh my goodness! She thought, her heart rate spiking through the roof as she jerked around at the sound. Through the crack under the door, she could see a set of legs blocking the morning light. Then, another gentle knocking at the door.

Claire wouldn't knock. Even without her keys, Claire wouldn't have knocked. Ooooohhhh my goodness. That's NOT Claire. Ohhh my goodness. Shondra's mind was flying at what felt like warp speed as she looked around the room for someplace to hide.

A louder knock coming from the door, Shondra nearly jumped out of her skin as she internally debated between under the bed and in the closet.

Yeah… maybe when you were five, Shondra, she thought to herself, knowing full well that she was far too round around the middle to consider the bed, and she ran to the closet. The accordion doors were slatted wood and would offer only slightly more protection than a curtain, but it was the only option. At least, it gave her a little more time.

Quietly closing the door to the bedroom, she turned the little knob on the handle and locked it. It wasn't much, but it was all she could think to do.

Opening the doors to the closet, the condition of the bed now made more sense. The closet was half-empty, looking as if it had been rifled through in a hurry. The floor at the base where she knew Claire kept her suitcase was also empty. All signs were now pointing to Claire having been here and gone.

From in front of the cleared-out closet, she could hear the locks turning and the front door opening. *Oh, for… this is literally the end of HALLOWEEN, you idiot.* Shondra thought, biting her bottom lip as she looked up and noticed that, unlike the classic slasher film she loved, Claire only had plastic hangers for self-defense. Useless. So she grabbed the only available weapon: a single thick-soled hiking boot.

Ohhh, yeah. You are totally dead.

Sitting in the near-dark, she tried to slow her manic breathing that a half-deaf person would be able to hear, and clutched the boot tight to her heaving chest.

A moment later, the door to the bedroom made an impressive pop and opened as well, the lock easily broken. Over the sound of her own heartbeat, she could hear extremely light-sounding footfalls walking up to the doors of the closet, and a sound that she was fairly sure was a sniff.

Seconds later, she heard a sigh and a familiar voice. "Hello, Shondra. It's only me. It's Mariska. It's okay."

While the two were, at best, occasionally begrudging acquaintances, Shondra's suspicions of the woman's true nature had only been increased by the ease with which she had entered the room and the fact that Mariska seemed completely aware not only WHERE she was, but WHO she was.

After some more silence, Mariska continued. "Can I open the door so we can talk? I got your messages. I'm… sorry that I missed your calls. I was… a touch preoccupied last night. But I'm here. It's okay, I promise."

"I… I like it in here. It's… cozy." Shondra protested, weakly.

"*Konechno*… of course." Mariska replied, a hint of irritation and a peppering of Russian in her voice as Shondra heard her walk over and sit on Claire's bed. "Okay. I am way over here. You are in there. We can talk like this."

Shuddering, Shondra bit her bottom lip and tried to calm down, now afraid she would pee her pants as Mariska continued. "I tried calling you back a little bit ago, but you didn't answer. Do you still have Claire's phone?"

"It's in my car, c… charging," Shondra replied, leaning forward to try and see Mariska through the slats, to no avail. "Oh… No, wait. I forgot. My car won't charge stuff if the… uh… engine isn't… Well, it's in my car and it was… uh… charging."

"Okay, that's fine. I didn't have your actual number, or I would have tried that too." Mariska replied, clearly trying to keep her voice as calming as possible. "So… why are you in the closet, Shondra?"

"You… you… you know!" Shondra shouted back, fear in her voice.

"So… Claire told you and you freaked out?" Mariska asked, already aware of the broad strokes from Shondra's panicked messages.

"Y… yeah, a little. She… uh… she… she SHOWED me. So…

I kinda freaked and my… my dog bit me when it happened and… I screamed and… Claire freaked out too and ran off. But… but she was… she was TALKING to me. Like, just talking like it was normal and I couldn't believe it. I was just..." Shondra said, her voice going at a breakneck pace.

"You were, as you said, freaking out. Anyone would. It's okay. But of course Claire was talking. She always does when she changes. She's still Claire and she's still your friend. I'm sure we can explain what happened when we find her. Have you heard anything from her?" Mariska continued, speaking as if everything was, in fact, perfectly normal.

"N… n… no. Nothing. I waited up all night and…nothing." Shondra said, her death grip on the shoe loosening as the conversation continued.

"That all said, why are you hiding from ME? What did Claire tell you about me?" Mariska asked, concern in her voice at her own question.

"Nothing. Nothing. Except that… except that you knew what had happened to her and…. And that you helped her. But that was it!" Shondra said, shouting the last part.

"Thennnnn, why are you hiding?"

"B… because… because… y'know… once you know Dick Grayson is ROBIN, figuring out who BATMAN is…. isn't…. isn't hard. You're…. You're…" Shondra said, re-tightening that grip on the shoe and scooching back against the wall.

Outside, Mariska sighed and paused before replying sarcastically. "Well… this is familiar territory. Look, whatever you think you know about what I am, what I am is Claire's friend. And… *chert poberi*… I would like to be yours as well. We had fun at the Halloween shop and you're silly, but you're nice. And you clearly care about Claire, too."

"Didn't you have fun, too, until things went off the rails?" Mariska asked, handling Shondra like a delicate vase.

"Uh… um… kinda, yeah." Shondra replied.

"So… whatever you think I am… it's like with Claire. You

know what she is now, but even then she's still Claire. She's not a *monster*, she's just… different. And it's not a bad thing, I promise." Mariska said, her tone getting a little lighter. "I'll be honest, she's a lot of fun when it happens and I can get her to relax. It makes her lighten up a little. She takes the stick out of her posterior just a bit."

"Wait, what?!?" Shondra exclaimed, confused.

"Okay… sorry. Not what you want to hear right now. Look, you saw what she became, and here we are, still dancing around the words. She is a werewolf. And yes, I am a vampire. But SHE'S still your friend and I am not going to hurt you. Ever. I promise." Mariska said, some frustration in her voice. "But… we need to talk if we're going to find where she's gone. And it's important, because I found out this morning that her *yebuchiy* ex is in town. Right now."

"Oh no…" Shondra gasped.

"Exactly. And if she thinks that you hate her now because of what happened... and her and I weren't speaking all week either… she is not going to be in a headspace to think straight if he tries fucking with her." Mariska continued as she stood up off the bed. "So… we… you and I… can talk more. I know you're terrified. I really do, but when she changed…tell me the truth."

"I know you were scared… but did you once for even a *second*… once she *talked* to you… think she could ever hurt you?"

There was a shuffling from the closet, and after a long moment of silence, the doors opened. Shondra stood there, a boot hanging from the hand at her side as she pursed her lips, trembling. "N… no."

A close-mouthed smile crossed Mariska's lips as she nodded. "And I never will either. Even if we don't end up getting along. But I'd very much like to try."

Chucking, Mariska tilted her head at the improvised weapon. "Nice. A boot."

"Well… she… she… didn't have anything else in there and… I had no idea… who was coming. Heh." Shondra replied with a nervous chuckle as Mariska continued to try and lighten the mood.

"So… you just… pieced together what I am? Nice."

"Y… yeah, well… y'know." Shondra put the boot down and then held both hands up towards Mariska as if she were a prize presenter on the Price is Right, gesturing to the entirety of the tiny, pale woman. "THIS. It's not… subtle."

"Touché." Mariska said, putting her hands on her narrow hips, looking around before looking back at Shondra. "I'll be honest, I'm glad she told you. I've been trying to get her to do so for months. And I knew you'd take it well."

"This is 'taking it well'? I… I was hiding in a closet with a shoe." Shondra said, eyebrow raised.

"You were hiding in CLAIRE'S closet, not your own. Because you came here, I'm assuming, worried about your friend. And here we are talking about it all. So, yes, give yourself some credit. I have seen… far worse over the years." Mariska said, nodding and smiling, clearly relieved at how it was going. "But… you said her phone was in your car? Maybe we can go looking for her. See if we can figure out where she ran off to. She often goes out to the state forest, particularly if she is stressed out."

"Uh… yeah… yeah… okay. Yeah. Uh… Wait, did you not drive over?" Shondra asked and followed hesitantly behind her as Mariska started towards the front of the apartment.

"Uber. I hate driving and don't have a car. They... disturb me. My village in Russia didn't have them when I was growing up, and now... It's… it's a whole... *thing*." Mariska said, stopping in the living room.

Turning, she looked at Shondra. The young, perfectly normal human still looked slightly panicked and extremely out of her depth. In a way, it was not too dissimilar from that day in the motel with Claire a year ago, minus the existential dread and depression. Regardless, she was standing there. She had come to her friend's apartment trying to do what she could to help, and that spoke volumes to the century-old vampire, who smiled warmly.

It was a smile that seemed to confuse Shondra, who cricked a brow. "Uh… what?"

"Sorry. Nothing, really. We… should get going." Mariska said, gesturing to the door casually.

"So… sunlight really doesn't bother you?" Shondra asked, legitimate curiosity overwhelming her fear for a moment while Mariska pulled the hood of her sweater up and pulled her sunglasses out of her pocket.

"Eh… it is not my friend, but no. I don't burst into flames or anything. That's just…"

Cutting her off, Shondra was beginning to return to her more familiar, mile-a-minute speech pattern. "Well… that makes sense. The whole 'sunlight kills vampires' cliche was actually created by F. W. Murnau for the movie, 'Nosferatu' as a flimsy ending to try and avoid getting sued for ripping off Dracula. But it stuck and became a part of the whole genre ever since it was codified by the Tod Browning film in the 30's."

Grinning, Mariska couldn't help but brag as she put her glasses on. "I know. I saw both… in the *theaters*."

"Okay… that's… uh… that's kind of awesome. I totally want to ask you a zillion questions, but we… uh… we really do need to find Claire. She's not here, but she WAS. Her closet was cleaned out and it looks like she might have packed a bag." Shondra said, filling Mariska in on what she had deduced in the bedroom.

"*Chert poberi*," Mariska cursed again, looking around the room as she tried to work things out. "So, she could be anywhere by now? Wonderful."

"Well, no." Shondra said, pulling Claire's keys out of her purse. "She left her car keys at my place with her phone when she took off, and it's still parked out front. So… that's good, right?"

"Yeah, I would imagine. Unless…" Mariska said, looking over to the key rack on the wall near the door. "She had a spare car key that she kept… right there."

Both women looked at the empty rack, then back at each other as they pieced together what must've happened before they arrived. Shondra sighed as she knitted her brows. "So… what does

'*Chert poberi*' mean?"

"Basically, 'damn it'." Mariska replied, rubbing the bridge of her nose with her fingers.

"*Chert poberi*," Shondra said with a defeated sigh.

Chapter Nineteen
⟨·⟩⟩◕⟨⟨·⟩

By the time Claire returned to Shondra's apartment, an exceedingly long walk carrying a suitcase in the Tampa heat, she was glad that her friend seemed gone. She had left her keys and her phone there the night before when she had split in a panic. Thankfully, her purse was still in her car when she came back with her spare set of keys.

It was enough. She had to leave.

She drove north up I-95, hours into her exodus and well outside of Florida, and her mind was a storm of memories, confusion, and fear. She couldn't understand just how she had ruined things so utterly, and so quickly.

Claire had already gone to Mariska's, hoping that whatever was wrong between them could at least be worked out, but the vampire who had been her closest confidant in the last year hadn't been home. Claire had no idea who to turn to. As it stood, she had one option she had been presented, and that was no option at all.

Hours earlier, she had found herself huddled in the woods, sitting pressed up against a tree, where he had left her as she pondered the fate she had spent a year dreading. Liam Docherty, her ex-boyfriend who had revealed himself to be a werewolf just before he had attacked and turned her, had returned for her as promised.

Thinking back to the last evening, Claire scowled behind the wheel of her car, disgusted that she had actually listened to him. Actually gave him the time to talk when she should have just kept walking away no matter how many times he stopped her. Instead, she sat and listened. And worse, she had *wanted* to.

It made no sense to her. Here, in the now, Claire's mind tried to understand how he could have affected her so strongly. Why what he was saying had made sense to her at the time. How close she had come to going with him when the morning came.

When she had begged him to leave her alone, he let her know that his van was nearby. That he would be waiting for her when dawn came. And when that sun began to warm the sky and cast its light over the trees of the nature reserve, she found herself slowly walking towards him. Following her keen nose toward the smell of him.

As she walked, she had felt a comfort, which was, ironically, extremely uncomfortable to think of now. But in spite of herself, she had wanted that comfort. She had wanted to go to him and wrap herself up in that scent again. She wanted to feel the way he made her feel in the time before he had attacked her that night.

Walking to the edge of the woods, she stopped as she looked into the brush. The hair that had covered her all night had fallen away in the underbrush and she was transformed once again. The legs that had been carrying her near forty miles an hour in the moonlight were now smooth and pink and scratched up from the dry brush she stepped through. And there, across the road just past the clearing was that damned van.

She had found him having sex with Beverly McLeish in that van a year ago, and it had made her angry enough to finally try leaving him. It was a dirty, dilapidated band van that he, Beverly, and his two brothers drove in from city to city to perform. Even when they were dating, she hadn't liked that van, and there, as she had stood in the woods looking at it, she despised it.

Yet, she wanted to run towards it. It was her escape; her shuttle to carry her away from the failure of her former life. And there, in the driver's seat, through the thick treeline, she could see him. Liam was sitting there, transformed back to the human visage she knew well. He was waiting for her, just as he said he would.

Struggling for what felt like an eternity, she looked down at herself. She was wearing only stretched and torn sweatpants and a ratty, shredded t-shirt. He said he had a change of clothes and he was waiting for her as he had promised. He called her beautiful when she was transformed. He extended a hand when everyone else she counted on for support seemed to have closed theirs.

As she began to step out of the woods, however, Claire paused.

She remembered that hatred in his icy blue eyes and the venom in his voice as he declared her to be his property. Property he had returned to claim. In that moment, just hours ago, Claire had stepped back.

She wondered if he could smell her the way she did him. His scent floated across the wind towards her and again, she remembered how much she had wanted him over the course of that bizarre night. But there, in the morning light, she had turned around and walked the other way.

She had walked for two hours, looking very much like a zombie on Halloween morning, and eventually reached her apartment to clean off and collect her thoughts. Her mind racing, she packed a bag and prepared to run, the same as she had tried to do a year ago. How could she go back to work on Monday and face Shondra? How could she continue where everyone she cared about had turned away from her?

Seven hours later, she crossed into Georgia, driving north with an eye on the only thing she could think to do; go to the family she had barely spoken to all year.

Her sister wasn't particularly happy about a last-minute visit in spite of her regular requests to see Claire, but she hadn't said no. At least she had someplace to go; a destination to focus on that wasn't Liam. It was something that she hoped could help recover at least some semblance of her old life before it all fell away.

Watching as the sun lowered in the sky, she clung to that thin hope as she realized that she would have to find someplace to eat soon and stop for the night. It was a full moon and she would have no choice but to transform again. So long as she wasn't hungry, she could control herself and lie low. A hotel room somewhere. A bucket or two of fried chicken. Someplace to hide for the night and lick her proverbial wounds as she struggled with the fear that her sister would close those doors as well.

Then she'd only have one option left…one terrible direction to run to. But she didn't want to consider that right now.

She didn't want to consider *him*.

Chapter Twenty

"No, no, Ms. Bryce. We should be back and done by next Monday."

"I know this was short notice, but... well... none of us saw my grandmother passing so suddenly, but she was... like, totally pushing a hundred. We honestly were surprised she held on as long as she did, really. My family...they're planning the funeral for this week and... well... I just... I couldn't deal with it by myself. You know how I get. I cried when that squirrel died in the breezeway of the building."

"And Claire just... insisted that she come to help me through this. Yes, yes, we both really appreciate it. We're driving up together. She's... in the back sleeping while I drive the first shift. We both really appreciate you giving us the time without warning like this."

"T... thank you. Thank you so much. We'll see you next Monday. Thanks again. Thanks. Okay. Thanks. Buh-bye." Shondra said, tapping frantically at her phone, trying to hang it up with the free hand that wasn't driving.

Letting out a massive sigh behind the wheel of her little Nissan Cube, she groaned melodramatically. "Do you think she knew I was making all that up, Mariska? I am... NOT good at lying."

"You *aren't?* I am *thoroughly* surprised. That, too, was a lie, by the way." Mariska smirked in the passenger seat as they drove their way north, doing their best to follow Claire Gribbald's exodus."If she said it was okay, it really doesn't matter if she could tell you were lying. You DID contradict yourself, though. Her death was completely sudden and she held on so long at the same time? You have a tenacious fictional grandmother."

"I soooo hope she doesn't check. My grandma died 5 years ago. I only had the one, and I took off for work back then, too. And it's not like we can fake an obituary with such short notice if she decides to look it up…" Shondra said, talking a mile a minute as she worked through the story she had fabricated to get her and Claire out of work for a week so neither would get fired.

Rolling her eyes and smiling more broadly, Mariska chuckled. "I can assure you that your boss isn't trolling the internet in search of evidence. It's fine. You will not need to add 'newspaper obituary forger' to your resume today. Breathe, or you're going to pass out. And since you're driving, that would most assuredly suck."

"Is… that a vampire joke?" Shondra asked nervously, still finding her footing with the woman she barely knew and didn't want to annoy.

"Not… intentionally, no. But, if it served the purpose of helping you calm yourself a little, I shall take full credit for it." Mariska replied, adjusting in her seat as she tried to get comfortable in spite of the cargo sitting in her lap. Looking down, she raised an eyebrow and held up Shondra's little chocolate poodle. "Did we really need to bring… this? I mean, there are kennels."

"Oh, don't you listen to the grouchy lady, Clive. You know I would never put you in a kennel, yes you do. You are being such a good boy, yes you are." Shondra said to the half-sleeping pup, who barely registered with what looked like a slightly twitching tail on an otherwise unconscious dog.

"Ugh… this is going to be a long trip. Why is your dog named… Clive?" Mariska asked, holding the dog up with a put-upon expression of mock indignation.

"Well, I got him from one of my neighbors whose dog had puppies. There were four of them she needed to find homes for, and out of all the little babies, he was the first to start barking. It was just so cute and he was so tiny, barking there. So… Clive Barker." Shondra explained, clearly proud of the pun.

Looking over, Mariska was resisting letting the smirk on her face show, so Shondra clarified. "Uh… y'know. The horror writer, from…"

"I know who Clive Barker is. I've seen Hellraiser." Mariska said with a grin, shaking her head.

"S... sorry. I just. I mean, you've been friends with Claire for a year now and we've really never talked. We've gone out with Claire together a few times, but I always figured you... just didn't like me. So I kept my distance and didn't press the issue, y'know?" Shondra said, still rambing as she did. "So... if you want... I can just turn on the radio and leave you alone or... ya know... whatever is best for you."

"That sounds like a terribly boring and useless way to get all the way to..." the platinum blonde vampire held up Claire's phone with her free hand. "Barley, Pennsylvania."

"Good thinking, checking Claire's phone. Otherwise we would have just had to... drive around at random trying to figure out where she went." Mariska said, side-stepping the observation for a moment. Shondra noticed, and she pursed her lips for a second as she replied.

"Yeah. Yeah. Well... I figured we didn't see her laptop in her apartment, so she had to have taken it with her, and thankfully she also has Facebook on her phone, so we could see that she messaged her sister. I... kinda feel a little bad about prying, though. I mean, that's her private... thing," Shondra added sheepishly.

"I understand, and under different circumstances, I'd agree. But.. I can't just let him get into her head again. That *zhopa* did so much damage to her, and she was just starting to put it behind her," Mariska declared, putting the phone down and scowling, clearly upset at the idea of Liam forcing himself back into Claire's life.

Looking over, Shondra had a quizzical expression on her face as she evaluated Mariska's attitude at the perceived threat to their mutual friend. "You... you really do care about her. About Claire, I mean. Like... I know you do, obviously, but... I'm glad she found you when all... when, y'know... she got... attacked. When this all happened to her. I'm glad she had a friend."

"She had more than one," Mariska said, matter-of-factly as she pet the snoozing pooch. "She's never stopped caring about you, Shondra. She was just… terrified. Liam and Beverly put… horrible ideas into her head about what it meant to be what she is: a werewolf. She's still afraid that she'll change one night and lose control; become that kind of monster they make movies about. And… she's been terrified that if you found out, it would be all that you would be able to see."

"Also, for the record? So far, I like you just fine." Mariska smiled more warmly. "I just didn't press the issue earlier because I didn't want to push Claire out of her comfort zone until she was ready. Maybe I should have, but…"

"But… she's been kind of a mess for a while now," Shondra interjected, relaxing as well while the statement hung in the air.

After a few minutes of a relative, but not strained, silence, Shondra spoke up again. "So… uh… do… do you mind if I ask you a question? I mean, it's okay again if you don't want to and I'm not trying to be annoying. I'm just… y'know…"

Cutting off the minor bit of rambling, Mariska replied with a slightly playful tone from the passenger seat. "I'm your first vampire. You just found out vampires and werewolves exist. We're also going to be in this car for a full day, at least. Just ask, or we'll both go mad from utter boredom."

"So… you said you saw Dracula in the theaters? Like, when it came out? I… uh… I know this is the most clichéd question I could think to ask, but…" Shondra said, hemming and hawing around the question before, again, Mariska interjected.

"I was… twenty-five when I was changed." She answered, looking at her reflection, which did, in fact, exist, in the window of the car, visible in the waning sun. "That was 1931, so you'll have to do the math, because I stopped counting in the 70's when it started making me self-conscious about my age."

Shondra chuckled at the little joke, and Mariska simply took the topic further, seemingly happy to do so.

"Since you know who directed it, you probably know that it

was the same year that Dracula came out. At the time, it was the only information I actually knew about vampires. I even was telling Claire the other day that because of that movie, I hid from the sun for almost a full year thinking I would burn up. I… hid from a LOT of things that I didn't have to."

Chucking, Mariska continued. "After I actually read the BOOK, I started experimenting and found out that sunlight did not kill me. All it does, really, is make me weak, nauseated, and sunburnt if I'm out in it too long uncovered. Really, it's more like…"

Gesturing with her free hand as she talked, Mariska waved her hand in front of the windshield. "A nice, sunny spring day for you feels more like noon in August to me, just without the sweating. I don't actually sweat anymore, which is absolutely a plus."

"Wow. You don't sweat? I… I don't know if that's ever come up in a movie." Shondra said, her anxiety beginning to be replaced by genuine curiosity. "So… uh… I guess you're really strong. I mean, you pushed Claire's bedroom door open like it was nothing and picked up that big cooler in the back… like totally super easy, and that thing… well, with what's in it, it looked heavy."

Glancing back, they had packed an ice-filled party cooler with all of the cans of blood that Claire had in her fridge, along with some more they picked up from Mariska's own house as they were heading out of town. "Yeah. So long as I'm well fed, I am… exceedingly strong. Not to brag, but the whole Underworld… werewolves versus vampires thing, is utter nonsense, really. Claire is quite strong too, especially when she's transformed, but I have that beat MANY times over."

"ON that note…" Mariska said, reaching back and grabbing one of the cans out of the cooler before noticing that Shondra looked a little weirded out. "Okay… this is going to be a very long drive if I am hungry because it is freaking you out that I need to drink this."

"I'm… I'm sorry. Really. It's just… it's still weird, is all. I promise. I'll be okay. I mean…" Shondra muttered a little, awkwardly trying to cover for her nerves as she started driving faster as a result. "Really. This is all still… just really, really new to me. I keep thinking it's not all settled in my brain and I'll just lose my… poop… once I stop to think, y'know."

"You sat up thinking about this all night long, last night," Mariska said, unscrewing the cap and taking a perfectly normal swig as Shondra caught a whiff of the salty-smelling contents, trying not to think about it too much. "You're not going to crack up, or you would have already. Give yourself some credit."

"Trust me when I say… you're taking all of this better than I've ever seen. And I've seen my share of people losing it over the years." Mariska said, a hint of melancholy in her voice that Shondra picked up on.

"Really? What… what happened?" She asked, eyebrow raised as Mariska pursed her lips and replied rather quickly.

"THAT… if you don't mind… I'd… rather not go into." She said, nodding.

"I'm s… I'm sorry. I didn't mean to pry." Shondra replied, turning her attention back to the road.

"Shondra, stop. I told you to ask questions, so you do not need to apologize. This one is just… not a memory I'd like to think about right now. That's all, I promise." In truth, Mariska was almost enthusiastic to open up to the refreshingly curious woman who seemed to be taking the revelations so well. It was nice to just be herself with someone other than Claire or even Beverly for a change.

To say nothing of the fact that she was more than a little egotistical. At least, enough to enjoy preening just a bit, which gave her a strange thought.

"So… would you freak out if I showed you the teeth? Ooooorrr… are you curious?" Mariska said with a hesitant grin. In the driver's seat, Shondra's eyes went wide as she bit her bottom lip.

"O. M. G! I was… I was a little scared to ask, honestly. I mean, I watched Claire change and… yeah, I freaked out because I didn't know it was gonna happen and… y'know… a complete surprise and all. But… uh… yeah. I was totally wondering because you've smiled a lot and they totally look normal but I figured something had to happen. I dunno." She rambled, excitedly. "I mean… if you don't mind?"

Rolling her eyes, Mariska shook her head. "You are very much a goof, Shondra. I don't mind. I asked you, after all. Hold on."

Licking her lips, Mariska opened her mouth wide and curled her upper lip back enough to show her teeth. As she did, her canines began to sharpen into points and push further down until they were extended a full half of an inch from the roof of her mouth. Once they were extended, she ran her tongue playfully over the tips for Shondra to see.

Watching, the young driver found herself wobbling past the lane lines and coasting into the middle lane of the highway they were on, now driving that much faster as she had let her attention drift. "Holy… okay. Wow. O. M. G., that is… that is kind of awe…"

There was a loud whooping sound as a siren began to wail and the cabin of the car filled up with the red and blue lights of a police car behind them. The shock of the sudden lights and sirens caused Shondra to weave even more before getting the little car under control.

"Ohhh. Oh no, oh no, oh no! Oh, we're… what are we gonna do? We're gonna get caught!" Shondra said, panic setting in as she looked ahead for a place to pull over.

"Breathe, Shondra. Just relax. What are we going to be caught doing? We're not doing ANYTHING. It will be fine." Mariska said, glancing over her shoulder with a wry grin Shondra wasn't yet used to seeing. "Just pull over and be calm. Everything will be fine."

"I am a black woman driving with a cooler of BLOOD in the back seat!" Shondra protested, glancing in the rearview.

"ANIMAL blood. WEIRD, but not illegal. At least I don't think it is." Mariska replied, pondering. "Look, just please. Trust me, okay? I won't let anything bad happen."

"They will invent a law to prosecute me under, and throw away the key." Shondra gulped, gripping the wheel tight enough for the faux leather to groan in protest.

"Trust me. It will be fine." Mariska nodded, her voice soft and calm as she too looked over her shoulder at the flashing lights.

"Uh... uh... okay. Okay. Pulling... pulling over." Shondra said as she tucked the small car up against the shoulder of the darkening highway as the sun dropped closer to the horizon. "Wait... what are you going to do? You're not... uh..."

"I already told you, I do not eat people. Neither does Claire. Calm your proverbial tits, woman." Mariska said, a little irritated at the implication, but giving Shondra a free pass in the moment. "Just let me do the talking, okay?"

"O... okay. Okay. I can do that. I can do that. Ohhhhh my goodness." Shondra said, her voice shrinking as she parked the car and waited. In true fashion, the officer seemed to take forever, making them wait long enough to have Shondra in near hysterics by the time the door to the police car opened and the officer made their way to the window.

Rolling the window down, Shondra had already pulled out her license and registration as the officer leaned into the window and began to speak. "So, I suppose you know you were weaving all over the road back there, and that the posted speed limit is 65 miles per hour? Do you have any idea how fast you were actually going back there?"

"Uh... um... heh... us... Yeah. I... we were going... uh." Shondra stammered, trying to smile and looking rather mad as a result. The officer raised their brow.

"81, ma'am. Can I see your license and registration?" The officer said flatly as Mariska leaned over Shondra's chest and looked up to the taller officer, making eye contact as she did.

Looking down, Shondra's eyes went wide as she watched Mariska's eyes turn red. She spoke to the officer with a wink and an exaggerated wave of her fingers in the air in an overtly obvious gesture. "You don't need to see her identification."

Gulping hard, Shondra silently mouthed, *Really?*, to which Mariska simply winked.

There was a pregnant pause for what felt to Shondra like an eternity before the officer replied flatly, "Yeah, I don't need to see your ID."

As Shondra's jaw fell open, Mariska continued. "You can just let us off with a warning since we're such nice girls."

"Okay, I'm gonna let you two off with a warning. Just keep it to 65 and be careful. Keep an eye on the road, alright?" The officer replied, exceedingly casually.

"We can go about our business."

"You can go about your business."

"Carry on."

"Carry on." The officer said, stepping back to wave them back along their way.

For a long moment, Shondra was frozen as Mariska playfully put a finger on the bottom of the rotund woman's chubby jaw, gently pushing it closed. "That's our cue."

"Uh… Huh? Oh.. Oh.. right. Uh-huh. Yeah, tooootally. Yeah." Shondra said, pulling carefully into traffic and watching as they left the parked police car in the distance before finally speaking again.

"YOU CAN DO THE JEDI MIND TRICK!?!?! Holy COW! That is… O. M. G.! That's… that's... " Shondra was virtually bouncing in her seat as Mariska smirked smugly in her own, Clive grumbling at the disturbance to his slumber.

"Useful, to be sure," Mariska offered, finishing Shondra's thought.

"Wow! Okay… that was… wow. Uh, though the line at the end is actually 'move along'?" she instinctively corrected.

"Ha!" Mariska laughed at the absurdity of her new friend's reaction, somewhat amazed that the young woman was so capable of dealing with it all so well and even with some measure of excitement. "Tomato, ToMAHto. Regardless, like I said, the situation is resolved. We are fine and all is well."

"Well… for us." Mariska said, as the sun dipped ever closer to the horizon and her voice dipped to a virtual whisper. "*Pozhaluysta, bud' v poryadke, volchonok.*"

Looking over, Shondra didn't need to know Russian or even the specifics of what had been said to understand the meaning. It was clear that Mariska was extremely worried for their mutual friend. "You really do care about her, don't you? A lot."

"Of course, I care about her. She's…" Mariska's flippant facade was all but gone now as she kept her eyes away from Shondra's. "She's my best friend. My only friend."

The words hung in the air between the two as Shondra nodded and considered the moment. "Was." She added with a gentle smile, as they pressed on. "Was your only friend."

Chapter Twenty-One
·))◐(('·

The sun was nearing the horizon many hours further north as Claire walked across the parking lot from the fairly average hotel. She had just gotten a room and was now making her way toward the Denny's connected to the gas station on the other side.

She knew she needed to eat WELL before the full moon crested into view and she changed. In spite of her anxiety over everything that had happened, she knew that she could simply wait out her transformation in the hotel room and leave at dawn. The sleep would be welcome, as she had been running on adrenaline for what felt like forever.

While Liam and Beverly may have 'Inceptioned' the idea into her head that she might lose control when the wolf was out, it hadn't once happened. Transformed, she was, in most respects, the same woman she was at the moment. A little taller. Stronger. Faster. Simply... MORE in many ways. The need to hunt or run or go a little wild often came up, but never overwhelmed her sense of reason.

What she found, more often than not, was that when she was the wolf, she liked it. She enjoyed feeling more in control of her anxiety. She enjoyed the increase in her confidence. She even enjoyed the freedom of the hunt; running wild and without care.

For a change, she enjoyed ENJOYING it. Over the past year, she had worked hard to learn to accept what she had become. Of course, that had all changed this past week, as events seemed to conspire to cause a rather swift backslide.

Stepping inside the mostly empty restaurant, Claire was reminded that it was Halloween as she noticed the waitress wearing a 'Bride of Frankenstein' costume. "Just one?" She asked, perking up and seeming excited.

"Yeah, please," Claire replied as the woman led her to a table near the window facing the residential neighborhood behind the building. She scooched her large frame into the tight booth and ordered a soda as the server left a menu for her. Her mind was on both the evening ahead and the evening behind her. On what had gone wrong and on what she could expect in Pennsylvania with her overbearing sister. It wasn't as if she could tell them what had happened, but she didn't know which way to turn, and like any frightened child, Claire was running home.

She still had a good hour to eat and try to calm her nerves as she looked at the houses and their decorations. A group of children, led by an older group of what looked like teenagers, were all dressed up in colorful costumes, heading from one door to the next, getting their trick-or-treating in earlier. Claire leaned on her hands and allowed herself a smile for the sight.

With the moon set to rise in a little while, her enhanced senses were heightened to nearly full capacity as her ear twitched slightly. She could hear the waitress coming with her drink from the other side of the restaurant. Stepping up, she set the glass and a straw down as Claire turned to smile, brushing a forelock of stray hair out of her face.

"How'ya doin' tonight, darlin'? Got any big plans?" She said, with a southern drawl and a pleasant and sincere smile.

Smiling back, Claire shook her head as she responded. "Not really. Hoping for a nice, quiet night in. On a… uh… bit of a road trip and am looking forward to just sleeping. A lot." Claire said, which was actually the truth, and did sound like exactly what she needed to try and get her proverbial head screwed on right.

"Long drive, huh?" The server replied softly, black bouffant wig with white streaks bobbing as she spoke.

"Yeah. Heading up to Pennsylvania to visit with family. But I needed some food in me and some sleep to keep going. Are you heading out later, or is this just for work?" Claire asked, indulging the pleasant woman in some small talk, hoping to get her mind off of the self-obsessing she was doing.

"Oh, this? Nah, This is just mah work uniform." The waitress replied, striking a hippy pose with a playful grin. "Ha, yeah.

Heading to a party after my shift, but ah love Halloween. Gettin' t' dress up as somethin' crazy and just be someone else fer th' night. It's mah favorite holiday, so since they let us, ah always dress up. Anyway, since yer lookin' like you could eat the ass offa horse, what can I get'cha, hon?"

Blanching at the woman's comment, which was a little too on the nose, Claire fidgeted as she grabbed the menu really quick. She already had an idea of what she wanted and gave it a brief check. "Oh, uh… let me… could I get the Lumberjack Slam with white toast, scrambled eggs with cheese and hash browns, please? Also, I'd like to add the T-Bone from the steak and eggs to that, please. Medium rare. I know it's an extra charge, but… uh… I'm really hungry."

"Wow, you sure are! Okay, hon. I'll put that right in for ya', all right?" The waitress said, writing out the order and heading back to the kitchen as Claire considered that she would likely stop at the big service station attached to the restaurant on the way out and stock up on a few bags of jerky as well. The waitress had no idea how close she was with her joke about Claire's ability to eat a horse. She never HAD, but on many a full moon, she had eaten her way through a wild animal or two, and in spite of doing so with a deer the night before, the anxiety was ramping up her appetite.

Claire could clearly hear the woman talking to the chef in the back. "Yeah, the thirteen-ounce steak WITH everything. She says she's hungry, I dunno. She sure looks it, so c'mon."

While she waited, Claire took a sip of her soda and looked around the restaurant. It was mostly empty but for a few families and couples peppered here and there, and she was glad for the relative privacy. Her mind was a minefield at the moment, and she preferred to have the ability to sit and think, even if what she found herself thinking about was less than pleasant.

Claire considered the laptop she had used to message her sister with and how her somewhat annoying older sibling was remarkably both happy for the impending visit AND put-upon by the idea that it was a major inconvenience. As a general rule, Ellie wasn't happy unless she was butting into someone's life, and clearly missed being able to do so with her 'wayward' sister.

Without her cell phone, which she had left at Shondra's apartment when everything had gone wrong, Claire had needed the computer to contact Ellie. However, the machine had remained closed and turned off since doing so. The sign at the counter said that the restaurant had free WiFi, and Claire was considering going to grab it and check her messages. That, or possibly send some herself.

She could talk to Mariska. Maybe even make sure that Shondra was okay. There was a strong pang of guilt in her belly at the way she had left, running from her problems to the only safe haven she could think of. A safe haven which, as she tried to avoid thinking of it, was no safe haven at all. What, after all, was she going to do? She absolutely couldn't tell her SISTER about any of this.

Sighing, Claire knew she was simply trading one problem for another to avoid facing Liam and Shondra. In truth, she was afraid to open the laptop. Part of her was afraid that there would be no messages from those closest to her, but the other part was more afraid that there WERE, and that she didn't want to read them.

As Liam's name crossed her mind, his face filled her memory. Denny's was the only restaurant for miles, but as she sat there, she knew it had been a tactical error as she flipped over the printed, paper placemat in front of her to the blank side. Staring at it, she found herself lost in the time before her life had gone off the deep end.

She had been in the corner booth of a similar Denny's back in Tampa, doodling on the back of her placemat, as she was wont to do. Lost in the moment, she was still waiting for her meal. A simple 'Moons over My Hammy' sandwich was more than enough to satisfy her back then, when her biggest concerns were bills and clients at work.

It was, as she remembered, a warm early Saturday morning. She had things to do that day, but at the moment was looking forward to a nice breakfast while nursing a coffee. With her hair in a loose ponytail and wearing nothing more elaborate than some jeans, sandals, and a t-shirt she had gotten from the Dali Museum, she was fairly average and unassuming that day; very unlike the group of loud, disheveled people who had come in and been seated a few tables away.

Claire glanced over with an irritated expression as they were making their excessively large orders. All four of them looked as if they had been rolling around in the dirt, and she had figured they must have been in some kind of fight, or something.

From where she was sitting, she couldn't quite make out what they were saying, but she could hear their thick, Scottish accents and was intrigued in spite of herself. Whatever they were talking about, they were clearly excited and energetic, laughing loudly while Claire watched.

The tall man with the long, slick black hair seemed to be the center of the others' attention, almost as if he were holding court. At least until one of the younger-looking ones nudged him and shot a side-eye to where Claire had been sitting.

Blushing slightly, she shot her eyes back down to the blank paper she was mindlessly doodling on, only half aware that he had become the subject of her restaurant placemat art. His deep, blue eyes locked on her, and he grinned just as she looked away.

"Here ya' go, ma'am." The voice of the server cut in, pulling Claire from the fog of her memory as her mountain of food arrived.

"Huh... oh. Uh, thanks. Sorry." Claire said, leaning back from the table so that she could spread out the veritable feast in front of her.

"No worries, hon. Almost hated t' interrupt you. You looked really lost, there. I... don't mean to pry, but are you okay?" She asked, seeming genuinely curious as she laid out the plates in front of Claire, along with caddies of syrups and jam spreads for her toast.

"Yeah. Yeah, I'm fine. Just drained. Been driving all day, is all. Thanks, though." Claire replied with a forced smile. The statement was technically the truth, as she had actually been up and functioning in one capacity or another for well over 24 hours now. If not for her enhanced metabolism, she would have crashed hard a while earlier. She was seriously looking forward to that hotel bed across the parking lot.

Looking over her meal, she decided to start with the pancakes as she considered that hotel room, thinking about the fact that she had never fallen asleep while transformed in the year she had been a werewolf. It was a strange observation that led her mind back to that night, which felt like a lifetime ago, now.

Doing her best to not be too obvious, Claire had continued to watch the curious quartet while she waited for her food. On the placemat in front of her, she had doodled the man she found inexplicably fascinating. The ballpoint pen from her purse couldn't capture those blue eyes she had spied from across the room, but she kept at it as she noticed him getting up from the table.

Listening, she could make out what he said to the others as he walked toward the front of the restaurant. "Be right back. I gotta hit th' head."

Glancing back, she noticed the other three were looking at her and talking amongst themselves as she blushed again and tried to look away, wondering what was taking so long with her food. However, that question faded quickly from her mind only minutes later as she felt warm breath on the back of her neck and his lilting, Scottish accent floated over her shoulders.

"Tha's no a bad likeness. I was wonderin' what ye were doin'." He said, leaning over her shoulder, having come up behind her like some kind of ninja. Turning with a sharp gasp, Claire all but leaped out of her seat at the surprise.

"Uhh… umm…" She hemmed and hawed, never having expected him to walk over and just interject himself into her space as he had.

"Sorry t' startle ye, but I couldnae help notice ye were noticin' me an' mine. M'name's Liam." He said with a pleasant and friendly grin as he rounded the table, putting one hand on the back of the empty chair opposite Claire. "Mind?"

"Huh? Uh… Uh, no. No, please. Yeah, you can sit. Sure." Claire stammered, thinking that she sounded like Shondra in the moment as she realized she must have been beet red at that point.

"That's really good, by th' way. I have'ta say, I'm impressed. yeve got some talent *theeeerre?*" Liam said, leaning on the table and looking not at the art, but at the artist. His deep blue eyes fixed on her own hazel ones. Claire felt like a thirteen-year-old girl as he dragged out the last word with an implied question at the end.

"Huh... Oh. Thank… thank you. Claire, my name is Claire." She replied anxiously, trying to get herself under control. She didn't know why she was reacting so strongly to the young man, but she could feel a growing heat in her middle as she crossed her legs. "I'm… I'm an artist. Well, a painter, but I do… um… graphic design."

"Well, I didnae need ye to tell me that yuir an artist, and a right hell a' one t' boot. I c'n see that fer myself. Me an' mine were curious as t' what ye were doin' over here, but I got t' say, I'm right flattered, Claire." He replied, his voice floating with a sing-song intonation as he used a finger to turn the impromptu portrait of himself to look at it closely. As he did, he gestured over his shoulder to the three left at the table who were all looking over at them, grinning wildly. "This is really fantastic."

Blushing even more, Claire fidgeted, smiling. "So, what… uh… what about you?"

"We're in town fer a gig at a little dive called the Pegasus lounge. We're doin' two shows this weekend." Liam said, leaning back to point. "The redhead grinnin' like a cat is Beverly. The tall one wit' the curly brown hair in th' back is m' little brother, Quentin. The little one wit' the sad attempt at a ginger beard is m' other little brother, Duncan."

"We c'n hear ye jus fine, arsehole!" Duncan shouted across the space as they laughed. At the time, Claire gave no thought to the fact that Liam was speaking at a normal volume and they could hear him from a ways away.

Laughing nervously along, Claire did her best to keep the conversation going with the man she found fascinating. "Oh, you're in a band?"

"Aye. The four 'a us have a band. Kinda a retro-punk meets metal thing. We're pretty new, but we're hopin' to git a few more gigs while we're in town. Lotta good bands came outta the region, so we're thinkin' we might be able t' git some momentum goin'. Git folks interested." Liam replied casually. "We did a gig last night that lasted fer hours. Hell, th' after-party only let out a little while ago. Part'a the life, an' all."

In the present, Claire scoffed at the memory. About half of the meal was gone as she tore through it, wanting to be done soon. She had lingered in her memories for too long and the sun was getting too low for her comfort. Thinking back, she realized she had actually met Liam immediately after a full moon, and it was the real reason for their disheveled looks and the fact that Bev's usual tightly-buzzed undercut had grown out a full inch and a half.

It was the first, admittedly understandable, lie in a string of them that would last for just over three months, where Claire had thrown herself at the man in spite of all the warnings. Not warnings that they were all werewolves; rather, the warnings that the man was a womanizing deadbeat who seemed to have every intention of burning through everything Claire had, both emotionally and financially. But on that night, all she had known was that Liam seemed sweet and charming. He had spotted her in the room and sought her out to talk and she had been almost instantly smitten.

She understood now that he likely had smelled her interest like a beacon from across the room, the same way she had more than once in the occasional nightclub or bar. As the memory played out in her mind, that knowledge made it that much worse.

"Ye know where the Pegasus is, Claire?" He asked, leaning in and tilting his head as the server brought Claire her sandwich.

"Thank you." She nodded, smiling before turning back to Liam, as she brushed some hair out of her face. There was a nervous chuckle in her voice as she said, "Yeah. It's out by Busch Gardens, I think. Right?"

"Aye, tha's the one. " He said, glancing over his shoulder towards his table as he shifted topics again. "So, we were up all night partyin', but what 'bout you? Why'r ye up so early?"

"Oh, I have to go in to work for a few hours. The company I work for has a deadline for a presentation on Monday. Not a huge deal, though. And, y'know, I don't have to dress up or anything. So, that's a plus." Claire answered, noticing that the others were now making their way over to the table.

"Really? What'r ye gonna do, ya dumbarse twatwaffle?" Duncan said as he rounded the table and slid over next to Liam with a smug smirk, "Ask her t' design us a new fookin' logo? B'cause tha's fookin' smooth."

"Not even," Liam replied, rolling his eyes and whacking his younger brother in the arm before turning back to Claire with a grin that had seemed charming at the time, but lingered as a predatory thing in her memory. "I was fixin' t' see if we could expect t' see her there t'night."

Walking past with Quentin behind her, Beverly slapped Duncan on the arm and gestured to the young man to follow her. "We're gonna head to the room n' git cleaned off, Liam. Catch up inna bit?"

Even then, it was obvious to Claire that the brothers followed Beverly's lead, and Beverly deferred to Liam. It would be a few months before she learned that it was a pack hierarchy she still didn't quite understand. And one she had no desire to be a part of.

"Aye, Bev. I'll be along." Liam said with an approving nod, as the others went up to the counter to get their meals to go and leave. It was now obvious in her memory that Liam had wanted some alone time with her. There would be time enough later to fold his new find into his little pack, and Claire would eventually get to know the others a little better. But on that morning, Liam was interested in Claire's attention.

As the waitress brought him his steak and eggs, the two talked for the better part of an hour and a half before Claire thought to pull away and go to the office as she had planned for her Saturday. She couldn't remember if she had plans for that night, but she had quickly abandoned them to begin the slide into following Liam around. To becoming "his".

Finishing her meal in the present, Claire remembered with crystal clarity how charming he had seemed. How friendly and open. How interested in everything she said and did. How complementary. Back then, he and everything about him was intoxicating.

Even last night, seeing him again. Seeing him transformed for the first time since the night he attacked her a year ago, in spite of all of her pain and fear, he was still intoxicating. Sitting there in that restaurant, as she looked at the sun kissing the horizon, she gestured to the waitress for her check. She wasn't really running because of what happened with Shondra.

It wasn't even Liam she was running from. She was running from the fear that if she saw him again, she would run back to him. Part of her wanted that, in spite of what he had done, and she couldn't understand why, nor what that said about her.

Claire walked over to the connected service station to stock up on snacks, ensuring that the wolf would have plenty of food as the night went on, just in case. She grabbed bottled water and about 8 packs of beef jerky before the bell at the front of the store jangled and something familiar filled her increasingly sharp senses.

The change was only fifteen to twenty minutes away at the MOST, but likely even sooner as the sky's color dipped from orange to a softer purple. Turning with a start to pay and make her way back to the hotel, she almost expected to see Liam or Beverly.

Maybe one of the brothers. Instead, she saw a middle-aged woman and man at the door.

She had striking, long salt and pepper hair and looked like she was dressing up for Halloween as Stevie Nicks with a long, wispy black duster over a black blouse and flowing skirt, though Claire suspected this was the woman's everyday dress. The man at her side sported an equally peppered beard with short-cropped hair and a simple red flannel shirt and jeans.

Both were staring directly at her as hard as she was staring at them.

Claire had no idea who they were. They walked towards the coolers to shop, still looking at her. As she looked back, she understood what her senses were telling her.

They were werewolves.

Aside from Liam and his pack, she had never come across any other wolves. As such, she had been unprepared for the sensation as her senses sprung to life, electric things. The hair on the back of her neck stood on end and she felt what was like the tingling of an adrenaline spike. It wasn't a fear reaction; rather, one of excitement. The wolf could recognize its own.

The two didn't say anything out loud to each other, but Claire could see them silently communicating. The older woman with the hair to her knees simply ran a finger across the face of her companion, smiled softly, and tilted her head towards where Claire was standing, frozen like a deer in headlights.

The man looked over and cricked an eyebrow, shrugging nonchalantly as the cashier behind Claire broke her intense concentration. "Uh... miss? You... checkin' out?"

"Huh?" Claire fell out of her reverie, turning and plopping her items on the counter. "Yeah. Yeah. Sorry, thanks."

He quickly scanned her items and rang her out, though it felt like it was taking forever as the sun began to disappear. Handing her the bag with her purchases, he added, "Wow. Are those contacts? I have never seen, like, yellow eyes like that before."

SHIT... Claire thought, dipping her head and taking the bag.

"Yeah. Uh. Contacts. Halloween, right? Thanks."

Turning again at the door, she looked over at the couple, who was grabbing a pack of wine coolers from the back. The woman looked over at her with a concerned expression, now, and seemed like she was about to speak when Claire ran out of the store.

Looking around, the panic was starting to settle in. She had, at best, ten minutes until the change would simply happen no matter what. But the couple's scent was still strong in her nose and she knew hers was strong in theirs. She suddenly imagined half a dozen possible scenarios, most of which ended with them coming to her hotel room to talk to her. Maybe ask her to go running with them. Maybe they would attack her, though that seemed extremely unlikely. Regardless, she truly had no idea and wasn't prepared to learn. With the weight of Liam's promise to wait for her, and that she was still to be his, Claire couldn't think straight.

A massive part of her wanted to turn around, go back into the store, and talk with the only two other werewolves she had ever encountered. That pull was powerful as she stood there, debating. The temptation was huge, but temptation was what had gotten her into the headspace she had been living in all day.

Plus, there was fear. She didn't know them, and the werewolves she'd known thus far hadn't exactly engendered trust in others.

Grabbing her keys out of her purse and refusing to turn and even look at the store, she ran to her car and threw everything in the passenger seat. The room was paid for, but she hadn't unpacked yet.

Fuck it. She thought, turning the key and taking a breath. *Find a rest stop and just sleep there. Put a fucking sheet over you if you have to, or just use the adrenaline boost to drive straight through. Sure. That's smart. A fucking werewolf driving a car down the interstate. Perfectly normal.*

Making a decision she feared she would regret, she peeled out of the parking lot, abandoning the safe haven of the hotel, and took off towards the interstate, hoping nothing else would go wrong.

189

Chapter Twenty-Two
·))●((·

Behind the wheel of the tiny Nissan Cube, while Shondra snored lightly in the passenger seat, Mariska lamented just how much she disliked driving. She was, of course, perfectly good at it. Being over a century old meant that she had learned many skills over the years. However, much like when she had learned to disco dance, she didn't particularly enjoy exercising the ability.

Shondra had been awake and functioning for considerably longer than 24 hours and was in desperate need of a rest, though. Mariska was also tired, but as long as she had blood, the ethereal vampire could keep going far longer than an ordinary human. Hence, the well-packed cooler with a significant supply in the back of the car.

Laying at Shondra's feet on a pillow and blanket by the floorboards, the woman's little chocolate poodle was snoozing as deeply as his owner.

In truth, Mariska had a hard time explaining why she didn't like driving. It was something linked with her perception of the world as a vampire. Like Claire, her senses were enhanced, but relied on a connection to the world around her. Yes, she could smell, see, and hear better. But those were both buttressed and connected through an ability to see the inherent energy in things. Life forces and temperature. Auras and the flow of the planet's energy itself.

Most regular humans had simple auras. Basic colors that were only ever the one thing. Claire's was a greenish hue that turned as golden as her eyes when she transformed. The aura of werewolves, as she had observed, was reflected in their eyes. Bev's aura was a brilliant emerald when transformed. Liam's was a vivid, pale blue.

Sleeping there, Shondra's was a dull lavender. Little Clive at her feet was an off-reddish brown.

The Earth itself gave off veritable rainbows for her; light and color that told her so much about the world around her. The flow of energies could be seen, and also felt, through her skin. ALL of her senses worked in unison to align to that flow and being in a car cut her off from much of it. As such, it made the act of driving feel like it would for someone suddenly forced to drive with frost on the window and horse blinders on.

It was a challenge, but one she could manage, as Shondra really needed to sleep, and they couldn't afford to lose any time. Having pushed through to dawn, the sky was now a bright blue again and the sun was getting higher in the sky. Thankfully, for her comfort, Shondra's car windows were UV tinted like Claire's and the mercurial vampire had her sunglasses on.

Stopping for little more than fueling up the car, they were making good time, though they were still hours behind Claire.

With any luck, Mariska thought, Claire would have to have stopped for the night, as it had been a full moon and she couldn't imagine her traveling while transformed, though physically there would be no real reason she couldn't. In truth, the visual of Claire driving along, fully transformed, gave her a chuckle. "Heh."

The vehicle's other occupant woke and groggily chuckled along. "Heh. Heh heh. W… wha'r… what are we laughin' 'bout?"

"Sorry to wake you, it was nothing." Mariska said softly with a smirk.

Lifting her neck up off of the little travel pillow it had been resting on, Shondra stretched it out as best she could, generating a few popping sounds. "Wha' time is it? How long was I asleep?"

"Well, hopefully, you feel a good bit more rested. You've been out for about five and a half hours. It is… just past nine forty-five." Mariska replied, glancing at the clock on the radio and reducing the volume of the music she was playing to help her pass the time. It was a selection of Tchaikovsky music streaming from her own cell phone; old fashioned, even for her, but playing 70's punk rock wouldn't have aided in Shondra's attempted rest.

"Yeah, yeah," Shondra replied, a bit more awake now and more herself again. "I feel better. I know you don't really like driving, but thanks again for taking over for a while."

At her feet, the little brown pup stirred and stretched as well as Shondra looked down and smiled. "Oh, good morning, Clive. Did you sleep well too, huh, little one? Huh? Yes, you did. You've been such a good boy, yes you have."

Rolling her eyes at the display, Mariska chuckled again. "Heh... Well, I'm sure you two need to take care of some business. We can pull over to do that and grab you something to eat?"

"That sounds like a plan. Dang, I still can't believe you don't have to... y'know... that you don't... um..." Shondra said, hemming and hawing around the specifics as Mariska interjected.

"Vampires neither shit nor piss. And yes, it is perhaps an even greater perk than the super strength. One of my favorites, really." She said, with no small bit of pride in the statement, as if it were a personal accomplishment.

"Ha. That's awesome!" Shondra smiled at the answer as her eyes went wide for a second. "Okay... um... actually, that kinda brings up a question if you... um... don't mind?"

"Shondra, I have already given you carte blanche to ask questions. Go ahead, I honestly do not mind. If I did, I'd have said so." Mariska shook her head at her traveling companion.

"Okay... so. I know about the Jedi mind trick and you've... like... totally got super strength. What other vampire powers or weaknesses do you have?"

"Should I be worried about this line of questioning? Planning to stake me while I sleep, eh?" Mariska leaned over with a grin and a wink.

"What? No! Don't be silly." Shondra replied with utter sincerity as she kept going. "Sooo. Can you fly?"

"I wish. I would not be in this car for the trip, I can assure you. I'd have just carried you and we'd be there already."

"Ohhhh no. I... yeah, no. I do not do heights. Heh. Uh... okay. Can you turn into... like, mist?"

"I don't even fart, so no. No mist."

"Hmmm. I can literally see you casting a reflection in the

rearview right now, so that's a no. Ummm… what about the wooden stake through the heart thing?"

"Technically, yes. My heart DOES beat to circulate the blood I drink, and without that, I could be killed. But it would have to be severely damaged beyond just a single puncture. I heal… very fast. Plus… a wooden stake would only ever be a factor during the day. At night… you'd hurt your hand trying to push one through my skin."

"Ah, right. Okay. So, back to the blood from before. You don't have to eat regular food and you get everything you need from blood. So… does blood just kind of… keep you at this basic physical level? Like… you don't gain or lose weight, or anything?" Shondra asked, genuinely curious.

"I could fit into my outfits from the so-called roaring twenties if I still had them," Mariska replied with another proud nod.

"So… it's like your body just stays at this… like... setting? That's… can you cut your hair?"

"I can, but when I feed, it will essentially grow back to what it looked like the night I was made. No new injuries. No scars. Nothing."

"Soooo, in the cooler, there's, like, deer blood. And… can you drink any animal's blood and get the same effect?

"As far as animals go, Pig is the closest to human in both taste and impact. I like deer. Cow… meh, it's… thicker and has more of an aftertaste. But the higher up the… evolutionary ladder… the more… functional it is, for lack of a better term."

"So, like… people blood is *better* for you?" Shondra asked, still more curious than anything as she discussed a point that Mariska would have assumed would frighten her.

"It is. However, it's a pain in the proverbial ass to get, so… I think of it like a VERY expensive meal I can't have all that often. Medical supplies have anticoagulants and that makes it taste positively foul. So… a long time ago, I found out about these people who… fancy themselves as vampires. Have clubs all over, and the like, and dress up like Lestat."

"Heh... Yeah, yeah. I've read about that before."

"Well... I have to admit... every now and then, I'll go, and make a MASSIVE, utterly shameless show of it. I'll reveal my fangs, and they climb over themselves to let me have a taste. The club makes money, they have the night of their lives, I get a fantastic meal, and all I have to really worry about is having to listen to a bunch of Anne Rice fanboys try to sound philosophical while they lisp around their fake fangs. Bless them."

Both women laughed at the scene Mariska had painted. The blonde vampire was really enjoying someone who was legitimately curious about her and not afraid.

"Okay... on that note, then. Do... do movie vampires get on your nerves, ever? Are there any who you like, or that get it right?" Shondra asked, jumping back into the questions.

"Well... pretentious or not, I DID actually like 'Interview With the Vampire'. Honestly, most versions of Dracula irritate me, aside from Gary Oldman. Admittedly, that might have more to do with it just being Gary Oldman, however." Mariska smirked and waggled her brows suggestively, which earned a chuckle from her attentive passenger. "Honestly, I don't mind most of the movies. I rarely take such things personally."

"Heh. Cool. That's totally... oh. Okay, so... you're a vampire, and Claire's a werewolf? So... uh... are there other kinds of things out there like that? Like other... y'know... stuff?"

"Monsters? It's a fair enough word in the pop culture parlance, though do not say it around Claire, for obvious reasons. Mythical creatures and the like. Yes, I'm likely not the best font of knowledge of such things, but fire away."

"Okay... there are wereWOLVES? What about... other hybrid creatures? Werecats? Werebears? OOOH... merpeople?"

"Heh... I have never met a werebear, but I've heard of some out west. The same in regards to werecats in South America. I have heard... and I repeat... HEARD... that there are also people who can turn into birds, but that and the bears are admittedly secondhand stories. As for merpeople, not a clue. As it turns out, our kind is as superstitious and vague as your own. Heh."

"Mummies?"

"I met a vampire in Greece in the… the fifties. She swore up and down that mummies were real, and warned me away from ever crossing into Egypt. She also had a girlfriend there who I think she didn't want me knowing about. Sooooo… take that, too, with a grain of proverbial salt."

"Ha! Oh my goodness, that sounds… Wow, you must have been to so many places. That's totally awesome. Okay… so. I mean… Oooh. What about ghosts? Are… are ghosts real?"

"Ahhh, yes. Those I have seen a few of over the years. They aren't really… everywhere. And sometimes I suspect that even when I see them, it is because they are allowing it. None have ever spoken to me, however. I will admit, between you, me, and Clive there, they actually unnerve me as much as anyone else."

"Oooooh." Shondra said, her jaw open wide with surprise. It was clear to Mariska that the woman was utterly fascinated with the details and she wished she actually had more to give on some of the topics. As odd as it seemed, she was enjoying the conversation.

However, it was a conversation cut short as little Clive began whining and scratching to be picked up.

Bending over and grunting past her prodigious paunch to pick up her pernicious pooch, Shondra asked, "Awww, here you go, Clivey. Good boy. Yeah, you gotta go tinkle? Mommy does, too. Especially after bending over like that."

She leaned towards Mariska with raised eyebrows and pursed lips. "If… um… you just see a regular rest stop, or whatever, we can pull over there first and then just get gas and food at the next exit. But… uh… yeah. That bend was not my best move. Thanks."

"Ahhh, understood," Mariska replied, as she scanned the road ahead for rest stops.

Looking out the window, the highway was winding, and the rolling hills, still dappled with autumn leaves, were a far sight different from the last view Shondra had before the sun had gone down the night before. "Where are we? How far did we get overnight?"

"God help us, we are firmly in West Virginia. Sad, because… West Virginia… but positive, as Pennsylvania isn't much further." Mariska answered with a sarcastic smirk. "Should be there by this afternoon at this pace."

Looking ahead, Mariska saw a sign for a rest stop in just a few miles and with a destination in mind, they quickly made their way there.

Pulling off the highway, theirs was the only car in the little rest area, tucked back off the road and surrounded by treelines that went back into the hillsides. There was little more to the area than about a dozen parking spots, some trash cans, a dog-walk area, and the two little concrete buildings where the toilets would hopefully be.

Seeing a spot near a mostly leafless tree, Mariska took the opportunity for whatever shade she could muster and parked. "Well, here we are. Might I suggest you attend to your dirty, sinful business. I'll walk Clive and make sure he's squeezed dry before we go, and then I can answer any further questions you may have."

"Don't squeeze my dog," Shondra said with a look of clearly fake shock on her face. "Okay. I'll try and be quick, but I might be fully loaded in here. Are you sure you're okay taking Clive? It's pretty sunny."

"It's really not that big of a deal, Shondra. Honestly. It's fairly chilly out and the sun isn't quite to the middle of the sky just yet. As I said, it doesn't light me on fire, or anything. It simply brings my abilities down to what are essentially human levels, and I doubt I'll need my full strength to wrangle so tiny a dog." Mariska said with a grin as she lifted up her hood and grinned. "I think I can manage."

"Well, okay. Here, hold my poodle. I'll be right back. Thanks."

Shondra said, grabbing her purse and handing the fidgety dog to Mariska, who held him up, away from her body. As Shondra headed quickly to the concrete slab marked 'Ladies', waddling as she held her knees together, Mariska hooked Clive to his leash and led him to the patch of dry, yellow grass nearest the car.

Standing there with a raised eyebrow, the thin vampire stretched. "How on Earth can a dog so little pee so much? Seriously, I am almost impressed, Clive."

The tiny dog looked up at her while continuing to empty himself. As he did, Mariska noticed another vehicle approaching and turning towards the rest area. Something about it made her hair stand on edge.

While it was still a good hundred yards away, it seemed to be traveling fairly fast. And with the light of day significantly impacting the sensitivity of her senses, it wasn't until it was almost on top of her that she realized why it looked familiar.

Screeching up onto the curb, the dingy old van came to a stop on the grass between Shondra's car and the restrooms. The vehicle she now recognized as the property of Liam Docherty and his band had barely missed Mariska as she scooped up Clive in one hand and made a run for the car.

As quickly as she could, she plopped Clive onto the passenger seat and shut him in for safety, his barking echoing through the glass. Looking over, Mariska snarled in contempt. "Liam."

"No' exactly." came the voice of Liam's younger brother, Duncan, getting out of the driver's seat. Mariska could hear the other doors opening as Quentin walked around the back.

The two brothers who she, at best, only tolerated before, started towards her, transforming right there in the parking lot. "But 'r big brother DOES say 'Hullo'.

Inside the small concrete rest-stop bathroom, there was no electricity, and the stalls were all equally filthy. Thankfully, Shondra's purse had a significant surplus of wet wipes and even a spare roll of toilet paper she had thought to grab at a prior fueling stop. As such, she had been able to clean up enough to take care of business by the time she heard the screeching tires of the van. "What in..."

She did her level best to finish up as quickly as she could, wiping with the wet wipes and pulling her pants up in a hurry. As she did, she heard the door open and close.

Whoever had just walked in didn't speak, and that silence sent a shot of fear down the woman's spine. Hesitantly, she whispered, "M... Mariska?"

"Nope." came a woman's voice with a Scottish lilt, unfamiliar to Shondra. Her heart skipped a beat.

From inside her tight stall, the last of the three in the rear corner, Shondra could hear heavy footfalls walking slowly towards her as she tried to line up her eyes with the crack in the door. "W... W... What do... what do you w... want? I... I'm... I'm not here alone!"

"Oh, ye are *now,* sweetness." came the reply, the voice getting lower and more gravelly as the footsteps began to include the tapping sound of nails on concrete. Shondra jumped, clapping her hands over her mouth to stifle a scream as she heard a screeching sound like claws on metal dragging across the doors towards her.

"Our little friend is right occupied at th' moment. So, f'r right now, it's jus' you..." The now-raspy, lilting voice said as she pulled the door open, popping the flimsy lock right out of the frame. "...N' me."

Outside in the parking lot, Mariska heard a bloodcurdling scream from the restroom and her anger boiled over. "SHONDRA! I'm coming!" She shouted, running forward in an attempt to sidestep the brothers. But in the daylight, she wasn't fast enough to avoid the wolfed-out Quentin, who grabbed her by the back of her hoodie and pulled hard.

Yanking her off her feet in mid-run, he tossed her hard into the side of Shondra's car, where she landed with a thud that dented the door. Her sunglasses had fallen off and the mid-morning sun was almost blinding to her, but she could still see the brothers smirking as they approached. She shook her head.

"Aw, no' so tough in th' day, are ye, bitch?" Quentin said smugly. "It's jus' us, girly. We saw t' tha'. Downed a tree in th' road a good mile back, so nobody t' interrupt us."

Inside the restroom, Beverly McLeish stood in the open door of the stall. Her t-shirt and jeans strained against her expanding form as she finished her transformation. Bright green eyes pierced into Shondra as she brushed a lock of red curls out of her face.

Backed up into the corner, Shondra was shuddering with fright, her eyes fixed on the creature growling before her, baring her sharp teeth and black claws.

Fear mixed with adrenaline as Shondra reached into her purse and fumbled through the contents. With a loud snarl, Beverly slammed a hand against the concrete wall next to Shondra's head, cracking it hard. "Listen up, ye little nugget. Ye an' me need t' tal…"

But before she finished talking, Shondra pulled a can of mace out of her purse and emptied it directly into Beverly's snarling face. The chemicals struck hard and deep, and the red-furred wolf reared back, screaming and grabbing her face.

The gap between the werewolf and the opening of the door was narrow, but with no other option and the knowledge that Mariska was weakened in the daylight, she let out a high-pitched scream to psych herself up and rammed herself into Bev as hard as she could.

Both women careened into the cold stone of the far wall and Beverly rubbed wildly at her eyes. Trying to get up and run, Shondra stumbled, fell over onto the hard ground, and smacked the back of her head against the door of the next stall. "AAAGH!!!"

"RAAAAGGGHHHH, Ye FOOKIN' little SHITE!!!" Beverly screamed and slammed one hand into the wall behind her. "I said t' FOOKIN' LISTEN!!!!"

Reaching her hand forward, with an open palm, she gritted reluctantly through pursed lips, "*Please!*"

Outside, Quentin stepped over casually and grabbed Mariska as she tried scrambling around to the rear door of the car. Her hand just an inch away from the handle, the much larger werewolf pulled her away. "GYYAH!!! Let... let go of me, you *govnosos!*"

"Where'ye goin'? Tryin' t' git t' yuir precious litt'e blood supply?" He bellowed, throwing her back down to the ground with a hard slam. Her shoulder let out a loud crack.

She screamed. It had been a long time since she had broken anything in her usually-powerful frame. The pain was as blinding as the sun itself as Quentin proceeded to strike the weakened vampire repeatedly with a series of hard kicks that tossed her back into the side of the little car. Under that weakening light, the impacts were causing legitimate damage as her pale skin began to show bruising and a trickle of blood ran from her lips.

He picked Mariska up off the ground by her neck. The curly-haired, fully-furred werewolf bared his teeth and snarled at the vampire as he pulled her close to his face. "Ye always thought ye were better'n us, but yuir no so tough now, are ye?"

"Not as thirsty as she is, right now, I'm thinkin'?" Bev's voice said as the ginger wolf walked around the front of the van, an arm on Shondra's shoulder and the other behind her back.

Turning towards her, the darker-furred Duncan hissed, "What're ye doin' out here, Bev? Liam tol' ye t' take care'a th' little lamb?

"Something like that," Bev said as she pulled out the can of Shondra's mace and fired it directly into the other werewolf's face. Mariska took advantage of the distraction to move. With all of her strength, she pulled herself close to the source of her pain, her fangs bared. Quentin's eyes rolled back as the tiny vampire bore down on his neck.

Putting her hands over her mouth, Shondra's eyes went wide as she exclaimed, "Oh my... FUCK!"

A few seconds later, Mariska released her hold on the werewolf, who had gone limp. He was easily two full feet taller than she was, but she now held him up effortlessly with one hand. Looking over to Shondra, blood dripping from her lips to her neck, she smirked. "Don't worry, I didn't quite DRAIN him, and wolves heal fast. He'll be fine. As for me..."

"There is one kind... one kind of blood you didn't ask about, Shondra. Werewolf blood." Mariska said angrily through gritted, red-smeared fangs. With a popping sound, her broken collarbone reset itself, and the purple bruising on her pale cheeks healed right in front of Shondra's amazed eyes.

Dropping Quentin, she stepped over to Duncan, who was still rubbing his eyes in pain, and reared back to punch the enormous wolf hard enough in the chest to send him careening into the side of the van with a massive thud, leaving an equally massive crater in the rusted side panel. Mariska wiped her face and looked at Bev.

"You're not going to make me hurt you, are you, Beverly?" The angry vampire's eyes flared red as she scowled.

"Agggh, fook no, love," Beverly said, rubbing her eyes as she handed the can back to the very confused Shondra. "I know how hopped up ye git on wolf blood. Peace! Tell 'er, will ya'?"

"It's okay, Mariska. I'm... I'm okay. She... she scared the.... the daylights out of me... but it was... it was for *their* benefit. She didn't know if they would be listening in. She... She wants to help." Shondra looked around, relieved to hear Quentin groan as Beverly leaned over and dragged the two to the back of the van. As she did, his fur fell off and he turned back to normal.

Tossing him in the back with a loud clang, she bit her bottom lip. "Ach... my fookin' drums. Dammit all t' hell. Git in there, ya' little fook. C'mere, you."

With Quentin in the back, still unconscious, Bev reached over and dragged Duncan to the door. He was wriggling and starting to stir, prompting her to bash his head into the rear bumper. "Take a fookin' nap, ya' right sheep fucker."

Slamming the doors shut, the ginger wolf-woman proceeded to

circle the vehicle and, one by one, shredded the van's tires with her claws as Mariska and Shondra watched. "So, you're here to help? Do tell." Mariska hissed.

Raising a finger and wiping her face off with the other hand, Beverly quickly shed her own fur and reverted to normal. It was a quick process that Shondra was still shocked to watch. "Liam… he sent us after ye, figuring ye were following Claire. He wanted us t' stop ye. Slow ye down, r' worse."

"And you agreed? Why the change of heart, Bev? Because I can tell you, I am seriously tired of you using me like this." Mariska said, scowling. Her eyes were still quite red and she was clearly very angry, and ready for a fight.

"Look, I heard wha' he told ye, an' he wasnae lying. We knocked a tree down across the road about a mile back f'r privacy, but tha' won't last f'rever. Can… can we git outta here, first? An' if ye don't like what I have'ta say in the CAR, ye can drain my ass an' leave me on the side'a the fookin' road?" Bev protested.

"She… probably has a point. We… we should probably go. Right, Mariska?" Shondra said, nervously, severely out of her league.

Sighing, Mariska pursed her lips as her fangs receded again. "Fine. Passenger seat, so I can sit right behind you. I can't believe you'd do this, Beverly. For HIM?"

"C'mon, I can explain on the way. Let's git outta here." Bev said sheepishly, clearly shamed by Mariska's words.

As they all walked back to the car, Bev got in first, followed by Shondra and Mariska. The nervous young woman, now back in the driver's seat, raised an eyebrow. "So… werewolf blood gives you back all your strength? Even under the sun?"

"Indeed," Mariska said with a somewhat disturbing grin. "It's… an intense experience. Very potent. EXTREMELY delicious."

"I'm sittin' right fookin' here, ye know?" Bev said, glancing over her shoulder towards her part-time lover, who had no love in her eyes at the moment.

"Oh, I know," was all Mariska said as they pulled back onto the road.

Chapter Twenty-Three

-)᛭)☾꒰꒱((

Oh my fucking god, you look like shit. Claire thought to herself, looking in the rearview of her car as she sat at a red light on the edge of the small, Pennsylvania town she had grown up in. Her physical condition was not too unexpected. After all, she had spent the last two nights transformed, and thanks to a mild panic attack as the sun set last night, she had only ended up getting a few hours of sleep.

A few hours sitting in her car with a jacket over her head in a rest stop in the middle of Virginia did not a restful night's sleep make. And as she paused at the red light to consider her ever-deepening predicament, all she could see was every misstep she had made over the last two days, compounding as she went.

Her hair looked like a rat's nest, having grown out a good four inches. Her eyes were sunken and bloodshot. Her entire demeanor just looked like hell, more than anyone's would after driving for approximately 24 hours, straight through from Florida to Pennsylvania.

She thought to herself that she should have stayed at that hotel. Before that, she should have talked with the couple in the convenience store who she could sense were werewolves. Aside from the night of her turning and the callous recitation of basic information from Beverly McLeish the day after, she had never seen another of her kind, much less two. Turning her back on information that could have been revelatory was boundlessly stupid. But even before that, she should have gone to Mariska's the night before Halloween, when she freaked out and ran from Shondra's house. In her heart, she knew that Mariska would have forgiven… whatever it was she was angry about.

Then there was Shondra. A thousand what-if scenarios ran through her head, some as simple as the idea that she should have not run after changing in front of her; others that she should have turned to her long-time friend right after her attack. An infinity of bad choices, each compounding the next, leading her back to the tiny little town where she grew up, fleeing from her ex to the presumed emotional safety of the family she had been avoiding. Giving up her entire life out of little more than fear.

As the light changed, Claire drove slowly through the Norman Rockwell postcard town she had worked so hard to get away from when she was younger. It looked the same. The main avenue of Barley, Pennsylvania flanked both sides of her car. Vintage streetlights and antique storefronts looked like something out of a period film from the fifties, except largely abandoned in the post-oil era in which they now existed. The economic depression of the region was half of what she had been so desperate to escape from, as it was stifling for a young woman to feel trapped in such a place.

Which was only made more ironic by the idea that she was returning to this town, desperate to escape her mistakes, and Liam.

The Scottish werewolf had told her he would wait for her, but he had made his intentions clear enough. After a year, he still felt that she was his to claim, that she was meant to be with him- and a part of her still wanted that, in spite of what he had done. More than anything else, that terrified her. Maybe she could recover what had been damaged with Shondra and Mariska, but the idea that on ANY level she would want to be with the monster who made her a werewolf shook her to the core.

She pulled up to the small, local eatery on the corner of the main drag through town. Parking, she sat there for a moment to collect her thoughts. The restaurant, a little seafood place called 'Gribbald's Wharf', was named for her grandfather, who opened the place up in the mid-fifties.

Growing up, her parents had taken it over, and it had been a regular hang out for her after school. Their mother had retained ownership after the divorce, but after she and her husband had died in a car accident, it became her sister Ellie's. It had been assumed for most of her life that the sisters Gribbald would run the establishment together.

Claire's lack of interest in that concept was one of the first major stress points between her and her family. She noted that the long sign over the door had been updated and no longer featured the logo she had created in high school when she had begun to show an interest in graphic design. Claire frowned and wondered if the mural of a New England fishing town she had painted in her senior year was still along the rear wall, or if Ellie had discarded that as well.

Okay, Claire thought. *This is it. Just go in and take your frickin' medicine. Talk to her and… what? What are you expecting to happen? You can't hide forever.*

Pulling her frizzy hair out and fixing her ponytail into something she hoped would look semi-intentional, Claire sighed. *Whatever. You aren't hiding. You're… trying to reconnect with the family… you can barely stand because you decided that salting the earth was a functional way to manage your life. Ugh. Just go in, already.*

Working up the nerve, she grabbed her purse and got out of the car with a pained stretch. The drive had been long, and a crick in her neck had persisted most of the day, outlasting her body's robust ability to bounce back. That, however, was nothing compared to the HAIR. "Oh, for fuck's sake? Really?! I thought I got all of this shit?"

Muttering to herself on the sidewalk outside the restaurant, Claire began brushing off the stray hair she found still clinging to most of her otherwise fresh wardrobe. Overnight, she had found a rest stop off the side of the road, where she changed when the moon had finally risen. For a couple of hours, she had even tried driving that way. It worked out that it was dark, her windows were tinted, and her transformation never actually impaired her ability to function or be herself, despite her renewed fears.

After a while, however, the adrenaline boost of transformation wore off, adjusting to accommodate her tail became distracting, and a growing concern that some minor traffic infraction would get her pulled over led Claire to find a secluded rest stop to park in for the night.

She parked as far from the brightly lit part of the lot as she could, and did her best to get as much sleep as was possible under the extremely unusual circumstances, pulling her jacket up over her head. When dawn came, Claire had woken up and transformed back to her human form in the car, shedding all of the freshly grown fur all over herself.

Running to the little bathroom of the rest stop, she had changed her clothes and did her best to clean out her car, but without a vacuum, there was simply too much to get it all. Looking back in the car, now, it looked like she was the owner of multiple shaggy dogs that all, coincidentally, had the exact same hair color as she did. It was a pain in the ass. But none of that was going through her mind as she finished cleaning herself off. Her mind was, instead, still lingering on the night she had just experienced.

It was unusual in a number of ways, not the least of which being that it was the first time she had ever fallen asleep as the wolf. It was something she had actively avoided, afraid that falling asleep might prompt her to somehow lose control of herself. So, while most days after a full moon had ended up with calling in sick to work due to needing sleep after staying awake the entire night before, this had been different.

Claire had been awake and functioning for almost two days straight at that point, and couldn't do it anymore. She had to try and sleep and, with little resistance from her exhausted body, it came easily to her. The dreams were an unexpected side effect.

Never in her life had they been as vivid or real. In the past year, she had been through more than her share of 'werewolf'-themed dreams, and occasionally, nightmares, but last night had been unlike anything she had experienced before. Last night was the first time she had been the wolf completely in her dreams.

She had found herself transformed; not into the form somewhere between the woman and wolf that she was used to, but into a genuine wolf. On all fours, there was nothing left of a human woman's form that she could see or feel. She never spoke or even tried, feeling no need to reach towards that part of herself.

In that moment, she felt whole and content, finding herself in a place she had never been before that somehow felt like home. Stretching before her was an expanse of endless, rolling hills of green glistening in the moonlight. The woods were thick and lush, reminding her of the places she had grown up around here in Pennsylvania, but not quite the same.

As she ran through those dream hills in her mind, she was not alone.

Surrounding her were others. She had not bothered counting or even paying them much special attention, as to her, they simply WERE. The other wolves were there for her, and she was there for them. It was as if she had known them her entire life, as familiar as any family. Together, they all ran for what felt like far longer than she had ever run before.

Standing there on the street corner in the midday sun of autumnal Pennsylvania, she could still feel the cold air of that dreamscape, the wet grass in what had been her paws. She could still see the eyes of the wolves she had run with.

What snapped her back to reality, though, was that she could still smell Liam. It had been over a day since he had tracked her and confronted her in that park in Tampa, but his scent lingered. For the last night, she couldn't get that aroma to leave her, like it was a thing alive, latching onto her. Like the man himself, it didn't seem to want to let her go, and it was driving Claire nuts as she finally worked up the strength to step inside the restaurant she had grown up in.

It was half-filled with faces she didn't recognize as she looked around. The place itself was largely the same. The old mural she had spent two months over the summer painting was there, but faded and chipped along the edges. The booths were not a dark blue as she remembered them, but a maroon color. The food smelled both familiar and completely new to her. The nose she had last smelled it with was a far cry from the equipment she now bore. The aroma literally made her mouth water as she licked her lips.

It was a strange mix of uncomfortable emotions as she stood there, hungry. The last time she had stood in the place had also been the last time she had spoken to her mother in any real capacity, and the memory still stung.

The bags of beef jerky she had secured were long gone, eaten overnight, and she was famished as she stood by the counter, waiting. There were two waitresses who she didn't know walking around in t-shirts with the new logo that she didn't like. They looked impossibly young.

"I'll be right with you, Ma'am. Is it just you?" The younger of the two servers asked, walking up. She was a short, chubby girl with straw-blonde hair and freckles on a round, smiling face.

"Uh… maybe two. It depends. Is Ellie... Draughter here?" Claire asked, taking a second to remember her older sister's husband's name.

"She's in the back, yeah. Is there something I can…" The young woman said, before being cut off by the voice from the kitchen as Ellie leaned through the window, looking genuinely happy.

"Claire!? I can't believe you made such good TIME! What did you do, drive straight through?" Ellie said, with a judgmental expression of cricked brows and a half-smile Claire was used to seeing. "Just seat her in booth 3, LeeAnne. I'll be right out."

"Okay, if you'll just follow me." The young server smiled, leading Claire to the back booth that was both the same and different from her memories. She remembered sitting here as a little girl, playing with toy cars under the table or dolls along the booth seat. She remembered doing homework or sketching the other people here when she was in high school. She remembered bringing the only person she ever tried dating while she still lived here, Marty Kline, to the restaurant for dinner after a Saturday matinee movie, only for him to spend half the time talking about trying to win his ex-girlfriend back.

The memories were all fresh, but the details were different. The table was new and the booths refinished. Ellie had clearly done a lot of renovating since Claire had visited nearly two years ago.

"There she is! Wow, look at you." Ellie said, emerging from the back in a black blouse and dress slacks. In truth, she had always been more interested in the business of the restaurant than she had ever been in the food, and it showed in how she carried herself. Holding her arms out, Ellie walked over, clearly expecting a hug, which Claire begrudgingly got up from the booth to provide.

As soon as her sister was in her arms, Claire found herself gripping the generally irritating woman more tightly than she had expected; tight enough to squeeze some of the air out of her older sister. Even in that moment, Claire's mind was still haunted by the smell of Liam lingering in her memory. Pulling back, Claire was unexpectedly emotional.

Ellie was a solid five inches shorter than her 'little' sister, though four years older. With hair a slightly darker brown, Ellie had hers cut into a much shorter, more professional cut that was swept off to the side, and she wore a pair of purple-framed glasses. She was a good deal leaner than Claire, a factor she rarely let slip by whenever they met.

"Look at you! I'm guessing you are still in that trap of eating out all the time instead of cooking at home? You look so worn out, Claire." Ellie said, that familiar judgmental tone settling in quickly as they sat down.

"Thanks. You look like shit too, El," Claire replied, more than a little sarcastically.

"CLAIRE!" came the instant and seemingly shocked reply. "Now, c'mon. I didn't mean it like that. You've been driving all day and night. It shows, is all I meant."

"Sorry," Claire acquiesced, even though she didn't believe her sister. She was simply too tired to argue the point. Besides, she was there for some kind of emotional support, and it would be counterproductive to piss on it right out of the gate. "You're right. I did drive pretty much straight through. But I hate stopping if I don't have to, y'know?"

The reply was only partially a lie, as the woman was notorious for pushing herself with deadlines and the like. "Soooo, is the food here still good, at least? You didn't screw with any of the recipes or shit, did you?"

Raising an eyebrow with a half-lidded pout, Ellie scoffed before going into something of a presentation. "Not near as much as I would have liked to. The prevailing opinion when it comes to little, local places like this is that you don't mess with established recipes and favorites. I watched a really good TED talk on menu development, though, that gave me ideas for rotating seasonal dishes as a way of expanding the menu over time to sneak in new stuff."

"Wait…" Ellie interjected, tilting her head. "Waaassss that just your way of saying that you're hungry?"

"It was *A* way of saying that. Y'know. On the road eating crap all night. I could eat." Claire smirked as she nodded. "Please tell me you kept the old surf and turf special?"

"Steak AND fish? We're going to have a big dinner later, Claire. Do you really want to fill up before then?" Ellie asked with a leading, almost maternal tone that Claire attempted to ignore.

"Trust me, I can eat two big meals back to back, not a problem," Claire replied with a mock-dismissive tone, making a hand-brushing gesture. Her sister had yet to bear witness to Claire's significantly increased appetite. That said, it was an appetite Claire knew better than to try and resist under the best of circumstances.

"If you say so, but Carlton is making a pork roast at home. Potatoes and veggies on the slow cooker. I don't want you to ruin your…" Ellie continued to protest before finally giving up, shooting Claire a sharply raised brow.

"Right. Whatever. I forget how stubborn you are." Ellie scoffed, rolling her eyes and choosing her next words at random, yet somehow hitting Claire right between the eyes. "Like a dog with a bone, really."

Calling the waitress back over, Ellie placed the order, including coffee for both women before they continued talking. "So... what's going on, Claire? I know this can't just be about me asking you to come home for Christmas? This isn't going to take that off the table, is it?"

"I don't know. I... figure I'll... still be free by then." Claire shrugged, having no expectations of a life to return to, much less a job, considering that she had not called or messaged work at all. "What? Can't I just want to visit my sister and her family?"

"Anyone ELSE, and the answer would be YES, Claire. YOU, and it makes me worried. You've gone out of your way to separate yourself from me... from us... so much over the last few years. Even more so since the funeral, that I doubted I'd ever see you again without heading to Florida myself." Ellie leaned on her tented fingers, her tone much more serious. Claire felt anger begin to flare up.

"I went out of my way to separate myself? Oh, did I do that all on my own? Really?" Claire retorted with venom in her voice. "Because I distinctly remember you siding with Mom right over there in calling me selfish for... forsaking the family business. You remember that, right? When she wrote me off as a lost cause and stopped talking to me?"

"Claire, it wasn't anything nearly that dramatic. Mom didn't agree with you running off to become an artist, and just because I didn't disagree doesn't make us enemies." Ellie sighed her response, largely ignoring Claire's tone. "I mean... I know you're obviously dealing with a lot, but you know, you CAN share some of that with me. I am the big sister, after all."

There was a long pause as Claire realized that she had to have SOMETHING to say to her sister and that in spite of the long drive, she was woefully unprepared. "Yeah... so... maybe. Yeah. A lot of stuff back home is... kind of..."

Taking a sip of her coffee, Claire fidgeted with the mug as she continued. "Falling apart. Shondra and I... we don't talk anymore. Work is... everything is difficult. And... I'm starting to seriously reconsider a lot of my life's choices."

"I guess I needed something resembling parental advice. Some... outside perspective." Claire finished.

Pursing her lips, it was clear that Ellie had a LOT to say and was restraining herself, as she collected her thoughts before replying with a sigh. "Wellllll... this is where I don't automatically default to 'I told you so'..."

"Which is a way of obviously saying it, just an FYI," Claire sarcastically interjected.

"BUT..." Ellie reclaimed the conversational momentum and continued, ignoring Claire's barb. "You have a lot going on, obviously. Big decisions and life-changing stuff to consider, and there's nothing wrong with needing to get help with it all. What's going on with... um?"

"Shondra!" Claire snapped, irritated by the flub of the name, which showed that Ellie had not paid any attention to her life for the past decade, really. She was beginning to realize that coming here might have been a massive mistake. It was a realization that increased her feeling of hopelessness, which she tried to push past. "C'mon, Ellie. She was my roommate all through school and my best friend ever since. I've told you about her a thousand times. You MET her when you visited, back before Grant was born."

The only reply was an eye roll and a perfunctory "Sorry."

"Yeah... anyway. I... It's hard to say, really." Which was the absolute truth, as Claire had no intentions of revealing her secret to her sister or family in any way. "But... it's like I... I lost track of who I am. Who I want to be, if that makes sense. And in the process, I seem to just be pushing everything away."

"And yeah, you don't have to frickin' tell me I've done that here, El. I know. I get it." Claire interjected the answer to the assumed comment before her sister could speak. That didn't stop the woman from following up with her own thoughts.

"You've been pushing everything away for years now, Claire. I mean, this isn't anything new, really. I have never been shy about letting you know what I thought about your moving away like you did, and I still think you made a mistake. But you seem to have built something for yourself down there that you enjoy. So, maybe that's why you're pushing it away?" Ellie commented, with considerably more penetrating insight than Claire was expecting.

"If there's something down there that makes you happy... even if you aren't ready to talk to me about it... then you... should probably try to make it work, I would think." she continued, much to Claire's ongoing surprise, before the elder sister reverted to form. "Not that I thought you running off to become an artist was a smart decision, when you had a solid foundation here to build from, but you've always been headstrong, Claire. You've always just... done whatever you wanted, whenever you wanted to."

"And the fact that I still have zero interest in helping you run a restaurant doesn't mean anything? I'm good at what I do, and I like it, Ellie." Claire leaned back just as the waitress brought out her rather significant lunch.

"Well, you certainly seem to have more than zero interest in the food. We don't even normally serve this for lunch. Do you eat like this all the time?" She commented, that same judgmental tone strong as she all but *tsk-tsked* her chunkier sister.

Cutting off a particularly large piece of the bloody steak, Claire shoved it in her mouth and began chewing in an exaggerated fashion. "Constantly." She muttered through a full mouth. "Which I can afford to do with my mad, phat artist money."

"You're impossible, Claire." Ellie groaned, shaking her head. "Look... I have work I need to do in the back, and you clearly... well... we can talk later, okay? I get off at six tonight, so I'll be home by six-thirty. Meet me there, then?"

Claire groaned internally at how easily things reverted to the way they had always been between the two, before swallowing the piece of steak and nodding. "Yeah. I need to stop over at the hotel off of the four-lane, though, and get a room first. But I'll..."

"Oh, nonsense. You can stay in the spare bedroom. It's all been worked out, and Carlton should have already changed the sheets. You're not staying at a hotel, Claire." Ellie protested, standing up and speaking authoritatively. "THAT, I insist on. So, are you going to drive around a bit? Check out the town? See any of your haunts?"

"I dunno. Maybe." Claire shrugged before raising an eyebrow. "Let me guess, you want me to NOT go to your house until you have a chance to go there first and make sure evvvverything is perfectly prepared?"

"You always make it sound like I'm some kind of order-Nazi, Claire. I just want tonight to go well, is all." Ellie scoffed before putting on an excessively large smile.

"I... love you, Claire. Okay?" She tried, softening her tone. As she did, Claire found herself wishing that her senses we not so keen that the hint of untruth in her sister's words wasn't so clear to her.

"Yeah..." Claire sighed. "Love you too."

With that awkward exchange, Ellie adjusted her blouse like it was a military uniform and headed into the back of the restaurant while Claire finished her meal as quickly as she could. It looked like she had an afternoon to kill in this town she had run away from.

Chapter Twenty-Four
·))●((·

Killing time in her old hometown wasn't something Claire had planned to do today. In truth, one of the first things she considered was just going to her car and taking a nap until it was time to head to her sister's house.

She decided against that, mostly out of concern for oversleeping after how poorly she had slept, but also due to being a little weirded out by the dream that was still rattling around in her brain. Deciding that distraction was in order, she considered checking her laptop in the back seat and trying to message Shondra, but had to pass on that idea after discovering that she had neglected to pack its power cord, and the machine had gone dead at some point during the drive up to Barley, Pennsylvania.

This left her with little to do except follow her sister's advice and see the sights of the place she had spent a significant amount of effort running from years ago, frustrated and yearning for more than the sleepy little town could provide.

Chuckling at the irony that she had returned home as a werewolf after a year of chaos and now figured a little quiet would do her good, she drove through the town. Passing the local high school, she remembered eating her lunch by the ramp of the loading dock behind the cafeteria, mostly by herself. She remembered cutting her leg on the fence when she tried climbing it and failed; embarrassing and painful. And she remembered crying behind the dumpster for the mockery at the expense of being the only six-foot girl in the locker room.

Many of the sites Claire drove past held memories with similar flavors for her, which only served to add stress to her already uncertain mind. Each place seemed to be a nostalgia center wrapped in a covering of mixed memories and regrets. It all served to remind her of why she had left to find a place where she felt like she belonged more, which led to Florida, and the life she was now running away from.

Rolling down the window of her yellow Pontiac Aztec, she took a long breath and let it fill her senses. The stories of the town filled her mind as a thousand different scents spoke to her werewolf nose, and she realized she was exploring the wrong part of her lonely little hometown. And doing so in a decidedly poor way.

Parking in town to stretch her long legs, Claire put on the light denim jacket she had packed and started walking up the hill that led up to the city park. While November in Tampa was as hot as most any month there, it was firmly autumn here. The leaves had already turned and begun to collect on the ground. It was a sunny day as she walked, but also a fairly windy one, and she closed her eyes to enjoy the sound of the dried leaves painting a virtual image of the rolling hills of the town.

They were always a pain in the ass to climb when she was younger, but in the here and now, she was better equipped for such physical activity. As she walked, the older, colonial-style homes gave way to the entrance to Baker Park. When Claire was younger, she had rarely cared to do things like wander in the park for a wide variety of reasons, not the least of which was basic safety. Of course, when she and her sister were MUCH younger, both would come here with their mother and romp at the playgrounds and swing on the swings. In the summer, the public pool at the top of the hill would open and they had spent many a day there. Unlike much of the rest of town, her memories here were mostly all positive.

She was, however, a different person then. Now, she could experience the park in a way that was impossible only a year ago. She felt more as if she belonged here.

It wasn't exactly the same as the rolling hills of the bizarre dream of the night before, but the dense trees of the woods that surrounded her as she strayed into them, away from the path, were close enough to bring that feeling back to her mind. Like the verdant grasses she remembered running through, these woods were calling to her. Standing amongst the trees, Claire exhaled to let out some of the tension that had been building. As the fresh, crisp autumn air filled her lungs, she started to feel normal again. The stress and anxiety that had felt so overwhelming for the last few days were abating enough for her to smile again.

She briefly felt that familiar tingle across her skin that suggested she liberate what was inside. If obeyed, it would be a release of the wolf for three days in a row, which she had never done before, but all things considered, she decided to keep that proverbial leash on.. The temptation was strong, though, not out of a need to escape this time, but purely for the joy of it here in these denser woods that seemed much more appropriate to her than the dry thickets and scrub pines of Florida.

Rather than run, however, Claire chose to rest, and sat on the ground with her back to a tree, closing her eyes again. Sitting there, her ears picked up everything, from the birds overhead to the chipmunks skittering through the leaves running down the hill. As the wind whistled through the remaining leaves in the trees, Claire's mind was clear for the first time in what felt like weeks. The tension she had been holding melted away, and it was a wonderful, relaxing sensation, if only for the moment.

Opening her eyes again, she took in the sight of the world around her. While once the leaves would have looked little more than brown, she could now see them in a rainbow of golds. The life force in the few remaining green leaves pulsed at her. Overhead, birds on their way south took flight, and in the blue of the sky, her eyes could see the swirling flow of air, lifting beneath those flapping wings. In the distance, she could hear the churning water of a babbling brook as clearly as if she were sitting next to it.

All of this and more as she simply sat there.

This was the truth of her experience of the past year. This was what she was now, and it wasn't a monster. It wasn't what Liam was. It was someone more connected to everything around her. Running her hands across the dried leaves to the cool earth below, she felt something she could only describe as a warmth that couldn't be measured in any real way. It consisted not of simple heat, but of breathing life.

A year ago, the world was just a place. A thing. Now, the world was a friend who embraced her, and in moments like this, she welcomed it.

One way or another, she needed to figure out how to repair what she had broken. She would have to go back and talk to Mariska and find a way to show Shondra that she was still Claire Gribbald, the woman who had been her best friend for years.

Thinking about it, once she settled in at her sister's for the night, she could still work to make things right. It was only Sunday, and work could still be called and a simple, feigned sickness should suffice if she left first thing in the morning. From her sister's house, she could call Mariska and possibly even Shondra and at least open the doors to working things out, as it was becoming clear to her that she had chosen to let that laptop's battery die. She had been punishing herself for her fear by cutting herself off from anyone that might support her, even going so far as to drive up to the one person she knew would offer support that would allow her to stay locked up in the shell of lies to which she had grown accustomed.

That secret, however, was out now, and she could see that she had handled it all in the worst possible way.

As for Liam, she didn't know what to do about that problem or the impossibly confusing feelings she was still grappling with, but she at least knew it needed to end. She needed to make a choice, and there among the trees, where she finally felt more at home, she felt that choice was possible.

It would be a problem to solve later. As the sun began turning a deeper gold and getting closer to the horizon, Claire started walking back down the steep hill toward where she had parked her car to head across town. At the gate to the park, she turned and wondered if she would be able to take the time to come here and possibly run before she left, a thought that brought another one of the first genuine smiles to her face in days.

Making her way back through town, it felt different to Claire, as the change in perspective helped her to take off the proverbial horse blinders coloring her experiences. The streets seemed friendlier and she found it just a little easier to remember the times she'd spent here. By now, Ellie should have been home for a good twenty minutes or so, but Claire walked at a leisurely pace across town to where she'd parked to give herself a little more time in the streets of the town she grew up in.

Passing by the shops of the main avenue through town, a few show windows were in the process of transitioning from the Halloween decorations straight to Christmas, as was common these days. There was the corner pharmacy and the library where she had spent hours studying art books. The closet-sized art supply store she had almost lived in during her teenage years was still there. She remembered getting whatever supplies she could afford, thanks to her first job at the flower shop across the street, which used to be a one-hour photo-developing shop.

Further along was the small movie theater that had played older films for two dollars over the summer, currently serving as a playhouse for the local community theater and taking advantage of the old vaudeville stage inside. It was powerfully quaint. Now she was glad to have come, even under the circumstances that had led her here.

In spite of herself, she was looking forward to seeing her sister and her family again. Her brother-in-law, Carlton, was a bit of a right-wing ass who she could at least tolerate, but Claire found that she was genuinely missing her now five-year-old nephew, Grant. It had been nearly two years since she had seen him. She probably should have gotten him something on the way, though she had no idea what he might have wanted.

Remembering that Ellie mentioned Grant beginning to show an interest in art turned Claire around on her heels, back to the little art supply shop. The windows had a protective film over them in order to keep the supplies from fading, and it had yellowed over the years. She was met by the familiar smell of charcoal and old newsprint as she opened the door.

Half hoping the owner would be there so she could reconnect with someone she only had fond memories of, she was disappointed when the person behind the counter was a younger teenager who turned with a disaffected shrug as the bell over the door chimed. Putting down his phone begrudgingly, he whined, "Uh, can I help you?"

"Just looking, thanks," Claire replied, not particularly caring to engage as she began perusing the tightly-packed shelves for something appropriate. There were, of course, plenty of art supplies for kids, but Claire found herself fixating on a nine-by-twelve bright red plastic clamshell clipboard. It had a smooth surface to put paper on, and opening the clip allowed you to put paper and supplies inside.

Claire thought it was perfect and grabbed it, some crayons, and a stack of colored paper that would all fit inside. In art school, she kept a similar set up in the messenger bag she used to carry so she could draw anywhere and hoped that it was perfect.

Bringing her finds up to the disinterested cashier, Claire half-smiled as she considered asking about the shop's owner for a second before her question was answered. Taking a breath, she sniffed the room involuntarily.

"That'll be twenty-three, ninety… uh…" the oily-looking teenager said, beginning to read her the total before noticing her odd behavior. Claire heard what he had said, but was now sniffing quite intently. There was a lingering scent that she recognized but couldn't quite consciously place until the front door of the store opened again.

Stepping in, an older man in his mid-sixties carried a bag of what smelled like sandwiches. A club and tuna salad. He was a short, pudgy man with bulbous features and a warm smile who began talking to the clerk with a pleasant tone, "So… they were out of turkey, Gary. I had 'em double up on…"

The man looked at Claire and his thick, deeply wrinkled face curled into a warm smile as he finished his thought, "...the ham. Claire? Claire Gribbald?"

Returning the smile, Claire realized that the scent of his Old Spice lingered freshly in the store. It was still connected to her memories of the shop owner, whom she had talked with so often as a teenager.

"Hi, Mister Martin!" Claire replied enthusiastically as he came over, plopped the bag of food on the counter next to her purchases, and put his hands on his hips. Looking the taller woman up and down, he shook his head.

"Holy cow, look at you. You haven't changed a day, kid." The older man assessed as the younger clerk began rifling through the bag of food, an irritated expression on his face. The expression caught the shop owner's attention who 'tsked' and rolled his eyes. "Go on, I can take care of this. Go. Take your break."

"Uh, right." the clerk said, grabbing his club sandwich and taking it to the little room in the back of the store that Claire remembered well.

"Ugh, I swear. I wish he had a tenth of your enthusiasm from back in the day." the older man griped, shaking his head before opening his arms up for a hug that Claire was all too willing to give. "I never had a better helper in here than you, kid."

Chucking, Claire gave the man a hefty squeeze before stepping back with a raised eyebrow. "Uh, Mister Martin, I never worked here?"

With another 'tsk', he scoffed, waving a hand dismissively at Claire. "Please. You were in here all the time, sitting over at the art desks and hanging around. You helped me change the displays and clean up. Heck, you did more to push my stock when folks would come in than I would, half the time. I mean, I didn't give you a fifty percent employee discount just for fun."

"Heh…" Claire chuckled as the memories filled in around her. She had spent many an afternoon shopping for supplies or talking with the man about her favorite artists, taking advantage of his detailed knowledge of what kind of tools they had used. In a lot of ways, she learned more from him than she had from her Art History teachers at school. "Yeah, I guess so. But I always felt kinda… I dunno… guilty for taking up all of your time and reading the how-to books for free, so I felt like I had to make it up by helping."

"Eh, I never complained." He replied, poking her in the arm as he went behind the counter to look at the register. Grabbing a pair of reader glasses off of the edge of the counter, he slipped them on and continued. "Yeah, this is all wrong. Lemme see… Yeah. Ten bucks."

"Mister…" Claire began to protest at the deep discount her old friend was giving her, but, again, his answer was an even sharper, 'TSK'.

"No 'Mister', anything, kid. You get your discount and you like it. Who's this all for anyway?" He asked, genuinely curious. "Did you finally have a little artist of your own?"

"Me… Shit…" Claire cursed as a force of habit before correcting herself with an embarrassed grimace. "Uh… sorry. I mean, no. No, this is for my nephew. I'm in town for… um… the weekend to visit, and his mom says he's getting into art."

"Ahhh! So you're gonna show him the ropes. Good on ya! The kid couldn't ask for a better teacher," he replied, as Claire fished a ten-dollar bill out of her purse and handed it to him. "Speaking of which, what have you been up to? How've you been?"

The question skirted dangerously close to questions she didn't want to answer. In the moment, however, Claire was happy enough to see her old friend that she found it easy to skirt around the unusual, hairy details. "I've been… pretty good. I'm still in Florida, doing graphic design, actually."

"You still paint, though, right?" He asked, eyebrows raised. While she technically hadn't abandoned her art, there was no reason to point out that since becoming a werewolf, she also hadn't been able to create as freely as she once had.

"Yeah. Not as much as I'd like to sometimes, but I get to put some of that creative expression into the day job, which is good." Claire responded with a smile and an answer that was, at least, *technically* true.

"Well, that's good, at least. You've always had talent, so it's good to see it not going to waste," he replied with a warm, paternal smile that Claire returned. They talked for a few more minutes, Claire asking him how his own life had been. They discussed the store and the economy. They discussed her family's restaurant from down the street and the town in general before Claire noticed that it was getting darker and that her sister was expecting her.

Saying her goodbye, he offered another hug and she took it gladly before heading to the door. She was glad to have come in here. Her newly enhanced senses had taken in all the details of the place she had spent so much time in, and all of those memories were now attaching themselves to that much more nuanced scent-memory. "Thanks again, Mister Martin. It was honestly great to see you."

"TSK," he scoffed once again. "Please, I'm nothing to see. Still… don't be a stranger, kid."

"I… I won't. G'night." Claire said, nodding with a warm smile before heading back out to her car.

The drive across town was short enough as the sun began to get lower in the sky. The full moon had passed, and tonight she would have control of herself, though Claire still tended to get a little nervous a couple of days before and after, as they tended to bring the wolf closer to the surface. That said, she resolved to work and keep herself from letting her sister get under her skin.

Pulling up, the house was a fairly large, two-story Victorian-style house with faded gray paint and an immaculately-kept lawn and front garden, though both were firmly in 'autumn' mode, with little growth. Parking, Claire grabbed the gift bag, her purse, and stepped out of the car.

Closing the car door, she brushed some rogue post-transformation hairs from her rear as a scent caught her attention.

Seriously? Claire thought as she shook her head. *He must have gotten his scent into my fur, or something. I swear I keep catching whiffs of him. I need to calm down and put him out of my mind and hopefully, that will finally get him out of my frickin' nose.*

Confident that she had gotten most of the discarded brown fur off her pants, Claire made her way up the well-maintained cobblestone walkway and onto the porch, where she knocked on the front door. From inside, she could clearly make out her little nephew's voice screaming that it was her as stomping little feet made their way to the door.

With keen ears, she could make out four heartbeats and cricked a curious eyebrow. Her sister was a notorious hostess, however, so it would not have surprised Claire at all to see some neighbor added into the mix.

After a second of struggling with the lock and the knob, the door opened and there was her nephew. "AUNT CLAIREEEE!!!!" He yelled, running out to give her a hug around the legs. With him, however, came another strong scent that made the hair on the back of her neck stand up.

"Hey, it's me kiddo! You're gonna knock me…" Claire said, looking down at the boy. He looked so much like his mother, with curly, dark brown hair and big brown eyes on a wide face. Her voice faded to a stop, mid-sentence. "...over."

As Grant stepped back into the doorframe, Claire noticed what he held under his arm, and it smelled impossible. It was a stuffed animal, about a third the size of Grant. A fur-covered werewolf Build-a-Bear-style doll wearing a pair of jeans and a blue blouse. Atop its brown, fur-covered head, was a topper of brown yarn hair pulled back into a ponytail that was disturbingly the same way she often wore her own hair.

On the doll was a scent she knew too well. It hadn't been lingering from before.

"W… what… what is that, Grant? Where did you get that, honey?" Claire said, her voice involuntarily dropping about half an octave and trembling as she forced the words out. Her skin was tingling and she hoped her eyes were still hazel as she stood there.

Holding the doll up proudly in front of his face, not noticing the fear setting into Claire's voice, little Grant beamed with excitement. "This is my Aunt Woofy! See… it looks like you, doesn't it?"

"K… kinda, yeah. kiddo, please. Tell me where you got that." Claire said, biting her bottom lip and shuddering as the smell grew stronger. From inside the hallway of the house, stepping softly into view, dressed in a nice pair of slacks and a black dress shirt, was Liam Docherty, a disturbing grin stretched across his face.

Tilting his head, his ice-blue eyes locked on Claire's as he spoke. "S'prise, beautiful."

Chapter Twenty-Five

"R'we really bringin' *her?*" Beverly McLeish groaned with sarcastic indignation from the passenger seat, pointing dismissively to Shondra, who was driving.

The little Nissan Cube was going about as fast as it could without slipping into a death rattle, which tended to happen anytime its nervous driver pushed it past eighty. The unlikely trio had crossed into Pennsylvania not too long ago and were hoping to get to Claire before it was too late.

From the back seat, tiny blonde Mariska was pouting and taking a swig of one of the bottles of blood she had packed for the road as she responded with a scowl. "No. WE'RE bringing YOU, Bev. Get it straight, you *shluha vokzal'naja.*"

"Hey! C'n ye cut it out, raggin' on me in Russian?! I'm tryin' t' help, y'know!" The wide-bottomed ginger protested, turning back to meet the eyes of her part-time lover, who looked more inclined to bite Bev's head off than acquiesce.

"That remains to be seen," Mariska shot back, tacking on another bit of her native tongue for good measure, "*Nochnaja babochka.*"

Groaning, Beverly sunk in her seat, which kicked up some ginger fur she had shed inside of her clothes. "D'ye know what that shite means? I ain't got a clue."

"I have Google Translate on my phone, but it's not, like, uh, y'know, the Universal Translator, or… uh… like… that. So, uh… no." Shondra said, her anxiety causing her to stutter.

"ACH, this is gonna be a long-ass drive. She cannae even translate yer 'Rocky and Bullwinkle' shite. An' she's jus'… a regular human. What the hell is she gonna do when we git there?" Beverly said, leaning her forehead against the palm of her hand in protest.

"We're not going there to fight, Bev. We're going to talk and explain to Claire that everything is okay." Mariska interjected, her tone becoming more sarcastic. "In spite of him."

"Look, I already said I was sorry f'r freakin' ye out, back there. It was jus' f'r show, so tha' Duncan and Quentin wouldn't suspect I was tryin' t' talk t' ye."

"Y… you… you enjoyed it." Shondra said, her voice dropping to a near-whisper as she forced herself to reply to the woman who, hours ago, had transformed into a werewolf and pretended to attack her in a rest stop bathroom.

A mischievous smirk creased her dimpled, freckle-spattered cheeks as the ginger wolf-woman shrugged. "I had t' make it look good."

From the rear seat, Mariska scowled harder, scritching Shondra's little chocolate poodle, Clive, who was sitting on her lap.

"Look. I don' know what else ye wan' me t' tell ye." Bev continued indignantly. "I tol' ye wha' Liam's doin' t' yer girl that's messin' with her head."

"Which is convenient, as it handily absolves you of a smidge of guilt, Bev. Until we talk to Claire, I am reserving judgment on if I think you're a lying sack of der'mo, or not." Mariska replied, leaning forward, causing little Clive to growl at the minor disturbance.

"Ha! Tha' meant SHITE. That one I caught." Bev said with a mock laugh, before realizing that nobody else in the car was laughing and changed her tone. "Sigh... Okay, yeah. Look, I know it don' make wha' I did right. N' I didnae tell ye as an excuse, rather a *reason."*

"I… I should never'a come over t' yer place wit'out tellin' ye what he was plannin'." She continued, honest contrition in her voice. "But I swear t' ye, tha' was th' only lie. I never meant t'..."

"You did, regardless of your intentions, Beverly." Mariska's voice dropped to a lower register as she cut Bev off mid-sentence. "So, just drop it. I don't want to talk about that. EVER."

There was a long moment of extremely awkward silence in the

small car, and Shondra glanced over to both, piecing together what hadn't been said. "Soooooo… uh… you two ARE… like… uh… totally a… like… thing, then? Like, a couple."

"No!" Both women snapped back in protest at the idea, each turning away from the other as they did. For her part, Shondra rolled her eyes and worked past her fear of the werewolf sitting next to her long enough to follow up.

"Well… uh.. We have a couple of hours before we get there. Maybe… maybe you should talk about it." Shondra shrugged, turning back towards Mariska for a second before returning her eyes to the road. "I mean… you… you can just tell me to shut up and I'll shut up. But it's… uh… kind of obvious you two are. y'know. Sort of, at least. And maybe…"

Sighing overdramatically, Mariska rolled her eyes and took another long swig of her can. "I don't see how I'm going to… what… get over that she SLEPT with me in order to distract me from her little leash-holder going after Claire. That's not just… something I can forget."

"And I'm a VAMPIRE. So… VERRRRRYYYY long memory." She leaned forward, her head right behind Bev's as she all but hissed.

"Believe me, I fookin' know." Bev grumbled in reply, leaning against the window as the sun began to reach the horizon. "Look… I did'na sleep wit'cha as a distraction. I was tol' t' distract ye… AN' I really, really wanted t' sleep with ye. It's… I mean… I know it's fooked up. I do… but… but…"

"I… I think she's saying she was conflicted." Shondra interjected, "y'know… between what she had to do, and what she wanted to do, and that she regrets the one, but not the other."

"How is this helping?" Mariska said, raising her eyebrows at Shondra. "Whose side are you on, here?"

"Yeah! Right. Tha's it exactly." Bev cut in, more worked up. "Th' nosey, mind-reading human is right. I feel like shite f'r wha' I did, love. Truly, I do."

Then, turning an eyebrow towards Shondra, Bev sniffed and

tilted her head. "Yer no' *actually* readin' m' mind, are ye? She is jus' a regular human, right? She ain't a *witch* 'r nothin'?"

"She's not a witch, and you're not off the hook, Bev!" Mariska said, pouting petulantly.

"Wait, are… are witches like… things, *too?* Like… real things?" Shondra perked up, still unabashedly fascinated by everything she was learning.

"Huh? A'course they are. Yuir best friend is a werewolf, she's a vampire, an' ye dunno about…" Bev began to exclaim before noticing Mariska shooting her *shut up* eyes from the back. "What?"

"Yeah, no. O… okay. I had no… no idea, okay." Shondra said, a little angry. "I... didn't know about any of this. She… she never told me. Well… until a couple of days ago."

"Turns out, in spite of me trying to help Claire realize she ISN'T some kind of monster for a year, *someone* put a bunch of horror-film nonsense in her head and abandoned her to figure the rest out last year. Someone told her she would lose control. *SOMEONE* told her to cut ties with the people she cared about because they could never accept her." Mariska again hissed in a low, angry, and accusatory voice.

"I didn't get any different when I was changed. Wha'? I was supposed t' hold 'er hand like a wee bairn and walk her through everythin'?" Bev snapped back, bitterness in her voice.

"*Perestan' bit dolboyobom, YES!*" Mariska shouted, waking up little Clive, who whined out a protest bark. "Yes, Bev! The *poshlaja svenja* did the exact same thing to you and you never once thought you should try and actually do BETTER when he did it AGAIN!?"

With her Russian accent leaking out as she yelled, the angry vampire put the puppy on the empty seat next to her so she could gesticulate with her hands. "You KNOW how I was made! That he abandoned me, and how badly I adapted. There was no way I could let her go through that, and I would have thought you would have done the same. But no, you filled her head with the same garbage Liam did for you. Why? You were hurt, so she had to hurt even more?"

Gripping the steering wheel tightly, Shondra was regretting her decision to therapize them, as a low, rumbling growl began to vibrate through the car from Beverly.

"And where yuir maker left eye… MINE WAS RIGHT THERE! TELLING' ME WHA' TO FOOKIN' DO!" Beverly snapped back, her eyes starting to brighten to the same frightening green as her voice dropped. Realizing she was starting to lose it, the more experienced werewolf pursed her lips and pulled back. "I didnae have a fookin' choice."

"N' neither will she. Yuir precious Claire." She finished, venom on her tongue.

"If you hate her so much, why are you coming to help her?" Mariska replied, her own voice flattening out.

"I'm nae here f'r her," was all Beverly would say in reply as she turned back to look out the window, silence taking hold in the car as they continued north.

Chapter Twenty-Six
-)) ⬤((-

"My doll? Mista' Liam gave it to me, Aunt Claire." Grant said, standing in the doorway to Claire's sister's house as he hugged sweetly on the little doll of a plush werewolf girl. The tall, lean man in the hallway stepped casually up behind him. In the doorway of the house, Claire's face had gone as white as a ghost.

She gasped and the bag of art supplies in her hand slipped out of her grip. It seemed impossible to her, but of course, Liam Docherty was there. He had said he would wait for her to return to him, but it was clear that was another in an endless string of lies.

Standing in a sharp, black dress shirt and slacks, his midnight black hair was pulled back into a looser ponytail than was normal for him, and the usual five o'clock shadow he sported was grown and styled into a neat, black beard. He looked like he had made quite the effort in putting himself together for this, though Claire was struggling to figure out why. In truth, she was struggling with everything, at the moment, as she stood there in shock.

It felt as if time had stopped before the sound of a loud clattering crash snapped Claire out of it. The plastic art binder in the bag had hit the floor. Claire blinked rapidly, trying to get a grip on herself, when Liam spoke.

Bringing up his fingers to the side of his face, he tapped himself in the head next to his eyes with a smirk. "Breathe, beautiful. ye don' want little Grant seein' those, do ye?"

Gulping, Claire shut her eyes for a second, realizing that she was once again on the verge of slipping and transforming. Her eyes had started to grow and turn amber.

"W… what the… what are you doing here, Liam?" she said, restraining herself from shouting, though there was an audible growl in her voice.

"All things in due time, beautiful," Liam smirked as he leaned down to pick up the dropped bag, peeking inside. "Ahhh, look at this, little pup. Yuir aunt Claire, I think, might'a brought'n ye somethin' special. Am I right?"

Pursing her lips, Claire reopened her eyes as she worked to control her breathing and calm down. As Grant looked up, his smile told her that she must have gotten the change under control. "Is it, aunt Claire? Did you get me something?"

"I… I did, Grant." Claire said, terror gripping her heart as Liam leaned over to hand the bag back to her. "Where's your mommy? I can show you your present after dinner, maybe."

Hesitantly, Claire took the bag as Liam stood back up, taking advantage of the moment to brush his finger against her own in the exchange. Claire had to restrain herself from gasping audibly as it felt like a jolt of electricity flew from his touch down her spine. Immediately, it felt as if she were somehow 5 degrees warmer all over.

The tension was, however, both broken and intensified as Claire's sister hopped into the room from the home's parlor with an overly wide, smug smile on her face. "I'm right here. And let me tell you, Claire, I had one heck of a time not spilling the beans about Liam, here. BUT, he asked me to keep it a surprise."

Of COURSE. Claire thought, chastising herself internally, which she was certain must've been playing across her face. *He must have been here all day at least. You dumb bitch, you weren't smelling him lingering on your clothes or fur. He had been here. He had already talked to Ellie. You fucking IDIOT!*

"Aye," Liam interjected with a raised brow and a facade of pleasantries as he rolled back on his heels, acting as innocently as he could. "I called yuir sister up n' tol' her I was flyin' in t' surprise ye. That ye were taking a trip up t' talk t' her about, well, ye know, US."

Gripping the bag more tightly, Claire's eyebrows tightened as she tried to not openly glare at him. "Us? What… US, Liam?"

"Oh, come on inside, Claire. You're letting all the heat out." Ellie said, pulling Claire into the doorway by the arm. It took a masterful amount of self-control for her not to flinch. Stepping inside meant being in an enclosed space with Liam. As if he could read Claire's mind, he took a hand and mussed up Grant's hair in a dog whistle gesture that only Claire understood.

"Aye, yuir sister an' her lovely husband have cooked up quite th' feast, beautiful. Right here in this lovely, peaceful home a' theirs. C'mon inside so we c'n all eat an' catch up." Liam said plainly enough, but the meaning was sharply defined. Claire shot him a glare that let just a hint of amber bleed into her irises. He sought out this place. He tracked down her family and got here before her. This was a message that no matter where she went, he would find her. This was a threat that nobody close to her was safe from him.

"Here, let me take that." Ellie said, taking the bag from the art supply store as she led them into the house through the parlor to the dining room. With a wave of his arm, Liam controlled the action, gesturing for Claire to follow in front of him. She realized that the trap was closing around her and she had pulled her own family into exactly what she was trying to run away from.

From behind, Liam put his hands gently, but firmly, on Claire's shoulders as they came into the dining room. Freezing in place like a deer staring into her own eyes in the night, Claire couldn't bring herself to move as he leaned in close enough for her to feel his hot breath against the nape of her neck. "Let me take yuir jacket, beautiful."

The sensation of a million tiny sparks all exploding under her skin brought the opposing feelings of an icy chill, followed by that same wave of warmth that, against all reason, flowed from her head straight to her middle. That heat caused her knees to go ever so weak, though she allowed none of it to show as he pulled her denim jacket slowly off her shoulders.

In the kitchen, Ellie's husband, Carlton, came out, untying the apron he had been wearing over his blue striped dress shirt and slacks. As he did, Ellie set the bag down on a side table in the dining room next to the main table, already set for five. "Hear that, Carlton? Why don't you say romantic stuff like that to me?"

With a stiff smile, the slightly older man with a boxy build and developing double-chin rolled his eyes mischievously. "Oh, I said it once. Then you said 'I do', and I've been off the hook ever since."

"Oh really? Is that how this works?" Ellie replied playfully as she walked past to the kitchen with Grant in tow. "C'mon, little guy. While your daddy is setting the table, we're going to get you all washed up."

With a dry and partially-practiced laugh, Carlton shook his head as he walked over to Claire, thankfully being the type to forgo hugs or overt displays of affection of most kinds. "Ahh, it's been forever. Hopefully, all is as well as we've been told. What can I get you both to drink? We have a pretty well-stocked fridge AND wine cabinet."

"Just a glass of water is fine with me, Carlton," Claire said, wanting to stay as sober as possible under the circumstances, as Liam hung her jacket up on a rack in the parlor before interjecting.

"Stap yer haverin', ye daft thing. This is a night f'r celebratin'." Liam said, sauntering back in to stand by her side as he wrapped a long arm around hers. "Two glasses a' yer finest, if'n ye will, my good sir."

"Ha! Good thinking. Well, you two get settled and we'll take care of everything." Carlton said, clapping his hands together and turning on his heels back towards the kitchen. "You called it, Ellie. Could you get the corkscrew out of the drawer while I grab a bottle?!"

As the oblivious family in the kitchen collected the fixings for the obviously well-planned dinner, Claire turned hard to shrug Liam's arm off of her. With a harsh, angry whisper, Claire spoke through gritted teeth. "How dare you do this! How dare you threaten…"

"I'm no' threatenin' anyone, beautiful. 'Cept maybe the little illusion yuir carryin' up in tha' head'a yuir's tha' I'm up t' no good." Liam replied, a good deal calmer. "Or are ye really angry at me tha' I sussed out that ye would want't try an' reconnect wit' yuir estranged, bonny sis? Tha' I decided tha' being alone was a god-awful idea an' decided t' do somethin' 'bout it? What EXACTLY did I do wrong, here?"

"You damn fucking well know!" Claire said, her face turning red and her eyes starting to go amber, before Liam stopped her.

"Rein it in, beautiful. They're comin' back. Unless'n ye wan' this t' go tits up in the worst way possible. If so, I'll do it right here for ye. Put an end t' the lies yeve been telling in one big, fat an' VERY hairy moment." Liam leaned in, his voice getting sharper as he did. "Calm down, have a seat an' le's have a nice, family dinner."

"Ut oh." Ellie said, carrying in a large crockpot of what smelled like a well-marinated beef roast that, in the moment, Claire figured she could take down by herself in five minutes flat. "What did you do, Claire? Really, you just got here and you look like you're spoiling for a fight."

"Ach, well, this'n is on me, Ellie. Ye know how'n yuir sister c'n get when she's sideswiped." Liam said dismissively, feeding into Ellie's tone. "Nothing a little wine n' good food wit' family won't cure, I'd wager."

"Right, beautiful?" Liam said, pulling out a chair for her. Another layer to the walls closing around her that Ellie was oblivious to.

For a moment, Claire stood there oscillating between barely-contained rage and inexplicably rising passions. Somehow finding calm in the narrow valley between the two, she put on a proper facade and took the offered seat.

After another few minutes of shuffling, table setting, and serving, all four adults and little Grant were in their seats, with Claire sitting next to Ellie, Liam across from her next to the small child, and Carlton at the end of the table. It was a layout that made Claire feel even more defenseless as they began to eat.

For the first few minutes, there was mostly silence as they got started. Reaching across with his spoon, Grant was trying to eat with the stuffed werewolf on his lap before his mother sighed.

"Grant, honey. Put your toy away or you're going to get juice all over it and then Mommy is going to have to go wash it. You can play with it after dinner, okay?"

He took on a pouty disposition, as he clearly didn't want to let go, but before the situation could escalate, Liam leaned over with what looked like a genuinely warm smile for the child that Claire found unnerving. "Yuir mum's right, little pup."

Across the table, Claire tensed up at his second use of the word 'pup', peppering in little cues that only meant anything to the two werewolves in the room.

"I tell ye wha'. Why don't'n I put yuir aunt Woofy right here in th' chair next t' me so'n we c'n all eat?" He said, gently but slowly taking the little plush off of Grant's lap with that same warm smile that Claire herself had fallen for.

As he did, the child's pout dissipated into a broad grin and a nod. "Okay!" Grant said excitedly as Liam sat the little doll up in a standing position to his left, high enough for its little eyes, golden marbles, to peek over the tabletop, aimed towards Claire's seat.

With a chuckle, Ellie shook her head, taking a sip of her wine. "Well… at least he's listening to someone, tonight. He's been so excited to see you, Claire. And isn't that so cute? He's barely put it down since he got it."

"It's… adorable." Claire replied through the facade of calm she was projecting, stopping herself from adding a 'fucking' in the middle of her statement.

"Isn't it? Where did you find that thing, Liam? I mean, Granty has never been much for stuffed animals, but he just loves that." Ellie asked, either not noticing Claire's somewhat hostile tone, or simply ignoring it, as she was wont to do.

"Ach, well, I came in from th' airport in Orlando, an' tha' thing's massive like some daft mall. N' I figured, since Claire here had talked so much about th' wee one, tha' I had best no' show up empty-handed." Liam said, taking a bite of his roast while pausing to chew and swallow. "So, they had one'a them places where'n ye can build yuir own little dolls, an I saw all the bits an' pieces that I couldnae resist."

Patting the little doll on its head, Liam smirked just a bit. "I mean, I'm thinkin' I did pretty well. Put together a wee little 'Claire' for'n yuir bairn here so'n he can have his auntie when she's no' around."

"Ha ha!" Ellie laughed a bit too much for Claire's comfort at the observation. "Well, you succeeded well, Liam. It's got the same little, angry pout she does so well. Look, she's doing it right now!"

Snickering, Ellie pointed to Claire's real scowl, thinking it was hilarious, and continued, "And making it a little… what… a wolf girl… is just so cute. The real Claire is a little growly more often than not."

It was everything she had in her to not ACTUALLY growl in that moment. Claire kept eating to keep herself physically occupied. The anger was the only thing keeping her head clear of the strange mix of rage and passion she felt while sitting there.

Even in human form, her senses were being assaulted by his scent. The smell of him permeated everything and even overwhelmed the aroma of the food. It was beyond intoxicating. Through it all, she still wanted him, and was beginning to hate herself for that.

Picking up on Ellie's comment, Liam couldn't resist twisting it. "Well, tha's 'r bonnie Claire, ain't it? Bit of a lovely beast, she is."

"Really?" Claire blurted out, her anger slipping out more than intended as Liam realized he might have overplayed his admittedly strong hand.

"Okay, okay. That was a bit much, I admit. Sorry, beautiful." He said, holding his hands up and smiling in a mock-surrender posture.

"Oh, calm down, Claire," Ellie added, seeming to enjoy her struggles. It was a long-standing dynamic in the family that Liam had been monopolizing. The haughty older sister continued. "We're just playing. Nobody is attacking you, so unclench your jaw and stop making everything more dramatic than it needs to be. Honestly."

"So, that roast has been in the slow cooker since about eight-thirty. My own marinade recipe, actually. Hope everyone is liking it." Carlton chimed in with a banal bit of casual dinner conversation in a thinly-veiled attempt to redirect the conversation.

"It's right lovely, there, Carlton," Liam said, taking another large bite and playing along with the shift in time. "Me own mum would be hard-pressed t' match it, I might be so bold as t' say."

"Well, from what you told us earlier, that sounds like high praise, indeed," Carlton replied, puffing his chest out proudly as his wife picked up the train of thought. "Yes. You... said your family owned a restaurant and farmland in Scotland?"

Cricking an eyebrow, Claire wondered just how long he had been there before her arrival.

"Oh, aye," Liam said, washing down a bite with some wine. "It's a bit more of a restaurant slash bed n' breakfast affair. But it's a part'a our family land, an' the farm we've had for... well... generations. But for as small as our village is, it's kinda a big deal, an' I've a brother whose food is th' stuff'a local legend."

"That just sounds so quaint," Ellie said, somewhat pretentiously, as she swished her own wine. "And you were saying that you stand to inherit that land and the business?"

"Aye, aye. I've been studyin' over here. Working towards a business license, an' the like. I've always wanted t' work th' family business an' take over f'r me mum and da on th' homestead." Liam said with a puffed-up bit of his own pretentiousness that Claire could see right through. "Finally take my seat as lord a' the clan n' all."

"A lord. Wow, Claire. I can't believe you found someone like this. You, of all people." Ellie followed up, judgment in her voice. Claire knew that her sister valued status and presumed position, and Liam had been feeding into that to make himself seem like the ideal catch for Claire.

"Welllll, t'be fair, all ye really need to claim that sad little title back home is a big enough piece a' land, really. But I can't wait t' share it wit' me girl here." Liam added, with false humility.

Claire's eyebrow shot up, confused with the story that she knew was at least a little invented. In the few months the two had dated, Claire had heard from Liam and his brothers about the farm and the business, which was all true. But he had basically run away from home and completely neglected to mention his band or that musical aspiration he was usually exceedingly proud of. As he looked over, he gave her something of a quick glare to remind Claire of the unspoken threat as he continued.

"Right, beautiful? I know you've been lookin' forward t' finally seein' th' land after all this time. N' I know me mum can't wait t' meet ye, too," he added.

"Oh, of course," Claire replied with mock enthusiasm as he smiled towards her. "I can hardly get you to STOP talking about how much you love your home. When were you planning on leaving?"

The smile on Liam's face spread wider as he rolled with the jab. "Oh, as soon as we can. Ye know, t' make th' announcement."

The knot in Claire's stomach tightened enough to turn graphite into diamonds as the implication began to sink in for her. "Announcement?" She said, flatly.

"Welllll," Liam said, his smile stretching into a rictus as his eyes went cold. "I know ye haven't told Ellie here, yet, as yeve been so stressed 'bout ever'thin', but it's part'a why I wanted t' come up here."

Reaching into his pocket, he pulled out a small box. She shook her head ever so slightly. As she did, with his brows, Liam indicated the reverse to her as he held out the box and opened it, to reveal a gold ring with a small, simple gem in its center. "We've been t'gether now f'r jus' over a year now, which I know ain't a long time, but it's been long enough f'r me t' want t' make real what we've both known in 'r hearts is what's meant t' be."

Forcing herself to make her face as blank as possible, Claire tried to breathe deeply, which only served to flood her senses with

241

Liam's overpowering scent and pheromones. She took a massive drink of her wine, trying her level best to think clearly as it felt like her head was about to spin off of her shoulders.

"C'mon, beautiful. I know what yuir feelin' in yer heart. We're made f'r each other." Liam finished. His voice dripped with honey, the melodic Scottish lilt resonating in Claire's mind and echoing in her heart. "Yuir mine. I figure it's right time t' make it official, don' ye?"

The last part was said with just a hint of edge to his voice as Liam overplayed his hand. In Claire's mind, he wasn't the smart-dressed facade of the man she had once fallen in love with, but rather, the black-furred creature that turned on her in that alley. As that scene replayed in her mind, her skin broke out in chills for all to see as she bit her bottom lip, remembering his words from that night: *'Fuck you! Ye don' leave me! Yuir MY bitch!'*

The forced proposal lingered there in the air, as did the inherent threat Liam represented in Claire's family's home. Staring at his deep, blue eyes, then over to little Grant, who could barely comprehend what was happening, Claire's mind raced.

The options limited, she couldn't just reject him right there without risking his wrath in a way that could potentially be deadly. While she hardly cared at all about Carlton, and Ellie was endlessly annoying to her, they were all still her family, and she couldn't let Liam hurt them. Saying yes risked locking her into a terrifying path. No matter how much a part of her was somehow still burning to take the man that had attacked her, mauled her and almost destroyed her life, her reason kept shouting for her to run again. With neither option being one she could entertain, Claire improvised.

Grabbing the bottle of wine on the table, she took a positively enormous swig, her eyes wide and shocked-looking as they locked on Liam. Swallowing the drink hard, she put the wine bottle down and let her bottom lip begin to quiver. The performance only needed to be convincing to her sister and her family, but if she was lucky, it would buy her time to make a plan or find some help.

With her emotions a cauldron of chaos, it wasn't particularly difficult to manage a few tears by blinking excessively, pretending the shock was settling in. Clasping her hands over her mouth, her voice was a cracked and warbling thing. "You… you want me to… Oh my goodness, Liam! I… I… I don't know what to say, I… I… OH MY GOODNESS!"

With a raised brow and a half-frown, Liam was processing the performance as Claire stood up quickly in her chair, which caused it to almost tip over behind her. "I… I… I have to… I'm sorry! I don't want to ruin dinner! *SNIFF* I… I have to think about this!!!"

Putting her hands over her face to cover up the lack of anything more than a few perfunctory tears, she began speed-walking out of the dining room to head up to the spare bedroom she knew had been prepared for her, as it had in past visits. Once out of sight of her family, Claire stopped pretending to cry, though she kept making the noises as she looked around the foyer at the base of the staircase.

She knew she couldn't leave. She had to confront Liam, and he likely wouldn't allow her to get far, but she needed to get him out of the same room as Grant and the others. This was all she could think about. On the shallow table by the door, she saw Ellie's purse. She continued to make crying sounds. She could hear that nobody had yet gotten up as she found what she was looking for and pocketed her sister's cell phone before cartoonishly stomping up the stairs, virtually screaming as she fake-cried.

Down in the dining room, there was a long moment of silence before all three looked up to the slam of a bedroom door upstairs that made Ellie, Carlton, and Grant flinch. As they did, Liam closed the ring box and pursed his lips. "Welllll, tha' coulda gone better."

"Oh, that's just Claire. She's… she's always been emotional like that. I'm sure you can talk to her and she'll listen to reason." Ellie said, pursing her lips and nodding, with an awkward tone to her voice.

"Oh, aye," Liam said, an edge in his voice that Ellie wasn't listening for. "I'm sure she will, too."

Chapter Twenty-Seven
⊶⟩◉⟨⊷

"Oh, for frickin' fucks' sake." Claire muttered to herself as she locked the door to the medium-sized guest bedroom that she had slept in a few times, noticing a duffle bag on the bed that reeked of Liam. Apparently, the plan was to be sharing this particular room, which was obviously an absolute no-go.

Against the side wall, there was an antique vanity with a tall, oval-shaped mirror where Claire looked herself over. Thankfully, while her heart was beating as if she were transformed and running at full speed, her eyes were their normal hazel color.

Over the bed, there was a window that she stepped over to and pulled open. The old wood stuck a bit, but it was easy enough to force up with her current adrenaline rush. There was a screen in place that she could pop out effortlessly if needed. The backyard sloped downhill and ran into the woods behind the house. It was a solid twenty-foot drop, which she could manage easily if she transformed.

For the moment, however, it was the fresh air she needed. The cold November night air came in with a light gust that Claire prayed would help her get some of Liam's scent out of her nose. Angrily, she pulled the comforter off of the bed, wrapping the bag up in it, and walking over to the small en suite bathroom, closing it in there to help get rid of the man's overpowering presence that seemed to cling to her senses like nothing else.

What the fuck is WRONG with you? Claire thought as she leaned close to the window, exhaling for a good 5 seconds before breathing in as deeply as she could. Repeating the pattern a few more times, she began to calm down and her head started to clear. *He frickin' MAULED you! He was a gaslighting, emotionally abusive asshole BEFORE that and he's threatening your frickin' family, and you're HORNY!?*

Calming down, she listened for a moment to make sure they

were all still downstairs before pulling her sister's phone out of her pocket. *Okay, just… get over yourself and call Mariska. Whatever's wrong, she'll understand and know what to do.*

Pressing the button on the side, Claire looked at the screen and muttered to herself, "Fuck. Aw, c'mon, El. Really? Of course, you have a goddamn password on your lock screen. Shit."

Taking another breath to try and mentally regroup, her stomach tightened back up as she heard familiar footfalls coming up the stairs. Pursing her lips, she began waving air in from the window frantically. She heard the most delicate of knocks on the door. From outside came his Scottish lilt, dipping and flowing in a sing-song rhythm.

"Suddenly there came a tappin', as of someone gently rappin', rappin' at m' chamber door," Liam whispered from the hall, causing Claire to roll her eyes and scowl.

"Really? Fuckin' POE quotes? Or do you only know it from watching 'The Crow'?" She grumbled, her raspy voice cracking as her anxiety began to rise.

"Look, jus' open up, beautiful." He said, more softly still, making sure his voice didn't carry any further than only her own sensitive ears could pick up. "I mean, we could have a nice heart t' heart wit' me standin' out here, but I'm thinkin' we might say things ye dinnae want yuir sister 'r her wee one knowin' about. Yuir call, a'course."

"Or I could just jump out this window and run. What's to stop me?" Claire replied plainly, wondering if he would answer her directly and acknowledge the threat of his presence to his family.

"Nothin' a'tall." was his reply. "I ain't here f'r anyone but you. Then wha', though? Keep runnin' from yuir truth forever? From what ye are, an' wha' WE are?"

"WE aren't anything, Liam." Claire countered, hissing through the door. "You saw to that."

Sighing, Liam took a second to reply. "Aye, I did. I fooked up, n' I know it. I lost control. I let all th' passion an' emotion in me build until… what happened, happened. Which... kinda hard t' talk about in the hallway, here."

Claire glared at the door for a long moment before she finally walked over and unlocked it. Instead of opening it, she walked back over next to the window, crossed her arms, and waited.

A second later, the door opened slowly and Liam leaned in hesitantly. Making a show of it, his eyes were wide as he waved a hand in. "Peace. So, does tha' mean I c'n come in? I admit I was half expectin' ye t' have collected her good dinner silver t' try an' stab me wit'."

There was no reply as he stood there waiting before finally stepping in and closing the door behind him. "I'll take that as a 'yes', then."

Again, Claire said nothing, as she worked to try and keep her head screwed on correctly and remember what he had done to her, and what he was doing in this exact moment.

"So, I'm guessin' yuir right pissed? I know I dropped a bit'a a bomb down there, but-" Liam continued before Claire cut him off.

"A bomb? You frickin' PROPOSED to me, Liam? Are you out of your mind?" She snapped back, her voice an angry, hoarse whisper. "And what the hell was all that bullshit down there about wanting to take over your family's farm and business? Since when have you given a shit about any of that?"

"Anythin' else ye want t' cram in there? Git it outta yer system?" Liam scoffed, putting his hands on his hips.

"Sure. Where do I frickin' start, Liam?" Claire growled. "Because, honestly, I'm still trying to get the smell of all the bullshit I had to swim in down there out of my frickin' nose. So, what, you flew in early and sweet-talked my sister into this bullshit dinner? Told her we were still together and that you were going to propose to me tonight?"

"I wanted t' show ye tha' I could clean up an' play nice wit' the normies an' be a right proper mate so I dressed oop an' put on m' best smile an' came t' make peace. Yeah, I got here b'fore ye, cuz I wanted t' surprise ye. Show ye I could change, even if it's jus' a little. N' I needed t' find a way t' get' ye t' listen t' me," Liam protested. "An' now, yuir listenin'."

"Yeah, I'm frickin' listening, Liam. So, now it's your turn to listen to me." Walking up to the ever-so-slightly taller man, Claire stuck a finger at him, rage behind her eyes as they shifted to the amber of the wolf. "You came here to remind me that you COULD. That you could interject yourself into my frickin' life no matter what. You wanted to show me that I couldn't get away from you, and trust me, that message is FULLY frickin' understood. I am NOT yours, Liam. I am not your fucking 'bitch', and I am not marrying you!"

"Wha', this?" Liam said, pulling out the box with the ring and dismissively tossing it on the bed. "That was f'r *their* benefit, beautiful. Don' you get it, yet? In every way that matters t' our kind, we're already paired. We've paired f'r LIFE."

His tone darkening, he leaned in, pointing directly at Claire's eyes. "That piece a' scrap on th' bed ain't my golden ring, beautiful. THESE are. Tha's MY blood ye carry now, like it 'r no."

Resisting the urge to swat his hand away for fear of the rush she had felt every time he touched her, Claire stepped back a pace in the room. "So, what? You *licked* me and now I'm frickin' *yours?* I don't think so, Liam! You had your shot and you ruined it in the most epic way I could imagine. And there's… no way I will ever...."

"Wha's wrong, beautiful? Where's that angry fookin' resolve goin'?" Liam sneered as Claire's focus drifted again, like it did every time he was near her. That smell in her nose pushed the anger down and changed its flavor to something Claire didn't want to acknowledge.

Panic edged in around the corners of her mind as she shoved back to no avail, hissing in the same angry whisper. "Get away!"

As expected, the touch sent a rush of electricity down her spine that made her knees weak and her mind reel. Between her legs, she felt that same warm rush that threatened to overwhelm her as she stumbled back away from him. "You… you, this is… you. What the… what the fuck are you doing?"

"I'm no doin' anythin, beautiful." He replied in a soft, sing-song lilt of a voice. "Don' ye get it? Yuir fightin' what ye are. Yuir fightin' wha' yuir heart is tellin' ye."

"You've been fightin' it f'r a year, now, an' wha's it got ye? Yuir miserable, tryin' t' deny yuirself a' wha' ye really want." he said, as Claire turned towards that window, desperation fueling the desire to try and leap out to freedom.

"Go ahead. Run. But then what? Where else ye gonna run to? I won't chase ye if'n ye do." Liam said, stepping to the other side of the bed, nodding as Claire struggled against herself, doing her best to stay focused.

"But yeve been runnin' f'r a year now. Runnin' without a place t' run TO. I c'n be that f'r ye, beautiful." Liam said, his voice even softer now and almost plaintive.

"Stop calling me that. You d… don't get to call me that!" Claire said, her voice trembling, which surprised her. "YOU gave that up."

"It's what ye ARE, Claire. How c'n I make ye understand tha', t' me, yuir th' most beautiful woman there is, in an' out. Like this… and like ye *really* are." He replied, stepping closer, slowly. "Gettin' t' see ye like that, free, and wild, and perfect was… like a dream t' me. An' I know ye dinnae wan' t' hear it, but it's th' truth. I'm sorry f'r the way it happened, Claire. I truly am. But I cannae lie t' ye, an' say that I'm sorry for what ye became. What ye are. B'cause what ye are is amazin', n' all I wan' is t' help show ye that."

"I'm no' askin' ye t' forgive me outright." He said, reaching a hand out ever so slightly as he stepped that much closer. "I'm only askin' ye to give me th' chance t' show ye how magnificent we could be t'gether."

Pausing, Claire stared down at his hand for a long moment, almost everything inside of her telling her to take it and accept what he was offering.

"Ye feel trapped, I know." Liam said, this time stepping to the side and sitting on the bed, while leaving just enough room for

Claire. "This life, I know how hard it is. But… neither a' us need t' be alone. I c'n help ye… help ye in ways ye jus don' know about. Way's… only I c'n really understand."

Fidgeting, Claire looked down at the empty spot on the bed for just an instant before the implication of his words rang in her head. "You can help me? You can… you *did* this to me, you piece of shit! But… but worse than that, after it happened, you all just frickin' vanished! Where was your help this whole past year?!"

"Would'ye have accepted it?" Liam shot back, his voice dropping back down again for a second before he softened his tone. "Will ye accept it now?"

"What the *fuck* do you think? This is frickin' *over,* Liam. I'm done with this!" Claire growled back at him, feeling angry enough to think straight as she stepped over to the door and away from Liam, who stood up again.

His earlier tone of reconciliation faded as he frowned in response, shaking his head. "Listen t' me. Ye dinnae know how this works, so I'll tell ye now…"

Reaching over, he grabbed Claire by the wrist and let out a growl of his own, his eyes shifting from their normal blue to the icy hue of his werewolf form. "This is happenin'. Accept it n' we can move forward…"

Immediately, Claire felt that warm rush again at his touch. This time, however, it was one among a phalanx of emotions that kept her focused enough to concentrate. Thinking back to her own fears in the karaoke bar with Mariska, her own words echoed in her mind: *'Sure… I could tell he was interested, but I don't know if that was real interest or just him reacting to the… y'know… the pheromones I pump out when I'm horny. It makes them… throw themselves at me sometimes. It makes them stupid, and that's not real. I mean, how am I supposed to trust if someone's interest is real?'*

"This… this is… This shit is *you!* Your… your pheromones fucking with my head. You're fucking with my head, and you KNOW it, you piece of shit!" Claire tried to pull her arm

250

free, but Liam held tight and pushed her back against the door with a thud. "But… I don't want this! This is stronger. This is… more than just that. I don't… How can you… how can you…"

Rambling, Claire couldn't find the words to express her jumbled thoughts as the sensation intensified. Her mind was in a fog and she was struggling even harder to think straight. The fog was so thick that she barely heard someone coming up to the door of the house downstairs. Liam ignored it and pressed his position.

"What, nobody told ye? I'm your fookin' MAKER, woman. That makes ye mine, n' that means your body n' soul r' hardwired t' *obey me*. So…sooner 'r later…" Liam leaned in close, sneering at her, "...yell *learn* t' jus' fucking *heel*."

From the other side of the door, there came a knock that caused Claire's blood to freeze in her veins. With everything going on, she hadn't heard anyone approach.

"Aunt… Aunt Claire?" came Grant's voice from the hall outside the spare bedroom. "Are you sad? I… I heard you yell."

With her back against the door, Claire's eyes darted as fear set in. She looked from the door back to Liam, who stared at her, his sneer curling into an ugly thing with growing canines bared as he whispered with a voice rough like glass over asphalt.

As he spoke, a scent other than Liam's, Grant's or her sister crept in from under the door. A scent she knew as well as her own that had found it's way to her. Claire immediately recognized it, and in that moment, felt her mind clear ever so slightly. "This... is... happenin', one way r' t'other. Tha' choice is yuirs, so make it."

There were no words or even a growl of warning as Claire moved. From thought to deed, only a couple of seconds elapsed as the window at the rear of the guest bedroom exploded in a rush of shattered glass and fur.

Transforming in an instant to take advantage of the surprise and overpower him until he changed as well, Claire made her choice and tackled him out of the second-story window and into the night sky.

Twenty feet below, two fully transformed werewolves slammed into the brush hard, disappearing in the darkness.

Chapter Twenty-Eight
⟨⟩ ꙮ ⟨⟩

"This is just typical Claire," Ellie complained as she put leftovers from dinner into Tupperware containers. Standing at the sink, her husband Carlton was rinsing dishes off to put in the open dishwasher. "I swear, she always does things like this. She takes any situation and works to find a way to make it all about her and ruin it for everyone else."

"Well, she did seem really upset, hon. Maybe they weren't quite as solid as he…" Carlton replied before being cut off by his insistent wife.

"Because she clearly wants to ruin that, too. I mean, she never even dated in high school and has barely ever talked about the idea since then. Mom and I used to joke that she had to be a lesbian." Ellie paused between tasks to take a sip of her wine and scoff. "You don't know her like I do, Carlton. She is a drama magnet. She insists on stirring up things that were working just fine. Now she has a boyfriend with a potential future beyond her silly little affectations of 'art', so, of course, she is thinking of pissing that away."

"Are they still arguing up there?" He replied, putting the last dish in the dishwasher and starting the machine's cycle.

"Yes. I think Grant is eavesdropping. Honey, would you go get him so he doesn't have to hear her mouth?" Ellie took another sip. "We don't need him picking THAT up from…"

As she spoke, a knock came to the front door. "Oh, what now? It's probably Mrs. Pearce from next door, coming to complain about Claire's loud whining."

Walking to the door, Ellie put her glass of wine down on the little table nearby as she opened it, expecting to see her nosy neighbor. "I'm sorry, Alice. I'll… oh… I'm sorry. Can I help you?"

She raised a curious eye at the short, rotund black woman with a large ponytail of wild curls, the wide-bottomed, taller ginger with a scowl on her face, and the diminutive, pale woman in the middle with platinum blonde hair.

"Yes, actually. You're…" Mariska said, leaning slightly toward Shondra, who nodded in approval, "You're Ellie, right? Claire's sister? My name is Mariska Baranov. We're friends of your sister's. She's here, right?"

"Hi, Ellie," Shondra said, waving with an awkward grin as Beverly simply rolled her eyes.

Looking confused and irritated, Ellie curled her lips as she tried to remember. "Oh… uh… Sharone, right?"

"Ach, she's a racist too. This just keeps gettin' better." Beverly said sarcastically. "Look, they're BOTH upstairs arguin'. I could smell 'em from the car, so let's just go and… oh, *shite.*"

Suddenly, there came the loud crash of the rear window upstairs blowing outward. Little Grant yelped from his side of the door in surprise, as the rest of them all turned with a jerk to the source of the calamity.

"An' tha's officially teats up," Beverly said, grimacing. "They're movin'! C'mon!"

"What in the hell is going on, here?! Carlton!!! Call the police!" Ellie said as she looked up to the base of the stairs. At the top, little Grant was trying to open the locked door.

"Aunt Claire! Aunt Claire!" He yelled, starting to cry, as downstairs, Shondra turned to Mariska.

"Mariska, we… we can start after them, but you… I think you have to get them under control, here." the nervous young woman said, biting her lip. The tiny vampire looked at her, surprised.

"Are you mad? He can tear you apart. And you know them, here… sort of. You should…" Mariska said before Shondra cut her off, scared but insistent.

"I can't stop them from calling the police. We have to keep this from getting worse. You have to use your… your… thingy. Get them to just… I don't know… but... " Shondra wasn't exactly used to taking charge, but her rambling made sense enough to Mariska.

"Right. I understand. I'll get them out of here and take care of it. You stay behind BEV, you understand? Stay behind her until I catch up." Mariska said, before turning towards her part-time werewolf lover, who nodded and filled in the implied order she knew was coming.

"Aye, aye, I'll make sure she's safe, love. I promise. Can we git movin', though, 'fore they end up in Ohio? C'mon." Bev said, as Mariska nodded her approval. Once it was done, the two women started running around the house to the backyard as Mariska turned back towards the angry and confused-looking Ellie.

Speaking, her eyes turned red. "Riiiight, I don't think calling the police is necessary, do you? I think you should… maybe go to the store? Get some… ice cream with the husband for the kid? Sound like a plan?"

The woods behind the house continued for a long while, getting deeper as the hill steepened toward the riverbed below. Through the dried leaves of the underbrush, Claire and Liam rolled downwards. The two transformed werewolves were locked in a tight embrace as they fell together, each bleeding from a combination of the impacts of the roll and their own bared claws.

Each was still wearing the clothes they had on in the house, although both outfits were becoming increasingly torn and stained from their interactions, straining against their larger, changed forms.

Hundreds of feet from the backyard of Ellie's house, the two tumbled into a clearing at the banks of the narrow river, where Claire landed firmly on top of Liam with a golden-eyed growl. "STAY AWAY FROM THEM!!! STAY AWAY FROM ME!!!"

While the impact clearly hurt, the black-furred wolf laughed through his initial grunt of pain. His voice was a jagged, ugly thing in the moonlight. "Who's threatenin' 'em, beautiful? Who wolfed out in th' house and smashed up th' room?"

Roaring with anger, Claire wanted to kill him. She wanted to tear into him and slice him and make him hurt for it all, but was fighting that urge as best as possible. All the while, that scent of his was pushing into her mind, making her ALSO want to tear what remained of their clothes off and take him right there in the mud of the riverbank.

The thought only made her angrier as she growled, "Do you seriously frickin' think that I don't know why you came here, Liam? But it's not going to happen! You're not going to HURT them and you're not going to get ME!!!"

"I already HAVE ye!" Liam growled back, his revealed fangs almost glowing against his jet-black fur as he grinned. Grabbing her by the wrists, he forced her hands up into the light. It was clear that she was only on top of him because he was letting her. On her black claws were glistening streams of red.

"Tha's MY blood, beautiful." He rumbled as Claire struggled against his grip. Even with her own strength, his was that much stronger. "Tha' anger yuir feelin'? Tha' RAGE? THA'S MINE! Tha's what I gave ye... an' it's what ye let OUT."

Pushing back off of him, Claire scrambled to her feet in surprise, looking at her exposed claws. As she did, Liam stood up, wiping dirt off of his torn clothes. "Ye thought ye could control it all. Control th' passion an' th' rage, but when it came down t' it, ye gave in, didn't ye?"

Stepping forward, his voice softened. "An' now yer scared about wha' tha' means? All year, you've had no real guidance. You've had second-hand advice from a fookin' vampire who meant well, but who don't know what it is... t' be what we ARE."

"Ye got angry and th' beast came out." He tilted his head as he continued. "So, now ye know wha' happened t' me. Now ye know tha' control ain't as easy as ye always want it t' be. Don' ye get it, beautiful? I understand. I've been where ye are righ' now. If'n ye just try an' trust me, I can help ye figure this all out. Hell, we c'n help each OTHER."

Standing there, Claire looked back up at him angrily. She was furious and she was struggling against his pheromonal assault that made her want to listen to his words in spite of herself. What he said was the culmination of her every fear over the last year; that no matter how in control she felt of herself when she was changed, she would lose control.

The sound of footfalls coming down the hill reminded her of something else, however. That smell she had detected back in the house gave her another kind of clarity that spurred her to action. It was that clarity of hope that came out when she replied.

"Really? This is... this is your frickin' Hail Mary play, Liam?" Claire said, her voice raspy and angry, but with a chuckle as she shook her head. "The bad movie cliché of 'we're not so different, you and I'? Are you frickin' kidding me? No."

Confused, Liam could smell who was coming as well, and he growled angrily at the realization. Seeing it, Claire continued, still transformed as she spoke. "No. I didn't lose control back there. I TOOK control. I didn't claw you out of anger, I clawed you to hold the fuck on and get you as far from that house as I fucking could, Liam."

"You waited to pull this shit until you thought I was alone. You tried to make me feel like I didn't have anyone in the world left so you could fill that void and get me to overlook every shitty fucking thing you ever did. For what?"

Stepping into the clearing from the woods, Shondra was panting as Beverly stepped in front of her as promised, transforming. Liam was being stared down by the two women he had made into werewolves. Looking over to the ginger-furred woman, Liam's growl became a low rumble as his eyes narrowed angrily.

"Ye fuckin' bitch! Ye think ye c'n betray me, too? Get over here... NOW!" He snapped.

"Hi, Shondra. Beverly." Claire said, turning and offering an awkward smile to the human woman who stood behind the other werewolf, who offered a frightened one in return. Claire now knew the fear wasn't directed at her as she turned towards Beverly. "Let me guess. Did he make you, too? Did all this fucked up shit to you, too? Used that leverage and his pheromones to make you do what he told you to?"

Looking at Claire, Beverly seemed momentarily confused at the words.. "Uh… wait, wha? Aye… aye. Uh… I… kinda came wit' them t' try an' tell YOU 'bout all that shite. Warn ye tha' he c'n get in yuir head."

"Thanks. Figured it out on my own, though. Thing is… it's fucking hard as hell… but neither of us HAS to do what he says. The only power he has is what we give him, and he can go fuck himself, because I'm not giving his ass SHIT, anymore."

"You NEED me an' ye KNOW it! Both of ye do!" Liam raged, roaring at Claire's defiance.

"N… NO!" Beverly said, her voice shaky as it was clear that those pheromones that had muddled Claire's mind were working hard on her as well, and had worked on her for years. "No, ye need HER, Liam! Ye always needed her! Why don' ye fuckin' tell her, already?"

"Get… over… here," Liam said, his voice a low, rumbling thing with just a hint of desperation.

"I… I… n… no. No. Liam. It's fookin' over. I'm fookin' done wit' ye." Beverly said, trembling there anxiously before turning to Claire. "He made me… made me ten years a'go. Like you… it was him losin' his cool. I turned his arse down in front'a his fookin' brothers an… an he couldn't handle th' rejection, so he did wha' he always does. But he got inta' me head after. He got me t' tell his FAMILY back home tha' I wanted it. He got me t' stay wit him and his little pack'a fuckboy wolves."

"But when they found out tha' he did it AGIN. Tha' he attacked someone else an' turned them… well…" Beverly continued before Liam roared at her, trying to cut her off.

"Shut the fook up, Bev! Shut th' fook up NOW, 'r I'll…" Liam took a step towards the ginger werewolf before Claire sidestepped between them to let the woman continue.

Inherent fear kicking in, Bev stepped back, bumping lightly into Shondra, who put her hand on the woman's fur-covered arm for support, whispering words of encouragement. "C'mon… you can do it."

Glancing back at the human woman she hardly knew who had maced her only a day ago, but who was now showing her compassion, Bev chuckled in disbelief before turning back to continue. "Yuir mum fookin' DISOWNED ye, ye right arse!"

"What?" Claire said, raising a brow, "Seriously?"

"He's outta the fookin' CLAN. See… he never tol' ye an'… an'… I shoulda… I shoulda told ye, too… but some'a us do got RULES. Th' clans back home set 'em up generations ago. An' this one loves breakin' the one in particular. He loves makin' his girls when they try t' leave him, after we find out he's a shite!" Bev stepped forward, taking strength from the assembled women to stand up to Liam. "See… he wasn't made, like us, Claire."

"He an' his dumbass brothers were *born* wolves. Their family back home… they do it right. They date wolves from other clans more often than not. And when they date regular folk, they only ever change 'em if'n they know th' score an CHOOSE t'take it on. He broke tha' rule TWICE, an his mum found out an' kicked his arse t' the curb last month. Th' only way back in'ta th' family… is if he could get ye t' mate wi' him, and say tha' this was all yuir choice. Otherwise… he's no' just disowned… he's a fookin' criminal. He broke th' number one law o' bein' a wolf, twice!"

"Found out?! Ye fookin' called her up an' told her, ye bitch!" Liam roared petulantly. "I'm th' ALPHA o' this pack, an' ye betrayed me!"

"He… knows that's… um… not really a thing? Right?" Shondra interjected sheepishly, holding up a finger like a student. "Alpha wolves. Like. It was a totally discredited study. The… the scientist that coined the term even said he was wrong. Wolves follow a *family* hierarchy that looks out for all members of the pack. I mean… y'know… regular wolves, anyway."

"Wait, what?" Liam cricked his head incredulously as Beverly pointed at him and shouted.

"HA! Fookin' *science*, motherfucker!"

Looking at Liam, Claire raised her eyebrow and shook her

head. As her confidence rose, she felt her mind growing more clear of his influence. His smell pulled less and less at her. "Seriously? You've gotta be frickin' kidding me. You're fucking pathetic, Liam. What happened to all your sob stories? You understood me? That was all bullshit, too, because of *course* it was. And now… you've got nothing. I mean, your mom sounds awesome, but you're a piece of shit. A very fucking alone piece of shit."

Raging petulantly, the hair on the back of his neck stood up on end as Liam crouched down, looking ready to leap at the women. Claire and Bev crouched down as well, growling as Shondra stepped further back behind Bev. Shaking her head, Claire stood her ground. "Just GO, Liam. Just fucking GO. You've got nothing here. I'm not going to help you make nice with your mom and I'm never… NEVER letting you back into my goddamn life! Period!"

"You bitches! I will fookin' gut yuir fat piggie friend there, an' then I'll head back up t' tha' house an' make sure…" Liam started to say, in a deep, low voice before the glow of two red eyes in the darkness of the brush behind Claire froze him in place.

"No. You absolutely will not," Mariska said, stepping into the riverbed past Claire and right up to Liam. In her hand, she was holding Liam's overnight bag that Claire had put in the bathroom upstairs. "And I think you know why, Liam."

Standing up to his full height, the jet-black, fur-covered werewolf growled and loomed over the barely-five-foot, whisper-thin vampire who had somehow snuck up on all three of the wolves. He was doing his best to look terrifying, and Mariska only chuckled.

"Your kind has codes against it, to start with. And while you may like breaking them, right now all you are is banished. Hurt them or raise a claw to Shondra or that family up there, and you know what will happen."

"Yuir own *kind* will come f'r ye! An' they willnae forgive ye," Bev interjected with a grim finality. Pushing past her own desires to succumb to his pheromones, she swallowed and continued.

"An'… an' they'll *know*. They'll know, b'cause all I got t' do…
All I got t' do is make one little phone call t' yer *mum*, Liam."

With widening eyes, Liam stared slack-jawed at Beverly, whom
he'd believed would always obey. A decade of giving in to his
demands had made her complacent, but now that the woman was
drawing strength from the other three women supporting her, she
was suddenly brazen. Staring intently, finding an inner strength
she had long since abandoned, she added to the ultimatum against
him. "Sorry. But… but I'm outta' yer fookin' shite band. Yuir on
your own, this time."

"Um!" Shondra said, her voice a squeak as she leaned out from
behind Bev, holding up a hand like a child in school wanting to
answer a question. "But… uh… actually, there's something else.
See… uh… I… I kinda checked the records on the drive up online
and… you were only here on, like, an education visa."

All eyes went to the rotund little human who stepped out,
gaining a little bit of confidence as she spoke. "And… uh… that
visa expired two years ago. I mean, you live pretty much off the
grid… but not completely. I mean… your band's tour schedule is
on *Facebook*. Uh, so… I already know you're working under the
table, and… well… it wouldn't take much to let Immigration and
Customs Enforcement know where you are."

Working up some more confidence, Shondra smiled slightly
and punctuated her point. "ICE, ICE, baby."

"Holy shite, tha's fookin'… *damn*, woman," Bev said, eyebrows
raised. She grinned as she made a fist and thumped her chest
lightly over her heart. "Respect."

"Heh… thanks," Shondra replied with a still-anxious but
slightly proud smile as Claire chuckled, stepping forward.

"So what's it going to be, Liam? We're none of us afraid of
you. I'M not afraid of you. And for the first time in a LONG
time… I don't fucking *NEED* you. I don't, and Beverly doesn't,
and we never frickin' will again. So just leave, Liam. Leave,
because I am done with you. *We* are done with you."

There was a long silence as Liam's eyes darted from woman to woman, in shock at the united front that they had created against him. He weighed his options. The human would be easy, and it was possible he could overpower both werewolves to exact a measure of revenge, but then his eyes fell on the diminutive vampire.

Seeing their eyes meet, Claire turned to Mariska as she all but dismissed the black-furred werewolf. "We've said all we need to say to this piece of shit. What about you?"

With a Cheshire grin, the red-eyed woman showed her fangs and chuckled. "I think I have one last point to add since it looks like he's thinking about doing something quantifiably stupid. He's wondering if he can win. If he can take us. All of us."

"You cannot," Mariska continued, stepping towards him again, as Claire had now given her carte blanche. "You are many things, Liam. You are charming and powerful. You are a … mediocre bass player, a womanizer, and for all intents and purposes, a rapist. But you are not a killer. You do not have the balls for that, little puppy."

"yer bluffin'. yuir no killer yerself," Liam replied, trying to make himself believe it as much as anyone else.

"You know nothing of me, child. See… your kind heals from physical trauma exceptionally well. And you all also taste, well, *amazing*. So, leave. I don't care where, so long as none of these women ever so much as smell you again. And if you are thinking you can hurt me or kill me, remember that you absolutely cannot. I am functionally immortal and you are so, SO very not. Should your path cross any of these women again, I will not kill you. What I promise you, is that you will *live*. You will live a VERY, VERY long time, in the kind of pain that only I can impart, and I will be the only person you ever see again. I can guarantee that if you push me…"

As she said so, Mariska reached forward with her free hand, grabbing Liam flat palmed against the chest, and squeezing. With a howl and a screech, Liam crumpled as Mariska closed her fingers, grabbing a chunk of his fur AND flesh, pulling down hard.

The enormous werewolf's knees buckled to keep that skin on his body, which put his eyes in line with the blazing red eyes of the angry Russian vampire, who finished her thought. "I will most assuredly push back. And you *will* live to regret it."

She leaned in and whispered in his ear. "Or… I'll just hand you over to your mommy and smile, as they deal with you in the traditional clan way. Your call, puppy."

As she let go of his chest, Liam fell backward into the river with a splash that made Claire grin. There was a lingering silence as the black-furred werewolf eyed them all, fear visible in his eyes, even to Shondra, who didn't have the senses to smell it like Claire or Bev could. Then, with pursed lips, he got up and looked at his torn clothes, realizing that he was firmly screwed.

Liam shrugged his shoulders, stepping back from where the women stood in defiance. His breathing was sharp and raspy as he took them in one by one. With a dry throat, he swallowed. "Fine. Fuckin' fine."

"You don' need me," He continued, a rattle in his voice which sounded so much smaller to Claire now. "I don' need you. Any o' you. Piss off, th' lot o' ye."

Shaking his head, he took another step back, clearly not knowing what to do next. Across from him at the edge of the river, Mariska simply tossed his bag over where it splashed in front of his feet. With a dismissive smirk, she replied. "It is settled then."

"Liam." Claire tilted her head and sighed. "Just go."

Silence lingered between them for what felt like forever, before the black-furred werewolf slung his bag over his shoulder and walked away into the darkness, his tail between his legs literally and proverbially.

Chapter Twenty-Nine

Standing in the moonlight at the bank of the river, Claire rinsed her clawed hands in the water. Cleaning the last of him off of her hands felt both like a literal need and a symbolic gesture as the others watched and waited.

Like Claire, Bev was still transformed. With the events of the last few days being so emotionally charged, she had reasons for choosing to stay this way for now.

Turning, Claire wiped her hands off on her pants, which hung low on her hips to allow her tail out while also hugging her far too tightly. It was uncomfortable, but hadn't been a priority for her until now, when she had the luxury to address it. "Ahh, fuck. This is too goddamn… hold on."

With one hand, she pulled at her waistband as she reached down to slash up the side of her leg with a claw, splitting the jeans along the seam. As they popped open, the scene was like an over-indulgent relative at Thanksgiving opening their pants at the end of the meal, and the groan Claire made was much the same. "Ooooh that's frickin' better. Damn."

To her pleasant surprise, Shondra chuckled at the display, which made her smile too. Mariska shook her head and sighed. "I told you denim was unforgiving, *volchonok*."

"I wasn't exactly planning to change when I got dressed today, y'know. This is… three days in a row, now." Claire joked back, shaking her head.

"Stretch denim, girly. Fookin' invest." Bev said, gesturing to her own pants with a grin. Pausing awkwardly for a moment, she cleared her throat and closed her eyes.

With the slightest of grunts, the ginger curls all over her body fell off into the cold wind as Bev shrank back to her human form. The entire process only took a few seconds, but when it was over, she was clearly worn out.

Bev walked over and looked up to Claire as she spoke. Her tone was as quiet and conciliatory as possible. "So… uh… yeah. Look. I… uh… I know I ain't yuir favorite person, all things considered. And… uh… when everythin' wen' down, I know I did ye dirty."

"I jus' wanted t' say tha' I was… sorry. I… I should'a been better than 'im. I shouldnae just left ye t' deal wit' all this by yuir lonesome like was done t' me." The usually-brusque woman was almost sheepish, brushing off fur that had clung to her clothes and hiking her pants back up to their proper fit. "An' I know it don' mean shite t' say it now, but…"

"He was in your head for ten years, Beverly," Claire said, still not perfectly okay with the woman, but understanding her far more, now. "And yeah… knowing that he had a specific pull on me… sure would have helped. But you were feeling that pull for years, and considering how close I came to taking what he was offering me earlier, I can understand."

"Aye…" Bev said, not quite comfortable with the moment as she fidgeted, letting the conversation trail off awkwardly. "So… uh… aye. He's a shite, an' we're both better off wit'out 'im in 'r lives."

Noticing that Shondra was watching, a bystander to these women who all shared something she didn't, Mariska shot Bev a glance and gestured back up the hillside towards the house before turning back towards Claire. "Well, I have got to get this mud off of my good boots, because this is just a travesty, *volchonok*. Will you be okay for a few?"

Realizing what her friend was doing, Claire nodded. Whatever drama had happened between the two of them was inconsequential at the moment, and Mariska knew that Shondra and Claire needed to talk in private. Nodding, Claire replied simply, "Yeah."

Motioning again, Mariska started up the hill with Bev behind her. "C'mon. We both need to clean ourselves up."

Shaking some mud off of her own very cold and furless foot, Beverly scoffed, following Mariska into the darkness of the trees.

"I'm nooo disagreein' wit ye, love."

After a long bit of silence, Claire stood in front of her best friend, holding her longer, fur-covered arms out at her sides as if to present her reality. "Uh… So… um… yeah. This is…me."

To her surprise, Shondra took the gesture as an invitation and fearlessly came over, wrapping her arms around Claire's middle in a hug. Sniffling, Claire hesitantly returned it. Lingering for what felt longer than it likely was, Shondra sniffled as well before pulling back. "Yeah...I kinda got filled in on the drive up here. I… I have your phone in the car, by the way. It's… uh… totally how we found out you were coming here."

"Shondra… I'm… I'm so sorry that I frickin' lied to you for so long. I just…" Claire said, her big amber eyes starting to well up.

"You were scared. You were scared that I wouldn't be able to accept you like this." Shondra interjected, finishing her friend's statement as Claire nodded sheepishly. "And… frankly… that hurt. It… it still kinda hurts. But I also get it. I'm not… I'm not mad, Claire. I'm not. I get it. I mean… if it was me… I can't automatically say I wouldn't have done the same."

"I'm sorry. I don't know how to tell you how sorry I am for everything." Claire said, wiping a tear from her furry cheek. "And… I can't believe you all came up here after me."

"Really? You would have done it for me. You… I need you to start believing that I'm not… I'm not so fragile that I can't handle this, Claire." Shondra replied. "Yeah… yeah, it's scary. Liam was scary. Beverly scared the… the heck out of me. But… she's not that bad, really. And Mariska and I got to talk a lot, too. And I'm glad. I'm glad I know everything now."

"So… now what?" Claire said. "I mean… I fucked up. I fucked up hard and just… I fucked everything up. I can't just…"

"Go home as if nothing happened? No. I mean… not with us." Shondra shook her head. The stout woman elaborated. "You can't… keep me at arm's length anymore, Claire. No more secrets. No more… protecting me. I took a road trip with a hundred-year-old vampire and a pissy lesbian werewolf. I can take

266

it. But what I… what I can't take is being on the outside anymore."

Reaching out, without hesitation, Shondra took the clawed and hairy hands of her friend. "If you can promise me that… then… then I want my best friend back."

"I… I promise. I really, really frickin' promise. I'm so…" Claire said, biting her bottom lip and nodding.

"I know. I am too. I wish I hadn't… y'know… totally freaked out back in my apartment. But that was then, okay? I… you don't have to apologize to me forever." Shondra nodded, her own eyes tearful as well. "If you're good… I'm good. WE can be good, right?"

"Right." Claire nodded again, pulling her hand free to wipe her cheeks.

"Oh my goodness. If you cry a lot like this, do you get those little tear stains in your fur like *Clive* does?" Shondra asked, interjecting some excited curiosity into the exchange to lighten the mood.

"What? Are you frickin' kidding? No. I…" Claire said, rubbing her eyes, noticing that there was a trail of wet fur beneath each eye. "Actually… I might. I… uh… never checked, actually. Heh."

Groaning, Claire started to pace at the river bed. "Shit. What am I gonna do? Do you think I can… just call in sick to work in the morning, or something? I just… I freaked out so hard. I thought everything was ruined and…"

"We… um… actually, we both have the week off." Shondra interjected, "I totally took care of it, so… Marcia is fine. I pretended that my grandma passed away. Uh… again. But, it's okay, Claire. Really."

"Well, aside from whatever damage was done up there at the house, but we can just… I dunno… maybe blame LIAM? Heh." Shondra chuckled again, shrugging and trying to not give too much credence to Claire's spiraling concerns.

"Thanks. Thanks, Shondra. Between you and 'Riska, I'd be totally fucked. I'd be totally fucked, and I took that all for granted." Claire ran her hand through her hair, still pacing. "I need to talk to her, too. I guess she's okay, but... actually, I still don't really know just what I did at the Halloween store that made her so mad."

"You never told me anything about her." Shondra pointed out, nodding as Claire raised her eyebrow.

"Wait, what?"

"Yeah. I asked her on the drive up. She was upset that I didn't know anything about her. You didn't tell me that you two sang karaoke, or even that she was Russian. She said that she felt ignored and cut out of a whole part of your life." Shondra continued, filling in the details Claire had been missing.

"Heh... that sounds about right. Shit... I really did just..." Claire said, clearly still trying to find a way to be self-recriminating before Shondra interjected again.

"Handle it wrong. Yeah. But... c'mon, Claire. I'm here. SHE'S here. None of that was important enough to stop us when you needed us to be there. And neither is this." Shondra gestured to Claire's fur-covered form.

"You're... really not freaked out?" Claire asked, looking down at herself.

"Total honesty... I was. I was, until Mariska explained everything. Now... it's... it's totally kind of awesome, really. I mean... I still have a zillion questions, y'know. But... yeah, I'm not freaked out." Shondra said, looking up into Claire's eyes with a warm smile. "I mean... look. I'm standing here having this... totally weird conversation with my best friend and she's a werewolf. But... you're still you. I mean. Nothing he told you is true. You're just... YOU. You're not some kind of monster. You're not losing control, or any of those horrible things he said to hurt you."

Nodding, Claire was threatening to cry again and she bit her bottom lip, which was somewhat of a challenge given her enlarged and sharpened teeth.

"When Beverly and I got down here... when I heard everything

268

he was saying… I was working up a big speech to try to talk to you. Convince you that none of it was true; that... that no matter what he did to you, none of it made you any less the Claire that was my best friend. It… I don't know if it would have helped… but I was totally running it in my head. Like… my best inspiring Star Trek captain speech, y'know?" Shondra continued, chuckling at the last part. "But… all that planning and you totally figured it out right here, on your own. You did it yourself, and I was so… I was so happy for that, Claire. And I'm happy for THIS."

"For… what?" Claire asked, legitimately confused.

"This. You could have changed back to talk to me. I mean, I know you can go back and forth easily any night that's not a full moon. But… you totally didn't." Shondra smiled broadly. "Because you ARE in control. Because… this is *you*. You're *all* of it… and this is… you claiming it, y'know? Mariska said that you like to… y'know… compartmentalize and talk about it like there's the normal you and the wolf. But… I mean… it's all just *you*, right? So… you talking to me like *this*... don't think I didn't notice how hard it was for you. It means a lot."

"Yeah…" Claire shrugged, rolling her eyes. "Also… it IS really cold out tonight and I don't have my jacket with me like you do. Soooo, the fur is a plus right now."

It was a joke designed to dismiss the emotion of the moment, and both women knew it. Were Mariska there, she would likely not let it fly. Shondra, however, just smiled and laughed, accepting the course change to take some of the pressure off of Claire.

"Oh my goodness. How do you do this back home? It is totally a sauna down there!" Shondra joked, referring to the hot, humid Tampa weather.

Laughing out loud, Claire was finally starting to feel better. "Yeah… it's… NOT great sometimes, I'll be honest. I can see some more road trips in my future after being up here. THIS is… like… werewolf paradise."

"Ha! I can totally imagine it." Shondra replied, noticing that the temperature really was dropping. "Just… no more solo ones, okay?"

"I promise," Claire responded, smiling more easily now. "So… you had a whole speech planned? I'm frickin' bummed I missed out on that."

"Well… I probably would have stammered and talked too much through the whole thing, with a bunch of long, weird, run-on sentences. But, yeah. I was thinking that maybe I would need to try and say something inspiring." Shondra said with a grin as the two turned to start back up towards the house. "But… like I said… turns out that you didn't need inspiration from me."

"Uh… bullshit," Claire said, stopping at the edge of the woods by the foot of the hill as she shook her head. As Shondra turned to look, Claire continued, "Everything I did, here tonight. Standing up to him. Standing up for *myself*. I… I didn't do it myself. WE did that, Shondra."

"Claire, you did all that before I got down the hill," Shondra said, confused.

"See… I don't know what all Mariska or Beverly told you about how my senses work, but… even now… I can still hear Beverly and 'Riska in the backyard. Bev is shaking fur out of her clothes and complaining about how cold it is and… ooo. 'Riska just grabbed her, and I think... Yeah, they're making out now." Claire said, her ear literally tilting towards the house.

Looking up in that direction, from where they were, Shondra couldn't even see the top of the hill through the darkened wood, much less hear a thing aside from the babbling brook behind them. "Wow. Really?"

"Yeah. So… when I was in that room with him and I thought I didn't have anything left to cling to… when all I thought I frickin' had left was HIM, you all arrived." Claire said. "My head was… like cotton with what he was doing to me, but through all of that, I smelled YOU first when that door downstairs opened."

"You… can tell my smell from the other side of a closed door… downstairs, and outside? Wow." Shondra said, trying to resist geeking out.

"Shondra… *your* smell. I can pick that out of a crowd. I can tell when you get out of your car at work when I'm already at my desk. I could smell you coming from the top of the hill and I could hear your heartbeat. It's… they're all unique. The smells and the sounds. You're unique." Claire scritched the back of her ear a little awkwardly. "And… it's one of my *favorite* smells. It… makes me happy every time."

"When I… in that room… I was ready to give up, Shondra. Ready to give Liam what he wanted, until I smelled you. You were HERE. You came. You didn't give up on me and… that was all that I needed to know." Again, a tear leaked out and darkened the brown fur under her eye. "That WAS the most inspirational speech I could have imagined."

"Y'know… heh." Claire said, trying to joke over the emotional moment. "I still kinda wish I got to hear it."

"HA!" Shondra laughed, also wiping a tear from her cheek. "It would have been totally… totally awesome."

"Oh, I have no frickin' doubt," Claire said as they started back up the hill. "C'mon. Stay behind me. I can see the path better and can help you up."

"Yeah, okay. Wow." Shondra said, taking Claire's hand for stability as they started up the hill into the darkness. "My best friend is totally a werewolf."

Epilogue - One Month Later
·)⟩◐⟨(·

The sun was riding the edge of the horizon and turning the warm Tampa skies a deep, golden red. It bathed Claire's bedroom in a flood of light while she sat next to the open window, brush in hand.

It had been a productive Saturday. She looked at the large, stretched canvas on her easel that was nearly complete. Lost in the moment, she worked with a deep and intense focus on the fields of color that filled her vision. Unlike many of her earlier paintings, which had always been more representational, there was no real clear or specific form on this one. Instead, she painted in blends of colors and abstract shapes. Movement and energy were driving her inspiration as she rinsed off her brush in the dirty brown water of the coffee mug at her side.

Leaning back to look at the piece, she squinted her large, amber eyes and took in the work. With her eyes transformed, she could perceive the canvas differently. She could see colors beyond what she used to, even detecting the heat of the paints and how light passed through them. It was a thing she hadn't let herself experience until now. She knew that her paintings would look different to human eyes…but she wasn't painting for anyone else.

On the floor around her easel were other paintings she had completed over the last few weeks, spread out so she could see them all. It helped her to take it all in, see if any of the pieces needed more work, and appreciate the efforts that had somehow stopped *feeling* like as much of an effort.

Aside from her eyes, the rest of her remained human. She was wearing a pair of black leggings and an old, paint-covered t-shirt with the neck cut open. Her long brown hair was in a messy bun atop her head as she pondered the colors only she could really see.

Since being turned, she had felt blocked emotionally and artistically; the inspiration to create was seemingly lost to her

272

forever. However, as she dried off her brush and dipped it into both the blue and the green on her palette tray to mix them up, she realized she had simply been trying to paint with the wrong eyes.

It was both literal and metaphorical. Of course, her enhanced eyes gave her a different perspective, but it was also part and parcel of the problem at the root of her issues. She was taking half of the woman she had become and caging it within herself. She was treating 'Claire' and 'the Wolf' as two separate things, and denying herself the greater perspective that came with an understanding that she was all things, all the time. She was Claire Gribbald, and Claire Gribbald was a werewolf.

The words Beverly had said to her in that hotel a year and one month ago echoed in her mind: "*Yuir never NOT the wolf, but th' wolf is never not you, either. So listen t' what ye hear. Take it all in and learn to understand it all. Ye may not be hairy but once a month unless ye choose t' be, but those gifts… an' they ARE gifts even if ye don' always think they are… are a part of ye now. All the time.*"

It took the intervention of those closest to her… and even Beverly… to help her understand that truth. It also took finally facing her fears and finding a way to move on from the trauma of her turning, but that night a month ago when she finally closed the door on Liam Docherty…she had opened another door.

Allowing the brush to flow as it wanted to, Claire wasn't so much painting as she was conducting the light in front of her. No longer concerned with form or representation, she allowed the passions that her newfound balance had given her. The wolf was fervor and fire. It was life, love, and freedom, and she had hidden a part of herself in that, which had locked down her ability to create. Now, that was all free. All parts of her were one, and with that realization came new inspiration.

Inspiration and contentment.

At least more contentment than she had felt in a long while. She had her life, her friends, and a future to look forward to as she finished the last addition of color.

Setting the brush in the water, she tilted her head and smiled. The light from the window was dimming and the room was awash in a purple glow that felt good as it ran across her face. The sun was all but gone and the moon would be high in the sky before too long. It was almost time to change.

She stood up and stepped away from the easel and towards her closet to pick an outfit. It was girl's night out and the thought put a grin on her face.

Walking through the parking lot, Claire didn't look all that different since the last time she had been to the little hole-in-the-wall karaoke bar. She wore cute skinny jeans and a snug black top with a wide scoop neck and three-quarter sleeves. Her hair was down, and to those who cared to notice, a good deal longer. She could immediately tell from the scent of the room that the rest of her group hadn't arrived just yet. She stepped up to an empty stool at the bar and took a seat.

Leaning over on her crossed arms, she set her small clutch purse next to her and smiled down the bar to the young bartender, nodding slightly to say 'hello' across the half-filled room. Like before, she could smell that he was interested.

"Hey, Claire. Good to see you out." He flushed a little, a nervous-but-friendly smile on his soft, roundish face, still peppered with the fuzz of a half-grown blond beard that Claire found cute. "What can I get you?"

"Just a rum and Coke for now, Sam. Still waiting on the others, so I don't want to lean into a frickin' pitcher until I know what they actually want." Claire responded, trying to set a good balance between being friendly enough to not shut him down, but not so much as to come on strong. She had a unique advantage in such scenarios that she tried not to use on purpose.

"Gotcha. One rum and coke coming up. Will you be starting a tab?" Sam asked as he pulled out a glass and started filling it.

"Please." she replied, sliding her credit card across to him while he finished his work. The bar was filling and Claire was hopeful that it would be a fun and relaxing night out. Looking around, she could smell the stories of the others there. The younger college girls in the back were already too drunk, clearly having 'pre-gamed' before heading out. The blonde was wearing way too much perfume, a bad knock-off of a much more expensive brand that left a caustic sting in her nose. There was a couple in their late 50's who clearly came on the motorcycle she had parked next to in the lot. Aside from the leather jackets, they had that unique scent of the open road, a potpourri of experiences.

It was like reading through Wikipedia in one sniff, as they had passed through the scents of so many others. The experience made Claire smile as Sam handed her the drink. "Well, here you go. Let me know if you need anything else."

"I will, thanks," Claire replied, smiling more widely. He was a big teddy bear who clearly liked her, and she wasn't against the idea of getting to know him a little better.

Turning as her ears picked up on the voices she had been expecting, she saw Mariska and Shondra walk in together, the rotund young woman in mid-sentence. "...which is what I was trying to do when the file crashed on me and I lost, like, five and a half hours of work. Thank GOODNESS I had backup files, but I was about to lose my mind and...:"

"Oh, hey, Claire!" Shondra said as she noticed Claire at the bar. Both women smiled as they stepped over to her. "I picked Mariska up on the way over. Do you believe that she walks every time? I mean... I KNOW she's not... y'know... in any actual danger. All things considered. But still, the idea was making me a nervous wreck, so I stopped by her house to grab her first. And besides, I'm the D.D., so, it just totally makes sense anyway!"

While they were talking, Sam came back over and took the others' drink orders, which consisted of another rum and Coke for Mariska that would end up going to Claire, and a Mountain Dew on ice for Shondra, who didn't drink.

"We adopted a *mother, volchonok*." Mariska smirked as she poked fun at Shondra's slightly overbearing nature, chuckling.

"You didn't seem to mind when I helped you reorganize your fridge last week," Shondra said, joking back. "Really, as old as she is, and everything was just set up in the least efficient way possible. A total mess."

"I knew where it all was, *mamochka*." Mariska rolled her eyes with a smirk. "It's my kitchen and I am a chef. I have a system, thank you very much."

"It's not a good system, Mariska, is all I'm trying to say and… wait… is that 'mother' in Russian?" Shondra raised an eyebrow as she walked over to give Claire a hug.

"You have your… Google. I'm not making your work easier for you." came the sarcastic reply. "So… our booth is quite empty. Shall we go mark our territory? Just don't pee on it, *volchonok*."

"HA. HA." Claire said as they made their way over to the table.

"Ah, I'll be right there. I just need to put some songs in with the DJ, ladies." Mariska said, stepping aside to go over to the stage where the three-ring binder had been set up with the song selections while Claire and Shondra got settled at the booth.

"Wow, Claire. Your hair looks… I can't believe how long it's gotten. It looks really nice." Shondra said, reaching over to touch Claire's much longer brown curls with a curious smile.

"Well… ALL my hair grows by about two inches whenever I change, and the rest of me grows fur. Since the hair on my head doesn't shed out when I change back, the growth just stays. I've learned how to trim it back myself more often than not. But this time… I dunno. I changed three days in a row, and once since then. I thought about it and realized I liked it longer, and why waste eight inches or so of growth if I like it?"

"I mean… I'm learning to accept the rest of it, why piss on one of the best perks? Ah, shit." she finished, prompting Shondra to laugh.

"Consider me jealous. You could, like, totally try any crazy haircut you wanted to, and if you hated how it came out, change a whole bunch and grow it back out. That is totally awesome." Shondra added with a wide smile.

As usual, Mariska simply walked over the top of the table to get to the rear corner of the booth after she finished putting her songs in, which was a bit of a surprise for Shondra, though she was learning to expect the unexpected from her new friend.

Plopping down to her seat, she reached over to Claire, sliding the woman's card back to her. "Here. Drinks are, this evening, on me. I insist."

"What? That's… you don't have to pay for us, though." Shondra interjected with a look of concern. "I mean, it's totally sweet, and all, but…"

"Nonsense. I asked you to leap freely from your comfort zone this evening." Mariska nodded, waving it off dismissively. "It was the least that could be done."

"PPPSSH! She isn't paying for shit." Clair scoffed with a wry grin, slipping her card back into her purse.

"Uh… I don't understand. What am I miss… ooooh. Oh, Mariska. You didn't?" Shondra asked, confusion turning quickly to comprehension.

"Yeah. You've seen her house." Claire chuckled, shaking her head. "I mean, it took me a little while to figure out how someone who barely works at a ramen joint always has money, but here we are."

"What need I spend money on? My pantry is staggeringly barren and I have little need for most utilities. I'm over a century old; hence, have a fair set of marketable skills. It has not been difficult to accrue a comfortable cushion of modest wealth." Mariska said matter-of-factly, a Cheshire cat grin on her pale face.

"That… and she does her whole 'Jedi mind trick' when she doesn't feel like paying for something. Which, y'know, is always. Heh." Claire interjected with a knowing chuckle.

"C'mon, really? Mar*IS*ka?" Shondra added in a chastising tone. "You have totally gotta stop doing that."

"I simply talked to the bartender and… may have made a suggestion that the evening was a special occasion… suggestively." Mariska shrugged, in spite of knowing she had disappointed her very human friend. "Sometimes it is... like a reflex action."

Feeling Shondra's mood change, Mariska knew the idea of that kind of mental manipulation was something she was less than comfortable with, almost on Claire's behalf. As such, she felt guilty in the moment. "I am sorry, *mamochka*. I... will do better. I promise."

"Thanks." Shondra nodded, and the mood lightened back up.

"So... I am not the only person singing tonight, I presume?" Mariska said, curling her lips and looking at the other two with mock-judgmental eyes. The lithe little vampire was dressed more casually than normal, with torn black jeans and a different pair of her trademark knee-high black boots with massive heels. Her top was a very worn, old black t-shirt with a white band logo that said *'Toxic Heartbreak'* on it. On her neck was a collection of about six different necklaces and chains, with even more bracelets on each wrist.

Claire and Shondra flanked her on either side of the booth, Shondra in a long, denim skirt and a turquoise turtleneck top, her curly hair pulled into two mirrored poofs on either side of her head. "I... I don't know. I mean, I've never... uhhh... SANG in public before, Mariska. I... I.... it's kind of embarrassing, isn't it?"

"It is GLORY and PASSION and FIRE, woman! You get up there and open your soul and bare it to the world in song!" Mariska replied, overdramatically, which caused Claire to snort in her drink.

"Yeah, but... uh... I've never... I mean... what if someone makes fun of me?" Shondra asked nervously.

"Then I murder them, and Claire eats the body," Mariska answered, matter-of-factly. Shondra's eyes went wide. "Oh, it is a joke, woman. I would very simply make them go up there after you and sing something themselves and regret it. You know, in that way I do."

Taking another sip of her drink, Claire chuckled at the idea.

"You laugh now, but you are getting up there too, *volchonok*." Mariska pulled out the flask of blood she carried in her purse to take a sip. "She protests too, *mamochka*, but she has a great voice. Like I've said before, it's resonant and growly and full of 'fuck me' energy. 'Bonnie Tyler', 'The Eurythmics', 'Joplin', she does wonderful on all of that."

"Oooh." Shondra said, excited by the prospect of hearing her raspy-voiced best friend actually sing.

"Indeed. If only there was a place she could sing transformed. With that added resonance… Mmmm, I can only imagine." Mariska said, smirking but totally serious otherwise.

"Calm down, 'Riska. You HAVE a girlfriend, remember?" Claire said, raising an eyebrow at the amorous vampire who scoffed in an exaggerated manner.

"Ugh. Yes, one who went back to SCOTLAND for a bit, leaving me completely bereft of proper fuckery for the next month and a half at LEAST." Mariska pouted in the corner. "Meaning I have to live vicariously through the love lives of YOU two."

Taking a swig to punctuate her point, Mariska continued. "I may starve, I'll have you know."

"How is Beverly?" Shondra asked, genuinely curious. The initial animosity between them may have dissipated, but the ginger werewolf was still not one of Claire's favorite people, and it showed on her face as she half-smirked at the question.

"Eh, she is fairly okay. The clan asked her to come out, and she insisted on explaining what had happened between her and Liam. She said that… if she were truly to make a fresh start, she needed to clear that proverbial air, and all. I mean… I do understand. It's just a little… lonely." Mariska said, admitting her feelings before changing the subject. "She did, however, give me a call earlier this evening that you may find interesting, *volchonok*."

Raising a wary eyebrow, Claire took a long sip that finished off her first glass as she swapped her empty with Mariska's full one. "I'm almost scared to frickin' ask. What was it, 'Riska?"

"Wellll, the clan…" Mariska paused, considering her words

carefully, "The clan over there apparently are taking what happened very seriously. Liam and his brothers have been blacklisted to a degree, as their mother has some level of pull with the authorities that deal with such matters for your kind."

"There are *authorities?* Like… *werewolf* authorities?" Claire asked, a legitimately surprised expression on her face.

"Apparently." Mariska shrugged. "Beverly has been at Liam's family home with his mother and his other siblings. Beyond the two we know, according to Bev, there are over twenty in total." Mariska's eyes went wide as she nodded on the large number.

"Hold the frickin' phone. Liam's mother has *over twenty* kids?" Claire choked on her drink, coughing for a minute to catch her breath before continuing. "That's… like… from a lot of pregnancies over many years, right? Not, like… uh…"

Glancing at Shondra, who looked almost too excited by the implication of the lingering question, Claire's voice dropped to a whisper. "...That's not, like, a frickin' LITTER or two, right?"

"Probably three. I mean… I've been doing a TON of, like, research on, y'know, regular wolves since, y'know…" Shondra interjected with all the same energy she usually would reserve for something like 'Lord of the Rings' trivia, "And… well… wolves CAN have litters between four and six…"

"*Shondra!*" Claire protested with wide eyes, "Too much information. Shit!"

At this point, Mariska chuckled, biting her bottom lip as she tried to keep it from becoming the full, belly laugh she wanted to let out. Failing, it came out as a loud guffaw.

"Ohh… Oooh, I can picture it. You looking like the one in the 'Hotel Transylvania' movies. Muumuu and house slippers with six little ones in there. HA HA HA HA!!!" Mariska laughed out loud as Claire simply scowled at her. "Ahh, relax. I suspect our Beverly may be exaggerating a smidge to muck with your head."

For her part, Shondra giggled, clearly picturing it in her head as well, "Well… hehe heheh heh… that would be cute. Ooh, would they be, like, werepups? Awwww, that sounds so cute. He he."

"Oh, fuck the both of you," Claire grumbled, throwing back the entire next drink in one long gulp. "It's official... if that's the case, I am never having frickin' sex again. No frickin' way."

"Um... so, can I get you ladies any refills?" Sam asked, walking over to the table to check on them as the laughing finally petered out. "Figured I'd come over and check."

"Yes. A double, Sam. TWO doubles." Claire said, handing him the empties as Shondra held a hand over her barely-touched drink to indicate she was good.

As he went back to the bar to get their drinks, Mariska leaned over with a raised eyebrow and a Cheshire grin on her pale face. "Well, I would surely hope not, *volchonok*. Poor Sam might just burst."

"Can we not talk about BURSTING, 'Riska?!" Claire rolled her eyes. "Ugh. Shit, I'm going to have to talk to Beverly when she gets back. There is still way too much I don't know about all of this."

"Well, baby steps." Mariska replied before realizing the poor choice of words. "Which is to say, you'll figure it out in due time, and I'm sure she will help. She still feels terrible about everything as it is."

"I'm sure she frickin' does." Claire replied, still clearly holding a grudge against the ginger woman. "Ugh, sorry. I promised I wasn't going to drag down the night. Sorry."

As Claire spoke, Sam returned with the refills, being sure to offer a wide smile to Claire as he did. "Well, here you go, ladies. If you need anything else, you know where to find me."

Waggling her eyebrows, Mariska smirked. "Don't worry about the conversation. You need to drag THAT one down. He is willing and you are hungry, *volchonok*."

"Yeah, yeah." Claire said as she took a sip and sighed. "And I'm not dismissing the idea. I'm just... like you said. Baby steps. I'm taking it slow. I don't even know what he's like, not, y'know, serving frickin' drinks? He may be boring as a stump."

Smiling like a victorious athlete, Mariska was beaming. "Ah, look at you! You are finally going to at least try and live your life again! Look at US, here together. You already are, and all joking aside, I am so proud!"

Holding out her flask, Mariska gestured to the other two women, unlikely friends in a strange world. Taking the cue, Claire rolled her eyes and smiled as she brought her drink up. Excited to somehow be a part of this unusual trio, Shondra thrust her glass of soda into the mix and they clinked their drinks together as Mariska continued, "I am over a century old, and I will… all things being equal… outlive you both. However, I have never been happier to have chosen to be a part of such women's lives. Thank you both."

"Awwwwww!" Shondra said, getting emotional at the sentiment as Claire smiled broadly, nodding.
"Yeah… I don't like to think about where I'd be without either of you, so I'm beyond glad to have such good friends." Claire added.

"Awwwwwwwwwwwwww!" Shondra repeated, biting her bottom lip. "You two suck. I am… I am totally lousy at stuff like this, but yeah. Yeah."

As they sat there, the DJ clicked on the microphone and announced the start of karaoke for the evening, telling the crowd the basic rules as everyone listened. And at the end of his spiel, he looked at his most regular singer, Mariska, to indicate that she was up.

"Well… it appears to have fallen to me to begin the true festivities of the evening, ladies." She said, getting up on the table to walk across towards the stage like a cat. "Just… remember how heartfelt all that was a moment ago as I start singing."

As Mariska hopped up and took the mic like a seasoned pro, Claire raised an eyebrow. "That sounds… ominous."

A few seconds later, the music started, and Claire recognized the familiar tune, though she couldn't quite place it. Mariska's voice was beautiful and polished as she worked the stage with swagger, looking directly at Claire.

"Wait… is that?" Claire muttered as Mariska kept singing, the familiar tune being matched up with lyrics she also recognized.

Both Shondra and Claire realized which song it was as Claire pursed her lips and Shondra had to stifle another chuckle. Laughing in spite of herself, Claire shook her head and shouted up to the stage, "Oh, fuck you, bitch!"

She chuckled and groaned at the same time, taking a swig of her drink. "I can't believe she's singing frickin' *'Hungry Like the Wolf'*."

The End.

Claire's story continues in:

LYCANTHROPY *and the* WOLVES of the HAVENLANDS

Coming Soon

Dee Fish is a Pennsylvania-based cartoonist, illustrator, and graphic designer. As a cartoonist, she is the creator of the online comic strip, **Dandy & Company,** the fantasy/adventure series, **The Wellkeeper** and the artist on the webcomic, **Giant Girl Adventures.** She has also inked the long-running, syndicated comic strip **Dick Tracy.**

Currently, she is the creator of **Finding Dee,** a semi-autobiographical webcomic about the trials, tribulations, and humor in coming out as transgender in your 40s.

As a graphic designer, Dee has worked on projects for clients \such as Coca-Cola, Sweet Tomatoes, Odwalla, Disney On Ice, Universal Studios Theme Parks and many more and has over 25 years of experience as a graphic designer.

Lycanthropy and the Single Girl is her debut novel.

Made in the USA
Columbia, SC
21 July 2024

c674ee90-ea70-41e6-9bf4-74130ee2b7b4R01